Acclaim for Brian McGrory
and his debut novel
THE INCUMBENT

"Riveting . . . that *The Incumbent* rises far above its genre does not make it any less effective as pure thriller. From the start, McGrory weaves a tension that grows taut as the drama of a frontier hanging . . . this first novel seem[s] the work not of a newcomer but of a master. As the best thrillers must, *The Incumbent* offers a tight, credible plot with a denouement as tense as a childhood dream of falling. What lifts it to art are McGrory's skill in characterization and his profundity of theme."

—*The Boston Globe*

"McGrory has crafted a noteworthy first novel with heft and heart. Equally savvy about the electoral process, investigative journalism, and human nature—yet still romantic at its core."

—*People*

"Brian McGrory writes prose with the economy and clarity that only the best writers can master. *The Incumbent* moves to its absorbing conclusion without a wasted gesture or a false note."

—Robert B. Parker, author of
Hugger Mugger and *Hush Money*

"The best political novel I've read in years."

—Neal Travis in the *New York Post*

"A superb first novel. . . . Fans of Baldacci's *Absolute Power* or DeMille's *The Lion's Game* should plunge into McGrory's enticing plot, following Flynn and his makeshift allies and enemies through a complex and credible web of deceit."

—*Publishers Weekly* (starred review)

"Riveting . . . a strong debut for a talented writer."

—*The Denver Post*

"Rarely does a thriller offer both such palm-sweating excitement and a genuine sense of the intrigue that infuses Washington, D.C. A completely fresh and hugely enjoyable political page-turner."

—Jeffery Deaver, author of *The Blue Nowhere* and *Speaking in Tongues*

"Thoroughly engaging. . . . McGrory's followers should be legion. . . . the denouement is extraordinary, and when McGrory could have taken the easy, clichéd way out of the story, he sidestepped the temptation and went for a resolution far more realistic and satisfying. *The Incumbent* is a wild ride."

—*St. Petersburg Times* (FL)

"With this astounding debut novel, McGrory has established himself as a prime author of political thrillers . . . a fresh, dynamic work that tops even *Absolute Power* and *The Tenth Justice.*"

—*San Antonio Express-News*

"A thrilling ride. McGrory knows his stuff as a reporter; he also shows us a real flair for suspense fiction."

—*The Boston Review*

"An astonishingly good ride. . . . Remember when David Baldacci hit that massive, first-time-novelist home run with *Absolute Power*—and Clint Eastwood snapped it up for film? *The Incumbent* is that kind of property, only the story is more intriguing and better-written."

—*Dallas Morning News*

"Our hero ends up scooping a story that's both deeper and murkier than Watergate. Bullet-fast and told tough, *The Incumbent* is *Eddie Coyle* meets *The Usual Suspects*."

—Chris Matthews, host of CNBC's *Hardball*

"Deserves to join that short list of books (*The Boys on the Bus*, *All the President's Men*, the novels of Ward Just and Charles McCarry) that give us a reliable dance card for that treacherous tango done by reporters and politicians."

—*Chicago Tribune*

"McGrory delivers in *The Incumbent*. Interesting people populate it, the plot is fascinating, and the ending surprising."

—*Houston Chronicle*

"Brian McGrory has written a terrific story about murder, ambition without limits, and presidential assassination. *The Incumbent* is a combination of Jack Germond and John Grisham."

—Mark Shields, syndicated columnist and political analyst for PBS and CNN

"A taut and electrifying look at Washington politics."

—*The San Francisco Examiner*

THE
INCUMBENT

BRIAN McGRORY

POCKET STAR BOOKS

New York   London   Toronto   Sydney   Singapore

A Pocket Star Book published by
POCKET BOOKS, a division of Simon & Schuster, Inc.
1230 Avenue of the Americas, New York, NY 10020

Copyright © 2000 by Brian McGrory

Originally published in hardcover in 2000 by Pocket Books

ISBN: 0-7434-0351-7

First Pocket Books paperback printing August 2001

10 9 8 7 6 5 4 3 2 1

POCKET STAR BOOKS and colophon are registered trademarks of Simon & Schuster, Inc.

Cover art by Tom Hallman

Printed in the U.S.A.

To my father, to his memory,
for teaching all those lessons with deeds rather than words

THE
INCUMBENT

ONE HOUR AND COUNTING until dusk, the time of the day Curtis Black liked best. The time when the distant sky left the illusion of light, but the enveloping haze provided the cover of dark. A time when if you knew what you were doing, if you knew how, and you knew why, the visual, visceral uncertainty of the moment served as your most reliable ally. For Curtis Black, it was a time of day to make his mark.

Black shook his Johnnie Walker along the top of the rickety Formica table, the cubes of ice smashing softly against each other and the side of the glass. He did this when he was nervous, and yes, he was nervous now. His eyes drifted vacantly across the diagrams spread out before him, then out the window at the waning afternoon light, then back to the diagrams, then at his watch. He took a small sip of Scotch.

Good help is hard to find. That's what he kept thinking, over and over again, that one thought interfering with his ability to concentrate on the task at hand. Good help is hard to find and harder still to keep. Kind of ironic, but the better you do, the quicker guys are to move on, to take their experience, the lessons they learned under you, and set out on their own. To succeed you have to keep moving, taking on new people, and every new person represents a new risk, every single time. But what else are you going to do? Go it alone? Go straight? Black took another sip and bore in on the closest diagram.

The armored truck would come down Prince Street and take a right on Hanover, then drive two blocks through what would be relatively heavy, early rush-hour traffic. There would be a dark blue delivery van idling in the spot where the armored truck usually double-parked, but given the time of day, given the foot traffic, the pickups, the drop-offs, that shouldn't seem unusual. As a matter of fact, the last two Tuesdays, Black had sat in that idling delivery van himself, positioned in that precise spot, to watch how the armored car driver would react, and both times the driver had pulled up in front, parked, and made his pickup from the Shawmut Bank.

It would be a two-man truck. In spite of his nerves, Black chuckled to himself at the thought. All that vulnerability, all that exposure, and just two men to withstand the world. The entire operation, from start to the safety of a successful getaway, should be over in ten minutes, maximum. Unless, of course, someone screwed up.

Which got back to the issue of Black's nerves and this recurring thought that good help is hard to find. He took another sip of whisky and stared out the window at nothing in particular, out onto Broadway in Chelsea, where immigrants locked in a losing battle against despair drove ancient cars down the litter-strewn street. Their plight escaped Black's notice. One small mistake by any one of his five guys, he was thinking, and the whole thing could turn to bedlam in a fraction of a second, and that one fraction of one second could haunt the rest of a lifetime. Maybe even dictate a lifetime. So it comes down to the execution even more than the plans, and the execution was in the hands of five guys he barely knew. He took another pull of whisky and continued gazing out the window, his chin resting hard on the cup of his hand.

By now, Black was oblivious to the diagrams. Rather, he was fretting about one of his men, a guy with the worrisome nickname of Rocky. The bad news was that this Rocky didn't seem to mind the name at all, at least as far as Black could see. The mildly good news was that the name came from Rocky's given name, Rocco. "Call me Rocky," he had said, jovially, that first time they had met for a hamburger and a beer over at the Red Hat. Black had just rolled his eyes. There are no résumés in this business, and no reliable lists of references. So much is done on feel, and suddenly, in the lengthening shadows of that crucial afternoon, Black didn't feel so good about this one.

Rocco Manupelli was a Vietnam veteran, an ex-con, and a former Mafia wiseguy who had done three years in the Walpole State Prison for armed robbery. Black had convinced himself that it might be good to work with a guy who had done time, because a guy who had done time will do absolutely anything not to do more, including getting something right, listening to the plans, not freelancing at the scene. But when they met, Rocky made only a passing reference to his stint in jail, and it wasn't even a negative one. He had made mention of how much exercise he had in prison, all that weight he had lost, as if he had gone to a frigging health spa. It was as if he hadn't minded, as if jail was as good as anything else he might have done, and remembering that fact was now beginning to scare the bejesus out of Curtis Black.

He took a final sip of whisky, draining the glass. He wanted more but wouldn't allow himself any. The goal was to calm his nerves, not dull them. He had to be aware, to be on top of his game, even if everyone knew that the best part of Curtis Black's game was in the planning, not the execution. One of his old cohorts, out on his own now (aren't they all?), used to say that his planning was always so precise, so exhaustively researched, that a trained ape couldn't screw up the scene. Indeed, it was so good that Black never saw fit to carry a gun. All that would do was add ten years to the jail term on the off chance he was ever caught, and the guys who worked for him, they were carrying anyways.

He focused for a moment on the traffic jerking up Broadway, at the elderly and unemployed walking along the gum-stained sidewalk, so slowly, because they really had no place they needed to go. He shook his glass once more, listening to the reassuring sound of the ice, then slid the tumbler along the tabletop just out of reach and bore in on the top diagram, envisioning the Wells Fargo security guard pushing a dolly carrying a duffel bag filled with cash. Everything goes right, and three men in ski masks jump out of the back of the blue van and surround him. A fourth man appears from across the street, comes up from behind, and disarms the second guard, who is standing beside the truck. Black would be directing the operation from the driver's seat of a getaway car, barking orders into a tiny microphone that the others could hear through their own earpieces. The idea was to keep the operation simple, let the men do their work, say nothing confusing. In a matter of three minutes, the men should be off the street and in the car, no shots, no worries. They'd leave the stolen van behind.

The knock on the door downstairs startled Black, even though he had been waiting for it. He looked at his watch and saw it was 4:25 P.M. Right on time. He picked up a photograph resting on the windowsill and smiled wistfully at the three people who were smiling back at him—a woman sitting on a sofa, holding the arms of a toddler who was courageously standing for the first time, and a man, a younger version of himself, kneeling nearby on the living room rug.

He pulled himself up from the metal chair, knocked his fist once against the top of the table, and ambled down the steep, crooked stairs to open the door. One hour to showtime.

one

Present Day
Thursday, October 26

IT'S ALWAYS ODD, MEETING someone famous. On television, they never look at you, unless they're giving a speech or staring at the camera in a commercial, and in those cases, they are perfectly made up, every hair in place, rouge spread across their cheeks by artists who make lucrative livings helping people appear better than they actually are. In newspaper pictures, they are staring down or straight ahead or off at some distant point, dead still, like a corpse. But in person, their eyes move as if some mannequin has sprung eerily to life. They have blemishes, hair is out of place, and your blood races the first few times they use your name.

It was like that on a perfect autumn dawn amid the rolling hills of Congressional Country Club, the type of day when the air is as crisp as an apple and the bright red and orange leaves look as if they were painted by the hand of God himself. It was just after 6:00 A.M., Thursday, October 26, when I wheeled my five-year-old Honda Accord into a space between a hunter green Jaguar and a Lexus. Before I could even pop the key into my trunk, a rather becoming woman flashed a Secret Service badge at me, spoke my name, and asked apologetically if I would raise my arms while she scanned my body with a hand-held metal detector. A couple of older members happened by, glanced at my car and at the agent frisking me, and shot me a look as if I must be some horrible criminal—or perhaps worse, a trespasser.

But their expressions changed abruptly when a man in golf cleats came clicking across the parking lot, looking all loosey-goosey with a putter in one hand and a can of Coca-Cola in the other. "Jack," he called out to me from about ten feet away in a voice as familiar as Sinatra. "Jack, Clay Hutchins. It's a pleasure to meet you."

The introduction was hardly necessary, but I wondered what else you do if you're him: Clayton Hutchins is the president of the United States. He was taking a break from the rigors of a heated election campaign to play an early-morning round of golf. Me? I'm a Washington-based reporter for the *Boston Record*, and if you ask my editors, a pretty damn good one. If you ask me, a very damn good one, but I'm trying to get that problem in check. And what was I doing playing golf with the president at his private club in one of the wealthiest towns in Maryland? Good question. One day I called his press secretary on a story about presidential pardons, a few days later I'm summoned off the campaign trail and onto a golf course with the president himself. I suspected I'd find out the reason soon enough.

"Mr. President, the pleasure is certainly mine," I said, somewhat flustered, reciting words I had rehearsed in the car on the way. "I'm quite honored by the invitation."

"What do you say we hit a few putts before we head out, Jack," the president said.

Some sort of valet in a jumpsuit came running up and

grabbed my golf bag. An advance man spoke into a walkie-talkie, and in the distance a caravan of golf carts moved around the practice green. Out of the corner of my eye, I saw the female Secret Service agent politely shooing away the two members who had given me the evil look, and I turned and graced them with a sizable smile.

As I walked toward the putting green with the president, past the ancient, graceful clubhouse, a man in a pair of knickers, a brightly colored argyle sweater, and a golf beret happened out the front door. The president leaned in toward me and whispered, "What a complete horse's ass, but he's the best the pro tour could do for me this week."

Louder, in that booming voice of his: "Jack, I want you to meet Skeeter Davis. Skeeter, this is Jack Flynn. He's the young man I told you about earlier. Skeeter's going to give us a few tips today, turn us into pros. Right, Skeeter?"

We all made proper introductions and swapped small talk and a few one-liners, though I fear mine weren't all that funny, tempered by some loose butterflies floating uncharacteristically about in my stomach. On the practice green, I retreated to my own little corner to take measure of the situation. Here was the president of the United States, in a pair of rumpled khakis with a navy blue polo shirt and a drooping yellow V-neck sweater, treating me like his new best friend. And Skeeter Davis, one of the country's foremost golf champions, ready to give me lessons. There were a dozen golf carts lining the green, some with burly Secret Service agents talking into their wrists and listening through clear plastic earpieces.

Two other carts carried four agents dressed in full black Ninja jumpsuits, armed with what appeared to be surface-to-air missile launchers and laser-trained automatic rifles. Over in the distance, on the other side of the caravan, were a few members of the White House press corps, mostly photographers with zoom lenses. There was a lot to think about here, but most of all, what I was thinking was this: Please don't duck hook my first drive into the woods.

"You boys ready?" the president boomed. His voice was like steel, meant to last, maybe even at times make history. He held his hand up toward the brilliant blue sky and briefly looked around at the pageant of colors that made up this fall morning. "It's going to be a memorable day."

On the tenth hole, Hutchins cut to the point. By then, he had already sliced six, maybe seven balls deep into the woods, in places where no federal employee had ever gone before. I started to wonder if the Secret Service agents were wearing their considerable gear to protect themselves against an assassin or Hutchins's errant golf shots. And after each ball floated aimlessly over the tree line and into the woods, I'll be damned if Skeeter Davis wasn't right there saying, "Excellent swing, Mr. President. Let me just make one small suggestion." I swear to God, Hutchins could have sliced a ball through the windshield of a school bus and caused forty third-graders to career off a cliff. The air would soon be filled with the sounds of ambulance sirens, and later, mothers wailing over the greatest misery they would ever know. And Davis would have said, "Nice swing, Mr. President. If you'd allow me to make one small suggestion."

Well, for what it was worth, my game was on, not that anyone really noticed. The Secret Service were looking for trouble. Davis was looking at Hutchins. Hutchins was looking at God knows what, but it wasn't me. Not until the tenth tee, when he asked Davis in a polite but imploring tone, "Skeeter, could you grab us all some lemonade out of that cart over there?"

As Skeeter made his way off, Hutchins turned to me with a businesslike look on his face and asked in a voice that sounded uncharacteristically timid, "How would you feel about coming over to the White House after the election, taking over as my press secretary?"

Jesus Christ. I was about to open my mouth, but to say what, I didn't know. Luckily, Hutchins cut me off just as I began to stammer.

"Look, you know my situation. I have no doubt I'm going to win this election. I'm two points up in our internal polls right now. That's off the record, I hope. But I haven't had the chance to actually govern yet. I have a staff I inherited, and they have no loyalty. Me to you, I don't think most of them are all that good. Not my type, anyways. Pointy-heads. Intellectuals. Wingnut conservatives. Think they know everything, when all's they know is what they read in those far right journals of theirs or get from all that hot air on the Sunday morning gabfests. I've got to get my own people around me. People I respect."

He paused, checking, I think, to see if his sales pitch was having any impact. I was still in shock, not sure myself if it was or not.

Skeeter came back, carrying three cups of lemonade over ice. After the brief talk of politics and such real-world considerations as career moves, he suddenly looked ridiculous in his knickers, knee socks, and sweater, like he was the host at some golf theme restaurant on the Grand Strand in South Carolina.

"Ah, you're a real man of the people, Skeeter," Hutchins said, grabbing his lemonade. Skeeter beamed, missing the irony. To me: "We'll finish this conversation later."

Hutchins then pushed a tee into the moist turf, took one of those funny half practice swings that some golfers do, then stroked his best drive of the day, the ball soaring a good 220 straight down the fairway before gently bouncing along the tight grass like a little lamb trotting across a dewy meadow. Davis seemed to be about to have an orgasm, shouting, "Perfect, Mr. President. Perfect."

I got up and duck hooked my drive hard against a tree ninety yards out, and from the sounds of it, the ball hit about four more pines as it zigzagged deeper into the woods.

"Would have made that offer earlier if I had known it would help me this much," Hutchins said, a twinkle in his eye. And as I made my way down the fairway, disgusted with my drive and bewildered over where this day was taking me, I couldn't help but begin to like the guy, or at least respect his ability to look for good staff.

"You're starting to suck, Jack."

That was the president, on the fourteenth tee, after I hit my fourth consecutive drive into the woods. He nurtured a reputation as a guy who liked to speak his mind, a no-nonsense businessman who had inexplicably flourished in the house of mirrors known as national politics, all the while remaining as blunt as he had been when he started out a political neophyte in the state capital of Iowa a mere ten years before. He wasn't much different out here, and these words were spoken with a lopsided grin and a dose of self-satisfaction.

Golf is like a political campaign, and a good political campaign is like life. You can devise great strategies and practice until you can't even see straight, but the game is long, and hazards will arise that you can never predict. There will be twists and turns that will torture the soul, ups and downs to test every cell of your very being, some of them absurdly unfair. And in the end, simple perseverance is often the key to who wins and who loses, who sits in the White House and who appears on Visa commercials in the Super Bowl, the lovable, powerless failure.

I bring this up because how could I predict on this day that the floor would fall out of my game because of an offer to be the presidential press secretary, one of the most visible jobs in America and a position that would eventually lead to great fortune for anyone who did it with even a modicum of success? There would be eventual book contracts, a sprawling office with plush carpet and a private bath heading the public relations division of a Wall Street investment house, grossly overpaying appearances performing punditry on network television. Not to mention that while you're at the White House, you might be able to work for what you believe in, perhaps even do some good for the country, if only for a short time.

Hutchins seemed to understand the reason for my golfing collapse, and he was reveling in it. There are two types of golfers, best as I could ever tell: those who just care about the score, the final outcome, whether the eight-foot putt hits dead center or skims by left, and those who luxuriate in the human element, the give and take, the frazzled nerves standing over that same eight-foot putt. The former usually are athletes, the latter are sportsmen, and I'd count Hutchins in the sportsmen's category, all toothy, even giddy, as the witness to my collapse, extending the occasional needle about being in need of a compass and a thermos as I made my way into the woods in search of an errant drive.

He, meanwhile, began hitting fairways off the tee with what I gathered was an unprecedented regularity. He began clicking his five iron off the fairway as pure as silk, his ball attracted to the green like a magnet. I heard one advance man suggest into his handheld radio that they might want to allow a network crew out onto the eighteenth hole for a candid look at the president at play, hitting soaring woods and deadly irons. I heard yet another aide use the word *miracle* on one particularly accurate approach shot, a seven iron from 140 yards that came within a club's length of the hole. Hutchins heard him, too, and shot him a look that would bring a Russian leader to his knees.

On the sixteenth hole, I skimmed four balls along the fairway and ended up inside a cavernous sand trap in front of the green, my ball pancaked hard into the grain. Hutchins, on the other hand, hit two beautiful shots, but caught a bad break and wound up in the same trap. It was as if we had stepped into a parallel universe.

"Here we are, Jack, together at last," he said, stepping onto the sand, so happy with life he hardly seemed able to contain himself.

Skeeter stepped into the trap as well and began giving us a few tips, looking, actually, far more at the president than at me: weight on your toes, club face open, come down hard into the sand an inch behind the ball and make sure you follow through. He demonstrated one shot and hit it within a few feet of the pin. Hutchins shrieked in delight. In my mind, I told him to go fuck himself— Davis, not Hutchins.

What happened next is the subject of considerable debate, a few moments in history that were to be picked over by news reporters, defense lawyers, federal prosecutors, and FBI agents for weeks to come. But before they all trampled my thoughts, making the rapid-fire events melt and twist around into each other, here are my recollections, virgin as an overnight snow:

I gave Hutchins a nod, indicating, You should hit first. He addressed his ball, and I stood about six feet behind him. As he finished what I thought would be his last practice swing, there was a dull crack. Water began shooting every which way.

"Fuck," Hutchins yelled. "Fuck." Two aides raced toward him with golf umbrellas and dry towels. On the other side of the fairway, I saw the Secret Service swat team leap from their carts and take aim at sites unknown with their automatic rifles. The four agents around us all pulled their guns and surrounded the president, serving as a human shield.

One of the agents, speaking furiously into his wrist, soon nodded and holstered his gun.

"The sprinkler system was mistakenly activated," he called out loudly. "It should be off in a minute."

Then I saw a golf cart carrying two maintenance workers race up the fairway toward a small shed in the shallow woods. One of the guys leaped out, and within a few seconds, the spouting water retreated into a light spray, and then to nothing, as the sprinkler heads ducked back into the ground. Several aides helped dry Hutchins off. The Secret Service agents walked away, the sense of impending doom having been replaced by a rainbow that hung in the air over the green. Hutchins returned to his ball and took one of those foolish half swings, eager to return to his game.

And then, much louder this time, *crack*. It was jarring not just for the sheer volume, which was immense, but for how out of place it seemed on this magnificent day, in this beautiful setting.

And then, again, *crack*.

I saw Hutchins fall hard into the sand. I saw the quick spray of blood. I heard Davis scream, though it was more like a wail, like something I had never heard before. I felt a strange sensation in my lower chest, as if someone had pressed a hot iron against me, then tried to dig the sharp end of that iron into my burning flesh. And I remember falling down hard in the sand myself.

Then there was bedlam. Three more shots, to the best of my count, though my hearing might have failed me, and the dull thump I heard as my body hit the ground may have meshed with the shots and shouts. Huge men rocketed across the fairway and into the sand trap, diving over the president, then squatting low and carrying him between their hulking bodies to an ambulance that had suddenly appeared beside the green. Paramedics were racing all around. I remember this because one of them kicked sand in my face as he ran toward Hutchins, and I wondered, Is this how I'm going to go, surrounded by rescue workers, choking on sand, bleeding to death on the nicest golf course I'll ever play?

Finally, three rescue workers slammed a stretcher down beside me and picked me up. In the distance there were screams, though they seemed to melt away as air rushed into my ears while the men ran me toward the ambulance. When I got there, they were loading Hutchins inside, and he was still conscious. I heard him, livid, tell one of the Secret Service agents: "This was going to be the best fucking round of my entire fucking life."

It's odd to say this, but the next thing I recall is my father standing over me—odd because my father is dead. He was with Gus Fitzpatrick, his fellow worker in the press room, who pulled a sheet across my chest, smoothed it out, and told me I was going to be fine. Then I heard a phone ringing—a loud, cutting ring that must have jarred me out of a deep sleep. You hear a phone, no matter where you are, no matter what has happened, and the reaction is always the same. Barely awake, I remember reaching for it, and as I lifted my arm, I saw, with horror, that needles, tubes, and wires extended up my forearm to my biceps, and there were ominous, blinking machines all around me. Still I reached, reflexively, and as I got my hand to the phone, a middle-aged nurse, breathless, appeared at the end of my bed, muttering, "Who could be calling this line?"

When I had the receiver in my hand, I found I couldn't speak, my throat still thick with the remnants of a long sleep. On the other end, there was the proper, crystal-clear voice of what sounded like an elderly gentleman, but not someone even remotely frail.

"Mr. Flynn, is that you?" he said.

I couldn't speak. I struggled to clear my voice and summoned the energy to mumble a rather warped "Yes."

"Mr. Flynn, I want you to listen carefully to me," he said. "Nothing is as it seems. Do not believe anything that they tell you. There are strange, complex motives involved in this shooting. I will call you again soon."

He hung up without my saying another word. The nurse, oddly exasperated with me, snatched the phone from my hand and slammed it down, then yanked the cord out of the wall. More gently, she pushed my head back against the pillows and stuck some sort of paper thermometer into my mouth. I had never been in a hospital before, but from watching television, it seems that they are always doing that, taking your temperature, health care workers as pollsters. I remember her departing, distant steps, the soft squeak of her rubber-soled shoes on the hard floor. Then I remember floating on a raft in a bobbing sea, very much alone, finally asleep.

two

SOMEBODY WAS POKING ME in the shoulder. As I slowly opened my eyes, I saw Peter Martin, Washington bureau chief of the *Boston Record,* quickly backing up from my bedside.

"You're awake," he said, in a tone that pretended to be matter-of-fact, but knowing him as I do, I knew to be anything but. "You all right?"

I didn't know. I didn't even know where I was. On the bedside table to my right, a laptop computer sat open and all fired up. Beside it was a large bouquet of yellow and red flowers, and beside that was an oddly shaped plastic cup with a handle that, it occurred to me even in my groggy state, I might soon be expected to urinate in. Outside the big window, it was dark, so I assumed it was night. Can't get anything by me.

I'm a reporter, so I figured I'd ask the questions, beginning with the obvious. "Where am I?"

"Oh boy," Martin said, shaking his head, then looking toward the door nervously, like maybe he should summon help. "You're at the Bethesda Naval Hospital. You know what you're doing here?"

I said, "Just help me out for a minute. I've been shot, right? Tell me what happened. Is Hutchins dead?"

Martin's never really been one to trot around the issues, and just because I was in a hospital, strapped to blinking machines that seemed to be sending all sorts of fluids coursing through my body, he wasn't about to start now.

"Jack, I hate to do this, but it's deadline. It's Thursday night, eight o'clock. The national desk up in Boston is screaming. You were a witness to an assassination attempt on the president of the United States in the middle of a cutthroat campaign, and we all thought it might be kind of nice to put this into a story."

Attempt. He said "attempt," so Hutchins wasn't dead, which was good. Neither was I, which, for me, was even better.

"Look, Peter, I'll do what I can. But before I do anything, fill me in. What am I doing here? What the fuck happened? Is Hutchins all right? Am I all right?"

Martin seemed to like that I was getting angry, evidenced by the look of relief that spilled all over his face. "Good, good," he said, as if to himself. "This is going to work out fine. Here's what I know, which isn't much. I'm counting on you to tell me more.

"You were out playing golf with the president early this morning. By the way, Appleton"—the editor in chief of the paper—"is curious as to exactly why you were doing that. So am I. Anyway, you're on the sixteenth hole. Evidently, the two of you were in a sand trap getting some little clinic from this pro golfer, I don't know his name. All of a sudden, you're shot.

"The FBI is saying that it was some militia member, disguised as a maintenance worker at the course, who pulled out a Colt .45 and shot you from the other side of the fairway. He wasn't a very good aim, luckily. The first bullet hit your club, ricocheted off, then grazed Hutchins's shoulder. A second shot struck you in the ribs. I think it broke your rib bone, or severely bruised it, but I'm no doctor. One of these typical situations when an inch either way and you're dead now. All I know is, the diagnosis is good, and you're expected to be out of here within a couple of days."

With that, Martin looked nervously at the door again, lowered his voice a bit, and said, "They really don't even want me in here now, so we should try to be as quick as possible."

"How is Hutchins?" I asked.

"He's fine. A slight shoulder injury, and now the guy's a national hero. A local paramedic told a network television crew that as they were loading him into the ambulance, he looked at them with a wide grin and said, 'What kind of jerk would shoot me right in the middle of the best round of golf of my life?' He's been slipping in the public polls for days, but now analysts are saying this shooting could win him the election. The guy's being talked about like a battlefield hero."

More and more, the scene was coming back to me—the loud cracks, Hutchins falling in a heap on a brilliant morning, the frenzy of activity, the piercing scream. "Jesus, how's Skeeter Davis, the golfer?" I asked, assuming he was the one who screamed. "He dead?"

"Dead? God no. I think he turned an ankle running for cover. He wasn't even hit."

"What happened to the shooter?" I asked, again, remembering another scream and late shots.

"Dead. Secret Service says he pointed a gun at one of their agents, and they mowed him down. Six bullets, I think, all of them in the head. This is a no-shit crew."

Martin was getting increasingly nervous, looking at the door, at the computer, at his watch, and at me, like some sort of caged animal. He's anxious by nature, but usually it's on his turf. Slightly bookish, with the soft, pasty look of someone whose father was a dermatologist constantly preaching the evils of the sun, he knows Capitol Hill front and back. He knows things about the budget process that cabinet secretaries don't know. He knows the ages of all nine Supreme Court justices and the years they were appointed. He can cite election statistics dating back to Eisenhower's first term. In a city where most bureau chiefs survive on brass and television appearances, Martin is the opposite. He survives on his brains and his willingness to work. But this was an assassination attempt, a glorified police story, and Martin really didn't have a clue.

"If you're well enough," he started, looking tentatively toward the door again, "we'd like a first-person account of what happened out there. It's a blockbuster. Biggest event in the world, and no one else will have what we have."

As Martin talked, a self-important young man in a navy blue suit strode through the door and abruptly asked, "Is your telephone not hooked up?"

I was fortunate enough to be born with a virtually bottomless reservoir of aggravation, which I dipped into to shoot him a look that should have stopped him dead in his tracks, though perhaps I shouldn't have been thinking in those terms on that specific day. He ignored it and quickly came around the bed to the phone, where he held up the disconnected telephone cord in the air, glanced angrily at me as if I had crossed him in some way, and plugged it back into the wall. Almost immediately, it rang.

"For you," he said.

Through the earpiece, a voice boomed out. "Jack, Jack, that you? For chrissakes, I'm five pars into the best nine holes of my life, and some horse's ass feels the need to take a potshot at us. What the hell is that all about?" Then came the sound of loud, wheezing laughter.

It was Hutchins. I'll be damned if I'm not the quickest thinker I've ever met, especially under duress. I motioned to Martin for a pen, and he searched furiously through a shoulder bag for a legal pad and a writing instrument, placing them carefully in my lap.

"I think that was my club pro, Mr. President, ticked off that you were taking me to the cleaners." I had a passing thought that maybe I shouldn't be joking with the president about killing him, not now anyway. No matter. I heard him cough, then laugh into the phone.

"You all right?" he asked, but didn't pause for an answer. "You ought to see this getup up here. It's a goddamned presidential suite, right here in the hospital. You should come up. My doctors, they think they're my mother. They won't even let me out of bed, and I've got a campaign to wage and an election to win."

I asked, "Mr. President, have you talked to the press yet?"

"The hell with that," he said. "Turn on CNN. My doctor's mugging for the cameras right now. He thinks he's Robert fucking Redford. They're showing your picture all over the place. I have Dalton"—Royal Dalton, his press secretary—"issuing a statement from me."

As I was shaking off the grogginess and moving around my bed, it struck me just how much pain I was in. My ribs felt like they were about to snap, and even normal breathing began to hurt. My arms throbbed from all the needles and heavy tubes sticking in them. My lips were so dry they were flaking, and I was near desperate for a drink of water.

But journalism is a funny business, and not in a humorous kind of way. There is no sympathy, only opportunity, and the fact that I was laid out in a hospital bed in Bethesda, Maryland, with a bullet hole in my chest and an injured rib that probably meant the difference between life and death was seen by my superiors as a major boon for the paper, and probably for me. And lying there, I began to see it that way myself.

"Mr. President, you mind if I throw a few questions at you for tomorrow's story?"

"You're in a goddamned hospital bed, and you're writing a story for tomorrow morning's paper?" Hutchins asked, incredulous. "Jesus Christ, you guys just don't give it a rest, do you? But what the hell, we're in this together. Fire away."

With that pun, he burst out laughing, then quickly calmed himself down. I proceeded to ask him a series of about half a dozen questions, and he easily, even poignantly, answered each one as I scribbled notes until I thought my throbbing arm might fall off. I had to give him credit: still lying in a hospital bed, he already had the patter of a reluctant hero. "They can shoot at me every day, until my last day in office, but I'll never bow to these haters and all that they represent."

I asked him about the likely impact on the election, which was only twelve days away. "Look," he said, "my doctors, my security team, they're telling me I'm going to be confined to the White House. Hear me clear right now. That's not going to happen. I was supposed to be in Baltimore, then St. Louis this afternoon. I'll be back on the stump, if not tomorrow, then Saturday. The American people have a right to see and judge the candidates for president. I'm not going to allow some hater with a gun to deprive our country of our God-given right."

All the while, Martin was circling my bed at an excitable pace, occasionally pumping his fist in the air as he heard bits and pieces of memorable quotes shouted by Hutchins. I was off the phone one, maybe two seconds when he placed the laptop gently in my lap and told me to tap away. "We'll go with two stories: your interview with Hutchins, which will include some analysis on election impact, and then your own first-person account. No time for art right now. This stuff should write itself. Just hit the keys as fast as you can."

And I did. I did, that is, until that same middle-aged nurse from earlier in the day walked through the door, a woman who looked remarkably like my Aunt Helda, and you can guess what she's like. She shot a glance at me sitting up in bed, and you could follow the angry progression of her eyes, from the sheaf of notes I now had beside me to the laptop computer to Peter Martin, and I thought she might slug me, but figured I was safe even if she did, given this was a hospital.

"All right, out," she said to Martin as she came angrily around my bed to grab the computer.

He was cool as a cucumber, and what he had to say, he said in a very calm way. "You touch that laptop, you make even one more step in its direction, I start screaming at the top of my lungs that you've just killed my baby. I'll wake people up from here to Chevy Chase."

Seeing the look on his face, knowing what was at stake, I believed him. Apparently, so did she. With nary a word, she backed up and stormed out of the room, I assumed, to get the security guards, though if she did, they never showed up. Martin, of course, closed the door to the room and locked it. Meanwhile, I typed. I wrote of Hutchins in his hospital bed, oozing bravado, accusing the militia of being haters. I wrote of his recollection of a flash and the sudden burst of pain. I wrote of his vow to return to the campaign trail by the weekend. Then I wrote my own account, beginning with the brilliant autumn morning, the pageant of colors, then quickly flipping to a blood-spattered sand trap and the Secret Service agents hurtling themselves into the line of fire.

When I was done, Martin took the computer and sat in one of those standard-issue hospital chairs, kind of low with an orange cushion back, and read, shaking his head all the while, rarely typing in any edits.

"Jesus Christ, I hate to tell you this, but you're good," he said finally.

"I know."

A visitor knocked, turned the knob, realized the door was locked, and then opened it with a key. He was a fifty-something man, fairly pleasant looking, actually, who said he was with the hospital's public relations department.

"Mr. Flynn, I have about fifty reporters downstairs in the cafeteria who are clamoring to see you," he said. "They asked me to invite you down for some questions."

Martin said, halfheartedly, as he plugged the computer into the phone jack and transmitted the two stories up to Boston, "Yeah, shit, I meant to tell you about that. You've become quite a little celebrity."

I was overcome by exhaustion and, conceited as I am, feared that in this condition I would look pale and bloated before the unforgiving eye of the television camera. "Can you take care of this tonight?" I asked Martin. "Tell them the doctor insisted I didn't come down, and tell them I'll be there in the morning to help as much as I can."

I was drained, mentally and physically. I'm a reporter, and tonight, that's what I did. It felt good. Still, something had changed. I had somehow turned into an unwitting celebrity, just for being there. My future was even in some doubt, though maybe a nice doubt, given this job offer I had received. Everything was so tiring, and I felt woozy.

Martin fiddled with the computer and made a call to the newsroom to make sure the stories had arrived safely. When he hung up, he turned to me in that pointed way of his and said, "Okay, so tell me. Why were you playing golf with the president of the United States?"

This was not an issue I felt like dealing with right then, but it was obvious, even in my semicomatose state, that I really had no choice. Lying in bed, I looked straight ahead and said, "I'm doing that story on presidential pardons that you and I discussed, trying to figure out if there's any rhyme or reason to the pardons that the White House gave out last summer, and then a new one last month. It's unusual for them to pardon convicts in the middle of a campaign, and there are a couple of names I'm curious about, so I call the White House press office.

"They're helping me out a little bit, and the next thing I know, Royal Dalton calls and wants to know if I play golf. He says Hutchins is looking for a partner for

Thursday morning during a quick campaign layover in D.C., and would I be available? If I play, he says, I might be able to lob him a question or two on the pardon issue."

Martin nodded, then asked the obvious question. "Did you?"

"Never got the chance," I replied. "I was waiting to do it after the round, and there was this small matter of getting shot."

I was so tired I could barely speak. Mid-conversation, I faded in and out of consciousness. I vaguely recall a doctor coming in, checking my pulse, fooling with the machines around my bed, talking softly with Martin. Two other visitors stepped into the room and showed the doctor badges. "FBI," I heard one of them say, the guy with the trench coat. Looked like he was from central casting. The other was a younger woman with luxuriant black hair and a business suit. I could barely hold my eyes open, but as I did, I saw her smile at me, a nice smile that showed sweet dimples on a face that looked vaguely familiar. The doctor chatted with them a while, and then they left. Martin then left with the doctor, giving my forearm a quick pat on the way out. Half-asleep, I remembered my earlier mysterious telephone call, a man's voice, a stern warning. Lies, everyone's telling lies. And I faded out again, this time to a place so blissful I would never find it again.

three

THERE IS THAT FINAL SCENE in *The Wizard of Oz*, when Dorothy regains consciousness in her farmhouse in Kansas, surrounded by her farmhands and neighbors—all of whom resemble the characters in her dream visit to the Emerald City. That's what I felt like, only it was the Bethesda Naval Hospital, not Kansas, and gathered around me were a pair of FBI agents, the hospital public relations director, Peter Martin, my pal Gus Fitzpatrick, a man in a white laboratory coat, who my deductive skills led me to believe was my doctor, and a few assorted friends from college and the paper. Everyone, it seemed, but the Joint Chiefs of Staff.

Martin stepped toward the bed and tossed the Friday-morning *Record* into my lap. "President Survives Assassination Attempt," the headline screamed, stripped across the top of the front page in big block letters. "Secret Service Kills Gunman; Believed to be Militia Member. 11th Hour Election Turmoil Expected." And under that, over two separate stories, "*Record* Reporter, Injured by Gunfire, Witnesses Event." And above another: "Hutchins: I Will Not Bow to Threats."

"We're the best paper on the biggest story in the country today," Martin said, absolutely exhilarated. "Forget country. In the world. We're being quoted all over the networks, all over the wires. You're a celebrity. The publisher and editor both wanted me to come down and thank you and ask if there's anything the paper can do for you during your recovery."

Martin paused, and the hospital public relations man spoke from the back of the room. "Sir," he said, "Keith Madigan, with Naval public affairs. I still have a room of about sixty reporters downstairs, and every one of them keeps asking when you're coming down to talk."

He had barely finished his sentence when the female FBI agent spoke out. "Samantha Stevens, special agent with the Federal Bureau of Investigation. This is Kent Drinker, assistant director. Before you go anywhere, we need to speak with you about the events of yesterday."

From the back of the room, the doctor was next. "Look, before anyone does anything, I have to talk some things over with Mr. Flynn and do some tests. I'm going—"

He wasn't quite finished, but I had already had enough. "Before I do anything, could I just get a moment alone with—" I looked around the room real fast for someone to talk to who could just give me a breather and explain how upside-down my world had become. I thought of Martin, but quickly backed away from the idea. Too nervous. If I chose any of my friends, the others would be insulted. "Gus," I said. "It will just be a minute, and then we'll take care of everything else. Doctor, I'll be ready for you right afterward. Agent, I have all the time you need, obviously." And I looked at the hospital PR man, forgetting his name. "And sir, if you could just tell my colleagues that I'll be down within an hour, well before deadline. Explain that I'm tied up right now with my doctor."

I noticed that all of the blinking, beeping machines had been pushed away from my bed, and the needles and tubes had been pulled out of my arms, replaced by small bandages covering gauze pads. I was glad I hadn't been awake for that. I felt better, physically. My chest still had the sensation that someone quite heavy was nonchalantly standing on top of it. But I didn't have that queasy, groggy feeling of the night before, and truth is, the pain wasn't all that bad and I felt quite rested.

As everyone but Gus slowly shuffled out of the room, politely pausing at the door to let each other go, the telephone rang, a penetrating ring that almost caused me to jump up out of my bed. I grabbed it before anyone else could, having a nagging, almost subconscious sense of who might be on the other end. The FBI agent, Stevens, must have sensed a change in my voice, because she shot me a quizzical look as I spoke my greetings.

"Mr. Flynn," the voice said, clear as a bell again, dignified, with impeccable pronunciation, like some sort of headmaster at a private school. I looked out the window as I held the receiver to my ear and noticed that the sun was shining brightly, illuminating a rich blue sky that marked what must have been another perfect autumn day. "Mr. Flynn, this is not a joke. This is not a game." He spoke those two sentences as if they were one, barely pausing, speaking dramatically, maybe even reading from something prepared.

"There are things happening all around you that you must learn," the man said. "I will help you, but I can only do so much. You will be leaving the hospital tomorrow morning. I will telephone you tomorrow afternoon, at your house, when you will have more time and privacy to talk."

How on earth did he know when I was leaving the hospital? I wondered. I didn't even know when I was leaving the hospital. I looked over in the direction of the door, trying to act as casual and unassuming as I could, and saw Stevens still standing there, overtly staring at me, almost as if she was trying to peer through the phone lines to see who was at the other end. I'm not sure why I immediately hid this caller from anyone. Maybe it was my lifelong distrust of authority. Maybe it was my knee-jerk need for privacy. Perhaps it was my simple love of secrets, especially ones that I could someday report in the pages of the *Record*. Regardless, I spoke in a loud, cheerful tone that sent a clear message to the caller that I was protecting him, and a contrary message to anyone in my room—read: FBI agents—that I had a friend, or at least an acquaintance on the line.

"I'll look forward to that," I said in a booming voice, with a forced smile. "It's really good to hear from you again. I can't believe you were this nice to call. Take care."

I hung up, and everyone kept walking out the door, except for Gus, who I think was both confused and delighted by my request that he stay behind.

"Gus, what is going on here?" I asked, cutting to the chase once everyone was gone. "Am I all right?"

"All right? You're a star, kid. You're not just going to be all right, you're going to be better than you ever were before. Your performance in today's paper is the talk of the country."

Gus is a national treasure. Every city, every newspaper,

no, every guy my age should have someone like Gus—a leathery-faced geezer of a man who has seen wars start and end, watched children born and, in one case, die, has witnessed fads come and go, all through the eyes of someone who knows what matters and, more important, what doesn't. Gus tends not to get excited by much. It's not that he doesn't care. In fact, he does. It's just that he's seen so much, remained so even, and is so confident of who he is and what he likes that he knows deep in his psyche what is truly worth getting excited over. Gus is a guy, in short, who you can trust.

Gus works in the pressroom of the *Record*. When I saw him standing in my hospital room, it was the first time in what must have been ten years that he wasn't wearing his ink-smeared hunter green apron draped over his work clothes. He was my father's best friend at work, back when they worked the overnight shift at the *Record*, keeping watch over the mammoth printing presses, recasting inks, and refilling the massive rolls of newsprint that rattled through the presses and turned into the next day's newspaper. It was, I used to think, and probably still do, the most important job in the world, the manifestation of which used to be on our kitchen table every morning, in black and white, when my father arrived home from work and I awoke to go to school.

As a kid of twelve, I told my father I wanted to work at the *Record*, and he immediately assumed I wanted to do just what he did. It wasn't until I was maybe seventeen years old, as we leaned against his car eating cones at the local Dairy Queen, having just come back from splitting a large bucket of balls at the driving range, that I explained to him I wanted to be a writer, a news reporter, perhaps even cover politics and go off to Washington. He didn't say much. No one in his family had ever been to college, let alone held a job with a title like Washington correspondent, and I'm not sure he knew how to react. When I was a senior in college, in Connecticut, he died of a severe stroke. He never saw me walk into the newsroom of the paper he had worked at for more than thirty-five years.

Gus did, though. After school, I did what all would-be reporters have to do: worked my way up through what would count as the minor leagues. I wrote for a small paper in Vermont for a year, built some clips, then took a job with a paper in suburban Boston and beat the *Record* day after day for a year and a half, until they had no choice but to hire me. That first day in the newsroom was the culmination of my loftiest dreams. There I was, among all the people I had read for so long—huge names in the industry, Pulitzer Prize winners, editors who had been to Washington, traveled overseas, jetted across the country on presidential campaigns. That first day I stood arranging a few books at my desk. I was dressed in a crisp Brooks Brothers pinpoint shirt, a neatly striped tie, the woolen trousers to a smart gray suit. Gus came walking up to my desk, limping as he does, given that he was born with one leg two inches longer than the other. I suspect he had never been in the newsroom before during business hours. I don't know if he had even talked to a reporter in his life. He was short and balding, and he stopped in front of me, staring with a long, proud gaze, a hint of a smile rounding out the edges of his lips. It was deadline, and Gus was wearing his apron during what must have been an early start to his shift.

He extended his hand to me, and I knew what my father would have felt. I moved past his hand into a soft embrace, and Gus wrapped his right arm tightly around me and hit me hard in the back, speaking into my ear, "You're going to be the best reporter this place has ever had." He stepped back and said, "Your father helped me get this job, at a tough time in my life. If I can do anything to help you, I will." Then he walked away, leaving a black ink smudge on my new shirt. Beside me, a rather bleached-out reporter in a bright bow tie, Troy Ellis, whose name I had read for years, usually over stories about academia and other intellectual issues, looked at me with shock, rolled his eyes in a superior way, and said in an exaggerated Brahmin accent, "My God, that looked interesting."

I was kind of caught. I was the new kid here, one day in the newsroom, standing among all these people who were my heroes, yet one of them was making fun of Gus. What the hell, I thought. "That, Troy, is someone more interesting than you would ever understand."

Troy didn't seem to understand even that, which I sensed was part of a pattern with him. He said nothing and turned back to his computer, me to my books, and that was that.

"Well," I said to Gus, who had settled into the orange vinyl-backed chair beside my hospital bed, "tell me, what on God's good earth is going on here?"

"What's going on here is that, through the luck of the skilled, you've just placed yourself at the center of the biggest story in America. There's nothing bigger. You're the witness to an assassination attempt on the president of the United States. From what I read today, you're his journalistic equivalent of a confidant. In my own humble view, this story is going to get a lot bigger before it fades away. The presidential campaign is in turmoil, and because of the militia? I mean, come on. The militia taking a crack at our president?"

"Doesn't get much bigger, does it?" I said. I was getting tired just thinking about it, the layers that would be involved, the assassination investigation, the impact on the race, the stories about American culture, reports from the hinterland on the antigovernment movement spreading across the country. And the reach for the explanation on how it came to this: the attempted murder of the president.

Gus said, "I want you to be careful. This little room is like a cocoon, but that's all over soon. You are going home tomorrow."

Jesus, I thought, the voice on the telephone was right. Gus continued: "Everyone's going to want a piece of you. The FBI is going to want a piece of you. The TV cameras are going to want a piece of you. Even the president is going to want a piece of you. You should enjoy it, but do your job. You're the best reporter I've ever met, and granted, I'm a bit biased. But do your job, and everything else will take care of itself."

These were the reassuring words I wanted to hear, and, lying in bed, I said quietly, "Thanks."

We made small talk about golf with the president and the FBI agent who had been in the room and the likely impact of this shooting on the campaign. After a while, Gus stood up from his chair to leave, and hesitated a moment at my bedside. He looked down at his feet as if he was not quite sure what to say. "You going to be all right at home?" he asked shyly.

Truth is, I wasn't sure. I hadn't spent more than three straight nights in that house in the last year. Suddenly I thought of my dog, alone there over the past twenty-four hours, and a wave of panic washed over me. "Jesus Christ," I said. "Do you know if Baker is all right?"

"The dog is fine. Your dog sitter came over and picked him up yesterday afternoon when she saw your picture on television. She said she'll bring him back when you get home."

I paused, basking in the relief. "I'll be fine," I said.

"I'll get the doctor. And I have to get back to Boston. The publisher was nice enough to pay my freight down here, but I have to get back to work tonight." And with that, a proud smile came over Gus's face. He gave my hand a long, affectionate squeeze, whispered, "Jack, do your job," then limped out of the room.

Cops and reporters are like oil and water. They share a like goal: to gather information for an ultimate presentation in the public domain. Police prepare for court cases. Reporters compile information for the pages of their newspaper. But how they go about it is vastly different. Police detectives prefer the privacy of an interrogation room, sitting at a spare table with graffiti marks dug into the top, surrounded by bare slab walls, illuminated by a single lamp, with some suspect or witness looking around at the sober surroundings and wondering what has become of his life and how he can quickly and drastically change it. Detectives can take the most theatrical, most sensational case and break it down into the dull sum of its scientific parts—semen and blood samples, fingerprints and fibers. They move with a painstaking method-ology gleaned from the pages of the police training man-ual they memorized when they ascended to the position so many years before. God forbid, publicity. That causes witnesses to be tainted, politicians to speak out, police chiefs to demand hasty action, and ultimately, protocol and common sense to be violated.

Reporters, meanwhile, like to interview people in action, capturing color and a sense of place. A good reporter can take the most mundane murder, inject it with a heavy dose of human emotion, massage it with a rapid-fire series of verbs, and end up with what the aver-age reader might be convinced is the crime of the century, at least until the next day's paper. Reporters are constantly looking at the whole at the expense of some of its parts, glossing over this angle or that aspect to play upon what editors call "the big picture." Good reporters move at breakneck speed, well aware of the competition from other newspapers or television stations. Best to have an incomplete story first than the entire tale last. And virtu-ally everything, they believe, is appropriate in the public realm, allowing readers to decide what is right or wrong, whether the grammar school principal is really a child molester or if the accusations of decade-old misdeeds are a piece of sad whimsy on the part of a psychologically unfit former student.

So it is all the more fruitful and delicious when a reporter is able to strike up a relationship with a police detective, and I take no small amount of pride in saying that much of the success I've had in my career—and, since you're wondering, I've had my share—has been due to my ability to get along with cops. My grandfather was a Boston police sergeant. One of my uncles was a Boston police detective. I know how to communicate with them in a way that Troy Ellis, for instance, never would—when to cuss, when to talk big, when to be respectful, how to engage them in some back and forth and involve them in my needs.

None of this, though, seemed to have any direct bearing on my new relationship with Samantha Stevens.

She didn't spend a lot of time on niceties when she strode into my hospital room, just a moment after the doctor had left. "Why don't we start with the basics?" she said. "What is it you were doing playing golf with the president of the United States?"

Her partner, who briefly introduced himself as an assistant director of the FBI, no less, stood impassively against the wall.

"He invited me," I said, taken aback, but trying to maintain composure.

"Why's that?" she asked, aloof, almost clinical.

I didn't like where this was going, mostly because I wasn't particularly keen on word getting out already about this offer to be press secretary.

"Why don't you ask him?" I said, and I watched as her very becoming face flushed red.

"Why don't I decide how to conduct the investigation?" she replied, just as aloof, just as clinical.

This wasn't quite unpleasant, but it wasn't far from it. I expected a nice, collegial little discussion, maybe share a can of orange juice and rhapsodize about what had become of a society where a collection of country bumpkins would think it's meaningful, even laudable, to kill the president of the United States and overthrow our democratic form of government. Instead, I was being treated like a suspect in a purse snatching.

Stevens was standing a few feet from my bed. I was sitting up on some pillows. Not that she gave me any encouragement to think about such things, but she looked even better than the day before, her straight black hair cascading across her shoulders and over the top part of a smart navy blue work suit. She had tiny little bags under her blazing blue eyes, and little crow's feet beside them, betraying the only signs of her age. She gave no indication whether she was pleased or displeased with how our little chat was proceeding.

"We are conducting the most important investigation in the bureau right now, Mr. Flynn," she said. "Forgive my manner, if you are for some reason offended by it. But I have to dedicate myself to getting to the bottom of this case as quickly as humanly possible. And such a mission doesn't accord me much time for excessive civility."

"Apparently not," I said. "If it would help," I added, knowing what I was about to suggest would do anything but, "I could call my lawyer and have him come down and sit in."

That seemed to take Stevens by surprise, not to mention her colleague Drinker, who I caught furrowing his brow. Me, too, actually. What the hell was I thinking?

"That would be a mistake for all of us," she said.

She paused, standing there with her arms crossed, then added, "Look, we didn't get off on the very best foot here. I just want you to understand the gravity of this investigation. We have vastly different interests, and I didn't necessarily appreciate reading your eyewitness account in the newspaper before we had a chance to talk. This is first and foremost an FBI investigation of an assassination attempt on the president, not simply some sensational story to help you sell more papers. Why don't we revisit this tomorrow, and I'm sure we'll make some more progress."

"That would be fine," I said, not wanting to be any more disagreeable.

She turned around to leave, and Drinker followed silently without even so much as looking my way. At the door, Drinker turned back around.

"By the way, who was that who called you earlier, when everyone was in the room?" His tone was soft, even pleasant.

"Oh, just an old friend of mine," I said, fumbling for an answer in a way that might have been obvious.

"What's the friend's name?" he asked.

I'm sure he saw the uncertainty on my face or sensed the flustered tone of my voice. "That's personal," I said eventually, and Drinker simply nodded as the two of them headed out the door.

four

THERE IS A SAYING ABOUT hospitals, except, of course, among hypochondriacs, that the longer you stay, the more things can go wrong. As someone who had never been in a hospital before in his life, I had already been in far too long, and when the doctor told me I could head home the following morning, I prevailed on him to endorse my departure for that very night.

The press corps treated me as well as I could have hoped, given that a few of the network stars were a bit miffed about being on the sidelines while an ink-stained wretch from an out-of-town paper basked in the limelight. I spent half an hour before the cameras, concentrating on good eye contact—never look down, make pleasant facial expressions, and never stammer *um* or *ah*—and was on my way home with my good friend and former college roommate Harry Putnam.

"Now what do you do?" he asked as his Audi rolled down Wisconsin Avenue, past the fast food restaurants and specialty shops all lit up on this breezy autumn night.

What indeed? For starters, there was the matter of my interview with this somewhat obstinate FBI agent, probably in the morning. More important, there was an anonymous call coming my way in the afternoon. Hutchins had been discharged from the hospital a few hours before me, telling reporters on the way out that danger be damned, he was heading back out on the campaign trail. I very much wanted to get back to work, despite these tight bandages wrapped around my aching ribs. There was much to do on this story, and I was in a prime position to do it. Most important of all, it was time to come to terms with my new reality of being home. It was time to stop running.

"Where do I begin?" I said. "I deal with it. No, I try to get ahead of it, all of it."

I fell silent, watching the Roy Rogers slide past, the Cineplex Odeon—Ten Screens, Free Validated Parking—the Chesapeake Bagelry. Harry, who knows me about as well as I know myself, sensed through my quiet that I was of no mind to have a deep, philosophical discussion about where I was in my life and where I might be heading.

"You want to stop for a beer, maybe something to eat?" he asked.

I did and I didn't. Mostly, I felt like being alone, to start to sort some things out, to prepare for what I thought would be an onslaught in the days ahead. "I'm going to take a pass on this one," I said, and he nodded his understanding.

"I'm around all weekend," he said.

We pulled up to the curb in front of my red brick townhouse in the heart of the East Village of Georgetown. Katherine and I had bought it two years earlier. I was enchanted by the enormous bowfront window with the small panes, and even though we first saw it in the dead of a humid Washington August, I pictured how it would look with a towering, lighted Christmas tree. She was smitten with the condition of the place, which was atrocious, so we could gut it and start anew, creating an interior in our own image—or, I should say, her image, with a few peripheral touches by me like, say, the doorbell.

Harry and I bade farewell, and I ambled up the stairs. This should have been a pleasant homecoming. I was a sudden celebrity, and even under the most trying of circumstances, I had re-proved myself to the newspaper, perhaps unnecessarily so, but in my business it was something that was always good to do. Besides that, I was suddenly on very good terms with the president—terms so good he wanted me to be his next press secretary. And beyond even that, I had days ahead of the terrific story of an assassination attempt a dozen days before a presidential election.

Still, maybe it was the lingering effects of the painkillers the doctors had put in my intravenous tubes. Maybe it was my complete physical, emotional, and mental exhaustion. But as I stepped inside my dark, empty house, I felt a sense of helplessness, of melancholy, and I craved a sleep that I knew I wouldn't get.

More than anything else, I missed Katherine, and thought to myself that this was no time to be alone. In a few days, it would be one year that she had been gone. We had been married three years and, like everyone else, had our ups and downs. We were far from a perfect couple, but for my money, we were more perfect than most. A friend of mine, wrestling with his own decision whether to get married, asked me once how I knew Katherine was the right person and that the marriage was happening at the right time. I said you never really know for sure. Look at the divorce rate. And I'm too independent to ever say, "I have to have this woman for the rest of my life." What I came to understand, though, was that I couldn't picture my life without her. So in a defensive gesture, we married, and it was the smartest thing I ever did.

We bought the house and renovated it top to bottom, inside and out. We bought a golden retriever and named him Baker. We had sex in spurts. There were weeks when we couldn't keep our hands off each other, when we would call each other at work and talk tawdry, as if we were having an affair, then steal off in the late afternoon, feigning meetings, and have sex in the waning sunlight of our second-floor bedroom. Afterward, exhausted, we would lie in bed, leaning on our elbows, and look silently out into our back garden, breaking the quiet to tell each other of our day. We would slowly dress in the descending dark and walk down the street to our favorite restaurant, La Chaumiere, still smelling of sex, our private secret. Of course, other times we were more physically aloof. One or the other of us was tired, or preoccupied, or just not around, and then we would enjoy our friendship, actually test the limits of our friendship, to eventually wake up one morning and feel the need to have sex. More than anything else, she was my friend, and trite as it is to say, she could make me laugh, knowing exactly which buttons to push at exactly the right times.

Her pregnancy brought on a real potpourri of emotions. She was constantly sick at first, dry-heaving at the very mention of food one moment and starving the next. I, meanwhile, was coming to terms with the thought of fatherhood. For most of my adult life I had taken pride in my dearth of worldly possessions, which were so limited that for years, when it came time to move, I was able to wrap the cord around the alarm clock and pack everything I owned into the back of my hatchback. Initially, the thought of the responsibility petrified me, sometimes making me as sick to my stomach as she was. By the sixth month or so, I had arrived at an inner peace and understood and openly appreciated the length of a woman's pregnancy, this nine-month readjustment period. By then, she was a glowing mother-to-be, all her new weight centered in her stomach. I couldn't wait to greet my newborn into our house, and privately I hoped for a daughter. I had a recurring fantasy of stealing home from work early one day, coming around the corner on foot, and running into my wife, pushing a carriage, Baker padding patiently and proudly beside them. I never actually figured out where that fantasy went from there, or if it even involved sex. I'm not sure if there is such a thing as a sexless fantasy, so perhaps I should reclassify it.

Anyways, it was all for naught. Katherine was due in mid October. By the second, I was a basket case, nervous to the point of being unable to work. So I stayed home that day and played with the dog and puttered around the house. Katherine, meanwhile, continued to make calls to her public relations clients from our upstairs office, sending out faxes and approving advertising strategies as if she didn't have a worry in the world. She did this right up to the time when she came walking out the French doors onto our back patio and announced to me that the time had come to head to Georgetown Hospital. She told me I was making her so nervous, I probably induced the delivery. I was wiping down our wrought iron outdoor furniture. Baker was sprawled on the cool bricks, in a patch of shade.

In the delivery room, as we began to run through all the breathing exercises we had learned in eight weeks of birthing classes, her pain seemed almost unbearable. She pushed and counted, counted and pushed, when suddenly a nurse monitoring her vital signs snapped up a telephone and had the receptionist page our obstetrician. The doctor came rushing in less than two minutes later, took measure of the situation, and told me in no uncertain terms to leave the room and have a seat in the waiting lounge. Worried sick, profoundly confused, I did as I was told, trying to meet my wife's eyes as I left, watching her face, covered in sweat, watch mine as I backed out of the room. She mouthed the words "Don't go." The doctor overrode her, yelling, "Please leave." In the waiting area, I sat staring at my feet for the next two hours.

Dr. Joyce was an attractive, late fiftyish woman with the look of competence you would never think to question and a reputation that placed her among the top ob/gyns in the city of Washington. As I sat there, lost in my fears, she came up so quietly I never saw her, took me by the hand, and began walking back toward the delivery room.

For a fleeting moment, all my dreadful thoughts gave way to the sparkling optimism that we were heading back to see my wife and newborn baby. I expected Katherine to be sound asleep, the effect of painkillers taking their toll. And I thought that our baby, boy or girl, would be kicking and screaming in a nearby crib. Already, I thought, I'm going to be pressed into service as a father. But before we arrived at the swinging doors that led into the maternity ward Dr. Joyce pulled me into a small conference room, bare except for a circular table, a few swivel chairs, and some institutional art—a covered bridge in what looked like Vermont is the one I best remember. She directed me into a seat, then leaned against a wall, looked me in the eye, and spoke, exhausted.

"There's no good way to say this, Jack. Katherine died during delivery. She had what is called a placental tear, and she died from internal bleeding. We did everything we could, and for a while, I thought we were going to be able to revive her, but the bleeding was too much."

A wave that began in the pit of my stomach worked its way up my chest and into my head. I had never felt so alone, so detached from everything and everyone I had ever known, in all of my life. I was physically devastated and emotionally incapacitated. I remember supporting myself on the table with my elbows as my head bowed in a storm of salty, silent tears. The doctor continued to speak.

"Jack, I can't imagine how tough this is, but I also have to explain to you, your daughter was stillborn. Once the internal hemorrhaging began, she never really had a chance."

I don't know if I passed out or if my mind just stopped functioning. I don't know if we were in that conference room for five minutes or five hours. At some point, I felt a weak sense of composure returning. I rubbed my palms repeatedly across my eyes and nose to soak up the tears and moisture. Dr. Joyce was still there. I vaguely remember her talking, but I have no idea what else she might have said.

She was looking forlornly at me, waiting patiently until I was ready to do God only knows what.

"Do you want to say good-bye?" she asked me. I was in no position to decide anything, but shook my head yes. She led me back into the delivery room, now empty but for a lifeless form on a rolling hospital gurney, and pulled back the sheet from Katherine's face. Her hair was still wet around her forehead from the sweat of her pain. Her eyes had been pushed shut. She looked like a doll, not a person. I clutched her cold hand and I kissed her cheek, and then her forehead, and then let my lips linger on hers until a tear rolled off my nose and onto her face. And I walked out of the room, forever changed, always something less than I should have been.

These were the thoughts that filled my mind as I prepared to go to bed. I poured some spring water into a cup and noticed that the plastic bottle was the only food I had in the refrigerator. I slumped down in my moss green couch and punched a code into the telephone to access my messages, and immediately a computerized female voice told me that my voice mail was full. There were thirty in all, from people I had never met, from my younger sister, from colleagues at the paper, from far-flung relatives, one from Gus, and the last message on the machine was from Agent Samantha Stevens of the FBI, who had a textured voice, almost a singer's voice. "I'd like to talk with you again as soon as you feel able," she said. "I'll call you again in the morning, or you can page me at this number—"

Without Baker trotting around, chewing on a rawhide bone or making his stuffed hedgehog squeal, the house seemed vacant, like a fishbowl without water. As I climbed the stairs to bed, there was an uncomfortable silence. Every step echoed off the walls. I thought about turning on the stereo, but there was really no music I wanted to hear. Arriving upstairs, I looked at all three doors. In the back, there was the bedroom, overlooking the patio and back garden. In the front, we had set up an office with a computer atop an antique library table and some nicely framed prints and old maps on the wall.

The middle room was the nursery. When I came home from the hospital after my wife's death, I pulled the door shut, and through some quirk of the human psyche, I hadn't been in there since. Friends, family members, have all offered, even pleaded, to clean the room out, to pack up the crib and the changing table and put the stuffed animals neatly in a box and carry them wherever it is that such things should go. I've always said no. "What are you waiting for?" they asked, repeatedly. I've never known, but maybe it was this, the night I came home a national celebrity.

So inexplicably, rather than go into my bedroom or the bathroom, I pulled the door open to the nursery, flicked on the light, and walked inside. I felt like I had stepped into some strange universe, into a part of my life that had ended before it ever began. The walls were a pale blue with the stenciled letters of the alphabet dancing down from the ceiling in various shades of violet and pink. There was a light layer of dust on the windowsill and atop the small bureau. The little blankets were still spread in the crib, waiting for our baby to come home.

Though shuttered for this many months, the room had the surprising aroma of newness in it—new woods on the crib and changing table, a new can of wet wipes that had been opened in anticipation of their use, new stuffed animals on the bureau. I stood there, not really frozen, just still, exhausted, then walked slowly around the room, peering into the crib, putting my finger on the play carousel above it, running my hand across the top of an elephant-shaped toy chest that was a gift from Katherine's mother. I thought about what would have—no, what should have—been: fatherhood, an ever-changing relationship with my wife, the adjustments and the laughs and the burdens and responsibilities. The meaningfulness of it all. I wondered if it would ever happen again. I couldn't picture it, starting from scratch in those first awkward days of dating, marriage to someone else, a new set of in-laws, another pregnancy. It struck me that even though she was gone, I still very much considered myself to be Katherine's husband. Fatherhood, that was different. It had ended before I knew what it was. And here I was, a visitor to a life I never had.

All these thoughts made me more tired. I only know I flicked the light out and sat down on the floor, on a Winnie-the-Pooh rug, all soft, never used. After sitting for a minute I spread out and lay down on my back, the sliver of light from the hall just missing my face, the furniture and toys just visible in the shadows. And I slept, fitfully, until the birds chirped outside and the sun hit me square in the eyes. When I awoke, I felt as if my melancholy had lifted, like a morning fog from a Maine harbor.

I was oddly lighthearted, as if I had gotten rid of

something I should have been rid of long ago. Maybe it was fear, maybe it was ignorance. I'm not really sure. I pulled myself to my feet, my ribs throbbing from sleeping on the floor. I kind of lurched out the door toward the shower. A small part of me felt as if I had just conquered something, but most of me just felt an unfamiliar sense of peace.

five

I PICKED UP THE telephone on the first ring.

"Have you seen the *Times* yet?" It was Peter Martin, being his usual personable self.

I replied, "I'm feeling much better, thanks. And how are you?"

"Look, this story is spinning out of control. You ready to come back to work?"

I cradled the phone in my neck as I tucked a fraying blue oxford-cloth shirt into my favorite old jeans. Someone banged on the front door, and I hurried downstairs with the portable phone still at my ear. When I opened the door, Baker, in all his glory, came charging inside.

He looked wonderful, I must say. He circled me twice, his tail wagging and slapping me on my knees. He suddenly lunged for his stuffed hedgehog, which was lying on the rug, and paced about the room with the toy lodged deep in his mouth. The hedgehog was squealing, the dog was snorting, I was down on one knee, smacking him lovingly on his side. "Hold on, Peter," I said into the phone, putting it down.

"What is going on there?" I heard him say.

"Kristen, this was really great of you," I said to the dog sitter, an adorable graduate student who lives down the street. "Let me grab you some money." Kristen had fallen in love with Baker in the local park nearly two years earlier, and told Katherine and me that if we ever needed a sitter, she would actually appreciate the chance. Ever since, she had proved to be one of the most reliable people in a life that seemed less reliable by the day.

"That's all right, Jack. I'll get it some other time. Here, I got you some bagels. I know you don't have any food here. By the way, you looked great on TV."

She seemed to be looking at me differently as she backed out of the door, and it made me uncomfortable. Television has a power that newspapers simply don't, an ability to convey celebrity on, quite literally, an ordinary jack like me. But before I could say anything, she was gone, Baker was sprawled on the floor with his fat face pressed up against his empty food bowl, and I was back on the phone with Peter.

"What's the *Times* have?" I asked.

Knowing he had my attention, he sounded more thoughtful now, a little less panicked. "It's kind of strange," he said. "They have a front-page story, quoting anonymous sources, saying that the FBI can't pin the gunman in the assassination attempt, identified as Tony Clawson from California, with a specific militia group. They ran a headshot of Clawson from some ID badge he wore at his job at Home Depot. Scary-looking guy. These same sources said that no militia group in the country has yet to claim any knowledge of the assassination attempt, which probably isn't surprising. Why would anyone want to say they knew, and be charged with aiding and abetting or whatever? But here's what I think is the most interesting part: about halfway through the story, the FBI spokesman says they *believe* that the gunman was a militia member. The *Times* doesn't make too big a deal about that, but to me, that seems like the feds are backing away from how definitive they were right after the incident. This opens up a whole lot of questions."

I was with him about 90 percent, but given the interruptions, the early hour—it was, I think, about eight-thirty Saturday morning—and everything else, if he quizzed me on what the questions were that the *Times* story opened up, I fear I'd have failed miserably. Still, I had an innate trust in Martin's abilities. He might be nervous as a cat. He may never have been around for a presidential assassination before. He may even be in well over his head. But he possessed wonderful powers of observation and a vast capacity to understand the business of journalism, and combined, that placed him in the right far more than it didn't.

"So what are you saying?" I asked, hoping to keep the ball in his court.

"We need to be on this. We need to be on this right away." His tone changed here, becoming softer. "I know you're not going to like this, but Havlicek is on his way out to California from Boston. The editor wants him on this story, and I didn't want to fight it. I didn't know how you were feeling physically and guessed you wouldn't want to make that flight. And minimally, he'll be good to do the initial sweep on Clawson, then go through documents, do some scut work. I don't think the extra hands can hurt on a story this big."

I was fine about it. Steve Havlicek was in his late fifties, a former Pulitzer Prize–winning investigative reporter with a sweet personality that masked a near manic drive to land stories that he knew no one else could get. He was the chief investigative reporter in Washington before I was, and Martin, looking out for my interests, was nervous that I would feel threatened by him poaching on my turf. In fact, Havlicek was an old friend, a quasi mentor, and I welcomed the help.

"We'll work well together," I said, and just about heard a sigh of relief on the other end of the line.

"You have a line in with the FBI on this one?" Martin asked. "The president? Can you flip any of these guys, put them on your side?"

My call-waiting tone sounded, and I took a pass on it. I figured I'd get enough calls today.

"The FBI agent seems pretty standoffish. That woman Stevens. She's going to be tough work, but I'll stay on her. I'm meeting with her at some point today. I'll spread some other calls out from home this morning and give you a ring if I get anything back. Have Havlicek give me a call when he gets on the ground in California."

It suddenly struck me: the anonymous caller. Maybe I had just lost his call by not picking up the other line.

"One more thing, Peter," I said, and then caught myself, quickly deciding not to tip my hand yet, not even to Martin. I had no real reason to keep it secret, but my instincts told me to maintain my own counsel on this right now, until I knew more.

"What?" he said, urgently.

My mind raced to fill in the blank. "Never mind" was not going to be good enough with Peter Martin. So I quickly came up with this: "You remember the militia stories I did last year? I made some good friends out west on that one, including one guy in Idaho, a militia leader, who is especially well plugged in nationally. I might be able to squeeze him."

It worked, strangely enough.

"Jesus Christ, that's right. Maybe you ought to just get out there and see whether this guy has anything. I'm going to check the flight schedules, and I'll call you later."

I hung up the phone, wondering what I had just done to myself. My caller ID read "Private name, private number." I checked to see if the caller had left a message on my voice mail. I was in luck.

Indeed, it was the shamefully aloof voice of Samantha Stevens, special agent with the FBI, requesting an audience at three o'clock that afternoon. "If that works for you, no need to call back," she said. "We'll just plan on meeting you at your house. See you then."

Immediately, I tapped out the number for the *Record*'s library up in Boston, and luckily my favorite researcher answered the phone, someone who would get me exactly what I needed.

"Dorothy," I said, in a singsongy voice that I always thought she liked, but who really knew? Actually, I probably sounded like an ass. "Jack Flynn here. Howaya?"

"Jesus, Jack, you're all over CNN. The networks are flashing your picture every other minute. One of the affiliates had a reporter in here last night interviewing people about you. I told them I thought you were a gifted writer, and was thrilled that you finally decided to confront your impotency problem."

Ah, that Dorothy, such a card. "You're a laugh a minute. Listen, here's what I need: can you pull me some good background stuff on one Samantha Stevens, an agent of the Federal Bureau of Investigation, the pride of this great land?" I continued, "And while you're in the system, could you see if there's anything on another agent, a man by the name of Kent Drinker, an assistant director?"

"Coming your way. I'll ship it through the computer?"

"Yeah. I'll look for it in a while. You're the best, Dorothy," I said, hanging up the phone.

Impotency. How would she know? I mean, how would I even know? You have to try to have sex to know you're impotent.

In the journalism business, we look at shards of people's lives and pretend we see the whole. We spend a day with someone, maybe just an hour, flitting in at some inopportune moment, maybe a drunk driving death or an arrest on child sexual assault. We talk to neighbors, get some quotes about the time the suspect returned a borrowed rake with a sack of warm nuts from a gourmet food store, then write as if we understand the very fiber of his soul. We look at silhouettes and pretend we see real flesh. I'm as guilty as anyone else, but I'm smart enough, or have been around long enough, to at least know that what I'm doing might not be entirely right.

Which is exactly how I felt as I sat in my study and scrolled through the computer file that Dorothy had sent me from the *Record* library. There was nothing on Stevens, not a blessed thing. But on Drinker, the stories were voluminous, most of them taken from the *Los Angeles Times,* and dating back several years. According to the accounts, Drinker worked as an FBI liaison to the U.S. Marshals' Witness Protection Program at the start of his career, rising steadily through the hierarchy. In an enormous promotion for largely thankless work, he was moved to Los Angeles, to take the number-two slot in the FBI's regional office.

He wasn't there but a year when a story broke in the *Los Angeles Times* that the special agent in charge of the region, a veteran FBI man by the name of Skip Weaver, had been blocking the promotions of Hispanic agents in favor of promotions for less experienced, less qualified white agents. The paper quoted from a batch of highly sensitive internal personnel documents that it said it had obtained from sources familiar with the office. Shortly after that, the paper conducted a review of FBI arrests in the region and found that the bureau arrested Hispanics in greater proportion than any other racial or ethnic group. This was enough to unleash a racial backlash the likes of which had not been seen there since the Rodney King riots. Black and Hispanic city councillors called for Weaver's immediate dismissal and presented the director of the FBI with a petition filled with 35,000 names. The city's race relations commission launched its own investigation. So did the FBI, but rather than investigate its personnel or arrest policies, it furiously probed into who had leaked the documents to the newspaper.

A federal grand jury was formed. Threats were made within the organization. Weaver virtually locked himself in his office, waiting for the culprit to be found. The reporter, a young man who thought his career had been made, was hauled before the grand jury. Next, he was brought into court and ordered to reveal his source. When he refused, the conservative-minded judge told him he faced jail time for contempt. Federal prosecutors treated him nicely, but outside court, several FBI agents informed him he would be charged with receiving stolen property and thrown in prison. Unbelievably, he caved, and informed investigators that Kent Drinker had leaked him the documents. When he tried to explain that Drinker was only trying to repair a grave injustice, that a few good, qualified hardworking Hispanic agents were being discriminated against, no one was around to hear him.

So Drinker was immediately called back to Washington. He was told he could face dismissal for stealing government property. He was reviled by a large segment of the bureau. In law enforcement, there is the code of silence, and he had just violated it, he had trampled it. In many quarters there, he would never be forgiven. He was assigned a desk job, menial work, really. That was all nearly a decade before.

For several years, apparently, he committed himself to the pick and shovel work of rejuvenation, keeping a low profile, going along, getting along, as much as they would let him, doing whatever he was asked. Eventually he played a key role in helping to solve a terrorist bombing in Nevada. And his fortunes took their sharpest turn for the better about four years ago, when Hutchins came to the White House as vice president. From the depths of penance, Drinker was pulled to nearly the pinnacle of the agency, named assistant director—a move interpreted by the national press as a message that the new administration wanted an honest, open government. For the past four years Drinker had launched an increasingly successful campaign for approval among the rank-and-file agents.

So what did this tell me? Well, perhaps it explained

why someone with as lofty a title as assistant director was helping with the street work of a major investigation, rather than supervising it from his office. Maybe this was another example of him trying to curry favor among his underlings by working in the trenches alongside them. And perhaps it explained why he had been so quiet with me in the hospital room that day, why he let Stevens ask nearly all the questions. Because he had been burned by reporters before, perhaps he quite simply didn't like us as a breed.

The telephone rang, and I just about knocked it off my desk in my haste to pick it up.

"Hey, old boy. I have to get on a godforsaken jet airplane and fly all the way out to Fresno, California, just to bail your fat ass out one more time." It was Havlicek, and if Martin was apologetic to me about his assignment on this story, obviously he wasn't himself.

"Not what I heard," I said. "I heard there's an issue over your output up there in Boston, and they decided to put you on this story to work with the master for a while. They want you to kneel at my knee. Watch and learn. Watch and learn." Now that this macho turf ritual was over, I cut to the point. "What do you have?"

"Nothing yet," Havlicek said, his taunting tone changing to one of honest bemusement. "I'm on an airplane. I'll be on the ground soon. I haven't worked in Washington for five years. Most of my people are gone from Justice. We're just trying to play catch-up with the *Times* for tomorrow. When are you on board?"

"Well, now. I have a couple of FBI agents coming over this afternoon, and I'm going to see if I can trade information with them, but it doesn't look real promising. I'll be working the phones all day, trying to find out anything I can on Clawson and the militia angle from here. If I get anything, I'll write it up, obviously, and we'll probably feed it into whatever you get. Otherwise I'll be in the bureau tomorrow."

"All right. I may give you a shout later today if I come across anything. Give me a call if you hear something worthwhile."

They arrived fashionably late for the interview, Stevens and Drinker. After a day spent accomplishing frustratingly little from my dozens of phone calls spread around official Washington, they were an oddly welcome sight. Poor Baker was nearly beside himself at the concept of female companionship at home. What a miracle. So I invited them in and offered them what I had, which at this particular time was water.

"Hopefully," Drinker said, as we had taken our seats in the living room, "all of us are in a better frame of mind today."

That, I think, was the closest I would get to an apology from this duo, so I accepted it gracefully and said, "I'm sure we all are."

The brief informalities behind us, Stevens briskly took up where she left off the day before. "I talked to the president in-depth about this earlier today, and he assures me that he initiated the invitation to you. He said he is a fan of your work and had some specific things he wanted to talk to you about. So it appears we have cleared up those questions."

Her tone softened as she added, "I'm hoping you can

run through with me just what it is you saw out there."

I regarded her for a moment. Her jet black hair had little wind-tussled wisps flowing in various directions, sexy, yet with a sense of casual innocence. It highlighted her translucent, alabaster skin. She was tall and slender, and her tan suit clung in some places and hung loose in others, making it appear that even when she tried being one of the boys, she was unmistakably a girl.

I began talking, and she scribbled furiously, turning the pages of her tiny notebook as fast as she could write, not even looking up at me or bothering to acknowledge my words.

"Very helpful," she said finally, when I had run out of things to describe. As witnesses go, I'm probably a pretty good one, considering that's what I do for a living. We met eyes a couple of times, and she never looked away. She even smiled once, when I did, when I talked about Davis screaming so loud that in the hospital, when I woke up, I had assumed that he had sustained some catastrophic injury, maybe even been killed. Drinker kicked in with a joke. "I talked to him yesterday, and he doesn't strike me as a real ruffian," he said.

We went over a few more points, though nothing big. The frost of the previous day seemed to be gradually melting away. In fact, as Drinker sat there mute, Stevens was adopting this odd air of familiarity; the banter growing easy, harmless. I didn't quite understand yet the difference in tone from the day before.

"Your house is beautiful," she said, looking around, in a signal that the interrogation had ended. "Great furniture. Great moldings."

"Thanks," I said. "My wife and I bought and renovated it a couple of years back."

"I know," she said. I shot her a quizzical look, and she smiled and shrugged. "Homework."

Finally, as the dog began snoring on the floor, I summoned the confidence to ask a question of my own.

"Do you mind if I ask something?" I said, adopting my reporter voice—confident and reassuring at the same time. "Can you guide me on the militia role in the shooting? There seems to be some discrepancy in public accounts on whether this was a militia-sponsored assassination attempt."

Stevens opened her mouth and began to pronounce the first syllable of what I expect was going to be an answer when Drinker firmly cut her off.

"We're not getting into these games," he said, looking at her, then at me. "Call our spokesman. You know who he is."

As they were leaving, as if on cue, Drinker again turned around in the doorway. "I don't mean to belabor the point," he said, his voice softer now, "but that telephone call yesterday in the hospital. You said it was a friend. But that came in on a direct-dial line. That friend couldn't have been transferred from the hospital switchboard. For someone to have called you, you would have had to have given your number out. The telephone records show that you hadn't made any calls to anyone, because you get charged by the call, so they keep careful records. And the nurses at your station said you hadn't had any other visitors the night before, except for the *Record*'s Washington bureau chief, Peter Martin. He's the only guy that would have known what number to call, because the hospital switchboard operator had orders from the FBI not to give your telephone number out to anyone who called on the main line. And Martin was in the room, so it wasn't him."

This all sounded confusing, but I think I knew what he was getting at. Basically, I was cornered and screwed. He left the obvious question dangling as to who was on the telephone. I wasn't sure why he was so concerned about it, but I marveled at his ability to ferret out something amiss, the only fib I had told throughout this entire episode. I had nothing to lose, so I gave it my final, best shot at staving him off, at least for now.

"Last I checked, I'm a witness, not a suspect," I said. "My calls are my business. I'm more interested in what your concern is."

Neither agent said anything, so I added, "I guess Martin must have given out my number. You've put a lot more thought into this than I have. It was just a call from an old friend."

He didn't push the issue this time, much to my considerable relief. He bade me farewell, and behind him, Stevens threw me what I took to be a cool parting look without so much as a verbal good-bye. So that was that, and I stood there wondering what it meant, all of it, the questions, the persistence, and more than any of that, this intriguing agent with the beautiful hair.

Nightfall brought Baker's evening walk. I grabbed a tennis ball, which he quickly scooped up in his mouth, and some money, which I hoped to spend on dinner if I could find an outdoor table at a Georgetown restaurant early on a Saturday evening. We walked and walked, the fresh air and exercise acting like an intoxicant after a day spent indoors. We stopped at our usual park, down on K Street, on the Potomac River, to toss and fetch. With my ribs taped up, I couldn't throw nearly as well as Baker could retrieve, and he didn't do well feigning his disappointment. Eventually, he settled into the grass and chewed on sticks.

For dinner, I took a place at a patio table at a small French restaurant on Thirty-first Street, Café la Ruche. I leaned down to tie Baker's leash to the bottom of my chair, fumbling with it because of the growing soreness in my chest. I looked up into the blue eyes of a fairly stunning waitress, who presented me a menu and cooed at Baker. "Dining alone?" she asked in a way that was inexplicably flirty.

"No, actually," I said, rising to the opportunity, "I'm dining with my dog."

She smiled a big smile, and I thought that I still had it, whatever *it* actually is. We chatted about what was good and what wasn't. She left and brought me back a Miller, took my order, and left me with my beer and my thoughts.

When she brought my food about fifteen minutes later, she reached into her apron and pulled out an envelope, handing it to me. It was blank, but sealed.

"A gentleman asked me to pass this along to you a few minutes ago," she said, quite casually.

I looked around curiously, first at the other diners, to see if there was anyone I knew, perhaps a colleague from the paper or a friend or someone who may have seen me on television and was passing along a note of support or disdain. Nothing. I looked out along the sidewalk and down the street—again, nothing. Before I put my fork into my swordfish, I carefully tore the envelope open to see what was inside. It was a typewritten, or rather computer-generated note, short to the point of abrupt.

"Meet me alone, at the Newseum, Sunday, 5:30 P.M."

Well, it provided the where, what, and when you hear so much about in journalism school, but it lacked the all-important who and why. I'd find that out, to be sure. I felt like I had stumbled onto the set of some James Bond movie. Again I looked around for the letter writer, but saw nobody that looked even remotely suspicious. I waved to my waitress, and she came bouncing right over.

"Can you help me out here?" I asked, attempting to sound casual, but my voice almost cracking from nerves. "I'm trying to figure out who this envelope came from. Are they still here?"

She put her finger up to her bee-stung lower lip and looked around thoughtfully. "I don't see him," she said.

"Was he a diner here? Where did he give you the envelope?"

"I was on my way into the kitchen, in a rush, and he just came up behind me and asked if I'd give this envelope to the guy outside with the dog. Tell you the truth, I didn't even bother to get a good look at him."

I was walking a delicate line here. I wanted to prod her further, but I didn't want to sound any alarms, though I'm not sure why not. "Older, younger? Do you recall what he was wearing? Any idea at all what he looked like?"

She was starting to lose interest and was looking across the patio at another table, where a woman was waving her hand at her to take care of some dining calamity. "I really don't," she said, walking away. "I'm sorry."

Over the dozen years that comprise my reporting career, I have had countless numbers of anonymous callers. You try to read into their voices, get a mental picture of what they look like, where they're calling from, and why. It's nothing so glamorous as the famous Deep

Throat of Watergate fame. No, I picture my callers as lonely people that life has left behind, semi-intelligent beings who wait with urgency for their morning newspaper, pore over every word of every story, and concoct terrifying scenarios in their own minds of what is happening to their world and to their own lives.

I had one caller leave messages on my voice mail at work for three months after TWA Flight 800 exploded in the sky. He told me, in the same detail night after night, that the CIA shot a heat-seeking missile at the plane from a rubber raft in Long Island Sound because an Iraqi spy was on board with a stolen briefcase filled with the intricate design details of the U.S. $100 bill. If the spy got away, the caller told me, he could have kicked the entire national and even international financial system on its side, so the CIA justified the deaths of a few hundred passengers because they were, in effect, saving the world as we know it.

Another time, an elderly-sounding man who told me he was from Cape Cod warned me that all Massachusetts State Police troopers were out to kill him because he once beat a speeding ticket in 1963 by proving that an officer parked on the side of the road had no basis on which to estimate his speed. From there on in, officers were required to follow speeding drivers to clock their speed— a decision that infuriated them, the caller told me. The spooky part about him was that an elderly gentleman had walked into a McDonald's restaurant in Hyannis during lunch hour one afternoon and pulled a gun. The man fired a wild shot, striking a blow-up Ronald McDonald doll in the head, causing it to explode and raising screams from dozens of children and their mothers eating lunch.

Ironically, or maybe not, a State Police trooper buying lunch pulled his gun and shot the man dead. I never heard from my caller from that day on, and always had a nagging feeling that it was him who was killed that day.

But this caller was different. For starters, he had somehow found my telephone number at the hospital within hours of my arrival, though Drinker explained how that would be a virtually impossible thing to do. He had spoken clearly, and made realistic, though cryptic accusations. He was not bothersome, and seemed to have a goal in mind. And beyond even that, my anonymous caller had followed me from my house, on my evening dog walk, all the way to this restaurant, where he slipped the waitress a note containing a directive on how I might learn more about the assassination attempt on the president of the United States. He meant business, and he seemed to know how to conduct it. This was all just terrific. I sat there on the restaurant patio, Baker blithely sleeping at my feet, spooning rice and swordfish into my face, wondering if he was watching me now, wondering why.

The walk home, to say the least, was an anxious one, every crunch of the leaves sending my head turning in search of any mysterious presence. A man in a sweatshirt carrying a briefcase walked about ten yards behind me. I tried maintaining pace with a young couple up ahead, figuring no harm would come with witnesses around. A van approached and seemed to slow down as I walked up Twenty-eighth Street, the man with the briefcase still behind me. I braced for some sort of confrontation—physical or otherwise—but nothing. Suddenly I didn't hear his footsteps anymore. I turned around, and he was gone, as was the van. I kept my eyes peeled for suspicious cars, but saw nothing. The couple ahead walked up the stairs to their house, leaving me all alone on what felt like an empty stage set, not a street. Baker acted uncharacteristically nervous, heeling close to my left knee.

As I arrived at my front door, that same van rounded the corner and slowly passed my house. I thought I spied the face of the man walking behind me sitting in the passenger seat. I hurriedly jammed the key into the lock and stepped inside.

"You're an idiot," I said to myself, even the sound of my own voice in the dark foyer raising the hairs on the back of my neck. I pulled the note from my pocket and read it one more time, then trundled upstairs to try to get some rest from this action-slash-melodrama that had become my life.

six

IN A WORLD WHERE precise planning and endless advance work serve as the foundation for success, every morning, a motley group of highly educated reporters and editors start the day from scratch, floating into America's newsrooms and bureaus at staggered hours, thinking big thoughts, working the telephones, pecking away at keyboards, struggling with word meanings and sentence flows, making and breaking careers and even lives in the communities they cover. In perhaps no other business, certainly not in insurance, not in the most prestigious law firms, not in the big-money brokerage houses on Wall Street, will you find so many employees living out their professional dreams. Reporting, to many, is not a job but a calling, and the privilege of doing it at a big-city daily paper makes them minor celebrities in their families, their circles of friends, and at PTA meetings, where another parent is liable to approach them in a quiet way and say, "You're a reporter for the *Record*. Can't you do something about this?"

Maybe. Reporters can pick up the telephone and reach governors, senators, captains of commerce. A few reporters, and I immodestly but irrefutably put myself in this category now, can reach the president of the United States. Reporters can drive to work in the morning and assume their day will be spent in the office, then by night end up on a flight to New Mexico for a week in the desert covering the mass suicide of a religious cult that believed Carl Sagan's death signaled the end of all virtue in the world. A reporter's story can cause the indictment of a mayor, the firing of a rogue police officer, the release of a prisoner wrongly convicted on false testimony. All this, and no license required, nothing but the ability to ferret out the elusive concept we call truth and to present it in a readable and hopefully stylish way. At the end of the day, when it all comes together—a front page, a sports section, a style page, feature stories, and the summation of hard news events—the publication of a newspaper is nothing short of a daily miracle, an act of democracy and freedom celebrated with a simple read.

Okay, so I'm biased. Why then, you might naturally ask, do reporters seem so unhappy? Well, there is the matter of pay, which is low, given the measure of responsibility they have. There are the foolish editors who fail to understand the brilliance of a reporter's idea or copy, the meek and self-righteous copy editors who take an evening's delight in catching a reporter's grammatical mistake. There are the mundane assignments—the Brockton City Council meeting, the routine drug smuggling arrest, the eighty-seventh inner-city murder of the year—set against the reporter's understanding of the better, more glamorous uses of his or her time. And there is the unimpeachable fact that reporters are natural complainers. It is what they do best, and when they are not complaining in print about the performance of professional sports teams or the lack of clout of the state congressional delegation, they complain about their own human condition, about the very same newsroom that once seemed to have so much romantic appeal. And finally and most importantly, reporters, as well educated as they are, are resigned to being life's witnesses, recorders of the great and not so great deeds of all those around them but rarely in the spotlight themselves. They do not set policy, they write about it. They do not run for office, they follow around those who do. As important as they are to the very essence of our country, reporters are relegated to the sidelines, not coaches, not really even fans, just supposedly impartial observers whose only voice is expected to be set in ramrod-neutral tones.

I mention all this because as I walked back into the bureau Sunday morning for the first time since I was shot, these were the sparring elements highlighted in my current situation. On the one hand, I had the president of the United States offering me a position as his press secretary, a move that would lead to great fame, policy making, a seat at the very center of power. On the other, I had what appeared to be a legitimate anonymous source ready to guide me toward the biggest story of my career, one that potentially led right to that same seat of power. Of course, I didn't know what that story was about yet, but such are the mysteries of a typical day in journalism.

This cerebral battle would have been lost on the likes of Peter Martin, who hustled up to my desk moments after I arrived in the bureau. "Thank God," he said, breathlessly. "Jesus Christ, we're getting creamed." While he spoke, he rubbed his hand absently across the side of his face, as if exhausted, though it was not quite 9:00 A.M.

"You see the *Times* this morning?" he asked. "Havlicek

could only say what they had yesterday, maybe advance it a little, but they're way out front again today."

I had read the *Times* already, out on my back patio after my morning walk with Baker. The story at issue was a pretty damned good one. FBI sources, quoted anonymously, said they had serious questions over the motive of the assassination attempt, mostly because they had no clear idea of who the would-be killer was. Havlicek was at least able to match the part of the *Times* story that said no family members of the attempted assassin Clawson could be found, no history, no criminal record based on his fingerprints.

"A good story," I said. Before I could go on, Martin stepped in to cut me off.

"Look, we need a larger piece of this. This is our fucking story. You were there. You were almost killed. Somebody's got to want to help us."

As he spoke, the telephone rang, and a pleasant woman's voice asked if I could hold the line for the president of the United States. Would-be assassins, broken ribs, appearances on CNN. Now Sunday-morning calls from my pal, the president.

"I'd be honored to talk to the president," I said, even though by the time I said that, the woman had already put me on hold, but the intended effect was not lost on those around me. Martin, pacing around as he spoke, looked at me skeptically.

"Quit fucking around," he said after a moment. "We have a shitload of work to get done."

I ignored him as the booming voice of President Hutchins filled my ear. I felt around my desk for a fresh legal pad, tossing aside a folder marked "Presidential pardons," as well as the last three issues of *Golf Digest*. "The hell are you doing back at work already? You nuts or something?"

"Mr. President, democracy needs to be protected every day of the week, injury or no injury. You know my devotion." He laughed at that, which I appreciated. He didn't seem like such a bad guy. Martin stood in front of me, his eyes glued to mine, like a retriever staring at a brand-new yellow tennis ball, all clean and firm. He sensed our best avenue to another story, and he was trying to will me in that direction. I was already there, waiting for my opening.

"I'm not heading out on a campaign swing until late this afternoon. You have a few minutes to come over to the house and chat?" Hutchins asked. By house, I assumed he meant the White House.

I knew full well what he wanted to chat about, but I also knew I could trade on that for another story, or at least the pieces of another story. And if I had this anonymous source filling my ear, it was good to get as much exposure to Hutchins as I possibly could.

"Of course I could come to the White House, sir," I said, speaking more formally than before. Martin pumped his fist into the air. I noticed a couple of other early-arriving reporters falling quiet and leaning in my direction for a better hearing vantage.

"Good. How about noon? We'll take a little lunch here, the two invalids. Just show up at the gate, and someone will guide you in."

Hanging up, I said to Martin as casually as I could, "Going in to see the president at noon."

He appeared ready to sit in my lap. His prior look of exhaustion had turned into one of exuberance. One thought did strike him, and he expressed it pretty clearly.

"Why?" he asked.

"Don't know. Maybe he likes my company. Maybe it's good PR for him, lunching with the injured reporter. Maybe he liked my stories Friday and is ready to spout off again. We'll see soon enough."

"Let's draw up some questions and angles before you go," Martin said. "We should still be scouting for something else, in case he fails to make news." With that, he left my desk in a half trot, half skip. He could have been floating on air. Next I saw of him, he was standing in his glass office, holding the phone up to his ear in a familiar position, a smile spread across his pale face.

By now, a few more colleagues were filtering into the room to cover the assassination or the election that it affected. One or two gave me a hard time about my new-found fame. Julie Gershman was first. When I was married, she was as reliable a flirt as you could ever desire, constantly looking me up and down, tossing seductive smiles in my direction at the drop of a dime. She was compact, tight as a drum, with red hair and almond-shaped eyes that looked like sex personified. And she knew it. After Katherine's death, she either stopped flirting or I stopped noticing. I think it was the former. I was treated with kid gloves after that, pitied, much to my disdain. I spent most of my time on the road, writing stories from afar, working out of hotel rooms, watching time fly by, stopping in the office only for a day or two at a stretch.

"Well, look who's here, the second coming of Christ," Gershman said, flipping her little Jackie Onassis haircut behind her ears. "Taking a break from CNN and the nets to check your messages in here, Jack? Calling Hollywood? I hear Brad Pitt wants to play you in the movie."

Well, this was certainly different, and I rather liked it. I had the telephone receiver wedged between my shoulder and ear, and cupped my hand over the mouthpiece. "Julie, give me a minute, okay? I've got Larry King on the line."

Actually, I was waiting for directory assistance, listening to a woman's tape-recorded voice repeatedly telling me to please hold, the next available operator would take my call. Why bog down my important colleagues in the mundane details of my day?

A couple of my pals plopped themselves down around my desk and made small talk. Everyone was laughing and carrying on, and I felt on top again, one of them, where I belonged, not the victim of a tragedy, but a reporter doing his job, and doing it damn well, getting breaks, like I always have. Havlicek walked into the bureau and stood over a desk on the other side of the room, having just arrived on a red-eye from the West Coast. "About time you ended that vacation," he bellowed across the way. Everyone laughed. I gave him the finger, just letting it float toward the ceiling as I calmly looked the other way, carrying on a conversation. A few minutes later, I pulled myself to my feet, grimacing at my sore ribs, and walked across the room. We met halfway, and he gave me a soft half hug, patting me on the back and saying quietly, "Welcome back. Time to get to work."

Newsrooms are inherently cluttered places, and Washington bureaus, while certainly smaller and slightly more sterile, are not much different. In a world of Internet searches and CD-ROMs, they are inexplicably filled with piles of newspapers, manila folders, and opened books strewn on chaotic desktops. The floors are lined with cardboard boxes holding files and stacks of photocopied documents. The men and women of the newsroom, the reporters and editors, have seen most of what life has to offer and look at everyone and everything with a healthy dose of skepticism. They're a tough lot to impress, tougher still to please. There is the constantly stale smell of overworked people. Phones are ringing every minute, with important—and self-important—professionals on the other end of the line. A bank of facsimile machines gives off an uninterrupted beep, and there is the omnipresent click of computer keyboards. And more than any of that, there is the mystique.

This place was all that and more. Located smack in the middle of downtown Washington, just a few blocks from the White House and, more importantly for my purposes, right next to Morton's of Chicago, the best steakhouse in town, the bureau was mostly one large open room, with about a dozen desks spread quiltwork, a healthy enough distance from each other that you could keep a conversation private if that's what you wanted. Off to one side was a large, plush conference room, and beside that was Martin's office. Both had walls of all glass, and both had vistas, beyond nearby office buildings, of Lafayette Park.

There were characters everywhere you looked. Erskine Berry was the *Record*'s chief economics reporter. He had covered Washington since Lyndon Johnson's Great Society, and padded around the bureau in a pair of orthopedic shoes, always dressed in a tweed jacket of some sort and a brightly colored bow tie, looking as if he were just about to settle into his regular leather chair at the Metropolitan Club. There was our Capitol Hill reporter, Julie, she of the perfect physique. Michael Reston covered the Supreme Court, and over the two years he had done that job, he had acquired many of the mannerisms you might expect from someone on the bench. He would cock his head. He would occasionally butt into a sentence, politely asking, "Don't you mean . . . ?" He smoked a pipe. Down the hall, at the reception desk, Barbara ruled with an iron fist. She considered me a surrogate son and over the last couple of days had left several messages on my voice mail at home. When I didn't return the calls—I'm not sure why I didn't—she sent a messenger over with an envelope bearing explicit instructions on what I should do and eat to return to health.

The carnival finally gave way to another day at the office. Havlicek and I agreed to make a round of calls and talk over our angles in the early afternoon. First thing I did, after going through messages and flipping through a large stack of mail, was punch out a number on my phone that got me into the depths of the J. Edgar Hoover Building, headquarters of the FBI. A familiar voice answered on the first ring.

"Ron, Flynn here," I said in my typically warm way. "Still stuck with the weekend shift, huh?"

"As I live and breathe, if it isn't the star of the fucking city," said Ron Hancock, a veteran special agent of the FBI.

I interjected, "I tell you what, first thing tomorrow, I'm going to sign a few glossies for the wife and kids and send them on over."

"I tell you what, I'll lay them down in the cellar, and the dog will piss all over them."

Well now, isn't that sweet. Now that we had the niceties out of the way, I cut to the point, even though I wasn't sure what the point was, but you never show the pink part of your stomach to a federal agent, not when you want to use them as a source of information. For all their feigned disgust with reporters, they're actually a bit afraid of us, and a little information goes a long way, if you know how to use it right.

"That's real nice," I said. "Listen, one question that's been bothering me since I woke up in the hospital fortunate enough to be staring into her pretty face: what's the line on Samantha Stevens? Good woman? Bad woman? Respected agent?"

Despite the threat to allow his dog to urinate on the likeness of my face, Hancock was a solid man, an even better agent, and a time-tested friend to the news media, or at least to me. He worked in the intelligence division of the FBI, mostly tracking terrorist activity in the country and outside, shaking down informants, keeping watch on suspected international criminals, plugging into networks of wiretapped information that the average citizen couldn't even fathom existed. I had met him a few years earlier, on a basic drug-smuggling case he worked in Boston. Bored with a pretty small-time investigation, he tossed me a few bones. I got things right and made him look good. We kept in touch ever since, and he was always willing to lend a hand. Working intelligence, he was clued into avenues all over the country. Perhaps more important, his natural curiosity made him something of an expert on the internal machinations of the FBI. If there was anything going on there, he knew about it, and his general sense of outrage usually spurred him to share what he knew.

He just kind of snickered. "I don't know a whole lot about Ms. Stevens, aside from the fact that the male agents seem to really like her. The brass must too, if they put her on a case like this."

For the hell of it, I added, "And Kent Drinker?"

"Well, that one's a little trickier. You know his checkered background, yet his renaissance here has been something to behold, and those who have worked with him have few complaints."

I said, "Yeah, his history, to say the least, is complex."

I intentionally left a void of silence open, hoping he would fill it with some information he might not otherwise have felt inclined to offer. An old reporter's trick. But Hancock's too good for that, and probably uses the same trick himself. So instead we just had an awkward pause.

Finally I asked innocently, "You don't even want to know how I am?"

He laughed a hearty laugh. "Next time," he said. "Right now, I've got to run."

I held the phone in my hand for a moment after he had hung up. Then, for a sense of structure, I typed what I knew into my computer. First, there was a gunman who no one really knew anything about, although the FBI immediately, seemingly without any foundation, had reported he was a militia member. Second, there was the matter of this anonymous source, telling me this shooting was not what it seemed, whatever that meant. Third, the outcome of a presidential election hung in the balance, affected one uncertain way or another by this gunman's errant shot.

"What do you think of Idaho?"

That was Martin, bursting my concentration. I slowly,

inconspicuously slipped a magazine over the typewritten note as I sprinted around the hallways of my mind, wondering what in God's name he meant by Idaho. Shit, I realized, the militia leader.

"I don't know," I said. "I've just been trying to piece together the holes we have right now. There are a lot of them."

"No shit. All holes. No answers. We need a break on this, and we need it fast. You think you should just get on a plane, try to break some news on the militia front? If it ends up that these groups are disavowing any knowledge of this gunman, it raises a whole lot of questions. Here's two of them: Who the hell is this guy, and why were the feds so quick to blame the militias?"

Good points, all, stated in Martin's typically concise manner. By now, the bureau had risen fully to life. Phones were ringing. Barbara was calling out messages over the intercom. Reporters were standing at their desks, pacing around, trading insults. I drank it in appreciatively as I sat there weighing my options. I didn't want to jump on a plane for the backwoods of America, specifically the Idaho Panhandle, not now anyway, not with what I had going on. I was due in the Oval Office at noon and at the Newseum at five-thirty that afternoon, for a meeting with my anonymous source that could change the direction of this entire story. Not to be overly dramatic, but it could change my career. On the other hand, suppose my source had nothing new? Suppose he was just another crazy? By heading out to Idaho, I had the distinct possibility of learning something more concrete, and we now had Havlicek working angles here in Washington.

"Why don't we hold off on a definitive plan until we

see what happens with Hutchins," I said, finding nice, neutral ground. "We'll see if he makes news, if he throws us in any direction. Then we'll decide if it's worth the trip west."

"That's good, very good," Martin said, satisfied. He turned around and walked away, saying to no one in particular, though I suspect it was meant for me, "Of course, that leaves us with nothing definitive in the works."

My meeting at the Newseum could fix that dilemma, but I wasn't quite ready to share that with him yet.

I quickly picked up the phone and, while poking through my electronic Rolodex, punched out a telephone number in Sand Falls, Idaho, specifically a ranch called Freedom Lake, headquarters for one of the most far-reaching militia groups in America. A young man, sounding no more than twenty years old, picked up on the second ring.

"Minutemen," he said.

I put on my sternest don't-fuck-with-me voice. "Daniel there?" I said, just about snapping the phone wires with my steely resolve.

"Who wants to know?" the kid said, sounding more punkish by the monosyllable.

"Jack Flynn from the *Boston Record,*" I said. I had met with Daniel Nathaniel—yes, it's his real name, God bless his parents—the year before, and we had hit it off in an odd kind of way.

"I'll have Ben call you back when he has time. He handles all of our news media calls."

"No," I said, my voice growing even sharper. "You'll go in and tell Mr. Nathaniel that Jack Flynn is on the line, then you'll transfer the call in when he tells you."

The kid put me on hold without saying anything, and next thing I heard was a ringing sound, then the voice of Nathaniel saying, "Do you know how hard it is to keep good soldiers inspired in a revolution, Jack? And you trying to scare my best receptionist right away."

"Sorry about that, old man," I said. "Here's the thing, though. I need some help, and I think you're in a position to give it."

"Jesus H. Christ. A celebrity like you is still doing the pick-and-shovel work for that newspaper? After seeing you on the tube, I figured you'd have joined one of the networks by now and be making a million large a year—half of that stolen in the form of federal taxes." He paused and added, "Go ahead."

"I need to know what you're picking up on this Hutchins assassination attempt. Where'd this Harvey Oswald wannabe come from? He one of your boys? He come from another state?"

"What I have would surprise you," Nathaniel said. "But you know I'm not going to talk about it over the phone like this."

Of course not. Daniel Nathaniel, like every red-blooded militia revolutionary, believed that the federal government, in its role of Big Brother, was listening to every conversation of every citizen every day, even taking pictures of those talking on the telephone with a new technology in spy satellite photography that allowed the lens to penetrate things like walls and roofs. I would have to hotfoot it to Idaho after all.

"What if I pay a social call on you?" I asked.

"That's better. You do that, first beer's on me. Next twenty are on that liberal newspaper of yours."

"You going to be around for the next few days?"

"Where would I go?" he said. "I'm in God's country out here."

"And this information, is it worth the trip?"

"Maybe, maybe not. But the pleasure of my company will make it worthwhile."

"Let's go over some questions," Martin said, once again appearing at my desk out of seemingly thin air. "We have to chase him on this militia angle, find out what he knows, where this investigation is headed. Would be nice to get him out there on the record on this stuff. Everyone else, especially the *Times*, is driving this thing with anonymous sources. Hutchins has avoided the topic in his public events. This is big."

"It is strange," I said, "these investigators now back-tracking on what they claimed was such a clear-cut motive. Maybe it's all nothing. But yeah, you're right, Hutchins might be our best avenue to breaking some new ground here."

We talked over some questions. Martin, for all his idiosyncrasies, and they are many, is good at that, cutting to the quick, finding the fault lines, gauging reader inter-est. I'm good too, and I possess the additional ability that he doesn't necessarily have, of dealing with people, and I'd have to lean heavily on that to steer Hutchins away from what I assumed was the point of this meeting—the offer of press secretary—and over to my purpose—the investi-gation into the assassination attempt.

At about eleven-thirty, I slipped into my navy blue suit jacket, put a microcassette recorder into my chest pocket, grabbed my White House clearance pass out of my top drawer, and headed for the door. As I walked the two blocks down Pennsylvania Avenue, I thought back to a running joke that Katherine and I had. We were figuring out how to decorate our upstairs study. She wanted colorful soft lines and a veritable jungle of plants. She said it helped her to create, all that growth and brightness. I wanted the feel of an English library, with hunter green walls and a leather club chair. We compromised, shooting for what she described as an Oval Office look. We refinished the moldings in bright white and hung old prints on pale yellow walls, and rather than an overwhelming desk we bought a nice library table at a little storefront antique shop near Middleburg, Virginia. Neither of us had a clue what the Oval Office actually looked like, except that it was probably oval, and our own little office was square and about one tenth of the size. When we were done with the decorations we toasted many hours of creative thinking with a glass of champagne, then effortlessly ended up on the antique rug engaged in a fit of wonderful sex. Nice memories, and soon I was there, at the guard shack, staring inside a sheet of bulletproof glass at a bored-looking member of the U.S. Secret Service.

seven

AT THE ENTRANCE TO the West Wing of the White House, a marine in full dress uniform stands so perfectly straight that visitors think he might be a mannequin, a toy soldier, until he snaps open the substantial door with a flip of his brawny wrist. Inside, in the lush reception area, an inevitably becoming young woman provides callers with an escort to their destination.

I don't know why I bring this up, however, because as a reporter I am required to enter through the press briefing room. It looks nice on television, when presidential spokesman Royal Dalton stands before a deep blue curtain with a White House emblem and rattles off the news of the day at his afternoon briefings, taking questions on anything from the subtlest change in U.S. policy toward Zimbabwe to whether White House aides are serving as the source of negative information about income tax and real estate questions faced by Democratic presidential nominee Stanny Nichols. (They were, despite Dalton's assertions to the contrary.) The podium gleams, the room looks spacious and official, and it appears as if American journalism—indeed, American democracy—is well served in that daily sixty-minute word fight when White House officials stand before a sometimes frothing press.

In point of fact, though, the room is an absolute pit—a bus station, others have called it, though they are quick to add that such a comparison may be slanderous to the well-meaning folks over at Greyhound. Years ago, this used to be the site of the White House swimming pool, where John F. Kennedy swam laps as therapy for his chronically ailing back. Richard Nixon, for reasons that have never been explained, filled the pool in and turned it into a briefing area. Now, burly cameramen allow their Starbucks coffee cups to pile up for weeks at a time before throwing them away. Their colleagues inevitably come along and choose a cup in which to deposit a wad of old chewing tobacco. The highly paid on-air talent toss their notes on the floor, assuming that someone else, as in the rest of their lives, is there to pick up after them. The threadbare rug is stained by the slush of too many winters and the sweat of too little air conditioning in the strangling Washington summer. And the chair backs are soiled by pencil gouges and graffiti marks, with declarations like "I should have gone to law school."

Sunday noon brought me through this very room, darkened because of the weekend. I climbed the few steps into the West Wing from the press area and announced myself to a uniformed Secret Service agent, who gave me a "So what?" look he seemed to save for all reporters seeking another bit of information to help along another story that was probably not very good for the administration. It was a look that made me want to grab him by his starched white poly-cotton shirt. But my ribs.

"I have an appointment with the president," I said, in what amounted to a verbal cuffing.

This made him take his task more seriously. He picked up the telephone, had a brief conversation that as best I could tell consisted of half a dozen prehistoric grunts, then led me past the Roosevelt Room on the right, past the Cabinet Room on the left, into an anteroom with two secretaries, one of whom greeted me with an enormous smile and unabashed pleasure at our meeting.

"Sylvia Weinrich," she said, holding out a delicate, perfectly manicured middle-aged hand. "It's delightful to see you. I must say, you've carried yourself with great dignity on television after the shooting. I don't know how I would have handled all that."

"Jack Flynn," I said, this time speaking the obvious. "I had the great advantage of not actually being hurt. Had I been, that might well have changed things."

We laughed politely at a joke that really wasn't all that funny, until Sylvia casually looked over her shoulder into an open door and said, "Why don't we just head right in. The president will probably want to get started."

She then brought me through a pair of wide doors into one of the most incredible places I have ever been: the Oval Office. The rug was such a colorful blue you could almost get lost in it, like the sea. In the middle was a bright eagle within the presidential seal, and beyond the rug on all sides was a shiny parquet maple-and-oak floor. A tall case clock ticked loudly by the door. Sunlight streamed in over the South Lawn through French doors and long windows. Magnificent paintings and portraits decorated the walls, including an unfinished one of George Washington hanging over the fireplace. Hutchins, in shirtsleeves—though elegant ones, I must say, with a fine blue pinstripe and presidential cuff links—stood up from his enormous oak desk at the far end of the room. It was a substantial, beautiful desk, a desk where presidents have signed declarations of war and treaties of peace, addressed the nation in times of crisis and triumph, plotted strategies to win reelection, to shape history, taped conversations that would haunt them to their graves. Hutchins stood up and boomed, "From the land of the living dead, Jack Flynn. Damned nice of you to come over."

I offered a simple smile at him and his surroundings, noticing Sylvia backing quietly out of the room. "A pleasure, sir," I said. "Thank you for the invitation." I found myself addressing him in that unusually formal tone, like on the golf course, and wondered if it was like that for everyone, especially in this office. I kind of presumed it was.

"Let's sit," Hutchins said, lowering his hand toward a blue-and-white-striped couch that I'd seen on television many times, though usually then it was occupied by a Middle Eastern king negotiating a truce or a Senate Republican having his arm twisted to back what always seemed to be billed as a landmark budget deal. Hutchins settled in a pale yellow upholstered chair set to the side of the fireplace.

"How are your ribs?" Hutchins asked as I lowered myself gingerly onto the couch. Then he answered his own question, as he tended to do. "Doctors tell me you're doing pretty well. Helps to be young and virile, huh?"

The door to the office swung open. Hutchins looked over, slightly startled, then watched calmly as the tall, courtly form of White House chief of staff Lincoln Powers came striding into the room.

"Sorry to interrupt, Mr. President," Powers said in that patrician Texan twang he has. "Have an important message I need to pass on to you." He handed Hutchins an official-looking memorandum, then turned back to me. "Well, you look even more handsome in person than on TV, young man," he said. "I'm Lincoln Powers, Mr. Flynn. Nice to meet you."

This TV thing, unbelievably, was starting to get old. I wondered how Walter Cronkite handled it all the time. I suppose it's different when you do it for a living.

Anyway, the story of Clayton Hutchins and Lincoln Powers was an unusual one—how the lives of two very different men intersected at a time of national crisis, and how they had bonded together ever since.

Hutchins's, mostly, was the amazing story. He had made his mark as a successful businessman in Des Moines, Iowa, taking a start-up technology company that produced personal finance software called Cookie Jar into the big leagues, eventually becoming a staple in households across America and earning its inventor hundreds of millions of dollars. Across Iowa, a state of significant prudence and few celebrities, Hutchins became a folk hero, lauded for his ambitions and his brains and loved for his massive acts of philanthropy. Some of the state's elder politicians took to joking that Hutchins's name became so commonplace on libraries, hospital wings, and school buildings that people might think he owned a construction company.

His was a uniquely American story—born and raised on a farm miles and miles from his closest neighbor, schooled at home, college educated later in life, entirely self-made in both the worlds of commerce and government.

His entrance to politics was unconventional, to say the least. A few months before the Iowa governor's race six years ago, a group of business leaders and citizen activists, dissatisfied with the lackluster candidates for the two major parties, got together and launched a massive draft-Hutchins movement for a third-party write-in campaign. Hutchins reluctantly accepted. Standing onstage with his two opponents at a series of debates, he had them so out-witted and outsmarted that the race seemed almost unfair. He won with 45 percent of the vote, fifteen points ahead of his closest competitor.

Hutchins came in with a refreshing ability to speak the truth and the simple promise that he would run the gov-ernment like a business and demand nothing but the best service at the lowest cost possible. He balanced the state's budget. He fired a string of high-level managers who had long been suspected of corruption. He spoke his mind, spoke it often, and spoke it well. Even *60 Minutes,* the bane of politicians countrywide, aired a glowing profile of Hutchins, calling him "one of the last great moderate politicians in America."

Two years later, the Republican front-runner for the presidency, Senator Wordsworth Cole, for reasons he didn't understand, found himself suddenly getting bat-tered in Iowa public opinion polls about a week before the caucus. Experts said it was bad organization and a stale message. Most Iowans were more pointed in their beliefs. They just seemed to think he was out of touch. So Hutchins unleashed the full glory of his power to help Cole win, and win he did, by a huge margin—a victory that analysts described as the watershed event in the cam-paign. From there, with momentum, he steamrolled into New Hampshire, and then across the country and all the way to the Republican nomination. Privately, at the

August Republican Convention in Miami, he promised to give Hutchins any cabinet post he desired as a reward for his crucial work.

Flash ahead to three weeks before the November election. The *New York Times* published a report that Cole's vice presidential running mate, Senator Steven Sugara of Wyoming, had been addicted to the prescription drug Prozac two years earlier, but had never disclosed the fact to Cole or, for that matter, to Wyoming voters. In a neck-and-neck race, the Cole campaign immediately went into a tailspin. But Hutchins met up with Cole on the campaign trail, counseled him that voters cast ballots for president, not vice president, and told him to publicly stand behind his nominee. He did, and staggered to a slim victory, but a victory nonetheless. They don't partially furnish the Oval Office or limit your miles on Air Force One because you only won by 2 percent. A week later, Sugara resigned. Hutchins was picked as vice president, and he continued like that for three and a half years.

He was a good understudy, a major fund-raising asset, a loyal and confidential adviser. At first, my brethren in the news media thought his personality might not fit the required role. Hutchins harked from the no-bullshit world of high-technology business, a place where risk led to the ultimate rewards and prudence was the hallmark of those left behind. He was offensive in almost every possible way, but not in the worst sense of the word. He was blunt. His voice was hard, as if it had been pounded by rocks. He was built like a fireplug, at five feet, ten inches, I'd guess, with a barrel chest and broad shoulders. His face was rough, his hair thinning, and he was anything but handsome, yet when he met with contributors or businessmen or even aides, he spawned many imitators, those who wanted to be like him, to dress like him, to talk as he did in words and tone. He was someone who seemed never to expect anything other than wild success, but when he achieved it, he gave the impression it would never change him.

As vice president, he was strong, but he knew his place. That meant he was fully aware he had not been elected. He knew his role was virtually meaningless compared to the president's. He accorded the president the same kind of reverent respect he expected from those under him when he worked in business. He understood that his most important function at its most fundamental level was simply to be there, to be ready, if the president should die. And that had happened this past August, one week before the Republican Convention.

President Cole dropped dead of a massive heart attack on the private tennis court tucked into the bushes on the South Lawn of the White House. It was a stunningly beautiful summer day. He had just put the finishing touches to his acceptance speech and was planning to take a week off with his family at their getaway house on Sea Island, Georgia. He stole out back for a tune-up game with a mid-level aide. Witnesses said he had just broken service and was poised to win the first set when he crumpled to the ground. By the time the Secret Service agents got to him, which was in seconds, he was already dead. By nightfall, Clayton Hutchins had taken the oath of office on the porch of the vice president's mansion on the grounds of the Naval Observatory. Like Jerry Ford, he became president without ever winning a single vote on a national ticket.

At a time of almost indescribable distress within the Republican Party and sorrow across the entire nation, Hutchins again proved to be a reassuring force. He accepted the nomination of his party by acclamation at a subdued convention in Chicago. He vowed to continue on the path blazed by Cole, a man he said he loved. He nominated Theodore Rockingham, a grandfatherly, even statesmanlike veteran of past Republican administrations, as his vice president. Throughout the autumn campaign, he remained silent as his Democratic opponent, the respected senator from Colorado, Stanny Nichols, got pelted by accusations over some decade-old income tax issues back home. It was still a tight race, but Hutchins was watching his poll numbers climb in the wake of the attempt on his life. As I sat in the Oval Office on this day, two months into Hutchins's presidency, victory in the election had become more realistic than at any other point in the campaign—realistic enough that Hutchins had just started thinking what he might do once he achieved it.

Back in August, one of the first things he did after taking the oath was place a call to Powers's sprawling cattle ranch, to plead with the elegant Texan to return to the White House for one last tour of duty on behalf of party and country. Powers was perhaps the most experienced, most respected political adviser in America, a confidant to Republican presidents for three decades, a former secretary of state who had blazed around the world on missions of war and peace. He knew Washington and he knew power, and he knew how to handle the latter within the curious circus of the former, and for that, I suspect, he had been an invaluable part of Hutchins's smooth transition. They were an odd pair, these two, a consummate government outsider and the ultimate creature of the capital, a virgin and a pimp, if you will.

"Sorry to cut in on you here," Powers said to me, as the president pulled a thick Waterman writing instrument off a side table and penned a note in the margin of the memorandum. As Powers took the papers back and walked from the room, a telephone console tucked on a shelf beneath the side table gave a soft, melodic ring. I looked down in surprise, having not seen anything there, and wondering who it is that calls the president. I answered my own question, watching a red light blink along a column that had various agencies listed: CIA, State, Chief of Staff, Treasury. The light illuminated beside the FBI.

"Yes," Hutchins said, sounding annoyed as he answered the phone. There was a pause as he listened, then he seemed to cut the caller off, saying, "Look, I appreciate this, but I've got several things going on right now, like a presidential campaign. I will call you later when I have time for a full briefing." He hung up without saying goodbye, then turned to me. "I get a little flesh wound in the shoulder, and everyone acts like I have to drop everything in the name of a national catastrophe. Life goes on, except, I guess, for that poor bastard who took the poke at me."

That would have been as good a time as any to cut in with a nicely placed segue, something original like "Speaking of the poor bastard. Any idea who the hell he is?" But I didn't feel comfortable enough yet, not with the president, and especially not here in the Oval Office, which was about as intimidating a place as I'd ever been in. I wondered if the word *fuck* had ever been uttered within these pristine confines, then remembered Nixon and assumed it had.

"So, where are you in terms of our discussion Thursday?" Hutchins asked, cutting hard to the point.

My eyes drifted around the room for a minute. All this time to come up with a pat answer, and I didn't actually have one. I looked out the French doors, into the Rose Garden, where the last of the season's hardiest flowers fluttered in the autumn breeze. I looked down to the circular drive, then beyond to the South Lawn, and imagined being here early on a Thursday evening, stepping onto the patio and walking across the grass to Marine One, giving a quick wave good-bye to the gathered staff, and lifting off for Camp David for a weekend of blissful seclusion, maybe a few holes of golf. Finally I looked at Hutchins, and from my sense of it, not a moment too soon, because he seemed to be getting aggravated with me. Searching for an answer, I punted. I decided to offer the truth.

"You have to understand, I've had a lot going on these past couple of days," I said.

"I understand that," he fired back, with a tone that meant understanding and accepting were entirely different. "I also have an election to win, then a country to run. And I need people like you with me, at least for the latter. And not just people *like* you, but specifically you. I know the timing could be better on all of this, but you owe it to this office, to your country, to put this at the forefront and make a decision."

I must say, a pretty good speech. "I just want to be sure. Tell me again what you have in mind," I said.

"No different than I said before. You come aboard here as the White House press secretary. My plan is to ship Dalton off to one of the agencies, maybe Interior. Seems like the type of guy he is. Sooner the better. He's Cole's boy, not mine, and I have to start putting mine in place."

I was coming to realize that this might be one of my last chances to get a handle on what might become of my life. Hutchins was not a guy who I could just pick up the phone and call with another question or two. "Why me?" I asked.

"You come highly recommended by a number of my operatives up in New England. I used to read you quite a bit when I was campaigning in New Hampshire and grew to be a fan. You also have a no-nonsense demeanor and a way with people that I really want to project to the public. I also don't have a clue what your politics are, which I like. A lot. In short, I think we'd work well together."

He was boosting my ego. I was, in turn, growing confident. "You have my apologies for not thinking this through already and my word that I'll do it as soon as I can. But sir, you have to know, there is an awful lot happening right now, for all of us, and my first obligation is to the newspaper."

"Don't I know it," Hutchins said, and he wiped the side of his head with his palm, looking momentarily as tired as I'd ever seen him look. "Do what you can. Here's the bottom line, though. I'm going to need a decision on Friday. That gives you five days. If not you, I have to move on and look for someone else."

He began to stand up and said, "You'll have to accept my apologies, but I've had something come up today, and am going to have to offer a rain check on lunch."

Time was running out for me. "Sir," I said, in as calm and confident a voice as I could. "Any idea who this dead would-be assassin is?"

Miraculously, Hutchins sat back down in his chair and looked at me for a long moment. "FBI still tells me they think he's a militia member, despite what all you guys are saying about the government's inability to link him with a group. Hell, the Secret Service has a security alert going. Their vast preference is for me not to even leave the White House. They want to make me a frigging prisoner of this place, only I have a campaign to run and win. I can't afford to play anything safe right now."

And that, ladies and gentlemen, is what you call news, and I felt myself making an excited fist with one hand as I jotted down what he said on a yellow legal pad with the other.

"We on the record?" Hutchins asked.

I nodded. "As far as I'm concerned, sir. Is that a problem?" I asked that last question politely, but with an almost challenging tone.

The president chuckled in a hollow kind of way. "You're some piece of work," he said. "I like that, though. I like that a lot."

I wasn't quite done here, even if he was. And now that it was gin-clear this was all on the record and that our conversation had become an interview, I pressed on with more bravado.

"And you're satisfied with the FBI in this investigation so far?" I asked, then quickly added, "And what is it that leads them to believe that this was a militiaman?"

"Two different questions," Hutchins said. He was putting his game face on, and it was a good one. "To the first one, hell, they're the single greatest law enforcement and investigative agency on the face of this earth. If they tell me they believe it was a militiaman who tried to kill me, then I believe it was a militiaman who tried to kill me. On the evidence they're basing that on, you know I can't get into that."

Good quotes, every sentence, every last word. Hutchins stood up. "Hold on a second," he said, walking over to his desk. He pulled a sheet of paper out of a drawer and walked back over toward me, placing it in my hands. "You didn't get this from me," he said. "And no, you can't take it with you."

I quickly scanned the document from the top down. It was on Treasury Department letterhead, Secret Service Division. It was dated October 18, a little more than a week before the shooting. It began, "Dear Mr. President, It has come to our attention, through the Federal Bureau of Investigation, that there has been a secondhand threat on your life. We would be glad to brief you in greater detail at your convenience. Until then, this memo is an advisory of several additional security measures being taken for your protection. . . ."

I soaked in every word, then scribbled it furiously into my notebook as Hutchins sat back in his chair, waiting patiently. When I looked up at him, he told me, "You didn't get this from me either, but I never bothered to get a briefing. I figure these guys know what they're doing when it comes to protecting me. They said they would prefer I didn't play golf that day, but advised me that if I did, they were confident they could guarantee my safety." He paused and softly chuckled.

Before I could ask any other questions, Hutchins raised his voice a bit. "You'll identify me as a White House official. Maybe I even rank as one of those *senior* White House officials you bastards are always quoting without names. Now I want you to think about our other issue. You owe it to me, and you owe it to yourself. And take my advice. Come over here and work in the White House. It will be the best experience you've ever had."

I stood up, and we shook hands. On the way out, the carpet was so thick it was like walking on air, or maybe it was the euphoria that comes with a nice news hit when you need it most. Within a minute, I was moving along at a rapid clip, along Pennsylvania Avenue, back to the *Record*.

This time, Martin was sitting at my desk when I glided into the newsroom, absently flipping through wire reports on the computer screen, biding time, waiting to learn what I had. At first, I didn't say anything. I put my notebook and recorder down beside him, slowly peeled off my suit jacket, and walked away to hang it up.

"Jesus Christ, c'mon, what do you have?" he called out after me. I hung my coat up before walking back and answering.

"Nothing. A big zero."

"What the flying fuck are you fucking talking about? You sit with the president of the United States in the Oval Office three days after he's been shot and nine days before the election, and you tell me you walked out of there with nothing?"

He was incredulous. His face, no, his entire body, had flushed to an extraordinary shade of crimson. His hands were actually trembling, and his voice quivered a bit as he talked. Needless to say, this isn't what he expected me to tell him, which explains why I did.

"Get a grip," I said. "And get out of my chair. I have a lot of work to do here."

He looked confused. I continued talking. "Would you call a high-level security alert a good story? The president saying that he was warned not to play golf that day? What if that same president said the FBI is still telling him that this assassination attempt was the result of the militia movement?"

The color—normal, human color—slowly returned to Martin, at least to his visible parts, though he still looked at me with suspicion.

"So you're saying this is what you have?" he asked, afraid to get excited in case I was pulling another prank on him. I suspect Martin had been tormented in similar fashion throughout most of his life, by larger fourth-graders, by high school jocks, by college fraternity boys. And I suspect he had gotten quite used to it, almost immune.

"This is what I have," I said. "The interview was brief. Every quote is precious. I was shown a document that will help our cause immensely. We're breaking some new ground with the security alert and the prior warning and putting him out on the record on the militia angle. I think this is going to work out well for us."

Martin looked stunned, but this time in a good way. "You're going to go hard as hell with it, right?" he asked.

"Oh, yeah. Straight ahead."

He moved away from the chair. "I'll go call Boston," he said, skipping off.

I settled in at my desk, spread my legal pad out beside me, and got comfortable, sore ribs and all. Over the course of the next ninety minutes, I took my readers on a brisk walk through a flowering garden, as an old editor of mine used to say. The prose flowed nicely, and after I shipped the story to Martin and he shipped it to Boston, I sat with my feet on my desk in a bureau ringing with the sonorous sounds of deadline, still reveling in the thrill of another successful story, a glow that is similar to those moments in bed after having particularly good sex with someone you're just getting to know. Or something like that. I wondered if this story would trigger another call from my anonymous voice, and if it did, what he might say. I was wondering what would happen an hour from then when I visited the Newseum. I was staring off at nothing in particular when Julie Gershman stopped by.

"Welcome back," she said in a flirty little way, and I knew immediately what she meant.

"Was it that obvious that I was gone?" I asked.

"Only to people who follow you closely," she said, ratcheting the conversation to another level.

"Well, it's good to be back," I said.

"Let me buy you a beer sometime soon," she said.

"Sooner the better," I replied.

"Good," she said, and turned and walked out, a knapsack on her shoulder, her short skirt flouncing with every sexy step.

"Idaho?" That was Martin, who had appeared magically at my desk, his euphoria ebbing toward the needs of the next news cycle.

"Today's Hutchins story does give Idaho more weight, doesn't it?" I asked.

"More than ever. I'll assume you're in the air tomorrow. Give a call when you get out there. We're back in the game."

As he walked away, my phone rang. It was Gus, just checking in, congratulating me on my coverage, just wanting to chat.

"You're a great man," I told him as we hung up. "I've got to run to an appointment now. Tomorrow I'm flying out to Spokane, actually to the Idaho Panhandle. I'll give you a ring when I get back."

I quickly punched out a number in Sand Falls. Eventually, Daniel Nathaniel came on the line.

"Tomorrow I'm in your neighborhood," I said, sounding firm, macho. "You going to make this trip worth my while?"

"Getting to spend some time with me is always worth anyone's while," he said. That answer was about as close as I'd get to absolute confirmation that he had something good.

eight

THERE IS AN EXHIBIT at the Newseum—a museum dedicated to the journalism industry, of all things—that allows tourists from, say, Iowa, to stand before a camera with the White House as a backdrop and broadcast their own news story on a nearby television screen, as if they were a real live Washington network correspondent bringing the day's events to the rest of the nation, windbreakers and sneakers aside.

I took limited comfort in this knowledge, figuring that my meeting with this anonymous source might actually give these network wannabes something to report on. At about 5:20 P.M., I paid my admission to the museum, which sits in Rosslyn, Virginia, just across the Potomac River from Georgetown, and began walking around the various exhibits. I didn't know, obviously, what this source looked like. I had to assume he knew me, and would seek me out if I just made myself visible.

Ends up, the Newseum closes at six, a fact I thought to be odd for a couple of reasons—first, shutting down a museum about the media right in the middle of deadline, second, because this early closing hour cut the time awfully close for my source. I had to assume that whatever it was that he had to say to me, he would say it quickly. As an echoey voice over the public address system called out that visitors should be prepared to leave within thirty minutes, I hung around an area where they posted front pages of newspapers from across the country.

I heard footsteps coming from across the hard tile floor, then a man called to me, "Excuse me, sir, but everyone has to start getting ready to head out now. We're closing down for the evening."

I turned to see a gentleman in a security uniform, complete with a hat. He looked startled when he saw my face, and added, "Oh, Mr. Flynn, excuse me. I had no idea it was you." He hesitated, then said, "Please, make yourself at home. We'll be doing some cleaning upstairs for a while, probably about an hour. Feel free to enjoy the museum in the meantime."

"Thank you," I said. So celebrity has its advantages.

I poked around for about thirty minutes, until it was quite obvious I was the only one in the place. I tried concentrating on exhibits on the history of newspapers and the evolution of network news, but to no avail. I could think of little more than what my anonymous source might have to say, and what it would all mean to this story. I was also growing impatient with his lack of punctuality, and come around six-twenty, resigned myself to the assumption that he wasn't going to show. It was either a hoax, or he got scared off, or he misplanned the encounter and couldn't get inside because of closing time. This was obviously not a pro, but then again, what is a professional source? I wondered if I should wait outside.

Suddenly, to my left, a wall filled with television

screens, twenty feet high and maybe twice that in length, popped to life, each set filled with the image of Peter Jennings broadcasting ABC's *World News Tonight*— hundreds of screens, every one a haunting image of the other. I'll admit, I like Peter Jennings, but enough is enough.

"Tonight, growing questions and few answers on Thursday's assassination attempt against President Clayton Hutchins," Jennings said, raising his eyebrows in that way he does when he disapproves of the direction of a story. "Tonight, an ABC special report."

His voice, his expressions, engulfed me. I looked around to see if anyone was watching me watch Peter, but the rest of the museum was empty, frighteningly empty given all the noise. I had the feeling of being alone in an amusement park, late at night, and having all the rides inexplicably spring to life.

"At the J. Edgar Hoover Building in downtown Washington, headquarters of the FBI, the official line remains that investigators continue to probe whether the shooting is tied to the nation's militia movement," Jennings said. "But within the FBI, sources tell ABC News there is currently a paucity of evidence pointing in that direction, though those same sources warn that new information is being gathered and multiple theories, including the possibility of a militia-related shooting, are still in play.

"Meanwhile, out in the field, those who know the dead would-be assassin, Tony Clawson, express surprise. We go now to Jackie Judd in Fresno, California, for a report on the life, and the death, of Tony Clawson."

The distant image of a Home Depot store flashed on all those screens, as the reporter's voice filled the Newseum and echoed toward the cavernous ceiling. Around a nearby bend, I heard what sounded like shoes on tile, then nothing but the reporter's voice, then more shoes on tile, then nothing again. I stared in that direction, looking for a person, a shadow, anything that would indicate another form of life in this room.

"Mr. Flynn?"

It was a loud, urgent voice emanating from the balcony above me, a shout almost, by necessity because of the television sets. My eyes bolted upward, but I could see nothing but darkness.

Peter Jennings droned on, oblivious to my situation, even though he appeared to be my only witness. "Out on the campaign trail, Senator Stanny Nichols, the Democratic presidential nominee, delivers a red meat speech to a labor union rally in the pivotal swing state of Wisconsin, as polls show President Hutchins creeping ahead in the aftermath of the assassination attempt—"

"Who is it?" I yelled back. Okay, stupid question, but sometimes you just ask the first thing that pops into your mind. And they're always asking that question in the movies.

"Stay right there, Mr. Flynn." For a second, it was as if Jennings was talking to me, but no. The voice, still at the clip of a holler, was younger than I had expected, given that the phone calls sounded like they came from a reasonably old man.

I stayed silent, waiting, but nothing happened.

Jennings: "Later in the program, in Bethlehem,

Pennsylvania, a fresh start for some old steel workers. As part of our *Eye on America,* we bring you the latest from an innovative job retraining program that is being billed as a model for our fading industrial nation—"

Still nothing. "Where are you?" I yelled, but got no response. I strained my eyes looking upward, then off into the distant expanse of the museum, but all I could see was the glow of so many television sets. Jennings's voice was so loud, so omnipotent, that it seemed to take its own visual form.

I'd like to think I'm nobody's fool, so it was beginning to dawn on me that if this was just some relatively innocent meeting between a reporter and a confidential source, I wouldn't be entangled in this situational melodrama. Problem is, that thought struck me just as I heard a loud crack—a sound that was becoming all too familiar these past few days.

I'm not sure whether I ducked or just flinched. Nor was I sure where the noise came from, which direction the bullet—assuming it was a bullet—was headed. Because of that, I didn't know which way to run, and feared that if I peeled off in any given direction, I might find myself face-to-face with my stalking gunman. Times like these, I wish I had just become a copy editor.

I looked behind me to see Peter Jennings's face blown out on one of the television screens, just about level with my own, and that image sent something tantamount to a convulsion through my body. It also prompted me to get flat to the floor and begin crawling toward the door, figuring that all things being equal, it was probably the best direction to head.

"The Gulf Coast of Texas braces for the late arrival of Hurricane Sally, which is expected to make land by dawn tomorrow—"

I strained to hear any other sounds, any other slight movements, most notably a gun cocking, but all I could really hear, Jennings aside, was the sound of my own heavy breathing. So I kept crawling to the entrance, about forty feet away, straightaway across the center of the museum floor. Every inch I covered I wondered whether I was an inch closer to safety or death.

About halfway there, I veered toward a heavy door marked with an illuminated sign that read, "Emergency Exit. Alarm will sound." Maybe sounding alarms wasn't such a bad idea. I paused on the floor for a few seconds, summoning the emotional and physical energy to bolt upward and blast through the door. My driving fear, gunman excepted, was that the door would be locked, but these are the risks you take in the name of salvation.

I braced myself on all fours and hurled myself against the door. It flew open, and a shrieking alarm filled the air. I found myself on some nondescript street in Rosslyn, empty after dark. I bolted around the corner of the building and could hear the alarm become muted as the door shut behind me. I ran the one block to the Metro station, gulping the fresh air of freedom and safety. A train was sliding toward the platform as I bounded down the escalator. The doors rolled open, and I grabbed my own pole to hold and stared out the rear window as we pulled away, staring, it ends up, at nothing at all.

• • •

By all means, I'm Irish. I have the ability to brood for hours at a time. If I ever needed bypass surgery, I'm convinced my doctors would open up my chest and find that my heart is an alarming shade of black. Not all the time, but often, I love to drink, to tell stories, to laugh hard when my brain feels soaked in Miller, or even worse, gin. But if you really want to see ethnic, take a look at Steve Havlicek.

He stands about five feet six inches, though he doesn't exactly seem short. His face is like a Rand McNally map of wrinkles, heading every which way from the downtown location that seems to be the middle of his cheeks. His hair, graying, is often matted against his big scalp or sticking up in various directions in shapeless wisps. He talks loud. He laughs even louder. He loves jokes, and he seems to have a general inability to be embarrassed by anything that life might throw at him. At home his wife, Margaret, his high school sweetheart, his same age, looks a decade younger. She is gorgeous, perfectly put together. They have two children, both grown and successful. From a distance anyway, and I suspect up close as well, they seem to have an ideal relationship, the type of love that tears barriers down rather than builds them up. Ah, but there I go getting deep again.

"Jesus, what a place." That was Havlicek, walking into the paneled Grille Room at the University Club, an establishment where I have remained a member in good standing for many years. He looked around the lounge and gave one of those soft whistles, like something on the *Andy Griffith Show,* and said, in a confiding voice, "High-roller city, huh? I bet lots of big guns come in here."

I don't think he quite understood the general code of conduct at all private clubs—one of understated appreciation. Members favor words like *comfortable* and *traditional,* and neither gawk nor mock each other, at least in a forum as public as the club bar. So I ignored that. I had arrived comfortably ahead of him, giving myself enough time to clean myself up in the marble men's room, knock down a Miller Highlife, and try to calm my nerves. "What are you drinking, Steve?" I said, rather shortly. Maybe I wasn't exactly calm quite yet.

Havlicek's gaze zeroed in on something across the room, nearly empty because it was a Sunday night. "Nice cheese tray," he said. "That for anyone? Even a nonmember?"

Lyle, the bartender, finally caught Havlicek's eye, God bless him. "Can I get you something, sir?" he asked, in that way that leaves the impression he might have a mouthful of marbles.

"You bet. What kind of beer do you have?" Havlicek asked.

The list was a long one, and I shot Lyle an interested look, wondering how he would handle this. "Anything you like." Okay, so he would handle it well.

"I like that," Havlicek said, warming to the place even more, growing comfortable, taking on a feeling of belonging. "I'll have a Heineken."

Havlicek wrapped his hairy hand around the ice-cold bottle and took a long gulp before Lyle could even hurry down the bar with a frosted pilsner glass. "That overnight flight and all that time-change bullshit wiped me out, so I didn't get much today," he said to me, his eyes meeting mine for the first time since he walked in.

Then, urgently, "Jesus Christ. What the frick happened to you? I thought I was a mess, but look at you, you're a fricking wreck."

"A tough day," I said. "Let me regroup first, and I'll tell you about it."

On a related matter, earlier in the afternoon, I had already decided to tell him about the anonymous calls and note, for a couple of reasons. First, he would probably be of help on it. He had one of the best investigative minds in the country. He had won his Pulitzer Prize a few years earlier for a series of stories detailing how a group of Boston housing inspectors were actually the biggest slumlords in the city, having arranged a series of property takeovers from prior shady owners, then operating the properties in the same way, free from the threat of inspection. Second reason was, it would be vastly unfair to withhold information from him on this story. If anyone did it to me, I would be furious, and that was the final yardstick. And given what had just happened to me an hour previous, I really had no choice anymore, for my own safety, and perhaps his as well.

"So we've got a dead assassin wannabe who no one knows who the fuck he is," I said as we leaned on the bar. "We've got the FBI immediately pointing the finger at the militias, and no one knows why. Basically, we've got nothing."

"Martin says you might fly out and talk to a militia pal of yours in Idaho? That might be a good idea, just to nail that angle down clean, be able to print that the militias definitively say they don't know who this guy is and that they wouldn't condone the shooting of the president."

"Thinking about it, but I'm not sure if that moves the ball far enough along. I do have a couple of other interesting developments—"

Lyle, at this point, came over with a couple of bowls of mixed snacks—some pretzels, wheat Chex, corn chips, and peanuts swirled together.

"Jesus Christ, this place is great," Havlicek said. He reached into his pocket, and I started thinking, Oh, no, please don't. But he did. He pulled out a fold of money and asked Lyle, "How much do we owe for that last round?" Confidingly to me: "I can bill this off to the *Record.*"

I put my hand gently on Havlicek's arm and pushed it down. "On me," I said.

"No, no, no," he said, determined, holding the money up high now. The few people around were looking. Lyle appeared frozen behind the bar.

"Really, Steve. I've got it. Besides, they don't take cash in here. Everything's on charge. I just sign it all away."

"You just sign your name, and that's it?" A pause while he calculated just what that meant, which, for him, was free food and drink. "God, I love this place."

Lyle looked relieved. I tugged Havlicek toward an empty dining table nearby, away from more potential trouble. Don't get me wrong. I'm not rich, and I'm not a snob. The University Club is my one true indulgence. Years ago, it was my refuge, a place to steal away for a few hours from the grind of work and the occasional frustrations of my courtship with Katherine. We were both enormous advocates of the need for our own time, private time, and I usually spent mine here, down in the gym working up a sweat, taking a long steam bath, then stealing up to this very grille room for a hamburger, a beer, and a wedge of cheesecake. Now, with Katherine gone, the club had become something of a second home for me, an anchor when I was constantly on the road, a place where I looked forward to coming and where Lyle would always greet me with a warm squeeze of my shoulder.

"Look," I said, after we sat down. "I've got some things we should go over."

"Yeah?" he said. He was looking at me square in the eyes, waiting, and I continued on slowly.

"I think someone just took a shot at me," I said. I saw the look of confusion on his face, and added quickly, "Let me start from the beginning. I've got an anonymous caller ringing me up. He made the first call right after I arrived in the hospital. He called me once on what must have been late Thursday afternoon, then again on Friday morning. Then someone—the source or more likely someone else—followed me to a restaurant in Georgetown last night and gave the waitress a note telling me to meet him at the Newseum over in Rosslyn tonight at five-thirty."

"What the fuck," Havlicek said. An eloquent one. "What happened tonight?"

I told him the details. When I was through, Havlicek said, "Jesus Christ. Some fricking story. You never saw the guy?"

"Not even a glimpse."

"You think it was the same source who's been calling you? You think this is all just some sort of setup?"

A pair of typically good inquiries. I shrugged.

Havlicek said, "What's he sound like?"

"He's older, and very eloquent. He's polite, but forceful. He sounds like he really wants to make a point. Sounds like he knows what he's talking about, but he hasn't really said anything of value yet."

Havlicek asked, "And was that the same voice that called out to you at the Newseum?"

"That's the thing," I replied. "I don't think it was. The voice there sounded much younger, much livelier, less formal."

"Probably two different people," Havlicek said, reaffirming what I believed in the back of my mind. "One person wants to help you get information. The other person wants to make sure you never get it. The good guy, assuming there is one, how did he leave it with you?"

I said, "Says he'll help me more as soon as he's convinced I'm serious."

"Well, the answer is to keep getting some hits on this story and slam them into the paper. Meanwhile, I'll renew my sources out there and work them over. And you should turn Idaho into a nice quick hit. Would be nice to have a turnaround on that, get it in the paper, generate some news and maintain this guy's interest in you."

Notice that although my life was on the line, calling authorities was never an option—not for Havlicek, not for me. There was a story at stake, and a peripheral investigation would hamper our chances at getting it.

A waiter came over with some menus. "I saw you on CNN, Mr. Flynn," he said to me. "You looked terrific." Mental note: add an extra tip on the sign slip.

Havlicek said, "Something's been bothering me." He looked at me hard and continued. "Why were you playing golf with Hutchins in the first place? Martin said you were working on some pardon story, but I didn't quite get it."

"Presidential pardons," I said. "Every year, the president pardons any given number of convicts. It's part of his executive powers, like vetoing a piece of legislation. At first, I was working a generic story, kind of the anatomy of a presidential pardon. Most of the pardons have easy explanations, like a convict in a questionable murder conviction becomes a model inmate after forty years and is freed to spend his dying days with his family, something like that. I came across one in Massachusetts, a guy by the name of Paul Stemple, involved in an armored car heist back in the late 1970s, that lacked an easy answer. So I asked Royal Dalton about it. He called me back with a vague explanation about the inmate having served twenty years already, but never explained properly the genesis of the pardon. Then, out of nowhere, he says the president would like to know if I might be available for a game of golf."

Havlicek cut in and said, "So you asked Hutchins about it?"

"Well, I planned to, yes. But before I could, we got carried away in another conversation, and then, suddenly, we get shot."

"Let me ask you something far-fetched," Havlicek said. "You don't think there's any way that Hutchins or his people might have staged this assassination attempt as some sort of preelection ploy, do you?"

I stared down into my beer and nodded my head slowly. "I'll admit, I've thought about that," I said. "But damn, come on. How dangerous is that?"

"Yeah, too stupid. Too stupid."

He added, "So somebody wants to help you. Somebody else wants to kill you, maybe because that first somebody wants to help you. You have to watch your back."

I nodded, and we both turned our attention to the menu. We ordered some smoked salmon, some calamari, a couple of hamburgers. At ten o'clock, Havlicek looked at his watch and announced he had to head back to his hotel and call his wife.

Watch your back. I started to walk outside, into the night, and then thought better of it. The dog was with Kristen, so I ambled up to the front desk, got myself a guest key, and slept in one of the overnight rooms upstairs.

FINALLY, CURTIS BLACK DECIDED it was time to break the heavy silence. For ten minutes, as he drove the intentionally nondescript blue cargo van out of Chelsea, then up and over the Tobin Bridge into Boston, no one had uttered a solitary word, not Black himself, not his three men sitting on the floor in the back. All of the men wore gloves, all of them were dressed in gray, all of them were packing a 9-mm semiautomatic weapon that Black hoped against hope they would never have to use. The fourth man would be meeting them on Hanover Street in the getaway car—a 1978 Lincoln Continental, stolen the week before and stashed since in a private garage. The fifth man would be meeting them on the Boston Fish Pier in a second getaway car, a Mercury station wagon with tinted windows.

Not that Black minded the silence. Better to be silent than jumpy, falsely jovial. Silence meant economy, and at the scene of a crime, there's nothing better than to be economical. The more words you speak, the more actions you take, the more opportunity there is for error and the more clues you leave behind. Better to cut into the fabric of everyday life with a scalpel rather than blow it up with a bomb, the goal being to grab whatever it is you want or need, then vanish in as straight a line as you came, leaving as little of life interrupted as possible. No need, in short, for undue drama.

Still, this silence felt almost morbid, Black thought. They had gone over their plan one final time, sitting around the little kitchen table of his Chelsea apartment. They had run through a checklist of actions, then made sure everyone was carrying his ski mask, his gloves, his gun. Each man's pockets were otherwise empty. Everyone knew his role.

"In an hour, we're a hell of a lot richer than we are right now," Black called out from the driver's seat. The unsubtle intent was to provide more incentive to do the job right—positive incentive.

He heard them move in the back, where the three guys were sitting on the floor and wheelwells, but still no one spoke. Eventually, someone—Black thought it was Cox—said, "You think we can put this money right back into circulation, or are we going to have to sit on it awhile?"

Black replied, "Well, I wouldn't try to open an account with it at Wells Fargo, and I wouldn't walk into the Bank of New England with a suitcase full of it tomorrow, but I think you can spend it if you're smart about it, buy plane tickets, maybe even a car, or whatever."

"I'm heading to Vegas tomorrow," Rocco said. "I'm getting myself a suite at Bally's. I'm going to eat a nice steak dinner, and I'm going to get a beautiful hooker, one of those little seventeen-year-old girls. I'm going to give her a little taste of what I'm all about, until she's giving it to me for free. Then I'm going to leave her in my room and hit the tables."

Black rolled his eyes in the front seat. How had he ended up with this farm animal? In another hour, he'd never have to deal with him again, and he never would. He made that promise to himself right there and then.

Black pulled his van off the bridge, looped around, and drove through the streets of Charlestown heading for the North End. The morning sun had given way to heavy afternoon clouds and the threat of rain, which all in all might be good. Clear the streets of passersby—each one a potential witness.

"About three minutes, and we're there," Black called out to the men in back.

Everyone had fallen quiet again, which was just as well. Black had made his point, and he'd heard all he could stand to hear from Rocco. Just pray to the good Lord he doesn't screw this up. Just get through the next half hour, and in every job in the future, he'd be more selective. He'd find better guys, pay them better money, keep them around longer. Maybe this guy Cox would prove himself today. Maybe he'd be someone to keep in the stable.

"Coming down Prince Street," Black said. "Two minutes."

Black checked his watch. It was 4:44 P.M., about twelve minutes until action. So many things to go wrong. But he had to remind himself: nothing ever did, not for him, not ever, not now. He was the most meticulous criminal strategist in Boston, a mastermind of bank heists and store holdups whose reputation within criminal and legal circles was held in virtual awe. This job, though, this job represented his most daring venture—a daylight armored car strike involving what he had already determined would be more money than he had ever pulled out of a single hit before. He was estimating the take to be anywhere from $600,000 to $1 million. This was a sleeper of a bank branch, a repository for Mafia money in the North End that was usually deposited every Tuesday afternoon after the weekend receipts.

"On Hanover Street. One minute to arrival."

He scanned the street, looking for anything unusual, anything he hadn't seen there in the last couple of days, but he saw nothing extraordinary. He was starting to get that feeling he always got during a hit, that lightness of heart, the singular focus of mind, the surge of concentration, when thoughts and words and actions mesh seamlessly into one. It was just another mark that made him so good at what he did.

He pulled the van over to the side of the street, double-parking in the precise spot where he had for the past couple of scouting missions.

"Arrival."

Pause.

"Standby."

Pause.

"Ten minutes to action."

A minute later, in his rearview mirror, Black saw the Lincoln pull up about two car lengths behind him and double-park, filling him with a sense of relief. Everything was running according to plan.

"Getaway car has arrived," Black called out, keeping his guys informed, even if the intricacies were lost on them.

Now it was just a matter of waiting—waiting for the Wells Fargo armored truck to pull down the street, to park in front of the van, for the security men to get out, one of them to walk inside the bank branch and come back outside pushing a dolly with a duffel bag filled with money. They had a plan. They just needed to follow it, Black told himself.

Four minutes later, Black broke the tense silence again. "Put your earpieces in place," he said, and the three men in back reached into their pockets as one and inserted small wires into their ears. "Test them," Black said. Then he spoke very quietly into his cupped hands. "Testing, one, two, three. Testing. Please acknowledge."

"Gotcha," Rocco responded.

"Fine," Cox said.

Stemple, the third man in the van, added, "With you."

Black said, "Car two, please hold up your hand if you can hear." He looked in his rearview mirror and received the signal he wanted.

Suddenly, a problem. In the mirror, Black's eye caught something he didn't expect. A meter maid—a man, actually—walking purposefully down the street with his ticket book in hand and a look of annoyance on his bearded face. A fucking meter maid.

"Stay down back there," Black said to the three men in the van. He cracked his window and watched in his side mirror as the man approached the getaway car behind him. He saw the meter man and his driver exchange words, then saw the meter man shrug, write out a ticket and carefully insert it under the windshield. Now the meter man was coming toward the van.

Black quickly processed this development through the calculator that was his criminal mind, and realized this wasn't necessarily harmful. The van, as well as the car, had been stolen the previous week. A ticket, assuming that the meter man didn't call the vehicles in, would be meaningless. Of significant concern, though, was the fact that the meter man may have gotten a good look at his driver, Sanchez, and was about to get a good look at Black.

Approaching the van, the meter man said in a loud voice, "Move it along. Move along."

Black looked the other way and ignored him, hiding his face with his arm in as casual a way as he could. Even as he did this, the ramifications flashed through his mind. This meter man would place the robbers at the scene. He would be asked to help with composite drawings. Those drawings would eventually be published in the newspaper and broadcast on television.

Black refused to turn around.

The meter man stood at the cracked window. "What's your problem? Move your van."

Black still ignored him. So the meter man wrote out a ticket with a flourish, stuck it under the windshield wiper, and proclaimed loudly, "That's fifty bucks right there, jerk." With that, he walked on. Black looked out the window, his hand still over his face. All he saw was the man's back.

At that exact moment, he also saw the armored car slowly, awkwardly, fill his side mirror, then lumber in front of him. His mind raced. It needn't be complicated. He had two choices. Pull the plug on the operation—drive away and forget the whole deal, at least for now. Or he could go on as planned and hope that the composite sketches looked nothing like anything that would matter.

In front of him, the armored car was backing up now, toward the van. Urgently, Black kept asking himself, Stay or go? Stay or go? The smart money told him to go, to pull up stakes, to just revamp his plan for another time and place. Why take a risk he didn't have to take? Shouldn't he take this as some sort of signal of a doomed operation? But what about the work that had already gone into this plan, the time and effort just to find a group of guys to carry it off, and then to train them?

Stay or go?

Did the meter man see anything he shouldn't have seen? Did he get a good look at faces? Would he remember them? Would he make for a good witness?

The driver's side door opened slowly on the armored car, as if it were opening a door into Black's own mind. He looked inside for an answer.

Stay or go? Stay or go?

Black said softly into his microphone: "Truck has arrived. Guard and driver getting out. Ski masks on. Four minutes to action."

nine

EVERYONE IS WAITING FOR something—waiting to graduate from school, waiting for a better job, waiting for the
holidays to come or to pass, for vacations to arrive, waiting for true love, for wedding days or divorce hearings,
waiting for injuries to heal or diseases to be cured, waiting
and hoping for mercy in the dying days of life. Me, I was
waiting too, though I wasn't exactly sure what for. After
Katherine died, I virtually left home and jetted around
the country with a laptop computer over my shoulder
and an Eddie Bauer duffel bag in my hand. My life
became a maze of distant, upscale hotel rooms, waiting
for room service or for calls to be returned, with nowhere
I had to be and nowhere else I really wanted to go. I
looked neither at my past nor toward my future as I lived
for a moment that I didn't actually want. I lost myself in
my work, hoping the pain would eventually pass, and
waiting was the only way I knew how.

Which is why I like flying. There is no shame in sitting
back and doing nothing but waiting. Even better, the wait
always brings results, except for those poor bastards
unlucky enough to be on the business end of an airplane
crash. I like to doze in and out while reading a trashy

novel. I like to stare out the window. I like to flip through the in-flight magazine, charting our course on the maps in the back, looking at the advertisements for hotels and restaurants in different cities. I especially like sitting in first class on long flights, when leggy stewardesses—I'm sorry, flight attendants—supply me with hot towels, newspapers, Milano cookies, a choice between salmon and filet mignon for dinner, chocolate sundaes served from a pushcart, and after-dinner drinks from those tiny bottles.

Monday morning found me in this precise situation, in the first-class cabin of a US Airways Boeing 757 destined for Seattle, where I would connect to Spokane. For breakfast, I ordered the omelette rather than the steak and eggs. Take my advice: always order the omelette. Beef isn't meant to be served to the masses 37,000 feet above the closest mesquite grill.

It struck me, somewhere between the Mississippi and the Dakotas, after breakfast was over and I had taken my usual stroll back through coach to gain a better appreciation for my lot in life, or at least for my expense account, that I had a particularly significant amount of waiting going on. There was the big picture waiting, as an editor might say—the wait for the emotional pain to pass and all that, and in some obscure way, I felt a little of that pain ebbing away now. I had begun to notice women again, even if I felt no particular desire to pursue any of them.

Perhaps more pertinent was the short-term waiting. I was waiting for a true break in this story, and I hoped that I might dig up some form of it on my trip to Idaho and the interview with the head of the Idaho Minutemen.

What I needed was to write a story that would trigger my anonymous source to fill my ear with some better information on what had the potential to be the biggest story of my life. And all the while, I was waiting to arrive at some sort of decision on the White House press secretary's position, though I couldn't help but feel that the story itself might ultimately decide my career fate. All this, for now, was good, productive waiting, if more than a bit tense, and it made the wait on the more serious matters go by with a little more ease.

On the ground at the Spokane airport, I rented a Pontiac Grand Am and headed west through Coeur d'Alene, then north up to Sand Falls. All the way, I traveled a near-barren two-lane highway, rimmed by towering pines and verdant hills—beauty that hides a land of inner desperation and the type of racism that is based on nothing more than raw ignorance. The boys up here, they'll rail against anything from the federal government to the blacks who steal the rightful jobs of the white men all across the country. Funny part is, most of the locals never vote, and I'd be willing to wager that a fair number of them have never met a black man in their lives. Their only enemy at work is their own laziness and incompetence.

Daniel Nathaniel was exactly this kind of guy. At forty-eight, he looked like a cross between the Pillsbury Doughboy and the Skipper on *Gilligan's Island,* minus their collective charisma and good cheer. He was a former undertaker who had lost his family funeral home to the IRS for reasons that were suspect at best. The agents had harassed him, taunted him, and ultimately led him to bankruptcy, taking a guy with a latent distrust of the federal government and sending him over the edge. After a brief prison stint for tax evasion, he had hooked up with a group of militant farmers and ranchers in his small town and formed the core of the Idaho Minutemen. Within months, he ascended to the position of commander, inherited a farmhouse in the hills around Sand Falls from one of the other members, and surrounded himself with a team of bodyguards and a driver. In exchange, he served as a source of everlasting wisdom and strength for his growing legions in the eternal war against the federal government. Truth is, though, he just didn't look the part.

I arrived at the farmhouse on Freedom Lake at about 1:00 P.M., and was stopped at a rickety gatehouse by an almost deathly skinny high school underclassman with droopy eyes.

"Stop right there," he shouted, stepping out in front of my rental car. I couldn't help but chuckle a bit to myself, knowing that once again I was about to step into an adult war fantasy of too many men with too much time. Trouble is, it really wasn't so funny, given the manifestation of all this hatred. One of their believers had blown up a federal building in Oklahoma City a few years back, and another just might be responsible for an assassination attempt on the president. More serious, that would-be assassin could have killed me.

With this pencil-necked postadolescent playing the role of Patton, I couldn't really control my disdain. Rolling down my window, I said in my most dismissive tone, "Let Daniel Nathaniel know that Jack Flynn is here."

"Is the commander expecting you?" the kid asked, equally dismissive. I didn't like that.

"I don't know what the commander is expecting. You'll

have to ask him that when you call to tell him I'm here." I had decided to save all of my patience for someone who could actually help me, meaning Nathaniel, knowing that with him I'd probably need every ounce of it I could find.

The kid looked at me without moving. I wasn't quite sure whether he was unclear on what to do next or unwilling to honor my request, so I asked him, "That a new squirt gun in your Batman belt? It looks really neat."

"Fuck you," he said, putting his hand on the handle of some sort of high-powered weapon, the details of which would be lost on a novice like myself.

"The commander isn't going to like you talking to his close friend like that," I said. I saw the kid's eyes shift. He walked away to get his two-way radio, which was sitting in the guard shack. He pressed a button and spoke, then released it, and all these horrible sounds came out, like a goose being bludgeoned on a golf course. I saw that happen once, but no need to go into the details here.

"What did you say your name was again?" he asked me.

"Flynn, you dope."

This time he was too nervous to talk back. After a couple of minutes, he approached my car window. "You want to go straight along this dirt road—"

"Yeah, I've been here before," I said, dipping into my reservoir of aggravation to add more exasperation to my tone.

I drove off along a dusty dirt road about two miles, through groves of enormous pines that separated the narrow lane from burned-out farm fields tucked into the hills. At the dilapidated farmhouse, two men in what looked to be police uniforms came running down off the porch to meet my car.

As one of them opened my door, he said, "Welcome, Mr. Flynn. Commander Nathaniel is expecting you." These guys were his bodyguards, and to that end, one of them frisked me through my clothes.

"You like having your hand on my crotch?" I asked as he worked his way down. He gazed at me with horror and what I sensed was a tinge of embarrassment, then continued silently down my thighs. Really, these guys were too easy.

"You're ready. We'll bring you in," the other one said.

They led me into the main room of the farmhouse. It was cold up here in the hills, and there was a fire burning in the fireplace. Nathaniel was sitting behind a large metal desk at the far end of the room. He stood up when I walked in and stretched his hand toward me.

"Welcome back," he said in a serious tone. "You here to enlist this time?"

What a card. I gave him a polite laugh. "You'd never take me," I said. "Flat feet. My father's black. Oh, and I'm gay."

He didn't laugh at my humor. Never has, come to think of it. And I saw his young bodyguards flash each other a look before scurrying from the room like a pair of rodents. Nathaniel's a rodent too, but he's a rodent in a position to help me out, so as we often do in the reporting business, I'd treat him with nothing but respect on this day. In journalism, this is called working toward the greater good.

"How's the fight going?" I asked as I settled into a plain wooden chair that sat atop the braided rug, which in turn covered ancient, scratched pine floors.

"We're going to win," he said, his voice flat, as if he

were advising me that the waterproof coffin vault would make my family considerably more comfortable about my mother's burial. "The government is weak—weaker than you think. And one day, we will rise to conquer."

I observed him closely, again unable to tell if this mortician-turned-tax-evader-turned-ex-con-turned-freak actually believed some of these things he said, or whether it was all tongue-in-cheek, done in spite, as he looked for the best deal he could find coming out of prison, wifeless, jobless, homeless, and broke. When I had met him the year before, I had been writing a three-part series on the burgeoning militia movement in America. Nathaniel, believe it or not, was one of the smarter ones, press savvy, and he allowed me into his enclave for a firsthand glimpse of the philosophies and activities of one of the more vibrant militias in the country. That story, widely circulated among members of the movement, single-handedly caused Nathaniel to soar within the loose national structure of the militias. Other news organizations began quoting him regularly. Other state militias called on him for consultations. Soon, he became a de facto national leader. And much as I hate to give him credit for anything, I must say that he has maintained some sense of modesty about it all, at least in his office, though perhaps that is due to nothing more than lack of money. Wall Street bankers and $400-an-hour attorneys don't normally join or bankroll their local militia, and that fact was readily apparent here.

I said, smiling, "Hopefully that day won't be today, because I was hoping you had a little time for me."

"All the time you need," he said, still flat.

He was fairly straightforward, I had learned, but like

many potential sources of valuable information, he could lapse into spates of caginess, and often had to be asked just the right question to provide the knowledge I needed. I had nothing prepared on paper to ask. I never do. I've spent a career winging it, and I wasn't about to change that style now. I decided to start broadly.

I asked, "So, what do you know?"

"About what?" he replied. Okay, so I sensed he was in his cagey mood.

"What do you have?" I said in a conspiratorial tone, as if it were me and him against the world, two partners with different views and from different walks of life, thrown together in this remarkable situation.

"Tell me what you need to know. I'll tell you if I have it. Then maybe I'll even tell you what I have," he said.

I rolled my eyes, but only to myself. He wanted to make a game over this, and I had no choice but to play along.

"You mind tape?" I asked, pulling a microcassette out of my jacket pocket.

He said, "My words are meant to last forever." I couldn't tell if he was joking. I don't think he was.

"Good. The president himself tells me that the FBI has evidence that the militia movement is behind the recent assassination attempt against him. I'm wondering what you know about this, whether you believe this to be true."

"Maybe," he said. Then he fell silent and gave me a look that said, Next question.

Maybe was an interesting answer, even as it occurred to me that I gave up time with my dog and flew across an entire continent so some goddamned jackass ex-undertaker with a camouflage jacket pressing against an enormous beer belly could play mind games with me. And perhaps play them successfully.

"What do you mean, maybe?" I said, trying to maintain patience.

"Maybe. Maybe means maybe. Possibly. Perhaps."

This was getting downright sophomoric, but I had to play along. Either that or I could start to slap him, but I quickly calculated that playing along might be better for my story, if not my health, given the information he might possess, as well as his phalanx of security goons at the ready.

"Help me out," I said. "I'm jet-lagged. I'm hungry. I'm stupid. Walk me through this thing. I'm not precisely sure what you mean by maybe, even if I should be."

He sat silent, cowlike, though I'm not sure if cows ever sit. After a while he cast his eyes on my microcassette, which was sitting between us on his desk, slightly off to one side.

I said, "You want me to turn that off?"

He nodded. So much for his everlasting words.

"What do you know about this?" I asked, my anxiety easing, but only slightly, realizing we were getting down to the business of doing business.

He paused again, as if collecting his thoughts. "I have some reasonably reliable information that this assassination attempt was sponsored by a group of freedom fighters based in Wyoming. They're a relatively new unit, inexperienced, with a commander who's hell-bent on making a national mark. This, apparently, was intended to be it."

I sat for a moment in a stunned but relieved silence. Daniel Nathaniel was essentially confirming the initial

FBI line on the shooting, cutting against the grain of most other stories since, including some in the *New York Times*. This was a significant development, not to be underplayed. A story indicating that a high-placed, well-up source within the militia movement was suggesting, if not outright saying, that the assassination attempt was militia-related would put me and the *Record* way ahead of the game. Sitting here in this cabin, it also gave me a surge of adrenaline, or maybe it was testosterone. Either way.

"Okay," I said, partly to Nathaniel, partly aloud to myself. Looking right at him, I asked, "How do you know?"

"What, you think I'm going to give away all my trade secrets? When you reported that time that the Michigan militia was on the brink of disbanding for lack of leadership, did I ask you how you knew?"

I hate when people I'm interviewing answer questions with questions. Puts me on my heels. Wastes my time.

"Different situation, different set of circumstances," I said. "You know that. I'm trying to get something into print. I have to make sure I can use it before I just go zipping it into the paper. Sometimes it's helpful to be accurate, even if it's just for kicks."

He said nothing, so I asked, "What's the guy's name in Wyoming, the commander?"

"Billy Walbin. Billy Joe Walbin to his friends. My understanding is he came up from Louisiana. He wears many hats, and maybe a cape, if you know what I mean."

I think I did. A too-typical antigovernment zealot who, for good measure, also railed against blacks, Jews, gays, and anyone else slightly different from himself. A Ku Klux Klan member sowing his oats.

I asked, "He accessible?"

"I don't know. Maybe not if one of his guys just took a potshot at the president and bought the farm."

I said, "I want to get this into print. I need to get this into print. Too many swirling questions about all this back in Washington. The FBI brass is saying one thing. The rank and file is leaking something decidedly different to the *New York Times* and the rest of the press. This assassination attempt is my fucking story. I was almost killed. I need your information to get something together on this. I need to know how you know."

In police work, detectives say you don't really need a motive, that they can try you just fine based strictly on physical evidence, especially with the advent of DNA testing, and I suppose much the same is true of reporting. Information, especially good information, is valuable no matter how you come across it. Still, it's always good to know the motive of the person giving it to you, if that's how you're getting it. Subtleties can be shaded, or accented, or even omitted, all for the sake of the proper pitch. As a reporter, I like to know what I'm dealing with, and why.

In this particular case, I sensed that Daniel Nathaniel might feel threatened by the burgeoning strength of the Wyoming militia generally, and of Billy Joe Walbin specifically. Fear is a good and trustworthy motive, when properly understood. I knew I could play this to my favor.

He said, "Take the information to the bank."

I replied, "The only place I can take it is to my editor, who's going to demand to know how you know. And unless you tell me, it will never see the light of day. Never. And think what a waste that will be."

After a pause, Nathaniel looked me in the eye and said, "I have a pipeline into his group, but if that gets into print, my source is dead, and maybe so am I. But I know this reliably. They held a meeting. They have been planning this for about six weeks. The information is good."

That takes care of that. I felt my hand balling up into a fist again. All that adrenaline. "What conditions are we talking under?" I asked.

Nathaniel knows the game pretty well, knows how to use the press to his advantage, like all those high government officials back in Washington who he claims to despise.

"A source familiar with the nation's militia movement," he said.

That seemed too vague, leaving open the possibility it was a law enforcement official. I didn't like it.

"No good. How about a well-placed militia leader?"

"And the day you print that, you can come out and cover the assassination of Daniel Nathaniel for your paper."

Fair enough, though I still grimace when people refer to themselves by name like that, as if their very sense of greatness transcends who they are.

"Right. An authority who monitors developments within the militia movement?" I suspected he'd like this, being called an authority and all.

He thought for a moment and said, "Good."

I checked my watch for the time: 2:30 P.M. Pacific, meaning 5:30 in Boston. West Coast stories are a killer, given the deadline issues. Much to my joy, or maybe relief, I had achieved more than I thought I would on this trip. The problem now was getting it into print.

"Let's go back over some of this," I said. "Have you had any direct contact with Walbin? Did he send a bulletin around to other militias that this was going to happen? Did he seek your advice?"

Nathaniel said, "Look, we're not the fucking King Sisters. You know us better than that. I mean, we don't all pick up the phone every night and make small talk with each other, telling everyone else what we're doing the next day. And some of these guys, they're just weird, I don't know what the fuck they're doing."

"You learned about this but didn't go to the feds with it?"

"I don't like the feds."

Good point. I pressed him but didn't get any more. He did say he had received calls in the last couple of days from reporters with the *New York Times* and the *Washington Post,* but hadn't returned them. I love it when people tell me that.

"I'll pass on your regrets when I see them," I said. Finally, I added, "I have to run. I appreciate your help. You around tomorrow? I'd like to call you for some more info, or some clarification. But I'm on deadline right now, right up against it."

"Call me," he said, nodding his head at me, still flat. He hit a button on his desk, and his two security goons came in. The interview was over. I bade a quick farewell to Nathaniel. It wasn't exactly friendly, because we're not exactly friends.

Outside, I drove down the dusty road as fast as the rental Grand Am would take me, slowing down at the guard shack on the way out only so the kid there could see me flipping him the middle finger. I thought I saw him reach for his gun, but was far out of view by the time he would actually have been able to pull it. He was probably just scratching a sore.

Decision time. No matter how I argued it in my own mind, I knew this story would benefit from another day of responsible reporting and thinking. Problem was, this was daily journalism, and responsibility and thought didn't have a fixed place here. I was caught in what is known as a cycle, when newspapers and networks breathlessly publish and broadcast scraps of information, half-truths, even nontruths, all, ironically, in the name of prominence and respect. This was about competition, not about reader enlightenment.

As I sped down the highway toward Coeur d'Alene, the pines smacking past me out my side windows, I replayed the day. The most prominent militia movement leader in the nation was saying, for the first time, that the assassination attempt was likely part of a militia-related conspiracy born in the hills of rural Wyoming. It was enough of a story to get the *Record* credit on the morning wires and network shows again. Whether it was enough to get this anonymous old man to call me again, I couldn't be sure. He hadn't called after my last Hutchins interview, which was beginning to make me nervous.

Still, there were many unanswered questions here, chief among them, Who was Billy Walbin and what might he have to say about this? Could Stevens or Drinker add anything? Would they? Was the FBI already on to the Wyoming angle, or would this be news to them? Right now, the story had more holes in it than Tony Clawson. On deadline on a Monday evening, I doubted whether I would be able to fill them.

It was only 3:00 P.M. here, but already the sun was getting weak, and I flipped the heat on low. I had a batch of calls to make on my cell phone. The first was to my travel agent, to see what time their last flight of the day left from Spokane. The destination of the second call was a little less clear. Should I put my hopes in Stevens, or in Drinker?

I had had more contact with Stevens, but doubts nagged over whether she had the stature, the authority, or even the confidence to leak me information of any great quality. Actually, I doubted that she did. Drinker was a more interesting case. From my research, I knew he had helped reporters in the past on significant stories.

It's like a narcotic, the modern information game. Suddenly, obscure bureaucrats or hamstrung officials can see their secretly leaked information appear in print or on television before hundreds of thousands of people, shaping public discourse, influencing policy, getting results. And all without attribution. Once in, always in, and I decided right then that Drinker would be my best shot, so I placed my next call to FBI headquarters in Washington.

"Director Drinker's office, please," I told the receptionist.

The phone rang six times before it kicked over to a woman's recorded voice, asking me to please leave a message. I hung up and called back the main number.

I said, sounding both confident and dismissive, something that came a little too naturally, "Hi, I'm trying to get Assistant Director Kent Drinker paged. Can you help me out?"

The man was anything but helpful. "Can't do that," he said. "If his secretary's not in, I can pass you through to his voice mail and you can leave a message there."

He seemed about to do just that when I butted in. "Look, this is Jack Flynn calling. I'm a witness to the assassination attempt on President Hutchins. I have some new information on the incident, and it is urgent that I talk to Drinker right away."

The operator hesitated for a moment, unsure of what to do. Then he said gruffly, "Hold on." A couple of long minutes later, he came back on the line. "I can try him, but I can't guarantee anything. You have a number he can call you back on?"

I gave my cell phone number, asked for his name in a not-too-subtle bit of pressure, and hung up. I had one other call to make, but kept the line open just in case.

As I cruised down the highway toward Coeur d'Alene, it occurred to me I was about as far away from home as possible, not so much in distance as in life, surrounded by all this wilderness, all this craziness. As the heater blew warm air on my feet and hands and the pale sun seemed to balance on the tops of the tall pines ahead, I wondered what Katherine and I might have been doing on this Monday night. Maybe we would have ordered food from an upscale delivery service and would be spooning little bits of mashed vegetables to our baby between taking bites of grilled swordfish for ourselves. Maybe she'd be pregnant again, glowing as she did the first time around. Maybe we'd be strolling the neighborhood, pushing the carriage with the dog padding along beside us, exchanging knowing, amused looks when we awoke about how much our lives had changed.

As I stared blankly out the window, the cellular telephone rang, thank God.

"Jack Flynn here," I said, my throat surprisingly thick

as I shook off my thoughts and brought myself back to the realities of death and life.

"Kent Drinker here. What can I do for you?"

Small talk, I assumed, carried no water with this guy, so I replied, "I'm running with a story tomorrow saying that an authority familiar with the inner workings of the militia movement believes the assassination attempt was orchestrated by an insurgent, newly formed militia unit in Wyoming. I'm trying to get FBI reaction, to see if the bureau has been pursuing that lead or has independent knowledge. Conversely, if you believe I'm wrong, it would be helpful to be guided away from the story."

There was nothing but dead air on the other end of the line—dead air that carried on so long that I began to wonder if we had been disconnected. "Hello?" I finally asked.

"Hold on," Drinker said. "I'm just trying to figure out what I can safely tell you."

Not the answer I was anticipating. I was assuming he would tell me nothing.

Another stretch of silence, then he added, "You would not be inaccurate in reporting that FBI investigators have been probing the relationship of a Wyoming militia group to this assassination attempt. I would be willing to say that on the condition of anonymity, as a senior law enforcement official."

Here we go again. "How about a senior FBI official?" I asked.

"No. I need at least some cover."

I asked, "How did you get turned on to the Wyoming group? What's your best link?"

"No way am I going that far with you," he said. "You

have enough for a significant story. You sure have more than your competition. That's all I'm going to tell you."

My mind was racing with more questions, but Drinker interrupted, saying in a clipped way, "I have to go. I've helped you enough." And then the click of his telephone.

It was abrupt, but it didn't really matter now. I had hit pay dirt. Immediately, I dialed up another number, that of directory assistance in Cody, Wyoming, the supposed hometown of the Wyoming Freedomfighters. They weren't listed, but a B. J. Walbin was, so I took it and called. On the other end, I got the expected rigamarole— the snotty kid asking my name and my intended business, a referral to their so-called spokesman, who seemed to be inaccessible.

"Handle this however you want," I told him. "But if I were you, I would inform Billy Joe that there will be a story in tomorrow morning's *Boston Record* that will highlight his role in a presidential assassination conspiracy. He might want to know about this before it runs. If he wants to know more, have him call me at this number."

I gave him the number and hung up before the kid could say another word. Fuck him.

Finally, I called Peter Martin at the office. I walked him briskly through what I had and told him where I wanted to go. He appeared in full agreement.

"How long before you can file?" he asked.

I said, "I don't have a word on paper yet. I'll have to write it from the road and hunt down someplace to transmit. Can you buy me a couple of hours?"

Other editors were sticklers for things like deadline times, story lengths, and the like. Martin, to his credit, was an advocate of reporters, and as part of that would try to get me what I needed to do my job well, which in this case was a few extra minutes, like maybe sixty of them.

He said, "No sweat. File to me. I'll buy you some time in Boston. Write the shit out of it."

I continued down the highway, urgently scanning the darkening road for a fast food restaurant, a bar, or even a mini-mart where I could pull over to put the proverbial pen to paper. So far, nothing. So I had started writing the story in my mind, getting through the first few paragraphs with some nice turns of phrase, when I spotted a faded red neon sign that announced "The Dew Drop Inn." It was a log building with just one window and smoke billowing from a chimney. The University Club of Washington it was not.

Outside were about a dozen pickup trucks and an olive-colored Buick LeSabre, vintage 1970s, which I assumed was owned by the town's one business executive. Nearby were another ten motorcycles—hogs, the owners probably called them.

Inside, the wood floors were dusty and seemed to scratch and slide underfoot. Everything was made of unfinished particleboard—from the beamed rafters to the bar to the simple booths and benches. Music played from a jukebox. Smoke filled the air, along with the smell of old beer and hot nachos. I stepped up toward the bartender as a few of the patrons looked my way.

I said, "White wine spritzer please, with a wedge of fresh lemon."

Just kidding. Mrs. Flynn didn't raise any fools. I ordered a Budweiser, specifically saying "Longneck," figuring, correctly, that's all they'd have here.

The bartender, a fifty-something gentleman with pleasant features and salt and pepper hair, popped it down on the bar. "Buck and a quarter," he said.

My, my, I thought. Maybe this place wasn't so bad after all. "You mind if I plug a laptop computer in over at that booth?" I asked. My goal was to get this bartender on my side, just in case I'd need him.

"All yours," he said.

I laid a pair of twenties between us and told him, "Hit the bar all around."

That gesture of goodwill bought me exactly what I had hoped: a few words of thanks from the boys, but mostly some privacy to sit back and type out a story as fast as I could, without interruption.

As I finished writing my second graph, my cellular telephone rang.

"Mr. Flynn, Billy Joe Walbin here," the caller said in a voice thick with a southern, good ol' boy accent.

I had no time for niceties or introductory, fruitless conversation.

"Thank you for calling back, sir," I said. "I am a Washington reporter for the *Boston Record*. I am planning on running with a story in tomorrow's paper saying that the Wyoming Freedomfighters, and you specifically, masterminded the failed assassination attempt on President Hutchins."

"Hey there, aren't you the boy, the reporter, who was shot in that thing?" he asked. Always nice to be remembered.

"I was, yes."

"Well, your story's bullshit. And I don't waste my time talkin' to the Jew media. You're all the same, all you Jew editors and Jew publishers and Jew reporters. Fuck youse all. Fuck you."

And just like that, the line went dead. So I inserted that in the story, minus the profanity. I quoted Nathaniel, anonymously. I quoted Drinker, anonymously. I back-filled all the details of the assassination attempt. I gave the whole thing a dose of context, and I was through, in time to make deadline, in time to get my flight back to civilization.

The bartender—Gerry, he had introduced himself as—cheerily allowed me the use of his telephone to send my story east. A few of the customers appeared riveted by my actions. Once it was gone, at 6:00 P.M. local time, I had some time to waste before my flight, so I ordered another Bud and took a seat at the bar. A rather large man in a leather biker jacket came over and asked how much memory I had in my machine.

"Can't remember," I said.

He laughed. The bartender laughed. With something of a beer glow from lack of food, I took it another step. I asked, more loudly this time, "What, you some kind of computer nerd?"

There was a long moment of absolute silence as the biker processed this question. I caught Gerry out of the corner of my eye put a couple of glasses down on top of the dishwasher and draw a little closer, in case there was trouble. At last, the biker burst out laughing and clubbed me on my back with his hand.

"Computer nerd—ha," he said, quaking in delight. All the other customers were laughing. Gerry was laughing. I was laughing. My pager sounded, and I took a quick look at it. "Great show. Peter," it said, his signal that he was done editing. I thought for a second about how Peter would do in this bar, and that made me wonder whether the nice clientele here would start with sodomy or would gnaw his legs off first for kicks, pardon the pun. Didn't really matter, I concluded. Another trip, another success. This one seemed so easy.

But life tends to throw you little curve balls when you least expect them, and one came at me at that moment in the form of the pimply guard from Nathaniel's compound, walking through the tired wooden door of the Dew Drop Inn. He spotted me at about the same time I spotted him, which is to say, immediately. I saw him reach instinctively inside his coat to make sure he was still packing his gun. I also saw no obvious look of worry on his face, which meant he was.

He came walking right over and took the bar stool right next to mine without actually looking at me and ordered a rum and Coke. I didn't think people drank those anymore. I was packing my computer away in its case when I heard him say, without ever turning toward me, "The little faggot's going to run right on out of here, huh? Scared?"

"Faggot's not exactly scared," I explained to him as I zipped up the case and put my arms through my coat. "Got a plane to catch." I turned to him and smiled what I thought was a pretty winning smile.

He apparently didn't think so. As my arms were just going into the sleeves of my coat, his left hand shot out, grabbed the back of my head by my neck, and tried slamming it down into the bar. Luckily, I was able to shoot my own left arm across the bar so my face collided only with my coat and my forearm, rather than the particleboard. When I pulled my head up, in a something of a daze, he kneed me in the crotch, causing me to double over in pain toward the dusty floor.

I'd been a reporter all my life, and the most violent situation I'd been involved in up until recently was when a pen once broke in my jacket pocket on the way to cover the statewide finals of a national spelling bee. But in the last week, I'd had bullets come at me twice, and now fists and knees. Time for a raise, or at least a clause in my union contract that would provide for hazard pay.

As I gasped for air, I could see and hear all the other nice patrons push their bar stools out and surround us in a state of collective surprise. He was one of them, a homeboy. I was the guy who no more than an hour ago had bought everyone a round of beer. There's no doubt they were shocked that the two of us would have any reason to fight.

I calculated in those briefest of moments that this situation could unfold in a couple of different ways. One, the entire bar could fall in line behind their own and kick the living Christ out of me, if not outright kill me. Two, they could recall that I had bought them the aforementioned round and side with me over some punkish kid who no one had ever particularly liked. Or three, they could stay neutral, which is exactly what they appeared to be doing. The group encircled us, but no one stepped in. One guy even called out, "Don't go too hard on him, Bo." Gee, thanks for the good wishes.

Bo didn't actually adhere to what I thought was reasoned, and reasonable, counsel. As I remained crunched down, trying to collect myself and protect my sore ribs from his onslaught, he took a roundhouse swing at the side of my face. I flinched back, and his fist grazed my cheek and kept going. That's when he glared at me and said something I thought to be quite interesting, even in my current state. He said, "I should have kicked the crap out of the last fed who came here, too."

Kicked the crap out of the last fed. We had someone who was confused, but potentially helpful, if I could just put him in a situation where he might find it in his best interest to provide that help. I didn't know what he meant, but I had a nagging, if unformed, suspicion. All the while, the crowd surrounding us continued to watch in confusion that now seemed to be transforming to glee. In retrospect, one more round of beers, and I think I would have had them on my side.

In an instant, I rose up out of my pain-induced crouch and faked a punch to Bo's greasy face. In a typical trait of youth, he overreacted, bringing both his arms up toward his head, exposing his entire midsection. I zeroed in with a ferocious punch to his stomach, so hard it virtually lifted him up off his feet and landed him on his ass, where he rolled into a ball.

Young Bo didn't seem to have a warrior's instinct. He stayed down, groaning. Pain shot through my ribs, but I had neither the time nor inclination to be burdened by it. No one in the circle of spectators made any move toward me, so I approached Bo, grabbing him by his stringy hair, pushing his face into the dirty floor, and asking, "What fed, Bo? What fed?"

He was actually crying now. Crying. I forced his head around in the grit, and he barely resisted. I also reached into his coat, felt around for a moment, and grabbed his gun. I put it on the floor and slid it far away from the two of us. No one else bothered to pick it up, which was a good sign.

"What fed?"

He continued to whimper and took a flailing shot at my face with his right fist. He missed. I pulled my left arm back, then rabbit-punched him in the nose, breaking it, I think, because blood came spurting out. The *Columbia Journalism Review* might not deem this the best way for a reporter to seek information, but fuck the *Columbia Journalism Review*. All their writers sit in offices in Manhattan thinking their big fucking thoughts without a rat's ass of an idea what it's like out here in the real world of daily reporting.

Young Bo yelped. I pushed his face around on the dirty floor again. "Tell me about the fucking fed before I break your fucking neck," I said, surprising even myself with the primitive tone of voice.

I pulled my fist back again, prompting Bo to squeal, "Stop. Stop. I'll tell you."

"Tell me."

Bo tried collecting himself. It wasn't a pretty scene. He was on the floor, facedown. I was on top of him, holding him by the scruff of the neck. A crowd of about twenty gawkers stood around us at a respectable distance. I tightened my grip.

"He was here last week," Bo said softly, through his whimpering. "No, two weeks ago. Guy wouldn't tell us his name or who he was with, but he had an appointment and we were told to show him right in. Someone said he was an FBI guy, named Kent, I think. Met with the commander at headquarters for about two hours, then left. Never seen a fed at the compound before. First him, now's you. I'd like to know what's going on."

"I'll tell you over tea sometime," I said to him, loud enough for others to hear, mostly because I thought it was a pretty good line. Then I whispered into his ear, "Until then, don't move a fucking muscle or I'll kick your fucking brains out." I got up, straightened out my clothes, pulled a $20 and a $10 out of my pocket and put them on the bar in front of Gerry, and said, "Set Bo up with his next couple of drinks, and buy the rest of the boys a round."

I gathered up my stuff and was off into the night with one immediate, crucial piece of business ahead of me. Hurtling down that two-lane road, I called Peter Martin's condominium in Arlington, Virginia. He answered on the first ring. Best I could tell, when he wasn't at the office, he was always home, though I'll be damned if I knew what he did there. Like everyone else in the newspaper business, he was divorced. I always figured he was just watching TV, probably CNN or C-Span.

"Flynn here," I said. "Kill that story in the second edition."

"What?"

"Something's going on with it, and I'm not sure what it is. But I think maybe we've been had. I just found out that Drinker might have been out here a couple of weeks ago, must have been before the assassination attempt. I don't know why, but I don't like it."

"We kill that story," Martin said, "and we look ridiculous."

"We leave it in for the full run, and we look even worse. We look negligent."

I explained my half-formed fears to him in greater detail.

There was a silence before Martin said, "I'll do what I can."

It was a long ride down to the airport, and an even longer walk to my room in the miserable airport hotel where I was forced to spend the night because I had missed the last flight. It all gave me just enough time to convince myself that by completely fucking up, perhaps I learned something about this story far more valuable than anything I previously had.

Tuesday, October 31

When I awoke the next morning, Tuesday morning, I was a jumble of uncharacteristic nerves. In reporting, rare were the times I screwed up, and rare were the stories when I was so dependent on any one person. But here, all my actions were geared toward getting a call from an elderly gentleman who was out of my control. I couldn't help but wonder if he read the version of the *Boston Record* with my story or without it.

For these reasons, the flight back to Washington seemed arduously long, even with another soft leather seat up in first class. From the airport, as they announced the final boarding, I called my message services at home and work for the third time of the morning, and it wasn't yet 9:00 A.M. Nothing. My pager sounded, and I fairly jumped through the ceiling of the USAirways Club. "Jack," the message scrolled across my Skytel. "Have important new information. Need to discuss tonight. University Club at eight? I'll buy. Steve."

I shook my head. It's 6:00 A.M. in DC, and Havlicek was already working the story. Maybe the source called him because he couldn't reach me. I picked up a telephone and belted out Havlicek's number at the bureau, but got no answer, so I left a message saying eight was fine. What could he have?

My only other wish of the morning came true: the seat beside me was vacant, meaning I was at no risk of having a chatterbox salesman spend the next six hours discussing the critical advantages of spreadsheet software for personal accounting. I admit, I'm not much of a good sport on airplanes. I don't make small talk with seatmates, and I don't encourage those who do. Only once do I remember really liking someone I met on a plane. He was an airport fireman, and taking off from Logan in Boston on a late-night flight to Las Vegas, he pointed out for me all the different spots on and around the runways where there had been, in his words, "aviation mishaps." "Look over there," he said, pointing his finger against the dark windows at something I couldn't see. "World Airways jet overshot the runway and slammed into a stone wall. Two dead, father and son. They were sitting in the front of the plane, just like we are. Assume their bodies fell into the harbor, and they probably were carried out to sea." Absolutely riveting.

I ordered the Sonoma chicken, having absolutely no idea what it would be, and opted for water instead of wine, assuming there might well be work to be done when the plane landed on the other end. Try as I might, with a book, computer hearts, the new November issue of *Attaché* magazine, I couldn't shake the questions: Had he called? Would he call? Was he real? What did he have? Is this, I wondered, what it is like to be a woman?

Ends up, the chicken was a smart move. Everyone who ordered the fish seemed to be sick as a dog, and I don't mean a nice purebred dog, like Baker, but some mangy thing with matted-down fur and funny ears, constantly picking up ticks.

A doctor came wandering up from coach to first class to make the rounds. He announced that they had apparently contracted a minor case of food poisoning and that life would go on, just not as well as if they had ordered the chicken. None of this seemed to alleviate any of the pain. The guy in front of me was groaning and moving about in his seat. I had to just get up and get out of there. Mother Teresa I am not. So I headed for the back of the plane on my usual walk. When I pushed through the curtain, everyone seemed so calm, so fresh. They had eaten these meager little boxed lunches—salads with three pieces of lettuce and a chunk of a tomato, a microscopic sliver of cheese lasagna, a hard chocolate chip cookie—and now they were fine. I wondered if this might all be the start of the revolution, right here on USAirways Flight 906. No time, though, for a revolution. I had a story to break.

I dawdled. I chatted with the stewardesses back in the galley, wondering if I sounded like the moronic middle-aged executives who always seem to get such a charge out of engaging the flight attendants. I probably did, but they didn't seem to mind. We traded hotel stories from Seattle.

"My fucking toilet wouldn't flush at two this morning," the blonde said.

My goodness. Such a pretty woman; such a tart mouth. I found myself pleasantly aroused as I made my way back up the aisle toward our mile-high version of *Chicago Hope.*

As I settled back into my seat, several people around

me were clutching their stomachs. The captain had come out of the cockpit and announced to them that he could land the plane in Kansas City if the passengers thought this was necessary, or he could carry on through to Philadelphia. The doctor advised them to keep going, saying that the airport wouldn't provide much more relief than this airplane, and that the sickness would pass in a short time anyway. I suspect he had a golf game back east the next morning that he didn't want to miss.

As I leaned toward the seat pocket for a book, I felt something crinkle beneath me. I reached behind my back and pulled out a single sheet of white paper, folded three ways, with my name written across it, by hand. This had an odd feeling of déjà vu, as I flashed back to that restaurant in Georgetown. I shot looks all around me to see if I could catch anyone watching me, however discreetly. Nothing. The woman across the aisle was sound asleep. All the other people within view appeared consumed by pain.

I gingerly opened the sheet up and saw just a few lines of perfect penmanship. "Dear Mr. Flynn," it began. "You are on the right track. I am here to help you. I will be in touch in the next couple of days to guide you. Do not believe what they tell you. The would-be assassin is not Tony Clawson."

Jesus mother of holy Christ. My informant was right here on the plane. I was within a few yards of him. Quickly I stood up and flagged a flight attendant hurrying by. I didn't have the time or inclination to be coy.

"Ma'am, did you happen to see the person who dropped this paper on my seat?" I asked, as I held up the folded-up note.

She couldn't have cared less. She said, "No, I'm sorry, we've been really busy," as she pushed past me. I scanned everyone's face around me, looking for some reaction. I got none. Then I stared at the sleeping woman across the aisle. Had she been there at the beginning of the flight? I couldn't be sure. Maybe she delivered the note, but wasn't the actual informant. I bore into her with my eyes, looking to see if she was faking, if this sleep was an act. But I couldn't see so much as a flutter of her eyes.

Clutching the note, I walked down the aisle into coach, determined, hoping to spook the writer into some sort of mistake. I looked around hard at virtually everyone, focusing even harder on the few older men. One man sat by the window doing a crossword puzzle, still wearing a blue blazer in his cramped seat. He looked proper enough to be my voice, so I stopped and stared at him. Eventually, he looked up at me and stared back. Our eyes were locked on each other when he asked, "Can I help you?"

It was a completely different voice than the one I had heard on the telephone. "My mistake," I said. "I thought I might know you."

I returned to the front, slumped down into my seat, and read the note again. The writer had repeated, generally, what the voice had told me before: "Do not believe what they tell you." Far more important were the first and last parts of the message. I was on the right track, this story would get much bigger, and finally, a piece of concrete information: the assassin was not who the FBI said he was. I would be contacted in a couple of days. Obviously, this guy meant business. Either he was on the plane, or an emissary was, at no small expense. He had followed me across the country. He watched me diligently, waiting for me to get up out of my seat so he could drop this. And then he sat back, immune to my desperate, silent appeals for help. Was this some sort of game to him? Was he just having fun? What was the point of catching me midflight, of not waiting until I was on the ground? Did he just want to show me how serious he was? And had he already read the story I had in the early editions today? Did he think I had screwed up? Apparently not.

I sat rigid in my seat for the next three hours, assuming I was being watched. As the stewardesses handed out cold compresses to the sick, the groaning all around me eventually stopped. When we landed, I carefully, self-consciously collected my carry-ons and walked off the plane.

When I jumped into a taxicab, I said, "Downtown, please." In that sense, I knew where I was heading. In another sense, I had no idea at all.

ten

By THE TIME I had made my way through the Grille Room, Lyle had already drawn me a beer, a Sam Adams OctoberFest, God love him, and God love the Boston Beer Company while we're at it. I could use whatever they had to offer tonight.

"You've become quite the celebrity," Lyle said to me through barely pursed lips. He wasn't admiring or condescending, but matter-of-fact, as if pointing out to me, with his years of Washington wisdom, that this too shall pass, like so many other things in life. Lyle had seen it all. That's just one of the reasons I like him. The frosted pilsner glass he slid toward me was another.

As I took my first pull of beer, he nodded toward the pool table, casually, never rushed. "Your colleague, Mr. Havlicek, I believe, arrived a while ago, and is engaged in a game of billiards."

I looked. Havlicek had just made a long bank shot. He let out a loud yelp and held his open-faced hand over his shoulder, as if to high-five his opponent, who happened to be Sinclair Shoesmith, the great-grandson of one of the club founders, a former secretary of state. I swear to God, Mr. Shoesmith—I've never heard anyone use his first name before—flinched back, as if he might be under attack from Havlicek. They don't high-five much over at the Chevy Chase Club or the Smithsonian Society, so I embarked on a rescue mission, though I'm not sure who was most in need of salvation—me, Mr. Shoesmith, or Havlicek.

I said, pulling up to the table, "Good evening, Mr. Shoesmith. Steve, good to see you. Do you mind if I interrupt the game before ESPN tries to put you gentlemen on SportsCenter? Steve, it's actually important we talk right away."

Havlicek hesitated, looking longingly at the table, while I tried to will him away with my eyes. "Good, let's talk," he said finally. "Terribly sorry, Sinclair, but I've got some work to do here."

Settled down at a table, he looked at me with a smile and said, "Good to see you, slugger. Strange trip, huh?" He then looked at me closer, at the bruise on my left cheek from my recent scuffle, and said, "Whoa, you look like shit. Everywhere you go these days, someone's taking a poke at you."

"Yeah, violent business we're in. I took a shot from one of Nathaniel's lackeys. The whole trip was something worse than strange. I've got some more news for you from today. First, though, I want to hear what you have."

Havlicek didn't seem overly concerned about my physical well-being. He pulled a manila folder out of his briefcase and put a pair of half-glasses on his prominent nose. "Good stuff," he said. "Not sure what it means yet, but I know it's good stuff."

Truth is, when it came to work, to journalism, to investigative reporting, Havlicek was as good as it gets. He had no fear, not just of government officials or mobsters or white-collar criminals much smarter than himself, but of failure. Where other reporters would assume that they couldn't find what they needed, Havlicek would scrape away, pushing a little more dirt back every day until finally he had dug a nice little hole to put someone in. He was tenacious and he was street-smart, and at age fifty-six, he hadn't lost a bit of speed on his first step or his ability to open it up down the homestretch. When I'm that age, if I'm ever that age, whatever it is I'm doing, I hope to have one-tenth of Steve Havlicek's passion.

Havlicek flipped through a sheaf of papers, saying, "Okay, Tony Clawson, Tony Clawson, where are you? There you are. Here, this is the photograph everyone was running of Clawson after the shooting. It came from a Home Depot security badge out in Fresno. He used to work in their landscape and garden department. Check it out: dirty blond hair, blue eyes."

I'd seen the photograph before. Not a great-looking guy, by any stretch. His eyes seemed wild, almost insane, as if he might club you over the head with a metal watering can, then leave you for dead by the terra-cotta pots, all because you didn't get your purchases to the checkout line by five minutes before closing time like the nice lady on the public address system had asked. Most people try to smile for their ID photos, especially when they're going to be wearing them on a badge. Clawson, I'd venture to guess, went out of his way to sneer. I'm betting the guy behind the camera just wanted to get him out of his office.

I said, "Okay." Obviously, the issue of Tony Clawson was of great interest to me right now, given the note, but I decided to hold back on sharing my own revelation until Havlicek was done.

One of my favorite waiters, Carlos, stopped by the table. "Mr. Flynn, a pleasure to see you again," he said. "Could I bring you gentlemen a bite to eat?" We ordered hamburgers and onion rings and an order of smoked salmon, along with another round of beers. Havlicek continued.

"So remember, the Secret Service shoots this guy six times in the head. Every one of them connects. You shoot a guy six times in the head, there's not much left. You have any idea what a guy looks like who's been shot six times in the head?"

"I really don't."

"Like this." With that, Havlicek slid a large glossy photograph toward me. It was a picture, I believe, of a man who had been shot six times in the head, the man specifically being the man they are calling Tony Clawson. My first instinct, quite beyond my control, was to vomit. Luckily my second instinct was to turn away to prevent myself from vomiting. In the photo, someone—I'm assuming the coroner—must have cleaned some of the wounds. Still, entire chunks of the man's face had been torn out. What remained was black and blue, almost beyond recognition as a human head. Oddly enough, and frightening beyond words, one eye remained in place, and that eye was open for the photo shoot.

"Pretty gross, huh?" Havlicek asked. "Sorry about this. But do you have any idea what I had to do to get this photo slipped to me?"

I was stunned into silence, trying to regain my composure. I wondered if I could trade that hamburger in for a little bowl of fruit salad.

Havlicek continued. "Take a look at that eye—"

"I don't want to look at anything in that picture again," I interrupted.

"No, really, this is work," he replied, straight as an arrow.

He could overcome any queasiness in the name of a story. This was the hunt, he was the hunter. "Take a look. What color does that look like?"

I couldn't believe I was doing this, but I found myself looking closer at it, bending my head toward the photograph, which sat on the table because I didn't want to touch it. I said, "Looks to be brown."

"Bing-fucking-o," he said. "Now take another look at the Home Depot ID photo. What do you see?"

"Blue eyes," I said. I paused. Dawn breaks on Marblehead. I added, "Holy shit."

The waiter returned with the food. Great. Across the table, Havlicek merrily spread some condiments on his burger and bit into it like a ravenous dog. I opted to let mine sit for a while, waiting to see if my stomach might settle.

I said, "But we can't jump to conclusions. One, this eye is barely an eye, and the color might be off in the photo, or if it isn't, he might be wearing tinted contacts."

Havlicek began talking with his mouth so packed with food that I was surprised that words could even get out.

"Right on all counts," he said. "Which is why I got my hands on this beauty."

He wiped his fingers on a napkin, then slid a folder marked "Confidential" across to me. I opened it up to see an autopsy report and thought to myself that this dinner conversation just kept getting better and better.

"Scan halfway down," he said, "to eye color."

I did, and there it was: brown. I smiled up at Havlicek as we locked eyes, his brown, mine an ocean blue. "So you have yourself an issue."

"What we have," he said, "is pretty good proof that the

man they shot at Congressional Country Club isn't the man they say is Tony Clawson, a California drifter with antigovernment tendencies."

Indeed, in the past couple of days, the FBI had been selectively leaking bits and pieces about the life and times of Tony Clawson. They put out word that Clawson had been to a couple of loose militia meetings in Nevada and possibly Wyoming. They said he had been brought to the attention of the FBI within the last eighteen months as a potential domestic terrorist because of his views and his criminal record, which included numerous instances of violence. Never, though, in all the stories questioning the FBI, in all the two-bit profiles of Clawson, was there any sort of new photograph of him. And all the while, in the name of national security, the FBI said it couldn't provide any more information, even anonymously.

"It's a different guy," Havlicek said. "I'd like to put that fact in the newspaper."

I took a bite out of my hamburger, and it felt like cotton-covered lead in my mouth. I forced it down, then pushed the plate to the side. "Carlos," I said to the waiter as he whisked by, "any chance you could just bring me some vanilla frozen yogurt?"

"You not going to eat that?" Havlicek asked, visibly concerned. I was trying to think of something to say that wouldn't make him feel bad. Instead, he reached for my plate and asked, "You mind?"

I let him take the hamburger, and pushed my chair back from the table to make myself comfortable. "What's it all mean?" I asked. "What the fuck does it all really mean?"

Havlicek said, his mouth packed with food again, "I don't have a clue. I just know what we have. If we know it, I suspect the feds do as well. We don't have a corner on curiosity, deductive skills, and intelligence."

"I've got two new developments on my front," I said.

"Go ahead," he replied.

"Second thing first. I heard from my anonymous source again."

"Jesus Christ," Havlicek said. "Talk about burying the fricking lead."

"Check this out. He gave me this."

I handed him the single sheet of paper with the hand-written note. Havlicek wiped his fingers again, put his half-glasses back on, and read through it, slowly. He looked up over his glasses and said, "Holy shit. We're really onto something, and now he sounds like he knows what he's talking about. He's for fucking real.

"But wait a minute," he added. He looked at the envelope and saw there was no postmark or mailing address written out. "How'd you get this? You meet him? You see him?"

I said, "On the goddamned airplane. He—or I should say, someone—left it on my seat when I went into the bathroom. It was just sitting there when I got out."

"Holy fuck. He was on the airplane," he said, partly a question, partly a statement.

"Could have been delivered by a messenger. I don't know. I asked the stewardess if she saw who dropped it there. She didn't. A bunch of people got food sickness up in first class, and it was chaotic. I walked up and down the aisle holding it, staring at people who looked suspicious, but got no reaction."

Havlicek said, "Let me just ask you two quick questions. Who in God's name is this guy, and what the frick else does he have?"

"I don't know," I said, my face pained and purposeful, on purpose. "I just don't know. But for all I know, he could be in this room right now."

"Jesus, you think he's a member here? That's a pretty high-flying anonymous source," Havlicek said.

"Point two," I said. "I think there's something strange going on between the FBI and this militia leader I know."

"Go ahead."

I told him the story. I told him of the interview with Daniel Nathaniel, the visit to the bar, the fight with this kid Bo, and of course, Bo's accusations and rantings about the fed named Drinker.

When I was done, Havlicek looked me up and down with laughing eyes and said in a tone spilling over with amusement, "You punched him in the kidneys and you broke his nose while he was down on the ground?" He made a shuddering motion with his shoulders. "Remind me never to cross you anytime soon."

"Not the kidneys," I said, indignant. "The stomach." I paused and asked, "You think the FBI could be working in some fashion with the head of the Idaho militia?"

Rather than answer, Havlicek asked, "So you pulled the plug on your story?"

"I didn't think I had any choice. You think otherwise?"

He was becoming serious again. "No. You did the right thing, the brave thing. But you should know about this."

He shuffled through more of his papers. God knows what he might be showing me now. He slid a computer printout toward me of an Associated Press story that began, "The *Boston Record* first published, then later deleted a story from its editions today asserting that a newly formed Wyoming-based militia group had sponsored last Thursday's assassination attempt against President Clayton Hutchins at Congressional Country Club. The story was pulled without explanation, in an apparent belief that the paper had published either wrong or unsupportable information. *Record* officials and editors could not be reached for comment today."

I bet those *Record* officials and editors were getting a real kick out of all this. Martin was obviously running interference for me, and that would also explain his multiple telephone messages to me throughout the day, which I had yet to answer.

"I had too many doubts," I said. "I admit, I rushed something I shouldn't have rushed."

Havlicek said, in that soothing way of his, "Fuck 'em all. By tomorrow, this is yesterday's news. We're onto even better things right now, and you know it."

I allowed my thoughts to broaden. I asked, half-rhetorically, "What is really going on here? What's this all about?" I didn't wait for an answer before I went on, allowing myself, this time, to become melodramatic. "We have some anonymous source who has told us repeatedly that things aren't as they seem, not to believe what others want us to believe. And now we have a point of fact where he is right, and a pretty fucking big one. The shooter isn't who the feds say the shooter is, at least it doesn't seem that way. So that means the motive may not be what the feds say the motive is. And now we have pretty good reason to believe that the feds have some bizarre, and possibly suspicious, relationship with the militia movement they are accusing of trying to kill the president. So where does that take us?"

"I'll have the cheesecake, some extra strawberries off to

the side, and another beer." That was Havlicek, speaking to Carlos, who had appeared at our table amid my monologue. I was about to get aggravated with him for his lack of attention when he cut me off.

"Look back at the Kennedy assassination," he said. "It's almost forty years after the fact, and people are still arguing over who pulled the trigger and for what reason. Now we have another presidential assassination attempt, and it is not unlikely that the same argument could take place all over again. Two big differences here, though. First, Hutchins wasn't killed, which will make this thing fade into history faster. Second, there was a reporter involved, namely you, who might help answer a lot of these questions before they slip off into some arcane debate among conspiracy theorists. For all we know, there is some mysterious force who tries to knock off our presidents every three decades. Maybe that's what this is all about."

Nothing much to add, and I was getting tired, so I said, in an unidentifiable accent, "Pret-ty strange. I've been out of touch all day. Anything happen in the campaign I should know about?"

"No. Nichols in California, Hutchins in the Midwest. The polls show Hutchins inching ahead, but probably not by as much as Nichols was expecting. The *Washington Post* had another story this morning on that suspicious real estate deal of Nichols's, though I'm not sure if the public cares. And Nichols has begun pushing for a final debate, probably because he sees the same poll numbers we do."

"You still think Hutchins could have cooked this shooting up?"

Havlicek only nodded. He said, "Don't be out of touch

tomorrow, not even for a moment. We don't want to blow a call from the anonymous one. I'm going to write up this autopsy stuff and put it in the paper. I'm nervous I didn't do it today, but wanted to run it by you first, make sure you didn't have something to add or subtract. This note makes me more confident than ever that we're right, that we're onto something big. I actually called my wife before I came over. I told her I wouldn't be home until after the election. My sense is, this thing gets a lot bigger before it goes away, and we're with it all the way through, me and you."

Samantha Stevens's recorded voice was more inviting than it had been before, and far more inviting, I should point out, than it had been in person. This time, there was a tinge of concern in her tone, as if something were wrong. And the very fact that she asked me to call her whenever I got the message, regardless of the hour, was telling enough. I sat on my couch and wondered what she had.

It was only 10:00 P.M., and the house felt emptier than I had expected in Baker's absence. First things first. I called Kristen, the dog sitter.

"Hey there," I said, trying to sound charming to make up for the hour and the fact I was about to steal my dog away. "Sorry I'm calling so late, but I kind of assumed you wanted to get rid of that no-good blond guy with the oversize ears you've been sleeping with for the past few days. Any chance of me picking him up?"

She was typically warm. "If you insist. I was about to head up to the store for a soda. Why don't we meet at the corner of N and Thirtieth in five minutes?"

Next, I dialed up Stevens. Ends up, she had left me her

pager number, which was interesting. Even worried FBI agents don't give their home telephone numbers out to key witnesses whom they have an enormous crush on.

Okay, so I made up the part about the crush. But it wasn't one minute before the telephone rang.

"Jack, Agent Stevens," she said.

Agent Stevens. Isn't that precious beyond words? Perhaps I'd like to be identified herein as *Reporter* Flynn, or *Journalist* Flynn for all you National Public Radio types.

In the time in which she inspired my disdain, she quickly caught her mistake. "Samantha Stevens," she said, this time in a surprisingly fetching tone. I was quickly over it.

"What can I do for you?" I asked.

She said, in a voice that lacked the familiarity that I was hoping for, "I'd really like to talk about a few things on this case. Would you be available to get together tomorrow?"

I said, "I've got a ton going on at work, obviously. Not every day presidents get shot in the middle of a campaign. Not every day reporters get shot either, thank God."

Nothing. Not even so much as a chuckle.

"What about tomorrow evening?" she asked.

This threw me off. She urgently needed something. If I were a betting man, I would bet it wasn't me. "That works," I said, sounding somewhat short of decisive for no particular reason. "How about a drink at the bar at Lespinasse, seven-thirty."

"Good," she said. "I'll see you there." She hesitated on the other end, then added, "Jack, can we keep this meeting confidential?"

"My favorite kind of meeting," I said.

• • •

I could see Kristen already standing on the designated corner from half a block away. Baker lay on the ground beside her, obviously exhausted by another full day of being a dog. He saw or sensed me from half a block away and pulled his face up off the curb, staring intently in my direction. I called his name softly, and he scrambled to his feet, then ran low and fast toward me, his tail wagging hard all along the way. When he got to me, he urgently ran his coarse tongue over my face in a show of thanks.

"Ahh, a boy and his dog," Kristen said as she came upon our little reunion. "How touching."

I said, "You saved me again. I can't tell you how much I appreciate this."

I handed her a check, which she reluctantly accepted without unfolding.

"I have a hunch I may have to fly out of here again soon on very short notice. Are you around?"

"I'm always around," she said, hesitated, then added, "Is everything all right in the house? You getting used to it again? It seems so, well, bare in there."

"I'm getting used to it," I said. "I suppose I should get used to it, seeing it is my life."

There was silence for a moment, the two of us just standing on a lamplit street corner. After a while, she said, "I miss Katherine."

That thought hung there in the crisp autumn air, adorned only by the gentle rustle of dead leaves and the faraway sound of a car door slamming shut. Kristen had only gotten to know Katherine for a short time. It was all so different then. Katherine and I were squeezing in our last spurts of relaxation before the onslaught of parenthood, flying to Rome for a weekend, to a wedding of a friend in St. John, up to Boston for a party in our honor with family and friends. There seemed to be a constant buzz in our lives, the air of expectation always present, the expectation being that life would always get better, that the very best days still lay ahead.

Kristen may not have known my wife very well, but she knew her well enough, and certainly she saw all this. When she said she missed her, I knew she was sincere.

"I do too," I replied.

We were quiet again for a moment. She said, in a tone of voice that was different, "I saw you two once." She stopped, then started again. "I saw you two once when you didn't know I saw you. It was at night. You were on M Street, probably going to eat or something. I don't know. Katherine was really pregnant, and she stopped you while you were walking. She kissed you on the street, then stared at you and you stared back at her and it was as if there wasn't anyone else in the world. I walked by and didn't say anything and you didn't see me. I didn't want to ruin the moment. But I thought, my God, how in love are they? I've thought about that moment a lot. I think about it when I see you alone, kind of struggling but not really saying anything about it. I don't know, Jack. I'm sorry for all this. And I'm sorry for bringing it up."

I stared at her for a moment, then away from her, off into the distance. Baker had lain back down. The night was quiet, the air feeling cooler by the minute. "Thanks," I said, softly, and I reached out and gave her wrist a squeeze as I said good-bye.

• • •

I live near the corner of Twenty-eighth and Dumbarton Streets, in what the silver-haired grand dames of the realty circuit would call the heart of the East Village of Georgetown. Coming around Twenty-eighth, with a block and a half toward home, I noticed a large black woman sitting in a beat-up old Toyota at the curb. The car engine was turned off. The first glimpse I got of her played in my mind like a snapshot. She seemed so out of place, just sitting there in her car as it neared eleven o'clock on a cool and lonely Tuesday night. When I spotted her, she seemed to be staring in my direction, as if looking for something, then she turned away as soon as we met eyes. It was odd.

Given what had happened at the Newseum, I knew this was stupid, returning to my house, walking the streets at night alone, pretending I was immune to danger when it was so painfully apparent in my recent history that I was not. But I had this stubborn Irish desire not to give in to the forces who were trying to intimidate me, or even kill me. That said, I was starting to feel afraid.

Halfway up the block, a man and a woman stood on the street, her leaning against a utility pole, necking.

I whispered to Baker, before we arrived within earshot of them, "I forgot that's what men and women do." The dog just kind of looked up at me, blankly. He was heeling tight, drawing his mood from mine. I think he assumed that men just mostly threw tennis balls, then took taxi-cabs to the airport.

As we passed by the couple, I saw the man look at me out of the corner of his eye. I looked away quickly and thought that that, too, was odd. Now it felt just plain creepy on these streets that I had walked hundreds of times at every conceivable hour. Most houses seemed to be darkened for the night, the windows shut tight against the chill of autumn, their owners sound asleep. I watched shadows flicker on the ground, looked warily at movement in shrubbery, and scanned both sides of the street for any other people in parked cars. Nothing. As I neared my doorstep, the street seemed so dark, so empty, and so quiet that it was like a Hollywood stage set, void of actors and light crews.

I pulled my keys out of my pocket, and a car rounded the corner, slowly. It was a man, alone, in a Ford Taurus or another car like it. He was looking in my direction as I was looking at him, and his car was barely moving at all. I fidgeted with the key in the lock and urgently pushed open the door. As I stepped inside, unnerved, I saw the car speed up and drive away. I shut the door fast, turning a deadbolt I don't think I had ever used before.

I quickly picked up the telephone and dialed Kristen's number. Baker stood by my side, looking around anxiously and up at me.

On the phone, one ring, then two, then three. *Come on, Kristen. Be there.*

"Hello," she said.

"Hey, it's Jack. I just wanted to make sure you got back in all right. It seemed kind of quiet out there."

She gave a short laugh that seemed a mix of curiosity and gratitude. "Jack," she said, pausing. "I'm fine." She laughed again. "You worry too much."

"Maybe I do." I said good-bye and hung up.

I pulled my sand wedge out of my golf bag on the way upstairs, then laid it down beside my bed, the closest thing I had to a weapon. I wondered what the NRA and PGA might think about this. Then I drifted off to sleep, and not very quickly.

eleven

WEDNESDAY MORNING BROUGHT a fresh batch of polls to an election that was just six days away—polls that showed Hutchins holding on to a three-point lead over his Democratic rival, Senator Stanny Nichols. To be sure, this was not Lincoln versus Douglas or Truman versus Dewey. Hell, it wasn't even Ford versus Carter. A week and a half before, when I packed my clubs into my car and drove out to Congressional Country Club, the presidential race was a statistical dead heat, pardon the pun. But the president had received a critical shot in the arm from that, well, shot in the arm. His approval ratings had risen nearly ten points, into the mid-60-percent range. Hutchins had suffered only a flesh wound in that blaze of gunfire; but Stanny Nichols saw his political career seriously injured.

Still, three points remained within that so-called margin of error that the boys over at Gallup always make sure we are well aware of. Despite Hutchins's good fortune, there was a sense of unease with him in the country, a lack of familiarity—and voters like to feel as if they know their president. Much of politics is about simple images, and some of that unease was erased out at Congressional Country Club when that nice paramedic was kind enough to poke Hutchins's words around and make him seem a nonchalant, combat-tested hero, cut right out of the American flag. Enough, anyway, to give him this three-point polling lead. Truth is, the closest Hutchins ever got to military action was probably playing with his GI Joe as a young boy and watching *McHale's Navy* and *F Troop* on TV. And the further truth is, voters were still nagged by a sense that they didn't really know the man.

The anxiety was evident throughout the White House. Lincoln Powers's mood was getting worse, not better. The president's campaign days were getting increasingly longer and more urgent. Aides seemed grim-faced, even in television interviews, as if the totality of events that was supposed to happen after that shooting didn't.

Give Nichols credit for hanging tough. He had been plagued by allegations of corruption—specifically, using his standing as a United States senator to receive a highly favorable purchase price on a Breckenridge chalet from the owner of a major ski resort, one of his top contributors, and then failing to pay the appropriate tax on it. Add to that his lack of national experience. When all of the major Democrats took a pass on the race because they assumed they'd be running against Hutchins's popular predecessor, Wordsworth Cole, Nichols was the only one who stepped in to fill the void. In another time, in another place, he would have been known as the sacrificial lamb. Here, he was the Democratic nominee.

After Cole died, Nichols had suddenly become a contender, legal problems and all. Smartly, he made the press a major issue in his campaign, saying it was time that the news media stopped hindering the rich dialogue of a great nation with two-bit tattletale stories about old and misreported events. It was a message that seemed to resonate with the voting public.

Meanwhile, Hutchins did his very best at playing the delicate role of national consoler, and his very best was pretty good. He had performed flawlessly in his brief tenure as president. He paid public respect to Cole almost every day, every chance he got. At the same time, in policy decisions, he made clear what he would always call his "respectful" differences. One of them was in the area of day care. Hutchins quickly signaled to Democratic senators that he would sign legislation restoring federal subsidies for child care, a decision, analysts later said, that would allow welfare mothers to return to work in greater numbers. Even the most conservative of commentators agreed with him that to create a foundation for a society without welfare, the government had to help poor people get out of the house.

Next, in an impromptu press conference in the press cabin of Air Force One, a correspondent from the Associated Press asked Hutchins about his opinion on abortion. It was the first time he had been asked about the issue as president. Until then, he never had the inclination or the reason to let his feelings be known.

"What the hell business is it of mine what a pregnant woman does to herself?" Hutchins growled at the reporter, in a voice that harked back to Lyndon Johnson. "Do I want her to have an abortion? God, no. That's not good for anyone—not her, not the fetus, probably not even for society. Am I willing to tell her you can't do this or that with your own body? No again. That's just not what I'm in public life to do."

His answer sent shock waves across the country. The prolife groups, who had always assumed that since Hutchins was a Republican vice president, he was on their side, went ballistic. They arrived in Washington en masse for an enormous protest on the Ellipse, carrying buckets of what they said were dead fetuses that they flung over the iron fence of the White House onto the South Lawn. The mainstream Republican Party was uneasy about his stand but quickly realized there was nothing anyone could do about it, and Ted Rockingham, ever soothing, worked his myriad personal friendships to help calm so many nerves. The nominating convention was already over. Hutchins was president, and like it or not, he was their candidate in the November election. And now he was three points ahead.

My desk telephone jarred me back to reality. It was early yet to be at work, evidenced by the fact that, at 8:30 A.M., I was alone in the bureau. As I reached for the phone, I prayed that this would finally be my conversation with the anonymous source.

"A little less than a week out from Election Day victory, and there you are on the sidelines, and we're giving you the chance to come on over here and get in the game." It was the voice of Lincoln Powers, sounding a little less southern and lilting than it usually did.

"You know what it's like to drive through the White House gates to work every morning?" he asked. "You know what it's like to be quoted in all the major newspapers every day, as someone who matters? You know what it's like to have a whole staff of assistants to help you out, worshipful little things who'll do whatever it takes to make you happy?"

"Anything, huh?" I said, playing along, being a guy. I added, "Look, Mr. Powers—"

"Please," he interrupted urgently, "you call me Link."

"Lincoln," I said, "the president asked me to carefully consider my decision, so I am doing just that."

Powers said, "Absolutely no rush. Meantime, I thought we might get together for breakfast or lunch, talk it all over in a little more detail, the plans I have for you over here."

I said, "That would be really nice, and helpful as well. But things are really pretty rough for me right now."

"I'll have my secretary call you," he said. "We'll set something up for tomorrow or Friday. Maybe you come over here and eat in the White House mess, see how the whole thing feels."

God only knew where the next two days would find me, but I didn't want to say that to Powers, so I replied, "Good, let's see how the days play out. Thanks for thinking about me."

"Before you go, just one more thing," he said, his voice changing, his tone becoming more serious.

"Sure," I replied.

"You didn't get this from me, and this may not be worth anything at all, but I know for a fact that the FBI has assigned a couple of agents to look into any possible connection between Tommy Graham and Mick Wilkerson and the assassination attempt."

The revelation stunned me. Graham was Stanny Nichols's campaign manager. Mick Wilkerson was his long-time chief political strategist. Together, they were the brain trust that had catapulted their candidate to the Democratic nomination. Perhaps this is what my anonymous source meant when he told me that nothing was as it seemed. Perhaps my anonymous source actually worked in the Nichols camp.

This didn't gel with anything else I had, but it was something to keep in mind.

"I appreciate the heads up," I replied, trying to contain my surprise.

"As I said, this didn't come from me."

As I hung up, I saw Havlicek pull up to his desk on the other side of the room, then neatly lay out his autopsy photographs and report around his computer, either to get everything within reach or to inspire himself. You could never tell with this guy. I, meanwhile, eyed my phone, picked up the receiver to make sure it was working, then began etching out questions on a yellow legal pad.

"What are you doing?"

That was Peter Martin, arriving at my desk, somewhat more at ease than usual.

"Nothing," I said, feeling like a little kid just caught stealing his sister's crayons. I still hadn't told him about this anonymous voice, and I had no plans to until I got something concrete.

"That's some hit Havlicek has for morning, no?" Martin asked, in a question that explained his good mood.

I said, "It's a great one. I'm going to work the telephones to see if I can help him out on my end. Otherwise, I'll be prepared to jump in and do anything I can in terms of follows. I suspect there'll be many."

"Good. I've got to tell you, I know we're in the throes of battle and all, but Appleton's none too happy about putting a story on the front page of the first edition yesterday, then having to pull it off. He's all over my case about it."

He let that sit out there for a minute, until I said, "I'm

sorry. It's entirely my fault. I'll send Appleton an e-mail or give him a call and tell him as much."

"No need. I've got us covered on it," Martin said, shaking his head.

I kept going anyway. "Look, Peter, I screwed up. I know I did. But I think someone was intentionally trying to screw me up, and that someone might be the militia leader and the FBI. This could be a much larger story, an exclusive story, because I made that mistake."

Martin started wringing his hands together, as he sometimes does when a veteran senator announces he's not seeking reelection or the president pocket vetoes a piece of tax legislation. He said, "Go on."

I told him what happened. I told of the talk with Nathaniel, of the phone call with Kent Drinker, of the, well, encounter with the kid named Bo at the Dew Drop Inn. "The obvious question is, why is an assistant director of the FBI paying a house call on one of the nation's emerging militia leaders a couple of weeks before a presidential assassination attempt in which the militia is blamed, at least initially?"

Martin rolled up a chair and sat down beside my desk. He said, "To concoct a story. That's what you think, right?"

I replied, "Well, maybe. But that presupposes that Drinker would know about an assassination attempt, doesn't it? So doesn't that become a little far-fetched?"

"That it does. So why else?" He paused, looking at me, and added, "Because Drinker had a tip about an assassination attempt? He wanted to check it out with the militia. That's still a good story, no?"

"Could be," I said. "But then, why the coordinated story lines now about this guy in Wyoming, Billy Walbin?"

We both sat there, baffled. My head hurt from thinking, hoping, waiting for this anonymous source. This wasn't so much journalism as algebra—trying to fit all the figures into a complex equation.

I said, "Havlicek and I were bouncing around the idea that this thing could have been staged, you know, like maybe some eleventh-hour election ploy."

Martin looked at me for a long moment, then shook his head. "I don't think there's any way," he said. "I think I know this city pretty well. I think I know politics pretty well. And I can't even imagine that anyone would dare pull such a stunt, and that it could be kept secret." He paused and added, "It would be one thing if Hutchins were down by ten points with less than two weeks left. But this thing was neck and neck. He didn't need anything this dramatic."

Good points, all, but I was increasingly unconvinced. The timing of the assassination attempt bugged me, the poor aim of the shooter, the resulting fanfare and rise in Hutchins's favorability ratings. Still, it was far-fetched, so I felt silly pushing it. I said, "At the least, we need to get someone out to Wyoming, ASAP, to pay a call on this militia leader, and I don't know if that's what I ought to be doing right now."

"You're right," Martin said. "And done. I'll send Phil Braxton"—another bureau reporter—"out there today."

"One more thing," I said. "I just got an off-the-record tip that Nichols's guys, Tommy Graham and Mick Wilkerson, are being looked at by the FBI as possibly having some sort of link to this."

Martin stared at me incredulously. "Link to the assassination attempt?" he asked, skeptically.

I shook my head.

"Who the hell is telling you this?"

"It's off the record," I said. "But it's coming from Lincoln Powers."

"Sounds like a stunt," Martin said. "Sounds like they're just trying to create some sort of negative buzz about their opponent a week before the election. We've got to be careful of that." He paused, then added, "And we also have to check it out." Then he got up and retreated to his office.

Other reporters were beginning to arrive at the bureau, including Julie Gershman, who walked in wearing a short, rust-colored skirt that inspired a sense of warmth in any man fortunate enough to see her, including me. I say this in a good way, as another indication that I was becoming whole.

She gave me a come-hither look—okay, so I have no idea what a come-hither look is, but I read about it once in my wife's *Cosmopolitan*—as she tucked her hair behind a tiny ear.

"We ever going to grab that drink, or are we going to continue to be two emotionless drones, coming to work, making small talk, going home?" she asked.

"Hey, you leave my lifestyle out of this, okay?"

She laughed. "Tonight?" she asked.

"Can't, unfortunately. Already meeting someone for a story. Let me dig myself out of this assassination story, and we'll get together then."

"I'm going to hold you to it," she said, and I hoped she was good for her word.

The telephone rang, and I fairly well jumped on top of it, only to find it was my friend Harry Putnam, wanting to head to the Capital Grille for steaks, cottage fries, some red wine, and cigars that night. Who am I, Dean Martin or something? Everyone thinks I'm available at the drop of a dime for an offer of a beer?

I turned up the volume on my ringer and roamed across the room, toward Havlicek. This felt all right in here today, better than I would have expected. We had some good hits behind us. We had one in the pipeline. Things were popping, and they would continue to be in the near term. Despite the debacle of Idaho, the looks I was getting, the comments, the backslaps, told me I was firmly back on top, on my game.

"Hey there, slugger," Havlicek said as I pulled up to his desk and caught a glimpse of the photos. I rounded the desk so I wouldn't have to see them.

I said, "I'll spread around a few calls on this, but only to people who'll keep the information close. I don't want to let word around on what we have."

"Good show," he said. "Let me know what you turn up. More important, let me know when you hear from your guy. You'll press him on the issue?"

"Of course. Let's just hope he calls."

Havlicek leaned back for a minute, taking his eyes off the computer screen for the first time. "He'll call," he said. "We've got him. He's in this thing, and wants to get in deeper, and he knows we're a good vehicle. If he doesn't know that now, he'll sure know it tomorrow morning when he reads this story."

At that precise moment, I heard my telephone ringing across the room and sprinted around desks and over one chair in my attempt to reach it. I felt like O. J. Simpson running through the airport, or maybe from a murder scene on Bundy Drive. I caught the phone mid-ring and breathlessly blurted my name. The caller promptly hung up.

Rather than stand there and agonize over what I may have missed, I punched out the number for the main switchboard at the FBI and asked for the office of Assistant Director Kent Drinker. Some, or even most, reporters would spend the better part of a full day preparing just the right questions and practicing the best tone to strike in this interview. I didn't even have anything formed in my mind. I just knew I was curious and angry, and that combination usually worked better for me than any other.

When Drinker came on the line, I said, "Sir, I'm going with a story tomorrow detailing the highly unusual fact that you paid a personal call on one of the nation's leading militia leaders a week before the assassination attempt on President Hutchins. I was hoping, for your sake more than mine, that you would see your way to providing me with some sort of rationale for your visit."

Well, that sounded pretty damned good to me, but probably less so to Drinker. All I heard on the other end was dead air, then some heavy breathing. I had half a mind to say, "Hello? Anyone home?" but wisely and successfully suppressed that urge.

Finally, he spoke. "I don't know where you could have gotten this, but you have wrong information."

"Well, if it is, then I'll run a correction. But I don't think that's going to happen. I have it solidly, reliably, and on the record that you were up at Freedom Lake the week before the assassination attempt. If you want to deny it or dispute it, you do so at your own peril."

Federal agents in general, and assistant FBI directors specifically, are not accustomed to being addressed quite like this. No, they're used to being the ones in control, calling the shots, making others sweat. That partly explained the enjoyment I was deriving from this call. The fact I was in the right explained the rest of my good mood.

During the silence that followed, I played out my vague theories. I believed that Drinker and Nathaniel had met. If they had met, it had to have been for a reason, and I had the nagging suspicion it involved the ease with which Nathaniel had offered me the details on the Wyoming militia, and the willingness of Drinker to confirm the story. If this were indeed true, I didn't know why. But what I did know, and all that mattered in giving me the upper hand in this discussion, was that a federal agent meeting with a militia leader a week or so before an assassination attempt made for significant news, whether I knew the reason or not. In the newspaper business, that's what's known as leverage.

Drinker said, "Can we talk off the record?"

Playing hardball, I replied, "No. Not now. Not until I get some sort of on-the-record explanation."

That was met with more silence. Eventually Drinker said, "Well, then, maybe I'll just refer you to the bureau flack."

"Fine," I replied. "Either way, there's a story in tomorrow's paper about you flying out to Idaho two weeks ago. You can either enlighten me or ignore me. Your choice."

"If I tell you the truth, if that truth gets published in your paper, it puts someone's life in imminent danger. I don't want that on my head, and I don't think you want it on yours, either. We need to be off the record."

In the news media, there are four conditions of discussions between sources of information and the reporters who seek knowledge from them. The first and most obvious is known as "on the record." It is also the best and most straightforward, meaning anything and everything that a given person tells you can be used in the newspaper, fully attributable to whoever said it. Unfortunately life, and especially the journalism that supposedly reflects it, isn't always so cut and dried. People might be fired for talking to reporters, or reviled, or even endangered, so all too often conversations between sources and reporters tend to be "on background." That means all the information is fully usable, attributable to some mutually negotiated title such as a "senior administration official" or a "ranking federal law enforcement officer." But the vague attribution not only masks the identity, it also shades the potential motives for spreading that information. Reporters have to beware, but often don't. The third condition is "deep background," which means a source will provide information to a reporter provided it is not attributable to anyone or anything at all. In this case, the reporter—or more often, a columnist—can use the information in an analysis as either opinion or fact. The fourth, and most extreme, is "off the record," which, in its purest form, means the source is providing the information only to give the reporter a better understanding of what is happening, but the information cannot be used in a story unless obtained elsewhere.

The problem with all this is that only the best reporters and most knowledgeable sources fully understand the intricacies of the ground rules. Most don't actually have a clue, and "off the record" too often means "on background" to the reporter or the source. Inevitably and invariably, people get burned, sources become irate, and inaccuracies end up in print.

Interesting gambit by him. I said, "All right. Tell me off the record, and we'll figure out afterward how to attribute it."

As if trying to get the words out before I changed my mind, he immediately said, "Daniel Nathaniel is a paid federal informant. I received a tip on an assassination conspiracy, and I went to him to try to measure its validity. We had worked together on other cases, and he's always proven helpful and reliable."

To say the least, I was stunned, though I tried not to show it. Here was a guy, Nathaniel, whose entire purpose in life was supposed to be rallying against the federal government he claimed to despise, and instead he was actually on the FBI payroll, squirreling away money made from informing on his militia brethren. And I thought I knew the guy.

In the verbal gap, Drinker said, "You see what I mean. You write this, Nathaniel's underlings kill him by tomorrow night."

That they would, but that wasn't my particular problem, or even my most significant concern. I asked, "So were the two of you on the level about this Wyoming militia leader, or was that a concocted story?"

"We believe it to be true, though obviously I don't have it hard enough to bring charges yet. But Nathaniel told me then what he seems to be telling you now. This is what he had heard."

I frantically tried making sense out of what he was saying, but trying to piece the information together felt like shuffling a deck of cards. "So are you saying that you suspected an assassination attempt was coming before the president ever got shot?"

"Yes."

"And you couldn't do anything about it?"

"Well, we tried."

I said, "I'd like to put that part on background, that a federal informant—unnamed in print—confirmed your suspicions of a conspiracy."

He paused for a moment, then said, "Sounds like as reasonable a compromise as I can get."

I said, "Two more things. First, on the record. You're sure that corpse you have is of a guy named Tony Clawson?"

Sounding taken aback, he said, "We have no reason at this moment to think it's anyone different." Back in the Watergate investigation, that's what *Washington Post* editor Benjamin Bradlee called a nondenial denial. Interesting.

"Second, on background, are you guys investigating any connection between any Democratic campaign operatives and this assassination attempt?" I threw that out there bald, trying to get an answer equally as blunt.

"Look, we pursue lots of leads and head down many different avenues in an investigation as comprehensive as this," he said. "I'm not going to comment or even acknowledge every specific one."

I wasn't sure exactly what that meant, so I said, "Specifically I'm wondering about Tommy Graham and Mick Wilkerson."

"Not going there."

I said, "I'll be in touch."

He replied, "If I were you, I would do that. This case is breaking fast."

We hung up, and sitting at my desk with nothing to

look at but the back of Julie Gershman's neck, I was left
to wonder, *breaking* as in *breaking news,* or *breaking* as in
breaking apart?

There is something intrinsically wonderful about the bar
at Lespinasse, a French restaurant in the heart of downtown Washington. The polished mahogany walls soar
perhaps thirty feet toward a frescoed ceiling. Portraits of
dead presidents gaze at waiters quietly shuffling across the
thick floral carpet. Soft leather chairs and upholstered
couches exude the aura of a corporate boardroom or a
private men's club, which, according to some women
activists, are one and the same.

If nothing else, it is a haven from the constant slights
and indignities of official Washington, where a twenty-
something receptionist for a freshman congressman will
answer a call for the press secretary from the *New York
Times* and ask impatiently, "And what is this regarding?"

Not here, not now, not when the nice members of the
Lespinasse management are fetching upward of $6 for a
cold beer, though they don't even carry Miller. For me,
that was a small price to pay for such comfort and civility.
For Peter Martin, guardian of the bureau budget, the
costs here always seemed a bit excessive, though as with so
many other finance-related matters, I largely ignored his
protestations with no discernible penalty. Once, when I
turned in an expense form for a $179 lunch for two here,
he looked the bill over quizzically and asked, "What, you
break a window or something?"

The bar seemed particularly soothing this evening. At
the very least, I was fairly confident no one would take a

shot at me. So I ordered a Heineken and slumped deeply into a soft settee with my eyes closed and my feet up and thought of the frustrating afternoon I had just left behind. I had made calls to anyone I could reach in the realms of federal law enforcement and national politics, asking whether Tommy Graham and Mick Wilkerson were being investigated in connection with the assassination attempt. From everyone I asked, I got only incredulity. In fact, I suspected I was starting to sound pretty stupid, and wondered if I was being intentionally led astray by Powers in the house of mirrors that was this story.

When I opened my eyes, I found the alluring figure of Agent Samantha Stevens looming above me.

"My God," she said in the way of a greeting. "You don't look so great."

"That's a risky thing to say," I said. "I feel like a million bucks. As a matter of fact, I've never felt better. I feel like I could go out and complete a triathlon right about now, which would make it my third this month."

She seemed unsure how to take this reaction, so I flashed her a sizable smile. "Long day," I added.

She looked typically beautiful, her face freshly washed and largely void of makeup, her jet black hair glowing in the soft light of the wall sconces, her short navy blue skirt revealing perfectly toned legs that seemed, as my friend Harry Putnam is fond of saying, to start on earth and ascend toward the heavens. She settled into a leather chair diagonally across from me. I was increasingly smitten by her, though I recognized the need to rein it in.

"I appreciate you meeting me on short notice," she said, speaking deliberately. "I know how busy you are."

I said, "You've piqued my curiosity. I've been racking my brain, wondering, did I miss something from the shooting scene, is there something I overlooked, is there something I heard or saw wrong?"

I looked at her expectantly, and she said, "Actually, it's not that at all." She paused, staring down at the drink that the waiter had just brought her, a glass of merlot, perhaps a whimsical one.

"I don't really know any journalists, professionally," she said. "I don't know if I'm supposed to do this, or if this is wrong, or what."

You have a crush, I said to myself. You've developed a crush on me, and you don't know how to tell me. Just let it out. You'll feel better. Just let it all go.

She said: "I wanted to ask you about that story you had in yesterday's paper that you ended up killing for the later editions."

Oh, well. She looked at me. I stayed quiet. She continued, "Obviously, I've read your story inside and out, and there are a couple of things I don't quite understand, as in, A, how you got that information, and B, why it is that you decided it wasn't any good. I thought you might be able to share."

This was an easy one for me, and something of an unexpected gift at a time when I needed it most. "I love to share," I said. "It's one of the first things my mother and father taught me to do. But when I share, I usually expect, and get, something in return."

She took a sip of her wine, then absently smoothed out her skirt, looked me in the eye, and said, "Okay. Why don't we start with that story. I'm interested in what else you know about Wyoming."

"Big, beautiful state," I said. "And I love the Tetons. There's a nice hotel, the Jenny Lake Lodge, overlooking the mountains, with a terrific fixed price dinner every night."

She didn't even pretend to find humor. "The militia," she said.

It was a curious question, but I was doing my best to hide any look of surprise. "No way," I said. "Let's start with you, and what you might have for me."

"Why?" she asked. "I'm the one who called you."

"I don't trust you." There, I said it.

"You don't trust me?" she asked, taken aback.

"I don't trust anyone, not my sisters, not my editors, no one." Quickly, I tried to break the mild tension that had formed. "Check that. I do trust my dog, but even that took me a couple of years."

She raised her eyebrows and leaned back in her chair. "What do you want to know from me?"

"We could start with the question of why you people couldn't prevent a presidential assassination attempt that you knew about in advance."

She remained silent, looking at me, waiting.

"Then we could take up the all-important question of the real identity of this would-be assassin, because you and I both know it's not this guy you call Tony Clawson."

Now her forehead was scrunched up in a look of confusion—whether feigned or not, I couldn't tell.

"The shooter's name is Tony Clawson. Case closed," she said snappily.

I shot back, "Read tomorrow's *Record*, then decide if you want to close that case so fast. Because you'll either learn something about your own investigation, or everyone else will learn something that you're trying to hide."

That, I quickly realized, was a pretty stern accusation, and I scanned for a chance to backtrack. Too late. Stevens's cheeks suddenly flared red, and her angular features for the briefest of moments appeared severe.

"I'm not hiding anything," she said, her voice almost seething. "I'm not covering anything up. I'm not even closing cases. I'm investigating an assassination attempt on the president of the United States—trying to find out about a crime that could have changed the direction of the free world."

Dramatic, yes, but probably right. "I'm sorry," I said. "I am not implying that you are. What I'm saying is, I have some serious questions. You don't seem inclined to provide answers. That's your prerogative. But still, you expect me to help your cause."

"My cause is to solve a major crime. I thought you might want to help," she said.

I said nothing in return. I wasn't really in the mood to deliver a lecture on the role of the press and so forth, which, in this case, seemed to involve making sure the FBI was doing its job and not pulling one over on the public.

She, in turn, hesitated, again smoothing out her skirt in what I assumed was a nervous habit picked up in some all-girl's school, or as we'd say now, all-women's, even if they were only sixteen or seventeen years old. All around us, the pace of the room had picked up ever so slightly, as a well-dressed clientele flowed in to chat about the upcoming election—Washington's version of a Super Bowl for the wing-tip shoes and wire-rimmed glasses set.

"I'll be straight with you," Stevens said, leaning closer so that the people around us couldn't hear. "I wasn't aware that the Wyoming angle was being treated quite this seriously within the bureau. I had never heard of Mr. Walbin before your ditched story."

Finally, something of significance—an FBI agent admitting to a reporter that she has not been fully apprised of the important details of her own investigation—a presidential assassination attempt, no less. I struggled to conceal my shock. Then, of course, I began wondering if I was being snookered, by Drinker or by Stevens.

"Are you aware of any sort of tip that the bureau had received prior to the assassination attempt?" I asked.

"No."

There was silence. We were leaning close, causing me to wonder what people around us might be thinking—that perhaps we were a couple having a serious conversation about our relationship, or discussing having children, or changing jobs, or matters of divorce. She seemed more vulnerable than I had seen her before, and, I sensed, more vulnerable than she liked.

She asked, "Why did you pull that story?"

"The honest truth is, I wasn't sure if it was true."

"How sure are you on the Wyoming information?"

I replied, "It's out there. It's in circulation. I keep hearing about it, and because I keep hearing about it, I have to run with something on it, because if I don't, someone else will, and I really hate the meaninglessness of second place in the news business."

She considered that for a moment, then said, "I'll be straight again. I'm hoping we might form some sort of relationship based on our mutual needs. I've never done this with a reporter before. But I've never been in an investigation where crucial facts were withheld from me."

"Have you approached Drinker or your direct superiors?" I asked.

"No. Not until I know more. I'm not playing from a position of ignorance anymore."

I liked that, this lack of blind loyalty, these street smarts. I said, "You should read tomorrow's *Record* carefully and tell me what you think."

"What do you have?"

I shook my head. "Can't," I said.

"I have some theories on this case," she said. She stared at me, her mouth slightly open as if not sure whether to elaborate.

"As in?"

"I'm going to pursue them on my own," she said. "At some point, we may be able to help each other."

I said, "Do those theories involve Tommy Graham and Mick Wilkerson?"

"No," she said, without even a flicker of hesitation.

Stevens took a sip of her wine, locked her gaze on me, and said, "Looks like I've given you more than you've given me."

I caught the waiter's eye as he walked by, thinking it might be time to get a check, get out while I was ahead, as Stevens was kind enough to point out. When he came to the table, Stevens quickly said, "Another glass of the merlot, please." I caught myself and added, "And another Heineken for me."

"So you've been a reporter your entire adult life?" she asked, displaying her knowledge of me and offering to change the tone of the conversation. I didn't say anything, so she added, "I'm tired, and you look like hell. Why don't we just have a drink?"

There's that Dean Martin thing again, but it wasn't a

bad idea. We sipped our beverages, we traded small talk about the newspaper business and the FBI and growing up in rural Indiana, as she did, as compared to South Boston, as I did. She told me she liked my house. I ordered a $19 shrimp cocktail and a $22 cheese and fruit plate, and could just about hear Peter Martin asking sarcastically, "What's this, two dollars a grape?"

Outside, she offered to drop me in Georgetown on the way to her Arlington condominium. Outside my house, she asked, "Could I use your bathroom?"

In the foyer, she knelt down on the floor, skirt and all, to give Baker an enormous hug and a kiss on his fluffy ears, telling him he was a wonderful boy all the while. In his excitement, the poor dog seemed ready to have a heart attack at the prospect of any company at this hour of the evening, let alone female.

"Don't you need to use the bathroom?" I asked finally as she stroked Baker's head with no apparent inclination to move.

She laughed and said, "No. I was just looking for an excuse to say hello to your dog. I absolutely adore him. Sorry."

We both smiled over that, and the telephone rang. It was about ten-thirty, and as I looked at the phone with a mix of longing and fear, she looked at me, amused.

"I'll just let that kick over to my answering service," I said.

"Déjà vu," she said with a mischievous grin. "Are you a character in an Anne Tyler novel or something? Why don't you pick up the telephone? A hot woman? An anonymous source? Maybe the president of the United States leaking to you again?"

She walked toward the telephone as I tried not to panic. Eternity seemed to descend on this living room, at least insofar as this ringing phone was concerned. It seemed as if it would ring forever. At last, she reached over and picked it up herself, saying in a playful voice, "Flynn residence, may I help you?"

Then she looked at me blankly and slowly put the phone back on the hook. "Hung up," she said. "I must have scared her off."

twelve

Thursday, November 2

THE DREAM WAS ONE of those hazy ones where the whole seems clearer than the sum of its parts. I remember realizing I was supposed to meet Katherine, but couldn't recall where or when or why. She wasn't at home and wasn't at work, and she didn't have her cell phone with her, so I sat at my desk in the bureau trying to figure out what time we said we would be getting together and where we were supposed to meet.

Then it struck me that maybe I couldn't reach her because she had gone to the hospital and had the baby. She hadn't called me because she wanted to surprise me with our new child. So maybe that's where we were supposed to gather, at Georgetown Hospital, in the maternity ward, to celebrate the most momentous day of our lives. So the real question was whether I should be angry at her for excluding me from our baby's birth or pleased that she was trying to make it a surprise.

Best I can remember, it was about here that the jagged sound smashed into my subconscious and stirred me into a state of semi-reality. At first I thought it was my alarm clock, but when I groped around my nightstand with a blind hand and shut it off, the sound kept firing away at my brain. Then I realized it was the telephone, and it occurred to me that Katherine might be calling to say she was dining with her sister and wanted to know if I would like to meet them for dessert. To say the least, I was confused. The bedroom was completely black and cool outside my comforter, and I glanced at the illuminated clock and saw it was four-thirty in the morning, which only added to the fog.

When finally I found the phone on my night table, the familiar, haunting voice on the other end knocked the last remnants of fantasy from my brain and brought me back to a reality I wasn't sure I liked.

"You're a hard man to reach, Mr. Flynn," the anonymous source said in that even, dignified voice that had echoed in my mind so many times over the last week.

My wife is dead, I thought, suddenly burdened anew with a sadness that I had shed for my dream. Before I could say anything to this voice, even extend a greeting, he kept talking.

"You must be careful not to be misled. You must realize, you are being fed lies, lies that mask important truths that will someday astound you. You must keep working, keep digging, and get at these truths."

The world, or at least this conversation, was becoming clearer to me as the cobwebs gave way to the importance of the moment. I had prepared for this call in excruciating detail, actually thought of little but, and I knew I couldn't lose the opportunity because I was tired and grieving for my wife.

"That wasn't you who wanted to meet me at the Newseum, right?" I asked.

There was a moment of silence on the other end, and

when he spoke, he sounded uncharacteristically flustered, his voice taking on a tone I had not heard from him before. "The Newseum? No, I don't understand."

This verified what Havlicek and I believed all along: that someone was trying to help me, even while someone else was trying to kill me.

I asked, "So you're saying you didn't have a note delivered to me at a restaurant Saturday night asking to meet you at the Newseum?"

"No."

I asked, "Then who would try to kill me?"

"Mr. Flynn, given the sensitivity of the information involved, there are people who will go to extremes to make sure it does not find its way into the public realm. There are people who would kill rather than see you get to the bottom of this story. I must warn you that if you continue to accept my help and pursue these leads, you are in danger. Imminent danger."

I said, somewhat less than politely, "You haven't given me any leads yet, only general guidance. I need specifics. If I'm going to be in danger, you might as well give me more help. It's not enough to encourage me. You know more than I do. You know more than you're saying. I need you to tell me what you know, or at least to guide me along so I can get there."

"That's fair," he said. He paused, and beside me, the dog, his head on the edge of a pillow and his body spread out on the bed like a person, rolled partially over to look at me, then closed his eyes again. I sat up in the dark on one elbow. The light from the telephone handset cast a small glow on my bed.

"I'm prepared to help you," he said. "I'm prepared to

bring you to the core of this situation. But it's crucial for you to understand, as we get further along, as you begin to realize what has happened with this assassination attempt, your own life will be threatened anew. Knowledge is power. That axiom is true. But in this case, knowledge is also danger."

Obviously my Deep Throat had a flair for the dramatic, and I wondered, given the tone of his voice and the perfect sentences he formed, whether he had resumed reading from some sort of script. If he thought he was scaring me, he thought wrong, but I sensed he understood this. The two most intriguing things you can say to any reporter worth the ink in his pen is that he may have to go to jail if he doesn't give up his source, and that his life is in danger. Best as I could understand at this early hour, he was offering me some version of a twofer.

"I've already accepted the danger," I said, finding myself speaking as theatrically as the source. "What I want is to get to the bottom of this story."

There was another long pause, and I thought I detected the shuffle of paper. I could hear him breathing softly into the telephone.

Finally, he said, "You've been to Chelsea, Massachusetts."

It seemed more of a declaration than a question, though I wasn't really sure, so I said, "Yes, I've been to Chelsea." And indeed I had. It's a tiny city of less than two square miles just over the Mystic River from Boston, jammed with decrepit slums and abandoned storefronts. It was the birthplace of Horatio Alger, a fact that had provided hope to waves of immigrants from Italy, Poland, and Ireland. Now that hope had turned into little more than despair for the Jamaicans and Mexicans who found themselves not in a job but in a cycle of poverty, their only refuge taken in an occasional puff of crack cocaine.

"You should travel there," he said. "You should find out everything you can about a man named Curtis Black. Learn about him, and you will have dug to the core of this case."

Chelsea. Curtis Black. The president of the United goddamned States of America. Silently, my finely honed reporting instincts were engaged in a full-blown war with my reverent tone toward this source. The instincts won, and I asked: "Just a casual question: what the hell does a Curtis Black in Chelsea, Massachusetts, have to do with an assassination attempt on the most powerful figure in the world?"

I thought this might anger him. Instead, he barely missed a beat. "Everything," he said. "I've given you all I can right now. It's up to you to find out why."

I asked, "Will you continue to help me?"

"As long as you're working this, I'll help you," he said.

"Will you ever reveal yourself to me?" I asked that question just out of curiosity. I assumed a quick "No," but instead, he paused again and said, "Perhaps someday, if I think it will help."

I wasn't ready for this conversation to end quite yet, though I feared he was. I asked, more lightly, "Have you seen today's *Record?*"

"No, I haven't."

"We have two stories," I said. "We have a story saying the trigger man cannot be the same man the feds say he is. Their ID, this guy named Tony Clawson, has eyes of a different color from the corpse.

"The second story says that the FBI had a prior tip,

confirmed by a federal informant, that a Wyoming-based militia group was plotting an attack on the president."

There was another long pause. The house was totally silent, outside of Baker's soft, rhythmic dog snoring. The clock showed 4:40 A.M. now. I thought I heard my source breathing more heavily.

"You have it about half right," he said, his tone slightly different, a little higher, with an edge, like a rubber band stretched thin. "You're going to want to find out about Curtis Black even faster now."

He hesitated, then, sounding more compassionate than businesslike, added, "Just take care of yourself. Be careful." Then he hung up.

At seven-thirty in the morning at the Washington bureau of a big-city newspaper, I should have been a good two hours out from seeing another human being. Except for the lawyers along K Street who bill by the hour and equate time in the most literal sense to money, this is a town slow to start at the beginning of the day. Congressional aides, federal officials, and news reporters don't typically arrive at work until just on the northern side of 10:00 A.M. Once they're there, they tend to work late into the evening, often until 9:00 P.M. or after, and invariably, once they are out, they will complain vociferously about the number of hours they dedicate to their job, because in a city that produces little more than monotonous debate—no automobiles, mutual funds, not even insurance—long hours are the closest thing anyone has to show for any sense of accomplishment.

On this morning, at the far end of the otherwise dark-ened newsroom, Steve Havlicek sat hunched under a single light at his computer terminal, staring intently at the words on his screen.

"One question," I said as I approached quietly and roused him from some trancelike state. "What the fuck are you doing here at this hour?"

"You know, that whole early-to-bed, early-to-rise thing," he said, jovial as ever. "Big story here. We've got work to do and no time to waste. Howaya, slugger?"

I just shook my head. I was holding a bag with two toasted bagels and offered him one. He didn't hesitate in accepting, and was already biting into the second half before I even got mine unwrapped.

"These stories are going to catch fire today," he said, his mouth full. "I've already got calls from the producers of Imus and the Gordon Liddy shows. When the boys over at CNN and Fox get in, they'll be all over us. This is officially hell day at the FBI."

Though Havlicek had done the lion's share of the work on the story of Clawson, he had given me a co-byline, partly out of professional courtesy, partly out of a raw shrewdness that my name might inspire the anonymous source to provide more help. Either way, it was the generous act of a very secure reporter.

I said, "Yeah, we have to start figuring out where we take this story next, though I suspect the reaction will give us a wild ride for the morning. What do you think the FBI is going to do?"

"They can't very well deny it," Havlicek said, looking at some point beyond me as he thought. "My bet is that they hole up over there at the Hoover Building and don't say a thing, or they simply say the investigation is continuing down many avenues."

"And the White House? I mean, Hutchins has to say something about this. This was an attempt to kill the bastard. He's got to weigh in with something stronger than he has full faith in the FBI."

"This will be a great day," Havlicek said. "Strap yourself in."

"Well, I've got something that might make it even greater. I got a call this morning from the anonymous one. The bastard woke me up at home at four-thirty."

Havlicek said, "Jesus Christ, you're burying the lead again. What did he say?"

I told him. I wove together the conversation about Chelsea and this guy named Curtis Black, and the source's kind words about our work so far. I told him of the danger he said we would face, of the shocking truths waiting to be uncovered. Havlicek was sitting in his chair just staring at me, his mouth agape, with, actually, some chewed-up bagel inside.

"Mother of merciful God," he said finally. He looked off across the room at nothing in particular, as if he were trying to fashion some thoughts in the dark space of the empty newsroom. "This is either one elaborate hoax or one wonderful newspaper story we're onto. Right now, all we can do is assume and hope to holy hell it's real."

I said, "We're in a rush, but I think I ought to hold off on going up to Boston, just for the day. This town is going to flip over these stories, especially yours, and we both ought to be around to handle the fallout."

Almost as if the scene were scripted, at that precise moment, on the small color television on Havlicek's desk, a photo of the front page of the day's *Boston Record* appeared behind a rookie anchorman still assigned to the early-morning shift on CNN. Havlicek saw me riveted to the television and grabbed for the remote control to turn up the volume.

"—The newspaper reports that the FBI has misidentified the attempted assassin in the shooting of President Clayton Hutchins last week—"

Havlicek hit the mute button, and I heard the ringing sound of my telephone on the other side of the room. I did my usual sprint and grabbed the phone on the fourth ring, barking, "Flynn."

"Why the hell didn't you tell me you had these stories?" It was the rather angry voice of Samantha Stevens.

"Excuse me?" I said, buying time, unsure of the right answer.

"I spill my fucking guts to you last night about not knowing about Wyoming, and you can't even tell me what the rest of the fucking world is going to be told in twelve hours?"

"Hey there, easy does it," I said. "Last I checked, you're not my editor. You're not even a subscriber, not that I know of, anyway. And if you'll think back, I did tell you to read the *Record* today. I told you that Clawson wasn't who you people say he is. As I recall, you told me, 'Case closed.'"

She said, getting angrier, "Look, I'm in a position to help you, but unless I know it goes two ways, you can go fuck yourself. Good luck."

With that, she hung up. No matter. My telephone was ringing off the hook here. Next up was my close, personal friend Ron Hancock of the FBI.

"Well, you've stirred up quite a hornet's nest," he said, flat, always flat, regardless of the words.

"Go ahead," I told him.

"The director has his entire top staff in his office now. There's so much chatter between here and the White House this morning that they might as well just hook up two cans to a piece of string."

I said, "That's interesting, but what does it all mean? Who is this guy you have over in the morgue, why is the FBI fucking up a presidential assassination attempt, and is the FBI fucking up, or covering up?"

"To questions one through three, don't know," he said, and I believed him.

I asked, "Do you think they're going to admit they made a mistake?"

"No idea," he said. "Those decisions are made about ten pay grades above mine. And let me tell you one thing: the FBI doesn't admit it made mistakes. If they do admit they made a mistake, know that it wasn't a mistake. Take that to the bank."

He paused, then added, "I wanted to ask you, you have anything else coming? Anything else I should know about as I work this from within?"

"Shot our load today," I said. "But I suspect there's a lot more work to do. I'll be in touch."

I hung up just in time to pick up another call.

"Sorry," Samantha Stevens said, sounding anything but. "I dropped the phone before."

"Right onto the cradle?" I asked.

"Look," she said. "I still think we can help each other. Let's keep our options open."

"Deal."

"Good. I have to go. All hell is breaking loose over here, thank you very much. I'll talk to you later."

When I turned around, Peter Martin was standing by my desk, almost levitating, he was so overjoyed, reading the latest wire service dispatch that recounted salient facts from the stories, with full attribution to the *Boston Record*. Thus far, no one, not the wires, not the networks, was able to obtain the photographs and autopsy reports that Havlicek had used to put our story together, so they had to repeatedly attribute all the information to the *Record*.

"We have this city by the balls today," Martin said, making a little vise grip with his chalky palm that made me flinch back ever so slightly.

I didn't engage. It was time for me to fill him in. "We have to talk," I said. "We have to talk about an anonymous source and a guy named Curtis Black."

He said, "The fuck are you talking about? We have a day of follows here on what may be the most important couple of stories this newspaper has ever broken."

"Let's go into your office," I said.

And we did. And after I was done with all the sordid details, from the first calls in the hospital to the uncertain encounter at the Newseum to the note on the airplane to the telephone tip in the dark of that very morning, Martin looked a shade lighter than Casper the ghost, only not as friendly. As I sat in one of his leather club chairs in front of his coffee table with my legs crossed and the weight of my upper body resting on one elbow, he paced around the office, silently, pushing his hair around so that it flew up at odd angles. At one point, he reached into his desk drawer and pulled out a bottle of Extra Strength Tylenol, throwing a few in his mouth without the benefit of water, as if they were Good 'n' Plenties.

He said, "I understand why you didn't, and I am not going to hold it against you, but I wish you had told me earlier."

I nodded.

He said, "Tell me your gut feeling. Is this guy on the level?"

"Well, he had the Clawson part right at the same time Havlicek was getting it. He's sure urgent about all this. He sounds educated. He's not spinning crazy conspiracy theories. He is going to considerable expense to make sure we take him seriously. I really don't know enough to draw a judgment, but I know just enough to know that we have to keep playing his game, or we're going to regret it for the rest of our careers."

"Yeah, you're right," Martin said, collapsing onto his couch, fading into the soft pillows.

"And what about this Graham and Wilkerson tip?" Martin asked.

"Been pursuing it, but I've gotten nothing back. Nothing. I just don't see it being true, or someone, somewhere would have given me a wink or a nod."

We both fell quiet for a moment, until he said, "Does this shooting ultimately win the election for Hutchins?"

While I considered an answer, he provided one of his own. "It seems like Hutchins has gotten a modest boost over this whole thing, but maybe not as good a boost as they expected. The public really doesn't seem to know what to make of all this confusion over the investigation. They've edged toward Hutchins in the polls, but it's been anything but decisive. I bet it's driving the White House crazy."

I nodded and said, "Yeah, I think you're about right. After the shooting, I know I thought Hutchins would jump ahead, especially with that Reaganesque quote that the ambulance driver remembered, though wrongly. The White House thought the same thing. And now, I don't know. I can't get my mind around how this is playing out, or even if the election had something to do with the assassination attempt."

"I suspect we'll find that out soon enough," Martin said. "I want you to hang in here today, mop up with Havlicek, and late tonight or tomorrow, you get on up to Chelsea and work like a tyrant on this guy Black. I have a hunch we'll know whether this information is any good in the next days or so."

I said, "Sounds like a plan." At least, it was the closest thing I had to one in this topsy-turvey thing we call life.

thirteen

IT WAS AROUND 1:00 P.M. when White House Press Secretary Royal Dalton slid open the pocket doors that separate the press office from the briefing room and walked awkwardly up to the podium. He was about an hour late.

Hutchins was laying over in Washington amid a week-long campaign trip. The room was electric this day. There is nothing that makes reporters happier than catching the government, especially a law enforcement agency, in a mistake or a lie, and this one about Tony Clawson could cut either way. Sure, other print reporters were frustrated at having been beaten to the story. The hell with them. Television reporters, they don't really care. The hotter the story, no matter who breaks it, means the more air time for them, and that means greater recognition—on the streets, at family weddings, and on the telephone with any of the young blond hostesses at the city's hottest restaurants when they call at five in the afternoon hoping for an eight-o'clock reservation, table for four.

Every seat in the room was filled with a reporter. Every inch of wall space was taken by cameramen who appeared layered on top of each other, creating a terrace of lenses, ready to beam this scene around the world in a matter of minutes. The lights were bright and hot, causing that unique—and, yes, unpleasant—odor of sweat and wool.

Dalton looked particularly uneasy today, his already pasty features washed even whiter, with the sole exception of the darkening circles under his beady eyes.

"I have a couple of policy announcements," he said, trying to maintain a casual demeanor as he looked around the room in something that more accurately approached fear. He went on to talk about a Medicare reform proposal that Republicans had been trying to sell for years, recycled, obviously, in time for some campaign season coverage.

After that, he opened the the session to questions, and first up was Moose Myers, senior White House correspondent for CNN. Moose was actually anything but. On the screen, he looked big and foreboding, usually because the camera shot him from close range, so he'd fill the picture. In person, he was five foot six, maybe five-seven in his favorite heels. I don't know why I bring this up. Whenever I talk to television guys, I tend to dwell on their features and come to the inevitable conclusion that aside from my reportorial pride, I could do that.

Moose asked: "Has President Hutchins talked to the FBI director this morning, and has he lost faith in the FBI's ability to conduct this investigation, given the revelations in today's *Boston Record?*"

Sitting smack in the middle of the room, about three rows behind him, I made a mental note to extend my thanks for that high-profile mention. It doesn't get much better than that. I actually had the feeling that a few of my colleagues were looking at me, and trust me when I say this is a tough lot to impress. You could walk on water, and the first thing most of them would want to do is inspect your shoes, and, finding them wet, ask, "Any reason why you went out and ruined a perfectly good pair of Cole-Haan wing tips?"

Dalton had obviously patched together a precisely worded answer to this question with senior White House aides and probably even Hutchins himself, then rehearsed it frontward and back over the past several hours. Here it came:

"The president," he said, "has spoken to Director Callinger of the FBI by telephone this morning. They had a pleasant and informative talk. They have been keeping in regular contact since the assassination attempt. You've all seen reports"—the *Record* stories, I'd point out—"that there has been a security alert here at the White House, and the president has been receiving regular updates on that.

"The president was assured today that the investigation remains on track and is moving ahead with significant progress. The president is obviously in no position to discuss the particulars of the investigation. He was the victim. He is not a detective. But I am told the FBI will have something more to say on this shortly."

Immediately, a dozen hands and as many voices filled the air. Myers, the CNN reporter, talked down his colleagues. Asking a question in this kind of setting is like a verbal fencing match. You have to stay at it longer and harder, and eventually the vanquished sit down and shut up. "Royal, you didn't answer me. Has the president lost faith in the abilities of the FBI, given what the *Boston Record* is saying today about the misidentified shooter and the fact that they had previously identified a specific militia group, but were unable to stop the assassination attempt?"

Every time he mentioned my paper, I subconsciously felt myself push my shoulders back a bit further. I also felt the urge to hug him, but those are my own private issues. If I really had, I could see CNN using that footage in a commercial for how revered Moose is by his colleagues.

"Look," Dalton said. "The president believes today what he's always believed, and what, I would argue, most of America believes: that the FBI is the most talented, most exhaustive, most prestigious law enforcement agency in the world. He hasn't changed his opinion because of a newspaper story in Boston."

Dalton spit out those last words as if they were some distasteful bit of phlegm that had worked its way from his throat into his mouth. But if he thought he could outsmart the gathered press—and pathetically, he probably believed he could—he was about to learn the folly of his ways. Immediately, the Associated Press reporter shouted out, "So the president believes that the FBI was right, that the dead man is actually Tony Clawson?"

Good one. Dalton hesitated at the podium. You could see him twitching if you watched closely enough. "As I indicated before," he said, gathering a dismissive tone, "the president is the president of the United States. He is not a detective. He does not involve himself in the particulars of this investigation. He leaves that up to the trained inspectors with the most successful, most notable law enforcement agency in the world."

The *Washington Post* reporter asked loudly: "Does the president still have faith in that agency and its director?"

Dalton: "He does not see any reason, at this juncture, not to have faith in the FBI. He wants to let them proceed with their investigation, which is certainly difficult to do, given the intense publicity and the second-guessing that we're seeing now in the news media."

My first inclination was to stand up and tell him that the story wasn't second-guessing, it was just laying out a set of obvious facts, most notably, that the FBI misidentified a would-be presidential assassin. My second inclination, the winning one, was that it might be unbecoming to stand and defend my own story. Significantly, Dalton had not called it wrong, and no one in the room thought it was.

The *Baltimore Sun* reporter, a twenty-year veteran of the press room who was demonstrably annoyed first with being beaten, and second with the mealymouthed responses from Dalton, asked, "Well, did the FBI director tell the president that they have the right identity or the wrong identity on the body of the alleged shooter? And is the FBI director prepared to offer his resignation?"

"You're not going to get much more from me on this one," Dalton said. "The president is a victim in this shooting. The particulars on this case will have to come from the FBI, and as I said, I think they'll have something for you people in a short while."

This was interesting. Dalton effectively passed on the question of whether the FBI director would resign because of a *Record* story. This was also becoming futile, though it would be another twenty minutes before anyone in the room would be willing to let go.

Basically, from my read, Dalton was shying away from saying that the president had full faith in the FBI. He had very purposefully not used those words, probably out of fear that the FBI had screwed up and knowledge that they were about to make an announcement to that effect. Dalton was also going to great lengths to distance the president from the investigation, repeatedly calling him a victim. This in itself was odd. White House aides prefer to depict the president as someone all-powerful, in control, not some hapless casualty of unfortunate circumstance. They were obviously being cautious about this, not setting anything in stone, leaving themselves an escape route. The question was, why?

As Dalton went around and around with reporters, my pager sounded. It's one of those high-tech beepers with the text messages that shows me the most recent wire reports every few hours. This message was far better than the norm, which usually consists of this: "Call Peter Martin immediately." I read my beeper twice to make sure I saw it right. "Jack, You're an asshole. Come see me ASAP. C.H."

I couldn't well get up in the middle of this briefing, mostly because the only way into the West Wing was directly past the podium, where all my colleagues, as well as Royal Dalton, would look at me with a mix of fear and loathing.

"Royal, is it the view of the president that the shooting attempt has hampered his ability to win reelection, or has it aided his cause because the country had the chance to see him perform in a difficult personal situation?" That was Jonathan Flowers with CBS News, with a subtle way of trying to reengage Dalton in the give-and-take, make him feel and act less like Larry Speakes, Reagan's press secretary, whose relationship with the news media was so awful that he would routinely stare down a particularly difficult questioner and bellow, "You're out of business." Then he'd ignore the reporter for the next week.

"I've said all I'm saying on assassination-related topics," Dalton seethed from the podium. He paused, then added icily, "Next subject."

Fuck him.

"Royal," I said, and I could feel all eyes riveted on me. I wasn't just some casual questioner here. My name was on that story, and there's the operating assumption from every other reporter and White House aide that the writer always knows more than he's written. "As president, as commander in chief, as someone generally charged with protecting our country and government, shouldn't President Hutchins be taking a keen interest in the progress of this investigation and the abilities of the investigators, given the potentially serious consequences on the well-being of the administration?"

I liked it. Dalton froze at the podium, furiously flipping through the briefing book of his mind for an answer. Finally, he punted. "Look, he is monitoring this regularly and closely. He is as concerned as anyone else with today's report. But he is also leaving the particulars of the investigation to those who are expert investigators."

This far in, and finally a usable quote. Hutchins is concerned. As Dalton sought other topics, on this day, there were a round of questions on the Medicare reform proposal, on the latest tax cut measure being touted by Nichols, et cetera. Eventually, the briefing tailed off into a blur of quiet mayhem, with reporters talking to each other and cameramen packing up their equipment and Dalton hesitating at the front of the room before he slinked through the door. I quickly pushed my way through the masses to a wall phone, dialed the White House switchboard, and quietly asked for Sylvia Weinrich, Hutchins's assistant.

"Miss Weinrich speaking," she said, answering the phone in her finishing-school tone, one regularly heard by world leaders, cabinet secretaries, and major contributors, though typically not by some harried reporter from South Boston.

"Hello, Miss Weinrich. Jack Flynn here." I spoke to her, I realized, as if I were talking to one of my former grammar school teachers, forming my words and thoughts carefully, all with a mix of respect and affection and the long-shot hope that she might like me and think I was smart. "The president, I believe, was kind enough to page me with an invitation to stop by. I was wondering if he had a convenient time."

It occurred to me just before she spoke that the page had been some hoax and that Hutchins had no intention of seeing me, all of which would have meant that I was in the process of making a general ass of myself. Luckily, she cleared that up in no time.

"Mr. Flynn, such a pleasure to hear from you again. My, you've been busy. I know the president wanted to see you as soon as possible. As a matter of fact, he has some office time right now and was wondering how soon you might be able to come in."

More than perhaps anyone else on earth, when the president beckons, people—congressmen, activists, titans of industry—drop everything and come, whether they want to or not. That's one of the perks of leadership. Me, I explained that I was in the building—a fact, I had a hunch, that they already knew. Marvelous, we both agreed, and in a matter of minutes, I was inconspicuously walking from the briefing room, through the West Wing, and into the Oval Office for the second time in my life, this time, though, unclear of my purpose and unprepared, I suspected, for what was to come.

He was sitting at that big oak desk, in shirtsleeves, wearing one of those pairs of half glasses that Havlicek had on a couple of nights before, looking dignified. He was reading a sheaf of papers in a black binder. The wan November sun streaked through the southern windows behind him and through the French doors that led out to the Rose Garden, where bunches of brightly colored chrysanthemums stood sentry against the early creep of winter. The room was bathed in light and warmth and quiet—just the gentle hum of moving air and the soft tick of the tall case clock. When Hutchins flipped a page, the sound was a relative explosion.

I sat on one of the two couches at the far end of the room, quietly waiting. Sylvia Weinrich had shut the door on her way out. My eyes scanned around from the jar of mints on the coffee table to the busts of Franklin Delano Roosevelt and John F. Kennedy near his desk to the biographies of Truman and Lincoln that were carefully arranged on the ancient pale yellow shelves. It was mesmerizing, this room, where history wasn't just made but prodded and pulled, nipped and formed. As the moments drifted into minutes, I started wondering if he knew I was here.

"Fuck, fuck, fuck." That was Hutchins, finally. He stood up from his desk, snapped his glasses off his face with one hand, and slowly walked toward me, looking haggard.

"You have any idea how much money this country sends to Israel every year in federal dollars?" he asked, not really seeming to want an answer. "Three billion. Three fucking billion fucking dollars. You have any idea how much private U.S. money is raised for Israel annually? Try another billion." By now, Hutchins was standing across from me, taking his seat on the opposite couch, talking softer with every word.

"How good are we to them? Cole just about promised fellatio to every senior Israeli official if they'd just be willing to meet with the Palestinians. Me? The second call I made after I was sworn in was to Jerusalem. No changes in policy, I said. They'd continue to be our best ally in the region. And how do they say thanks to all this money, to all this friendship, to the promise of all this history if they can reach a simple accord with people they know they'll be living beside from now to fucking eternity? They build tunnels and housing on sacred Palestinian land. They know the reaction they're going to get. They know they're fucking things up. Then they just shrug and ask me, 'Are you with us or not?' And what can I say? 'Yes, I am, though, gee, I was hoping you might behave differently.' Well, you know what? Maybe I'm not with them anymore."

This scene was astounding for a few reasons, most notably that this was five days before a monumental presidential election. Hutchins should be standing before cameras, basking in the glow of favorable public opinion polls, looking down the pipe to four years in the White House in his own right. Granted, he was only taking a brief breather here, but the respite should not be spent laboring over the finer or broader points of the muddled and immovable Middle East peace process. It crossed my mind that the *Record* story might be one reason why Hutchins wasn't happier. The reality of his life was another. He was childless, wifeless, and really had no one with whom to share the moment aside from a group of aides I don't think he particularly liked. So here was Hutchins, alone with a reporter he barely knew, fretting about issues he had frustratingly little control over.

I hadn't said anything yet, and Hutchins didn't appear interested in my opinion, so I sat in silence, watching closely the sad, almost sour look on his face, the toll of this job, listening to the words flow into what seemed a pool of self-pity. His reputation was that of a hard-charging bull, a man whom I once wrote had a steak-house charm about him: straightforward, with few garnishments. Today, he appeared wilted, like some hound dog on a hot August afternoon.

"And you," he said, more politely now, paternal. "Where are you on our proposal? You make up your mind yet? You ready to do the right thing and join the team, help make history? I'm about to win four more years. I'll be able to do anything I want, go anywhere I want to go. I probably won't even run for reelection. I might just use this term to kick an awful lot of ass and let things fall where they may. You could be there, every step of the way, for every kick and all the applause that follows."

Hutchins paused, staring out the French doors. His feet were up on the coffee table. He held his half glasses in one hand, letting them dangle by the stem as some people do, occasionally flipping them around. He reached up and rubbed his eyes with two fingers, massaging them hard as if he were trying to push them back into his head. He looked as if he were about to lose the election rather than win the damn thing.

I said, "I'm putting an enormous amount of thought into your offer, sir. But I think it's fair to warn you that I don't think this is an appropriate time for me."

Hutchins just kind of looked at me for a minute, allowing his eyes to scan over my face, probing, silent.

"Howa your ribs?" he asked, surprising me.

"Much better," I said. "I'm getting a lot more comfortable."

"Hasn't affected your work, for chrissakes," he said, getting that mischievous smile again, looking at me hard, playfully, waiting for a response.

I smiled. "Busy time."

"Oh, it's a busy time all right. It's a busy fucking time."

He let that hang there, and the two of us sat facing each other, waiting for reactions.

I broke the silence. "Sir, do you have any reaction beyond what Dalton has said on the performance of the FBI? Are you worried they're going to botch this shooting?"

He resumed his serious look and tone. "I can't help you on this one." Then he did. He repositioned himself on the settee and said, "Look, they're the FBI. You hope to God they know what they're doing. You believe in your heart that they do. You look at their record, at their history, at their tradition, and at their reputation, and you just have to believe they're going to get things right."

Nice little quote that my paper will have exclusively—certainly a lot better than that patter of Dalton's.

"Here's the point, though," he continued. "You're a smart kid. I want you in my trench, not shooting at me from someone else's. If it takes money, I promise you, we'll max out on your pay. I'll dip into my own pocket to supplement it. I'll give you hiring power over at the press office. You bring in whoever you want. You know you have my ear. I'll give you virtually open access to the Oval. You come in here anytime you want and talk things through. You'll be one of my most important advisers, cutting across the board."

Holy shit. Essentially, what he was now offering me wasn't just the position of press secretary, though that slot alone was pretty damned good. He was talking about senior presidential adviser, at the very center of his inner circle, a fixture in the Washington power structure. Senators would have to kiss my ass. Network anchors would vie for my time. My financial future would be set. This was interesting, though probably not interesting enough to sway me. The story—this assassination attempt and all the mystery that surrounded it—was too good. My roots in newspapers ran too deep.

"It's all very flattering," I said. "I really will think about it."

My deadline was supposed to be the next day, Friday. "Take whatever time you need," he said. "The sooner the better, but I'd rather have a yes in a week than a no in a day."

I said, "I don't want to leave you hanging. I'll move as quickly as I can. But like I said, right now, to be perfectly honest, I'm leaning against it."

There was a moment of silence. I gazed around the room again, thinking this could be in some way mine, this hold on power.

With the quiet mounting toward God knows what, my curiosity got the better of me, and I took a chance. "You don't look so good, sir. Given that the polls show you creeping ahead, I would think you'd be in a better frame of mind."

He focused on me—bore in on my face, still silent, his gray eyes locking in on mine, not in an angry way but almost in some odd way pleading, but for what, I had no idea.

"Are we talking, me and you, or am I talking to 700,000 *Record* readers?" he asked.

I think he inflated our circulation figures, not that I mind. "Me and you, sir," I said.

He sighed loudly. "This job, it's not what you might think. Hell, it's not what I had thought. There is the swarm of attention, and in the middle of that swarm, the sense of total isolation. There is the dangling prospect of accomplishment, matched against the overriding reality of constant failure."

He paused for a moment, looking out toward the Rose Garden. He continued, "Look, it sounds foolish to complain about all this, and there's a lot that's great—this house, the limousines, the helicopter, Air Force One, Camp David. I have a staff of valets who'll help me put my boxers on in the morning if I ask them to. They lay out my clothes every day, freshly pressed, always nice and clean. I can play golf at any frigging private club in America without even calling for a tee time. But for the rest of my life, I'll never be able to sit at a bar and order a hamburger. I'll never be able to go for a Sunday-afternoon drive. I can't even go for a walk in my own neighborhood. Hell, I don't really even have a neighborhood. I am the neighborhood."

He was on a roll. The stream of consciousness seemed to be turning into a tidal wave. "I'm not a professional politician. Maybe that's my biggest problem, at the same time it's my greatest asset. I didn't spend my entire life praying and scheming to be president. I didn't ask for this job."

He paused, and I cut in, my tone noticeably sympathetic even if I didn't yet feel any great sympathy. "Sir, with all due respect, you did ask for this job. You're in the process of asking for it right now, in this election."

He seemed not in the least bit offended. "Yeah, you're right, I am asking for it," he said. "But tell me this, how do you not ask for this job when you know you could have it? How do you turn your back on being in every history book of every junior high kid in the country from now until the end of time? How do you walk away from that?"

Fair points. We sat in silence again for a moment. He was brooding; I was stunned, for a variety of reasons. I had never seen him this reflective, this thoughtful. He usually put forth the veneer of a fraternity brother, ever mischievous, involved only in the moment. I recalled his great delight at watching me drive the ball into the woods at Congressional. I remembered his fascination with the presidential suite at the Bethesda Navy Hospital. But you always knew that below the surface there was an inner, driving force with this man. It was part of his great charm.

Still, I didn't know it ran this deep, or this purple. Here was the president of the United States, heading toward probable victory in an election just five days away, outright depressed at the prospect of four years in the White House. I thought back to past presidents, how they arrived and how they left. John Kennedy embodied a new age of Camelot. Three years later, he was shot and killed, his brains spattered across that convertible limousine in Dallas. Lyndon Johnson was broken by the Vietnam War. Richard Nixon fulfilled his greatest dreams with his election in 1968, outdid himself in 1972, and then left in disgrace two years later, standing at the entry of Marine One on the South Lawn, his staff and friends on the grass below, giving a final, two-handed victory sign, his suit jacket awkwardly scrunched up below his arms as his face was formed into a forced, bittersweet smile. Ford was only given a taste of power. Carter was given only a little more than that. He arrived so young, with so much promise. He left a gray-haired man obsessed by a group of hostages he was unable to help until he couldn't even help himself. Reagan may be the only one who left with his heart intact, though even he was ridiculed in his parting days. Bush rode higher than anyone before him, the victorious conquester of the Gulf War, only to be brought down by economic forces he failed to understand. Clinton embodied a new generation of leadership, with all its hopes and with all its failings, and in the end, his entire life was torn asunder in a clash between the weakness of his own personality and the immense personal responsibilities of the office.

"Look, I'm unloading too much," Hutchins said, interrupting my stroll through history. "I'm tired from the campaign. Maybe I'm intimidated by the work ahead. And when a guy takes a shot at you out of nowhere, you start thinking about the fragile nature of life. Bottom line: I'm going to be fine."

Hutchins slapped his two hands against his knees, in a sign that the conversation was over. I hesitated, then rose slowly from the couch, assuming this was my signal to leave. He stayed slumped down. "Your wife, she died, right?" he asked, and the first thing I thought was, it would be a hell of a question to get wrong.

I said, "She did, about a year ago."

I was standing now. He was sitting, deep in the couch, showing no signs of getting up. He said, "I'm sorry." There was a silence. I started to turn around to leave. He added, "I hope you find someone else. No matter who you are, no matter where you've been, no matter where you're going, life isn't meant to be lived alone, not for normal human beings, anyway."

I nodded at him. "I think you're right," I said. I walked slowly out the door, leaving him slumped into the couch, looking painfully sad. As I left, Sylvia Weinrich walked in carrying a silver tray holding a can of Diet Coke, a crystal bowl filled with ice, and a frosted glass. She smiled as she passed me. I turned to see Hutchins walking slowly to his desk.

• • •

"Hey there, slugger."

That was Havlicek, looking up from his computer, the headset to a microcassette recorder covering his ears as he transcribed a tape.

He asked, "You hear about the FBI statement?"

"I've been out of touch for the last hour," I said. "What did they say?"

Peter Martin approached from his office and leaned on Havlicek's desk without saying anything.

"Very interesting," Havlicek began. "They issued a bull-shit response that the original identification of Clawson was only tentative, and it only became public because it was released by a junior agent who was speaking without authorization. They also said they had realized in the past forty-eight hours that this initial identification—their words—was wrong, and they had reopened that facet of their investigation to learn the identity of the attempted assassin."

I asked, "So they still don't know who the guy is that they killed, this dead person in their morgue?"

"They won't say. They said that because of the initial, false release of the tentative ID, they will make certain that in the future no parts of their investigation are released to the news media until they are ready. They claim that today's story hindered their investigation, so they're going to button down even tighter."

I laughed a sneering laugh. "Those pricks. They screw up, then blame us for hindering them. What a bunch of jackasses."

"Bingo. But at least they've essentially confirmed our story. This makes for good print tomorrow. On Wyoming, they have declined to comment, except to say they did have a security alert at the White House. They were adamant that they do not discuss anything to do with any federal informants."

Martin spoke for the first time. "This also means that every paper in the country, including the *New York Times* and *Washington Post,* have to mention us in tomorrow's stories, giving us full credit. The FBI made sure of that today by admitting this and blaming us at the same time. This couldn't be better."

"Well, yeah," I said. "It could be better if we could prove those bastards are lying, that they really didn't know they had the wrong ID, or that they did know, but they misled us on purpose." For the first time, I brought up the Hutchins session. "And they'll all have to follow us again tomorrow. I have exclusive quotes from the president. I sat with him in the Oval Office this afternoon while he unloaded to me."

I reviewed those quotes for them, and Martin made a move as if he might hug me, then apparently thought better of it. He clenched his fists together. "This keeps getting better," he said. "We are on a colossal roll."

The three of us fell quiet for a moment. It was nearing 4:00 P.M., so we divvied up the workload. As I've said, Havlicek is the best, most dogged reporter I know, but he writes as if English is a second language. With that in mind, Martin delicately suggested that he type up what he had and ship it to me, and I would combine it with my White House reaction and meld it into one story.

But even the best-laid plans sometimes fall victim to circumstance. As I settled in at my desk, before I even checked my voice mail and computer messages, the telephone rang.

"Jesus Christ, you're tough to reach. I thought you quit." It was the ever-personable Ron Hancock.

"Been in with the president all afternoon," I said.

"Yeah, right." He just kind of snickered. I was about to argue, but decided to save the energy.

"They're feeding you a line of crap from over here," he said. "It's bullshit. They were calling this victim Tony Clawson right up until six A.M., when the news broke from your paper that they had the wrong ID."

"Can you prove it?" I asked, starting to get excited but trying to keep myself in check. You don't want to show these guys too much, even if they're trying to help.

"I'm an FBI agent. Of course I can prove it. What's your fax number?"

I gave it to him, and he said, "Go stand by your machine. I'm sending you something right now. You don't know where you got it from. If you go before a grand jury, you'll tell them nothing. If you get called by the fucking director, you'll tell him nothing. If they stick bamboo shoots under your fingernails and make you eat boiled horse dick for dinner, you'll tell them you love it."

There are weeks, even months, in this strange business of newspaper reporting when absolutely nothing goes right—when the only guy who can prove a tip that you know is true has gone off hiking in the Himalayas and ends up freezing to death in his base camp, or when a blockbuster corruption story you've been working for a month ends up on the front page of the *Los Angeles Times* because you've decided to take an extra day of writing to smooth out the tone. There are, of course, those times when there just aren't any tips or good stories, and the whole world seems set in different shades of gray. It's times like this that your sisters call and say they haven't seen you in the paper much lately, is everything all right with your job?

I mention this because this obviously was not one of these times. In fact, on my way to the facsimile machine, unsure what I was about to receive, I kept quietly pumping my fist down at my side, as if I had just scored the winning basket for South Boston High in the Christmas tournament against Charlestown. This was better than sex, though truth be known, I was probably a bad judge of that, given the duration of time since I last had any.

By the time I got to the machine, it was already spitting out a plain sheet of white paper with the typewritten words: "For Jack Flynn. Personal and Confidential. For Jack Flynn's eyes only."

What followed was a detailed FBI internal case summary dated the day before, stamped late in the afternoon by whoever received it, which discussed the identity of the killer as Tony Clawson. Hancock, the rascal, had whited out some key parts about the investigation. Even while he was trying to help me out, he still had some allegiance to the FBI and didn't want the case blown. I respected that. I notified Martin and Havlicek. There was much backslapping and hand-wringing, and in the end, the three of us pored over every word of the story that I began by writing.

"Nice clean hit," Martin said when we shipped the story to the national desk. We were standing in his office. It was pitch-black outside. The bureau was mostly empty. The soft light of his desk lamp cast a warm glow. "I'll assume you're on an early flight to Boston tomorrow."

Before I could answer, Havlicek appeared in the doorway, smiling. "No *I* in the word *team*," he said.

I furrowed my brow at him, expressing confusion.

He shrugged. "I don't know what it means either. My Little League coach used to say it all the time. Just seemed to fit here. Let's head out. Drinks are on me."

"I'm in," Martin said.

I craved solitude and sleep, but couldn't really say no without looking like a curmudgeon. I was the youngest guy in the group, and so was expected to be a part of these things. "Where to?" I asked, as Martin put his coat on.

Havlicek said, "University Club. Love that bar."

So I guess the drinks would be on me, then.

"Give me five minutes," I said.

At my desk, I clicked through my electronic Rolodex to the telephone number for a dining and drinking establishment in Chelsea, Massachusetts, appropriately named the Pigpen.

"Sammy there," I said, in a tone as gruff and hard as I could gather, which wasn't particularly difficult to do.

The sound of tinny music was prominent in the background, as was the constant din of discussion, which, in the case of the Pigpen, I can guarantee you was taking place at no cerebral level. As if the guy who answered the phone was trying to play some part in a movie, he said, matching my gruffness with impressive skill, "Who wants to know?"

"Jack Flynn."

I heard the receiver hit a hard surface, probably the bar, which I silently expressed thanks wasn't the cradle. After a minute, someone picked up on another line, and the background music sounded a little louder.

"What the fuck do you want now? I thought I made you into some big-time Washington reporter these days."

A word about Sammy Markowitz: he is about sixty,

bald but for a little stubble around his crown. He has droopy eyes and bad teeth and smokes Camels all day, every day, sitting in a back booth of the Pigpen, which he owns, drinking Great Western champagne, playing gin rummy with any and all comers. He has a face that sags down to a formless chin, and all things considered, makes Don Rickles look like an Olympic athlete. He is also the most powerful force in Chelsea's most important industry—bookmaking—and therefore has the endless respect of the city's many hoodlums and wannabes, the entire police force, even the mayor, whom he graces with a $10,000 bonus every Christmas Eve.

Many years before, I dedicated weeks of my life to researching his bookie network, in a story I hoped to do about the anatomy of an illegal gaming operation. Truth be known, I was making very little progress penetrating the layers of insulation he had built around himself, and was about to abandon the story, when one night I arrived home to my Commonwealth Avenue apartment in Boston's Back Bay and was greeted on my doorstep by what looked like an Italian undertaker in need of a shave and some manners.

"Someone would like to see you," he said. "Come with me."

I didn't seem to have much choice, courtesy of the gun in his hand, so I went, thinking this would make a good lead in a story that I didn't actually have. He brought me to the Pigpen, to Markowitz's table, where I was told in no uncertain terms that I should drop my research and walk away from the story. Unfortunately, or maybe not, he had caught me on the tail end of a night out with the boys at the Capital Grille, and I was feeling the bravado that only a full bottle of Duckhorn cabernet can really instill.

"What's in it for me?" I asked him.

He paused, taken aback. Looking me up and down in a bit of disbelief, he eventually said, "What do you want?"

"Well, you're asking me to walk away from a good story that I've put a lot of work into. You have something else for me?"

He paused again, scratching at his face and exposing his bad teeth, then asked, "What about police corruption?"

"Police corruption is good. I like police corruption."

In a matter of days, he played a critical role laying out a story on a group of a dozen Chelsea police officers who had led a decade-long reign of terror on the community they were paid to protect, ranging from thievery to assault to torture to, in at least one case that I was able to report, murder. The story resulted in the indictment, conviction, and imprisonment of the dozen cops, the resignation of the police chief, and the recall of the mayor. I was named a finalist for the Pulitzer Prize, and Markowitz remained very much in business. I hadn't spoken to him since.

"I'm well, Sammy, thanks, and I hope you are too." No reaction, so I continued. "I need five minutes from you, and I need you in a cooperative frame of mind."

"What do you want from me?" he said, his tone and attitude largely void of the joy that I would expect to hear from anyone I hadn't talked to in this long.

I said, "I'm looking for someone, and it's crucial I find him. I've got more than a hunch you can help me."

"Yeah? Who?"

"I'm in your town tomorrow. What if I just stop by?"

"Yeah? Well, maybe I'm here, maybe I'm not."

He's always there, so I took that as something as close to an invitation as I'd get. "Good," I said. "I'll see you tomorrow. Drinks are on you."

Next I called Diego Rodriguez, an assistant United States attorney in Boston and a sometime source of information, leaving a message on his voice mail that I needed to speak to him tomorrow, in person, preferably in his office. And with that, a day that felt like it should be over was really just starting.

fourteen

FRANK SINATRA WAS SINGING "The Best Is Yet to Come" as I strode through the wide doors of the University Club grille and up to the bar, where Peter Martin and Steve Havlicek were talking animatedly about whether Carl Bernstein had received his proper due covering—or rather, uncovering—the Watergate affair. I had just been out in the hallway calling my dog sitter. My first thought coming into this conversation was that maybe I should bow out straight away and head home for the night.

But good manners prevailed, as they so often do, at least with me. Lyle was there, working his typical magic. Actually, what Lyle was doing was reaching deep into the coldest ice chest in the District of Columbia, pulling out bottles of Miller Highlife, and pouring them into frosted pilsner glasses. Seems like magic, especially when he's doing it for you.

Frank seemed to be hitting all his notes especially well in this particular rendition. It was my wedding song, and to that end, I felt a certain kinship to it, but I wasn't sure how I felt about hearing it here tonight. I guess all right, but the song can't help but bring back memories, fond and sad at the same time.

Katherine and I got married by a justice of the peace in a secluded corner of the Boston Public Garden as dusk settled on the second Saturday of October. The leaves were brilliant shades of orange and red. The air was slightly cool, perfumed with the sense of passage. About eighty friends and family members gathered to watch us, and after the brief ceremony, we all strolled up the Commonwealth Avenue mall two blocks to my friend Roger Schecter's condomonium, where we ate a catered feast on his moonlit roof deck, danced to a five-piece swing band, and toasted a future that shone as bright as all those autumn stars. Who knew then that just as stars flicker, futures do as well?

The wedding itself was part of a whole weekend of festivity. The night before, at our rehearsal dinner in the downstairs dining room of Locke-Ober, one of Boston's most venerable restaurants, I stood up with three glasses of cabernet already flowing through my system and made a toast. "I'm a cocky sort," I began, to some snickering from a couple of tables filled with my wiseass friends. "I expect to accomplish a lot in life. Maybe my newspaper reporting will make me famous. Maybe I'll win a prize. But this marriage," I said, "this relationship, is the greatest accomplishment I will ever have, and I plan to guard it and nurture it and always be more grateful for this than anything else in my life. I am in love," I said in a bit of uncharacteristic openness, "and this love is greater than I could ever have imagined."

Katherine, when I sat down, had tears in her eyes. So did my mother, but I think that's because the nice general manager, subtle as he was about it, had just delivered the bill. The room was silent, then filled with applause. Later, a group of friends headed to the bar at the Tennis & Racquet Club, where I was also a member in good standing. I remember Frank Sinatra singing "Get Me to the

Church on Time" as I ran into Katherine in the hallway to the rest rooms. I suggested to her that we follow tradition, that on this night we sleep apart, two remade virgins awaiting their big day. She put her hand on the back of my neck and pulled my lips down toward hers, kissing me hard. She pulled her mouth away ever so slightly, still holding my face close. "Not a chance in the world," she said. Okay.

Back to our wedding reception. Roger being Roger, and, well, the roof deck being his, he got up midway through the evening and gave a toast of his own. He raised the issue of his vast portfolio, as he sometimes tends to do—a fortune that extends into the tens of millions of dollars, all money made in timely investments in some Route 128 software and Internet startup companies. "For all my material wealth, for all I'm financially worth, I have nowhere near the happiness that these two have," he said. "Look at them. Look at what they have. They have a joy that no amount of money can ever buy. They are wealthier than I ever hope to be, and on this night, I'm not ashamed to proclaim my jealousy."

That was nice. I think I saw one of my sisters wipe a tear off her cheek. Later, I handed the pesky wedding photographer a twenty-dollar bill and told him to go buy himself a couple of Scotch whiskies around the corner at Joe's American Bar and Grille, and take that Polaroid with him. Katherine sidled up to me along the railing of the deck. The Hancock Building and Prudential Center were on one side of us, the Charles River on the other. She put her hand on my cheek in the only moment of privacy we had had all night. "You're the only thing I've ever wanted in my entire life," she said. She stared up at me, her eyes glistening and growing wet. After a minute, she stood on her toes and kissed me warmly on my ear, whispering, "I will love you, Jack Flynn, every minute of every hour until the day I die." That's when I felt a flashbulb go off again, and I thought to myself, My God, I love this woman, and boy, can that photographer toss back twenty bucks worth of Johnnie Walker fast.

"But it was Bernstein who had all the personality. People wanted to help him. People told him things they wouldn't tell Woodward." That was Havlicek, still engrossed in one of the more inane conversations that I had ever had the misfortune of hearing.

"Boys, boys," I said. "Why don't we sit at a table and start over on something that might actually matter to somebody."

My mood had quickly declined. But we sat down, and they shut up, and that seemed to make things a little better. A minute later our waiter stopped by the table with a basket of onion rings, some smoked salmon, and a couple of hamburgers. In the three minutes it had taken me to make my call, these guys had ordered the left side of the menu and put it on my tab. I started to say something, then figured, why bother. Havlicek's mouth was already filled. Martin was cutting up several onion rings with a fork and knife.

"Carlos, could you bring me over a swordfish sandwich?" I said.

Havlicek looked up from his plate, alarmed. "They have swordfish sandwiches? I didn't see any swordfish sandwiches on the menu."

"Not on the menu," I said, immaturely restaking my claim to a club that I felt sliding away. "They make them up for me, special."

There was a pause, then Martin asked, "What time are you heading north in the morning?"

I said, "I figured I'd grab the six A.M. flight, get me in around seven-thirty. I'll be on the ground reporting by nine. This voice seemed to think that we didn't have a whole lot of time to waste on this thing."

"How we supposed to know?" Havlicek added, accidentally spitting a caper next to my fork, which I found more than unappetizing.

"We don't. We trust," I said.

They seemed to be thinking about that for a while, as if trust, to newspaper people, anyway, was such a novel idea. They ate. My swordfish arrived. Martin eventually asked, expansively, "So who is this guy and why does he want to help us so bad?"

We didn't answer, so Martin asked, "He some conspiracy theorist with a few good hunches? He someone in the White House, one of Cole's old loyalists trying to kick up trouble? Is it some agent of Stanny Nichols, like these guys Graham and Wilkerson, trying to leak out their opposition research, and if so, why be so covert?"

Havlicek looked down at his plate, I assumed in thought, but I realized it was because he was sopping up the last drops of burger juice and mustard with the remnants of a roll. "Don't know," he said. "But maybe we're working this puzzle backward. Maybe we ought to be trying to figure out what he has, and see if what he has holds up, before we worry about who he is. His identity could be the least of our issues, provided his information is any good."

Havlicek meant this in a friendly way, three guys sitting around a table with a few beers and some red meat discussing a good story. But Martin took it as a slight challenge to his intellect, as editors tend to do. When you're not on the street working a story, when you're not writing for the paper or producing anything of great consequence, you tend to get territorial and defensive about the power and value of your ideas, mostly because that's all you have.

"Look, I know what matters," Martin said. "I'm just figuring maybe we can shortcut this thing. And more than that, I'm just curious over who's spending so much time and money trying to help us out."

"So am I," I said, interjecting in my role as diplomat. "I'm curious as to who this guy is and what he's got. Keep in mind, it's me he's following around. It's me who was shot at over at the Newseum."

Carlos came over dangling dessert menus, asking if we were interested, prompting Havlicek to just about jump out of his chair at him. Frank was singing "Hello Dolly" by now, and very well, I might add. Waiters were carrying plates of prime rib and shrimp. The room was filled with the gentle clink of china, the hum of conversation, staccato bursts of laughter. Out of the corner of my eye, I caught an unusual sight—unusual, at least, for this particular club: a beautiful woman coming through the doorway, alone, and taking a place at a corner table. I turned to look, and my heart almost came through my chest. That was no beautiful woman, it was Samantha Stevens, special agent with the FBI, smiling at me from across the room as she slid her chair in, crossed her long legs in front of her, and gently placed her purse on the floor.

• • •

If you think it's tough to get Steve Havlicek out of a dining room when a free dessert is still on the line, think again. It's not just tough, it's impossible, a feat I wouldn't even try with a John Deere tractor and a pair of field oxen.

So with the last bits of their chocolate mousse cake gone, the boys finally took leave. I made my way across the room to Stevens's table, flashed her my attempt at a Frank Sinatra smile, and said, "Didn't realize you were a member here."

She was drinking red wine on a tab I had carefully and quietly established for her with the waiter, and reading the *Wall Street Journal*—the Money and Investing section, to be exact. "I've always wanted to go to a bar where they pump testosterone in through the heating vents," she said, not exactly answering my question. "Let me ask you, has anyone ever gored themselves on the moose antlers?"

"Not that I know of," I said. "Actually, the women members here, and yes, we do have women members, they all seem to really like the moose. I'm not sure if that says more about the aesthetics of the moose or the quality of our women membership."

She gave me an exaggerated frown, comfortable enough, it seemed, that she didn't have to laugh at every joke that ever so slightly missed the mark. With another clever introduction out of the way, I took a seat at the table and said, "This is an unexpected surprise."

"Most surprises are unexpected," she replied. Good one. I made a mental note to stop using that cliché after all these years.

She swirled the wine around in her glass and said,

"Sorry to intrude on your sanctuary, but I need to talk to you in confidence again. May I?"

"Of course you can," I said.

She stared down at the wine rolling around the edges of her glass as she nonchalantly twirled the stem in her hand. After a moment, she looked up at me and said, "I'm being excluded from every major decision on a case that is supposed to be partly mine. I don't think I'm even being shown working copies of any reports. Drinker's barely speaking to me, and he seems to have carte blanche to do whatever he wants on this case, in whatever way he wants to do it. I don't even think my boss is clued in. Drinker speaks only to Callinger. I think they're the only two guys who know what's going on."

I let that sit out there as I processed it. I was still leery of being played for the fool, and harbored suspicions that this was some sort of a setup, an attempt to get me to divulge that I was working with an anonymous source, and maybe even Ron Hancock. I reminded myself, You don't know this woman all that well.

"Do you and Drinker talk every day?"

She shrugged. "He might stop by my office and ask me to do something like call this militia outpost or some gun store or something that seems peripherally connected, at best. He's not really one to make extensive chitchat even in the easiest of times."

"And you're really not seeing reports? You think about going to Callinger?"

"I did," she said. "I said it was bothering me, the way this investigation was being handled. I said I felt cut out of the loop on it. You know what he said? He told me to just stick with it, that it would be over soon enough, and not to worry about how it's going, that there were already plenty enough people worrying for me."

The chairman was singing "Fly Me to the Moon" now on what must have been some double album collection. A few guys at a nearby table had sparked up some pretty expensive cigars, something mild, something Dominican, from the scent of them. There was silence between us as Carlos stopped by to pick up our empty glasses and replace them with full ones.

Stevens took a sip of her fresh wine and said, "I'm hopeful, perhaps naively so, that if you have any information, even unsubstantiated information, about FBI wrongdoing on this case, that you might pass it on to me to investigate."

That was a tough one. I could just tell her, No, you're wrong. But why? And more important, why brick off a potential source of valuable information? Reporting was often about negotiation, and I still hadn't figured out where I was in this particular situation. So I lied, in the name of good journalism.

"I don't have anything right now, except what I've written for tomorrow morning's paper, which is a story quoting from an internal document saying that the FBI was identifying the shooter as Tony Clawson at least as recently as yesterday afternoon."

She just stared at me with that one, then took a sip of wine, absently lifting the glass to her lips.

"Right now," I said, "everything I know, my readers know. I tend to be like that. I don't keep secrets very long."

"Well, there's no way that I'm going to just sit back and watch while this investigation spirals out of control," she said. "It's an embarrassment for the bureau."

She looked me in the eyes and added, "Let me ask you something. That story of yours today. Do you know who the federal informant is?"

An interesting question, meaning, apparently, that she didn't.

I replied, "Yes. I agreed not to publish the identity so the informant wouldn't be killed, as could well be the case if word got out."

She nodded, still looking at me. She asked, "Is it Daniel Nathaniel?" The question betrayed her profound irrelevance in this investigation, or at least I thought it did.

I didn't answer. I only looked back at her, in silence. She added, "If it is, don't say anything."

I didn't, and she eventually looked away.

She spread a hard gaze over my face and said, "Then I have something else."

Her tone had changed, as did the look in her eyes. I felt a lump form in my throat, as if something were about to happen, something of significance. My impulse was to blurt out the question, What? but I stopped myself, not wanting to appear too eager, too needy. I coolly met her gaze and said, "Go ahead."

"I got access to some computer files." She hesitated and said, "We're on background here, right?" I nodded. She went on. "The files detail all federally paid informants, meaning, if someone's on our payroll for giving us information, they're recorded in the ledgers. Obviously, this information is sensitive, so not everyone is listed by name. Some just have descriptions, like, I don't know, 'Miami dockworker.' You know?"

She paused to collect herself. "The point is, Drinker told me about telling you of how Daniel Nathaniel is a federal informant. Well, he gave me the information in one of his rare written reports. Anyways, this guy Nathaniel, he's not on the list, despite Drinker's assertion to you that he was. I can't find his name, and I can't find anyone who fits the description. There's not even a militia member on our ledgers from Idaho."

I drank that in for a moment, stunned at the baldness of Drinker's lie and the fact that his colleague Stevens would call him on it, at least with me. What did it mean? If Drinker was fabricating, it meant that he worked with Nathaniel to concoct the story about the Wyoming militia, in all likelihood to hide something else. What was it they were trying to hide? That was the real question.

Much as I wanted to pursue it right there and then with Stevens, some inner voice told me not to. I think that voice was simply one of distrust. "That's, well, more than interesting," I said, dropping it at that.

We sat in a long stretch of silence, until she said, far more conversationally, "You ever have a week where everything in the world is out to screw you over?" She half smiled.

"Actually," I said, "I've had years like that."

She nodded sympathetically. "So I'm in Nordstrom's last night. I'm over there buying my father a birthday present, and I'm in the men's shop. I catch sight of this guy who looks so familiar that my heart realizes who he is before my brain does. You know what I mean? There's a woman with him, and she's holding a pair of pants up to his waist while he's pulling on a new suit jacket. They're smiling, and they're so happy. And it hits me like a club over the head, that's my ex-husband, and he's with another woman."

"Wow," I said, more for my own shock than in empathy with hers. I couldn't picture her with a husband, never mind an ex-husband, mostly because I had always associated her with being single and available. This opened up an entirely new way of looking at her. So with nothing constructive to add at this point, and feeling slightly voyeuristic, I asked, "What did you do?"

"I was going to just turn away, but he saw me. We met eyes, and he called to me, 'Hey, Sam, how are you?' I had no real choice but to go over, much as I just wanted to crawl into a hole. I walk over there, and the woman, she's still holding the fucking pants up to his waist, just kind of standing there not knowing what's going on. We talked a bit, though I'm not sure about what. My mind was just swimming. He introduced me to her, but just by name. He didn't say, 'Julia, I want you to meet my ex-wife, Samantha. Sam, I want you to meet my girlfriend, Julia.' I don't think I said more than a dozen words, and I just got out of there. I didn't even buy my father's present. I punched the dashboard of my car so hard I almost broke my hand."

I felt myself recovering from my own surprise, at least enough to ask a couple more worthwhile questions. She was facing me with her elbows on the table, her chin resting in her hands. She looked strangely comfortable unloading to me.

"When's the last time you saw him?"

"About a year. I hadn't seen him since we walked out of divorce court last fall and shook hands good-bye."

"You obviously miss him," I said, thinking the statement trite just as the words left my lips.

"I don't know if that's necessarily true," she said. "I

think I miss my old life, or what I thought my old life would become, which was happily married, looking forward to starting a family, sharing, growing old with someone. Staying in love. Or maybe just not being alone."

"What's his name?" I asked.

"Eric." I hate the name Eric, but thought it best not to mention that.

She said, "You know, I'm not pining for him or anything like that. I'm really not. To be honest about it, I don't even think about him all that much anymore."

I started to say something, though exactly what, I'm not sure. She kept talking right over me, which I think was a good thing.

"It's just weird, seeing this guy, the guy I married, the guy I figured I'd be with for the rest of my life, to have children with, to send them through college, to retire with, it's just so fucking weird to see him with another person, like I'm so replaceable, like he's moved on, found something better, and I'm stuck, struggling with myself, no different than I was before. Or if I am different, then I'm just worse. That's what's so bad about all this."

I had half a mind to reach out and put my hand over hers, to comfort her with my eyes, to let her know she wasn't as alone as she was feeling. I held back for a variety of reasons, one of them being the continuing suspicion that I was being fed a line, another being the general inappropriateness of a reporter and a federal agent having any sort of emotional, never mind physical, involvement.

Still, I'm not a mule, so I told her, "Look, I hope you don't mind me saying this, but my bet is you're not like you were before, that you've grown a lot since you two split. The only difference is that you haven't found any-one yet, and maybe he has. And maybe you haven't found anyone because you're a little more discriminating. You don't want to make those same mistakes."

I paused, then brushed against inappropriateness, unable to contain myself. "I mean, look at you," I said. "You're stunning looking. You're a goddamned FBI agent, and a well-regarded one at that. You will have more opportunities to meet men, and good men, than you could ever imagine. The right one will come along, prob-ably when you least expect it." Like, say, right now.

She stared straight ahead. Around us, the grille was gradually clearing out, the laughter giving way to the background music. She looked up at me and said, "I know you're right. Sometimes it's just lonely."

"I know lonely," I said. "I've driven off to the hospital with a pregnant wife about to have a baby girl, and I drove home that night all alone, both of them dead."

She locked her eyes on mine and said, "I'm so sorry. I know that. My issues, they're trivial in comparison."

I said, "No, we all have our own issues, our own prob-lems, our own obstacles to overcome. You mind me ask-ing what went wrong with you guys?"

She thought for a minute, contorting her face ever so slightly so the skin was drawn even tighter over her cheek-bones. She said, "I don't want to go there now."

I felt a slight rebuke, until she quickly added, "Some other time I'll tell you."

"Check, Mr. Flynn?" That was Carlos, in another dis-play of his impeccable timing. I said, "Yeah, that would be great."

• • •

The last drops of distant daylight had long since drained from the early winter sky as Baker and I arrived at Rose Park in Georgetown for what used to be our regular game of fetch, a ritual that I had missed this last week because of the press of work and the looming danger. Used to be, this was my hour of calm. Out in the park, in the chill air, with nothing more than a dog who bore a remarkable resemblance to a small golden bear and the distant flicker of television lights in people's windows, all the bullshit seemed to give way to my own clear thoughts. And it was during this time out here when I so often came to realize where I had been and where I still had to go. Perhaps foolishly, I decided on that night to give it another go.

Baker tends to show his emotions more than me, despite his English lineage. As soon as we stepped on the soft grass, he tossed the tennis ball excitedly from his mouth, gawked as it hit my shoes, stepped back four paces, and sat, the look on his face one of unbridled joy at the event that was to come. I wished for the millionth time that I could get as excited about something, anything, as Baker did about shagging down this ball.

For kicks, I sometimes pretended I was playing quarterback for the New England Patriots, directing the team toward victory with my head and my heart. I don't want to throw the term *multitalented* around too loosely, but let's face it, I'm a full-service guy. On my first throw, he scooped the ball up in his mouth and whipped his head around as if he were breaking the ball's neck, if it had one, which obviously it didn't, but that's not really the point. That instinctual feat accomplished, he tossed it back at my shoes and set out across the field again as I led him by ten feet or so with another perfect throw. He caught it on the first bounce. Grogan to Vataha. We were quite a team.

Standing there searching for the kind of peace that comes with perspective, I decided to bring a little misery to my night and take a quick inventory of all that was going wrong. I had an enormous story that seemed to be slipping out of my control. I had an anonymous source who might be about to send me on a wild-goose chase or into the throes of danger. I had someone taking an occasional shot at me. I had a fetching FBI agent with wondrous hair and pouty lips showing an inordinate amount of interest in me, though I wasn't yet sure if this comes under what was going wrong or what might be right. Too early to tell which way it was cutting. And I should add, at that moment, I also had an ominous-looking man in a tan trench coat walking purposefully across the otherwise empty field, heading exactly in my direction. I suspected I might soon be adding his visit to my list.

In regards to the approaching man, Baker spotted him just seconds after I did, and, being the faithful protector of all things Jack, bounded angrily across the field, barked loudly, and then grabbed the man's leg, bringing him down in a heap of blood and pain.

Actually, I lie. Baker joyfully trotted up to the guy, dropped the ball at his feet, and stepped back in wondrous anticipation of the throw he assumed was to come. The man kept walking, ignoring him.

"Be careful," I called out. "He's vicious."

"I'll be all right," the man said, getting closer, his voice, familiar, just slightly louder than conversational.

"I was talking to my dog," I said with a shallow laugh.

And out of the dark and into my life once again stepped

Kent Drinker, assistant director of the FBI. Coincidence? I wasn't sure.

I added, for no particular reason, "You really should have called ahead and made an appointment. I'm rather busy out here."

"I don't need a whole lot of time," Drinker said.

That was good news. It was Thursday night, the end of a long day, and the dual feelings of exhaustion and uncertainty mingled in my mind and created an uncharacteristic sense of uneasiness, the type of mood when you begin questioning everything you've ever done for reasons that you're unable to fully understand.

I said, flat, "What can I do for you this fine night?"

"I was hoping I might get some help and give some help," Drinker said.

That sounded interesting, though rehearsed. I picked up the ball and tossed it for Baker, then watched his form as he hurtled across the field in pursuit. I turned my gaze to Drinker and regarded him for a moment. He was tall and athletic, with looks that spoke to the word *Everyman*, or at least to that of an everyday federal agent. He had close-cropped hair that I would bet he cut every couple of weeks. His eyes were gray. My guess is that he lived a spare life of simple pleasures, when he pursued pleasure at all. I'm not sure why, but I pictured his wife as a southerner, probably from one of the Carolinas, old-fashioned bordering on obedient, a stay-at-home mother, as if there was any other choice.

"Everything I have, I think I've given you already," I said. "My impression is that I was a pretty good witness, despite what you might think."

There was a long pause between us, broken only by

Baker once again presenting me with the ball, and me once again throwing it.

"Look, I've dealt with reporters before," Drinker said finally. "I suspect you know that already. And I was more than helpful in my day. I also got more than burned. My whole fucking career got fried. And now I've been given a rare second chance in the bureau. I'm out here doing the best I can. I'm trying to solve a presidential assassination attempt after the Secret Service put six bullets into my prime suspect and rendered him useless to me. And I have you and your paper staring over my shoulder second-guessing me every step of the way, getting in the way of a good investigation."

He paused for just long enough that I thought he was done, then added, "I need some room. I need some time. And I need some help."

This was curious. I considered his words, then said, "I give you some time and space and whatever help it is you're talking about, what do I get in return?"

"I can help you on this case, just like I helped that reporter out in L.A., only I'm hoping you're a little more loyal, or at least reliable to your sources."

I said, "I think Benedict Arnold was slightly more loyal than the last reporter you dealt with."

He almost smiled in spite of himself. I looked him over for a moment. Despite my finely honed abilities in the area of character judgment, I couldn't get a full handle yet on Kent Drinker. I wasn't sure if he was driving events in this case, or if the events were driving him, whether he was mishandling the investigation or deftly trying to conceal some larger truth. Not knowing hurt. It left me unsure whether he was friend or foe. I wanted to believe the former. My natural tendencies always caused me to suspect the latter, especially from public officials.

The raw facts were these: he had misidentified the presidential assassin. He had showed an inordinate amount of interest in who had called my hospital room. He had apparently consorted with a militia leader to concoct a story about motive, and then lied to me about it. About an hour ago, I had learned that he might have lied to me about that militia leader being a paid informant. He had a direct line to the president of the United States. He had iced out even his top subordinate, Stevens, and was seemingly a one-man show in trying to solve the case.

Or trying not to solve it. I didn't know, and thus, my dilemma. And this thought popped into the front of my mind from one of the deep recesses: had he really iced out Stevens, or was I being played for a moron? Wouldn't be the first time, though that's not really the point here.

He kicked softly at a small stone in the field and said, "You drew too hasty a conclusion on Tony Clawson."

"Yeah?" I replied, my tone ranging from disbelief toward the incredulous.

Drinker ignored that and said, "You were right about some parts, wrong about others."

I played this through the journalistic calculator that was my mind. "Let's see," I began. "Essentially, you publicly named a suspect who didn't even have the same eye color as the guy the Secret Service shot dead at Congressional. Help me out here with what we might have gotten wrong."

He asked, "Can I talk to you off the record?"

This again. I said, "I'd rather talk on the record and keep things on the up and up."

Drinker stayed silent for a moment.

"Once more, I'd like to, but I can't," he said. "I'd be fired in an hour, especially with my history. I want to stress, I have some information that's important for you to know."

Well, I didn't know whether to believe him, believe Stevens, or believe my own instincts, which told me not to believe anyone. The worst he could be doing was lying, so I told him, "Okay, on background, attributable to a law enforcement official."

"No way. There are only about three people who know what I know. I'd be fingered immediately." He paused and added, "My advice would be to take what I have and try to confirm it on your own."

There was a lengthy silence between us as I mulled my options, which were limited in number and scope. The last thing I expected on this night was for Drinker, who I regarded with little more than suspicion, to offer an enduring alliance and perhaps give me my biggest break on the case. Obviously I was wary for every good reason, but it wouldn't serve me well just then to shut him off.

In the quiet, Baker settled down in front of us and chewed on a stick. I looked up briefly and saw that the sky was now a solid sheet of black.

"All right, off the record," I said.

Without much hesitation, Drinker started talking as if I had just turned on a spout. "We have a fucked-up situation. I'll admit up front, this shooting has nothing to do with the militia. You have us cold on that. And the dead shooter is not the Tony Clawson we offered up in that Home Depot ID, the California drifter. Good work on that, by the way. Sometimes I wish my people were as thorough."

"So you were lying last time when you told me Nathaniel was a paid informant?"

"I was protecting the truth."

I wasn't quite sure how to respond. So I didn't.

He continued, "It's a different Tony Clawson. And it's his background that's so interesting and so potentially devastating, especially to my agency."

Okay, so this was getting better by the syllable. I stayed silent, hoping the dead air would prod him to continue.

He stayed silent too. FBI agents must learn reporter tricks up at Quantico or something. I finally said, "Devastating, how?"

He shook his head purposefully. "Can't go that far," he said. He paused, then added, "Find out who Tony Clawson is, or was, and you'll know exactly what I mean."

Everyone had a suggestion. I thought of the words of the anonymous caller early that morning. *Learn about Curtis Black, and you will have dug to the core of this case.*

Baker came swaggering over and dropped the tennis ball at Drinker's feet. Drinker looked at me, then picked up the ball, gave it an underhand toss, and said to the dog, "Go get it," as if he needed instruction.

In the momentary silence, the voice of my anonymous source filled my mind again. *Nothing is as it seems.* A good warning, it increasingly seemed. So the obvious question now, beyond the obvious questions about Clawson, was what in God's name Curtis Black had to do with Tony Clawson.

Drinker turned his attention from the dog to me. "I need to ask you one more time, and I'm hoping you'll decide to cooperate. Who was that on the telephone in your hospital room that day?"

I didn't utter a word. In the void, Drinker added, "Look, I'll admit, we have a full-court press on you in trying to find the identity of your caller. I tried the hard approach. Stevens is trying the soft approach. You've been more than resistant. Here's the truth: I think I know who called you that day. That person's been in touch with you since. That person can screw up this entire investigation and, in effect, screw up the entire story that I'm more than ready to help you with. You help me, I help you, and you'll in fact be helping yourself."

Well, note especially his reference to Stevens, because that's the last clear sentence I heard him say. After that, it was as if I had just been kneed in the gut. So perhaps my first instincts were right: Stevens and Drinker really were in this together, trying to play with my mind. Or perhaps not. My head was starting to hurt. So much for the mind-clearing benefits of my evening dog walk.

I said, "Truth is, I really don't know who was on the phone, and that's all I'm saying about it right now." I regarded this as my best strategy. If I gave up any more details, my value to Drinker would likely lessen, and I'd receive less help. Simple journalist survival skills.

Drinker looked me over carefully. "There's a lot at stake for both of us," he said. With that, he turned around silently and walked back across the field from whence he came, his tan raincoat fading and then melding into the dark of the night. He left behind a couple of questions: Who the hell is this Tony Clawson, and is Drinker as good a friend as he wants me to believe? I knew then that the answer to the former would probably reap the answer to the latter. Now it was just a matter of doing the work.

CURTIS BLACK SAT IN the front of the van as if he were watching a movie, transfixed by the developments unfolding on the screen. And just like a movie, everything was proceeding as if it were all part of a tightly written script.

The driver stood casually beside the armored Wells Fargo truck as if he didn't have a worry in the world, oblivious to everything going on around him, including Black's attention. He even pulled a cigarette out of his shirt pocket and lit it, took a few puffs, let it fall to the pavement, and stubbed it out under his black shoe. His cohort came from the back of the van, pulled out a dolly, and walked into the Shawmut Bank, where he would collect the day's receipts. If all went according to plan, he should be visible in the door in about seven minutes.

"Be alert," Black said into the small microphone pinned to the wrist of his shirt. Inside the van, the three men crouched against the back door.

Black continued staring out the window. The hazy dusk had grown thick, made to seem even darker by the moonless sky. A mist gathered on the windshield. The streets appeared slick with water, reflecting the glare of car headlights and store signs. All in all, Black thought to himself, ideal conditions for a heist.

Black regarded the armored car driver for a moment. He was about forty-five, maybe fifty years old, ruddy from all that time standing outdoors in weather just like this, stout, boyish, as if his wife made his lunch for him every day and packed it in a brown paper bag. He had big forearms, probably from lifting bags of money back at the warehouse. Imagine that? Black thought to himself. Here's a guy making $10 an hour, and he spends his days lugging other people's money around to the point that it probably hurts his back. Life can be ironic, and irony can be cruel.

Black shot a quick glance at his watch. The guard had been inside the bank for four minutes now. According to the plan, he should be approaching the door in roughly three minutes. Black's three men continued to crouch against the van door.

"Sanchez, come on up," Black said into the microphone.

The driver of the getaway car opened his door and walked up to the side of the van, his ski mask on top of his head like a wool hat, with the part that covered his face not yet pulled down. He stood beside the van, waiting, looking at the ground, concealing his face from any passersby.

And just as planned, the guard appeared inside the door of the bank, pushing a dolly with a duffel bag. He turned around and opened the door with his backside.

"Showtime," Black announced into his wrist. "Go."

In a blaze of action, the rear door of the van burst open. The three men jumped out into the moist winter air, their black masks shielding their faces. On the pavement, they fanned out, then sprinted toward the guard at the bank door from different angles. There was to be no mistake: this was a relentless commando raid. Shoot one attacker, and there were still two others to finish the job.

"Freeze," Stemple yelled. The guard jerked his face up and was instinctively reaching for the semiautomatic pistol in his side holster when Rocco hit him with a body slam at full running speed. The guard sprawled out on the pavement, dazed. When he rolled over to get up, Cox was already on top of him, stripping his gun away, then pushing a jackboot down on his throat.

"You even move your tongue and I'll fucking rip your fucking Adam's apple out," Cox seethed. The guard stared upward, helpless and wide-eyed.

Meantime, at the van, Sanchez yanked his mask down over his face and approached the driver of the armored car from behind. His sole job was to immobilize the driver, preferably by putting him in a headlock, and knocking him unconscious with a knee to the face. Black had chosen Sanchez for this role because of his immense physical stature. He was six feet, two inches tall, some 220 pounds of raw muscle, a veritable mountain of a man.

Black watched from the seat of the van as Sanchez headed toward the armored truck at a controlled but rapid clip. He saw the driver reach for his sidearm. Just as the driver pulled his weapon out, Sanchez made contact, grabbing his coat and preparing for the headlock.

It was misting out, and that presented an unexpected problem. The drops of moisture had balled up on the driver's water-repellent jacket. Sanchez's hands slipped, causing a couple of seconds of uncertainty.

The driver, considerably shorter, squirmed loose. Sanchez

lost his balance—not enough to fall, but plenty enough to leave a gaping canyon of opportunity for any decent shot. Barely stopping to aim, the driver fired his gun in the direction of the bandits in front of the bank door, a wild shot but a shot nonetheless. The report felt like an explosion to Curtis Black, the sound echoing off the facades of the ancient stores and carrying down rain-slickened Hanover Street like a rolling ball of thunder.

As Black sat with his panoramic view from the front seat of the van, the moment seemed to freeze before his eyes. Sanchez stood a few feet from the driver, trying to regain his balance. The driver stood with the gun in his hand, taking aim again at the bandits. By the bank door, Stemple and Rocco, grabbing the duffel bag filled with money to lug to the getaway car, had fallen to their knees at the sound of the shot. Cox took shelter by crouching down behind the incapacitated guard.

Any and all semblance of control had been lost. Every minute of meticulous planning had become nothing more than a distant, disconnected memory, irrelevant to the events at hand. Never in the life of Curtis Black had he felt the raw terror he did at this instant, watching his heist spiral out of control, his destiny in the hands of four men he neither knew nor trusted.

He watched as Sanchez regained his balance, then shifted his body weight in preparation to lunge at the gun-wielding driver. On the sidewalk, he saw Stemple and Rocco reaching inside their jackets, though now he couldn't tell who was who. They both wore those ominous ski masks. They were both dressed identically.

"Hold fire," Black yelled into his wrist microphone. "Hold your fucking fire."

Crack.

Another shot, another echo rolling down Hanover Street. Passersby screamed, though Black hardly heard them. They dove behind cars, scattered down the sidewalk like frightened animals. Black scanned the scene frantically, looking for the source of the shot, afraid to know the answer. There was no good answer.

That one second felt like an hour. Black watched in horror as the driver dropped his gun, then crumpled to the wet pavement. Blood began flowing from a grotesque cavity in his neck, the liquid trickling out into a puddle of crimson that formed beneath the man's face. Sanchez stood over him for a moment, looked up at Black in the van, then bolted back toward the getaway car.

Stemple and Rocco ran toward the car with the duffel bag, their bodies slung low to the ground by the weight of the money. Cox crouched down low to the guard, lifted his gun up over his head, and swung it down violently at the guard's face, crushing his nose. He then stood up and sprinted after Stemple and Rocco.

Black flung the driver's-side door open on the van, lowered his head to conceal his features, and raced the ten yards back to the getaway car, where he snapped the rear door open and settled into the backseat. Rocco and Stemple flung the money into the trunk and got into the back beside him. Cox settled into the front. Sanchez drove. The group squealed away, a tiny band of silence amid so much chaos.

Success and failure. Maybe a million dollars in the trunk. One man dead, five lives in so much jeopardy.

In a parking lot at the end of the Boston Fish Pier, where the group switched getaway cars from the Lincoln to a stolen station wagon, Black paused for a moment in the darkening night.

"Who killed him?" he asked, in something just short of a shout. "Who killed him?"

No answer.

The new driver, who had met them at the pier, took in the scene with panicked eyes. It wasn't supposed to be like this, he knew. The mood was supposed to be one of restrained celebration. It was his job to sweep them quietly out of town.

"What happened?" the driver asked nervously.

No answer. Rather, the men silently but hurriedly folded themselves into the new vehicle, ignoring the question. Stemple paused at the door, turned around, and flung his gun far into the harbor. Black could only shake his head. What was the point now? he wondered. Would it do any good to merely yell at a man who had just committed cold-blooded murder? Instead, he leaned against a light pole and vomited into a plastic trash bag. His life, he knew, would never be the same.

fifteen

A THIN, COLD MIST descended on downtown Chelsea, the tiny droplets balling up on my coat and in my hair, leaving a sheen on the potholed street so that the gaudy yellow neon lights of the Wall Street Check Cashing store reflected every which way I looked.

Grown men, mostly Asians and a few Hispanics, gathered aimlessly on street corners, some of them talking loudly, others just staring straight ahead. In front of the Goodwill store, one of the only successful businesses on this strip of Broadway, a man with a makeshift bullhorn read from the Bible, emphasizing the word *Christ* whenever he got the chance, almost singing it. No one seemed to notice him. On the street a few feet away, an ambulance slowly rode by, its siren blasting at full throttle. The man with the bullhorn yelled above the din.

With this as my backdrop, I pushed against the heavy wooden door into the dark haze of the Pigpen, which looked and smelled just as I had remembered it from a few years before, which is to say dirty and of stale beer. There was a fog from cigarette smoke both fresh and old. Wan daylight filtered through tiny, yellow Plexiglas windows. Outside, the sound of the siren faded as the ambulance rolled down the street. Inside, the bartender looked me up and down and said, "You need something?"

"Sammy around?" I asked, quickly figuring that small talk wouldn't get me very far in this establishment. A couple of barflies, middle-aged men with stubble on their faces and defeat in their eyes, looked my way. Across the room, I saw Sammy Markowitz sitting at his usual booth in the back, smoking a cigarette, flipping through a sheaf of papers that I assumed were the prior day's bookmaking profits. A banker's lamp glowed on his table.

"Not here," the bartender said.

I said, "You must have missed him come in, because he's sitting right over there." I began walking in Markowitz's direction when a sizable gentleman in an ill-fitting black sport jacket and a T-shirt stood up from a bar stool and blocked my path.

"Like the man says," he told me, "Mr. Markowitz's not here right now."

It's never easy, this thing called life. Or maybe it's just the journalism part that always seems so tough. I was face-to-face with this goon, so close I could smell the beer and beef jerky on his breath. I was too short of time to be nice and too smart to be rude. So I said to him, "Perhaps you could go tell Mr. Markowitz that his friend Jack Flynn is here. We talked on the telephone yesterday, and he invited me to stop in."

The man, who bore a remarkable resemblance to an ape, if it would ever occur to an ape to dress this bad and hang out at a bar all day, looked me up and down. The synapses in his tiny brain were firing so hard that his whole head looked like it might well explode, all in an attempt to calculate what awful things might happen to him if he approached Sammy Markowitz and announced the presence of a visitor named Jack Flynn. Finally the bartender said, "You stay with him, Sal. I'll see if the boss is here."

A minute later, common sense and patience prevailed as I was led toward the back of the restaurant, where Sammy Markowitz stood to greet me, clasped my hand, and said, "To think, a few years ago I almost had you killed. You've turned out so handsome."

Understand that this man was a known murderer, someone who, as mob legend had it, once broke an adversary's neck with his bare hands in the middle of a game of bocce, mostly because of one bad roll. He recruited teenagers to a life of crime and suffering. He wrought havoc with his illegal bookmaking, destroying entire families, leading supposed friends to bankruptcy, making them virtual slaves to his organization with high-interest loans.

And yet, I'll admit, there was something terribly winning about him. Perhaps it was his appearance, which, as I've said, was Rickles-like. He seemed oddly meek for a guy who struck such fear. He could be self-deprecating. And most of all, he could just be funny, as if he was playing the role of a mob chief in a situation comedy, understanding all the ironies, knowing his own faults, not taking any of it, or himself, all that seriously.

"My dog thanks you for rethinking your plan," I said. "And so do I."

We engaged in the typical small talk, about the Celtics and the new Boston mayor and a few reporters who were covering the organized crime beat. He extended sympathies over Katherine's death. His own wife had died of cancer in recent months, and I expressed regret over that.

Then he said to me, rather unceremoniously, "So what do you want?"

"Curtis Black," I said, examining his face carefully while I spoke the name. His eyes shifted a little bit, but I couldn't be sure if that counted as a reaction. "I need to find Curtis Black." I paused for half a beat, then added. "This one's important to me."

He looked at me for a moment, matching my stare, an unlit cigarette dangling on his lower lip. He picked up his lighter off the table, a heavy, gold-plated thing, monogrammed with the letters *SG*, and lit it, watching the smoke from his first exhale float aimlessly toward the ceiling. Finally, he said to me, in no particular tone of voice, "Don't know him."

"Bullshit," I said, and was about to continue, but he cut me off.

"Hey, hey, keep that down," he said, a small smile forming at the edges of his lips. "People don't talk to me like that, especially in here."

"You know him," I said. "And like I said, I don't ask a whole lot from you. You haven't heard from me in three years. But I need you right now. I'm asking for your help."

I made a mental note that should I keep experiencing this ascending fame, and should I someday have the occasion to write my memoirs for some sort of seven-figure advance, I might well leave this scene out, this pathetic groveling before a known killer.

Markowitz put one finger up in the air, and one of his goons shot over to the table about a second later. Without ever looking at him, Markowitz said, "Bring me another split." To me: "Why are you asking about him?"

Truth be known, I couldn't really say, mostly because I didn't quite know yet. In fact, I was hoping he could tell me.

I said, "He's into something. I'm not 100 percent sure what it is yet, but I know it's something of consequence."

The man in black returned with a thin bottle of sparkling wine, Best Western, and emptied it into a lowball glass that was sitting in front of Markowitz. He walked away without offering anything to me.

Markowitz looked unimpressed by the whole scene, his vacant eyes just kind of gazing back at mine. He asked, flat, "What do you know about him already?"

"Very little."

And that was the truth. Before I got on the airplane, I had called Dorothy at the *Record* library and asked her to pull up anything and everything she could find on Curtis Black. She left me a voice mail saying she had only found two short news briefs, both of them from the *Record*. The first one was about the arrest of Curtis Black and several other men from Boston's North Shore for a 1979 armored car heist in Boston's North End in which a guard was shot and killed. The second one was about their arraignment in U.S. district court. She shipped the stories to my computer file, but I hadn't logged in yet from my laptop.

I added, "I know he's into armored car robberies, or he was. Beyond that, I don't know much of anything. I wish I knew more, which is why I'm sitting here with you."

Markowitz simply looked at me, dragging on his cigarette, knocking his knuckles absently, softly, on the scratched surface of the wooden table.

He said, after what seemed like a forever pause, "He's not around here anymore. I don't know what I can tell you." As I stared at him, Markowitz added, "And you're asking the wrong guy."

"What do you mean?"

"You want to know about Curtis Black, you should go ask our federal government. They're the ones who know about him."

"Because of the charges?" I said, in a half question, half answer, hoping to lead him somewhere, though I'll be damned if I knew where.

"Because of the charges and everything else," Markowitz said.

He was cryptic, trying to tell me something without actually saying it, playing a game that wasn't intended to be any fun.

I asked, "Is Black in jail?"

Markowitz said, "No, he's not, and that's what you might want to talk to your federal government about."

"Sammy, come on, I need you on this. What do you mean?"

To this, I got nothing. "I've gone as far as I can go," he said. And when Markowitz wants to shut down, he shuts down hard, and not even someone of my estimable interviewing skills will be able to sway him to the contrary. I knew I had pushed as far as I could.

"When I know more," I said, "you mind if I come back at you?"

He said, "You know where to find me," which was his way of saying I could. "And you know how I work," he added. "I confirm, but I don't provide."

And I headed for the door. Markowitz had told me to go check with the federal government, so that's exactly what I decided to do next.

• • •

Across the Mystic River from Chelsea, Diego Rodriguez looked resplendent in his Louis suit, standing in his small fifth-floor office in the U.S. district court with the perfect view of the harbor and the distant runways of Logan International Airport.

We exchanged the type of needling that only old battlefield friends can indulge. We had been involved in a lot of cases together over the years, a lot of good stories, and Rodriguez had proven himself a reliable and informed source.

"I have a hunch and a hope," I said, cutting to the quick. "My hunch is, you know a thing or two about a former armored car robber named Curtis Black. My hope is you can share it with me."

No reaction whatsoever. Rodriguez was leaning back in his chair, behind his desk, his legs stretched out before him. I was sitting across his desk in a wing chair, overlooking his remarkable view.

Diego Rodriguez was a federal prosecutor assigned to many of the most glamorous cases in his office. The fact that he was Hispanic gave him opportunities. The fact that he was good brought him a remarkable track record of victory. For me, he had provided a constant flow of information on cases ranging from Irish gun running to mob surveillance. He never violated his own office, never put a case in jeopardy, but he respected and understood the role of the news media, and he respected and liked me. Ours was, in many ways, a good and beneficial relationship.

Which is why I was so surprised when he said, simply, "I'm not sure I can help you with this one." He sounded uncharacteristically stiff and slightly embarrassed at his refusal—not defiant, but apologetic. It was a tone that made me take stock before I forged ahead. Still, I had neither the time nor luxury to pull any punches.

I asked, "Do you know who I'm talking about?"

Rodriguez reached for a can of Coca-Cola on his desk, took a pull from it, then nodded. Almost as an afterthought, he said, "I know him."

I told him, "Look, Diego, I need you. This one is important to me. This one could be important to a lot more people than just me. Help me out. Please."

I fell silent. He was silent. There was nothing in the room but the gentle purr of warm air flowing through the vents.

"I wish I could," he said.

"You can," I said. "Just like all those other times before. You help, I keep my mouth shut until the hereafter."

He didn't smile at all. He looked at me and said, "You know the case, right? That armored car hit in the North End. That's all public record, and I assume you've looked it up."

I breathed a sigh of relief that he had opened up this much. I replied, "I'm vaguely familiar with it, yes, but I haven't gone through the actual trial records or transcripts yet."

In this business, a shard of information, used correctly, sometimes gets you the entire picture, or at least something reasonably close, so I added, "My understanding is that Mr. Black didn't do any time."

"This goes a lot deeper than that," he said.

I was leaning over toward him so far that I could have toppled out of my chair. I was trying to will the information out of his head and into my ears. "How deep?" I asked.

With that question hanging in the balance, we sat in

silence for a stretch. The day outside became a pale glow and was turning the corner toward dark. The only light in Rodriguez's office was from a small lamp on his desk. Neither of us seemed to mind.

Rodriguez looked like he was about to say something, then hesitated. He tapped his Coke can. Then he just shook his head.

"I can't," he said. That was followed by another long pause. He added, "I'm not trying to play games with you. I am truly sorry. But all I can tell you right now is that you really don't want to be mucking around in this."

I asked, "What the hell do you mean by that?"

He simply shook his head again. "Sometimes people change," he said. He said that with an odd look on his face, his eyes boring into mine. "Sometimes people change, and it's tough to keep up with them."

Then he stood and added, "I've got to run to court. Just take my word on this. You don't want to push this too far."

The nice members of the Copley Plaza Hotel's management team saw fit to upgrade me to a suite overlooking Copley Square, specifically the St. James Suite. Take my word on one thing only. When the hotel desk clerk assigns you to a room with a name rather than a number, you're going to like where you're going.

Once upstairs, I took a brief tour of the room, made myself familiar with the contents of the minibar, quickly perused the room service menu, and called down for a hamburger. Then I settled in at the desk and fired up my laptop.

The stories were sitting in my queue, as promised, the first one headlined "Five North Shore Men Arrested in Fatal North End Wells Fargo Heist." I quickly scanned through, seeing Black's name at the top of the second paragraph, then Rocco Manupelli, who the story described as a rising member of the New England mob. My eyes scanned through the rest of the list of suspects, from Marcio Sanchez to Joe Cox and then to the name that stopped my heart cold: Paul Stemple. Paul Stemple. I knew the name. It rang so familiar in my mind, but I couldn't place it. Paul Stemple. Paul Stemple. I had the feeling I was running down a barren hallway, opening doors into darkened rooms, frantically searching for something that I wasn't even sure was there.

And then, bang. It was as if someone had flicked the tines of a fork against a fine crystal glass. Paul Stemple. He was the same man who had received the presidential pardon, the man whom I initially intended to ask Hutchins about at Congressional Country Club the day of the assassination attempt. Paul Stemple connected to Curtis Black. Curtis Black connected to the shooting. These seemed to be answers, but the answers were only a prelude to another whole set of questions, this one so much more confusing. I stared at the computer screen until the letters turned fuzzy and seemed to evaporate. At that point, I stared at nothing at all.

Someone knocked at the door. At first I jumped in surprise, then recalled my call to room service, which now seemed like an eternity ago. *Paul Stemple and Curtis Black.* I cleared off a spot on the desk for the food tray, pulled the door open, and had begun to say, "Bring it right in here, please," when I saw that the person on my threshold wasn't the waiter, but was none other than my old friend Gus Fitzpatrick. He had a sheepish look on his face, a faint smile that seemed to express some embarrassment over an arrival without prior notice.

"They told me in the D.C. bureau that you were in Boston for the night. I figured you'd be here," he said, still standing in the hall.

"Gus," I said, "what a welcome sight. For God's sakes, come in."

We shook hands, the shake turning into a soft embrace. On his way to the couch, he looked around in a mild state of awe at the resplendence of the suite, even whistling softly. "Am I going to have to lay off half my overnight crew so our star reporter can afford to travel in this kind of style?"

"It's a free upgrade," I said.

We settled in, he on the couch, me on a soft chair. The walls on the room were painted a regal yellow, the carpeting was a deep shade of red. The fireplace was marble, the window a bay, the art on the wall portraits of people who I had some vague idea I probably should have known, but didn't.

Gus said, "So you, my friend, are hitting home runs every day of the week. You're knocking this story out of the park. You have any idea how proud I am? You know how proud your father would have been?"

"Oh, c'mon. Thanks. But the more I find out, the less it is I seem to know. The story is just so—" I paused, looking for the right word. My mood was completely colored by the recent, confusing revelation of Paul Stemple. I was getting that feeling of exhaustion again. "Elusive. I just can't piece the damned thing together. There's always another part we don't know."

"From the looks of it, young man, you're on a run. You're finding out things that other reporters aren't getting. Look at you. You've had a couple of interviews with the president over this thing, right? Why are you being so hard on yourself? You're the most important reporter in the country on the most important story of the moment."

Maybe Gus was right. Maybe not. I wanted to feel good about what he was saying, but all I really felt was tired. The trip to Boston hadn't proven particularly fertile. Markowitz had provided little help, if any at all. Rodriguez had given me even less.

I said, "Thanks, Gus. I'm really grateful for that. Maybe I'm just too much in the thick of it to step back and appreciate what's going on."

Another knock at the door. I let the room service waiter in, and he left the tray on the coffee table. Gus declined my offer to split the hamburger—a welcome act of gastronomic altruism so markedly different from my recent experiences back in Washington.

As I ate, he asked, "So what is it, Jack? Why all this frustration on your part?"

I chewed on the burger while I pondered the question. "Because," I said when my mouth was empty, "it feels like I should know a lot more. Every time I learn something, it usually means there are three other things that don't make sense. Everything seems so within reach, but so far out of my reach at the same time."

He looked at me sympathetically. "You have to take it one step at a time. You can only do what you can do. And you have to be careful."

That sounded strange to me. "What do you mean, be careful?" I asked as I salted my pile of French fries.

"Just what I said," he replied, meeting my gaze. "This can be a dangerous business. You know that."

"Don't I," I said, softly, as much to myself as to him.

"You're tired, Jack," Gus said. "You're tired and you're frustrated. You've done great work. You're about to do even better work. Get some rest. Some good things are going to happen to you."

He stood up, motioning for me to stay down. I got up anyway. As he walked toward the door, me trailing behind, he asked, "You ever wish you could just completely change your identity and become an entirely different person?"

It struck me as an odd question at an odd time, but interesting nonetheless. "Right now I do, yeah," I answered.

"You shouldn't," he said. "You have a great life, young man. You have an even better life in front of you." With that, he squeezed my arm and walked out the door.

I finished my hamburger in the silence of the suite. *Curtis Black and Paul Stemple.* What did this bizarre connection mean to the story? *Curtis Black and Paul Stemple.* They are cohorts in a failed armored car heist some two decades ago. They are both charged in the death of a guard. Over twenty years later, the president of the United States is shot.

I'm told that Curtis Black is somehow key to the shooting, though I have no idea how or why. Mobsters won't talk about him. Neither will federal prosecutors. I am warned not to—what did Rodriguez so unartfully say?—"muck around in this." I can't find Black. He's apparently not in prison. And Stemple, he is for some reason pardoned by this president just before the assassination is attempted. And there is no apparent reason for this pardon. Nothing is overtly explained.

So what is the connection? Could Black have master-minded the assassination attempt? Could he have been angry over the Stemple pardon and sought revenge in some way? Could he be acting on behalf of another one of the armored car robbers still in jail, someone who was denied a pardon?

All these questions made my head hurt. I turned to see the light shining from my laptop computer off in a dark corner of the room. I leaned my head against the back of the chair to give my mind a rest.

A new identity. It was an interesting concept Gus had raised. Perhaps I'd become a mutual fund manager, make a filthy fortune traveling the world, analyzing businesses, picking stocks in a market in which it didn't seem like you could easily miss. Maybe I'd become a professional golfer, the now obvious dangers of the course aside. Spend every day practicing nine-iron shots with my personal pro, then heading to the putting green to work out the kinks in my stroke.

A new identity. Someone else had raised that same point today, or something like it, no? Who was it, and why?

Yes, Diego Rodriguez, in his office, at the end of our meeting. "Sometimes people change," he said. I specifically remember that funny look he gave me, the way his eyes locked on mine. It was a non sequitur. It made no sense. And he said something else. He said that when people change, it's tough to keep up with them. Tough to keep up with them.

And then there was Markowitz. I had asked him if Black was in jail, and he said no. I asked him why, and he said I should ask the feds about that. Ask the feds why Black isn't in jail.

It was as if all these pieces of a puzzle started zipping into place, forming a picture that still wasn't clear—but a picture nonetheless.

You know how I work. I confirm, but I don't provide.

I grabbed my coat, my computer, and my overnight bag, which I still hadn't unpacked. I deftly sidestepped the coffee table and bolted out the door. Finally, knowledge—or at least the best substitute I had, which was educated guesswork.

Water dripped from my hair as I stood over the booth of Sammy Markowitz, who looked up at me, bovine, a pencil in his hand and a financial ledger spread out before him.

The forgiving hues of night did little to improve the aesthetics of the Pigpen. Actually, they did nothing at all. The smoke was thicker than it was that morning. The jukebox was every bit as tinny. The crowd was larger, more of the same, and thus more unpleasant. This place made my old fraternity lounge at Wesleyan seem like Le Cirque.

"So soon?" Markowitz asked, not really surprised, not really anything.

I had neither the time nor the will for the bullshit small talk. "Tell me this," I said, determinedly. "Tell me if I'm right. Curtis Black turned state's witness, entered the witness protection program, and changed his identity. That's why he's not in jail. That's why the feds would know more about him than you do." Pause, then, "Sammy, you've got to tell me now."

My voice rolled out of my mouth as pointed as barbed wire, but it seemed to have little discernible impact.

Markowitz continued to look up at me, completely unimpressed. Here I was with what may well have been the most important revelation of my life, aside from that time over a bottle of gin and the better part of a lime that I decided I had to get married, but that's not really the point here.

"Sammy, you'll confirm, but you won't provide. Those have always been the rules."

He replied, "I don't have to go by rules, kid." He let that hang out there, defiantly.

I rested the palm of my hand on the table, prompting one of his goons to come over. Sammy shooed him away—a good sign.

"Yes or no, Sammy. That's all I need. A goddamned yes or a goddamned no."

He stared up at me in silence, taking an occasional puff from his cigarette and blowing the smoke out of the side of his mouth, away from me.

"I need it," I said.

He took a final drag on his cigarette, looked it over in his fingers, stubbed it out, and said, "Yes."

I asked, "You know who he is now, who he became?"

Markowitz sat with both his elbows on the table, still meeting my gaze with a blank look. He averted eyes to take a sip of his cheap champagne, then looked back at me.

He said, "No one does. Black disappeared in the program. You probably know as much about where he went as anyone right now."

I knocked my fist against the table twice as I turned around to go. "Thank you," I said, and made a straight line for the door, for the street, for my idling taxi that would take me to the airport for the triumphant flight out of town. I placed a call to Lincoln Powers at the White House from my cell phone and told him I'd neared a decision and would like to meet the president one last time. He sounded pleased and told me he could give me a few minutes the following morning in Illinois, on a campaign stop there.

Next stop: Chicago.

My next call was to Havlicek. "Hey, old man," I said.

"Jesus Christ, where are you and what'd you learn?"

"I'm in Boston, on my way to the airport for Chicago. Going to meet up with Hutchins tomorrow. Find out as much as you can about the federal witness protection program. I'll explain more when I get in tomorrow afternoon."

I heard his voice as I hung up the phone, and it occurred to me, rolling across the rain-glistened streets of Chelsea, that in my business, the only thing more dangerous than knowing nothing is thinking you know more than you actually do.

sixteen

A HIGH SCHOOL BAND exploded into a rousing rendition of "Hail to the Chief" as I walked inside the ballroom of the Chicago Sheraton. A pair of stocky Secret Service agents in trademark dark suits escorted me along the side wall to a holding area cordoned off with velvet ropes near the side of the dais.

The crowd of several thousand Republican partisans was up on its feet cheering wildly. Hutchins, who had just walked out onto the stage, had a smile on his face as big as Lake Michigan. He waved his arms back and forth above his head, stopping only to point out people in the audience whom he recognized, giving them a thumbs-up sign as he mouthed their names. He actually did this to me, letting his eyes linger a moment on mine before turning his palm up toward the crowd as if to say, "Look at all this." He appeared elated, the antithesis of that last time I called on him in the Oval Office.

And why shouldn't he be? He was barnstorming across the country in a rousing campaign swing, unveiling a series of commonsense policy initiatives designed to take the public discourse beyond the routine stalemate of partisanship to a place he called "The American Way." At every stop, in cities like St. Louis, Cleveland, Houston, and Atlanta, there wasn't just enthusiasm but adulation. Pollsters said his lead had increased to about five points, give or take. It was a combination, they said, of the honeymoon that any president gets when he takes over at a trying time, his survival of an assassin's bullet, and his newly floated battery of ideas.

And those ideas flowed with abandon, ignorant of traditional party lines. In a bald appeal to the American mainstream, he warned the Republican-controlled Congress not to send up any more bills that would curtail abortion rights, lest they wanted to face another veto and anger a president of their own party. He told the Democratic leadership not to even think about turning back welfare reform. He proposed a sweeping overhaul of Social Security that would allow young workers to invest their money privately in Wall Street and be virtually guaranteed a long-term rate of return double that of anything the government had ever provided. And he proposed health care reform that was met with enthusiasm by key members of both parties, the U.S. Chamber of Commerce, and the AFL-CIO.

How popular had he become? That morning's *Chicago Sun-Times,* a bratty little tabloid, had endorsed Hutchins on its editorial page, and also had Hutchins's photograph splashed across its front page, with several of his proposals bulleted down the side, all under the fawning headline "Clay's Way." A *Washington Post* endorsement described him as "a leader with the common sense of Mark Twain and the political instincts of Franklin Roosevelt."

"These aren't Republican ideas," he boomed from the podium in Chicago. "These aren't Democratic ideas. These are American ideas." The crowd fell into a near frenzy.

"Not a bad little reception, huh?"

That was Royal Dalton, the White House press secretary who had taken the job in the first days of the Cole administration and was about to lose it in the first days of the Hutchins administration, though I'm not entirely sure if he realized that fact yet.

Speaking of which, my intention was to reject the press secretary's job. I'm a newspaper reporter—always have been, always will be. I don't look good on television. I don't particularly like politics, mostly because I don't particularly like politicians. I disdain the idea that, as a press secretary, I'd ever have to suck up to someone like myself, some cynical reporter whose bullshit meter jumps off the charts at the first sign of any insincerity and virtually explodes at the suspicion of a lie.

That said, I'd use the rejection as a chance to ask some much-needed and belated questions.

"Kind of reminds me of Nixon in Egypt about a month before he resigned," I said to Dalton. He looked at me quizzically, then decided to ignore the remark.

"So I have you slotted for about fifteen minutes with him, after this event. He'll go up to his suite in the hotel for some private time, and you're due to be brought up there right after him."

Dalton was having to speak louder. The crowd had broken out into a chant of "Clay's Way, Clay's Way." Hutchins stood on the podium pretending to be mad that they had interrupted his speech, holding his hands up in a plea for quiet, peering over the crowd with a mock sour look on his face.

"Ladies and gentlemen," he shouted into the microphone. "You have to let me finish. I have to continue across the country. I have an election to win, an agenda to put into place. I have to get back to Washington, victorious, to make sure those career politicians aren't misusing any more of our money and dampening any more of our American dream."

My God, how campy. But the crowd went crazy, the sound of the applause and the cheers swirling toward the cavernous ceiling, mixing with the red, white, and blue balloons that floated in the netting overhead.

Dalton said, "It's been like this at every stop. I've never seen anything like it."

I gave the press secretary a quick up and down. He was dressed in a gray chalk-stripe suit with a brightly colored bow tie pinned up against what looked to be a remarkably expensive shirt, the type that had French cuffs adhered by monogrammed gold cuff links. As I may have mentioned, he had a rather puffy, pasty look to him, no doubt honed by years spent in conservatories playing the piano as a child or reading Shakespeare in his room in boarding school, or tucked away in some corner of a library at his Ivy League university. He made George Will look like the Marlboro Man.

"On background," he said, "between you and me, over in the West Wing, we just have to watch out that he doesn't get too carried away with this populist message." He gave kind of a knowing laugh, mostly through his nose, as if he had just said something funny, though I wasn't sure what it was. "We just have to make sure he doesn't start believing all this centrist pablum he's throwing out. God, President Cole must be rolling over in his grave."

On stage, Hutchins appeared to be on a roll himself.

"Look," he said, speaking with no notes in front of him, winging it, enjoying himself. "Let's make a deal. I like deals. Deals are what helped me get rich before I came to Washington. Here's the deal I want to cut with the American people. I talk about the American dream an awful lot, and I do it for a reason. I happen to think the American dream is the backbone of this wonderful country. The role of the government isn't to make sure you fulfill that dream. That's too easy for the people and too hard for the government. It's unrealistic. No, the government's role should be to make sure that every American—and that's every single American, black or white or red or brown, male or female, young or old, gay or straight—has the *opportunity* to pursue his or her dream. So here's what I want to do. I promise you, I guarantee you, I will work until the day I leave office to make sure that every American gets the education they need to pursue their dream. That means the best primary and secondary school education, that means the best post-high-school education, that means the constant availability of job retraining for those who lose their livelihoods and are forced to look for something else, something different, a little bit later in life. I also promise you, we will not allow discrimination—not here in America, not under this administration, not because of age, sex, race, or even sexual preference."

The crowd was silent, listening intently, perhaps in a collective understanding that they were witnessing a rare moment of political improvisation. Dalton, on the other hand, had an uneasy look to him that bordered on actual fright.

"Here's what I want in return. I want you to be

Americans, to go back to our roots. That means showing compassion for those less fortunate. That means helping those who can work find a job. Let's break this cycle of dependence once and for all. Let's never return to the welfare state that we became. On the other hand, let's not be cruel. Some of us need a helping hand, and to give it, that too is the American way."

A roar of applause, and Hutchins, looking businesslike now, waited patiently for it to stop.

"Let's end the crime. Let's end the discrimination. Let's put our time and our money where it ought to be put, and that's toward making this country a better place to live, where opportunity is available for the asking, and dreams can be fulfilled by those willing to work toward fulfilling them. That's the deal I'm ready to cut with you. That's the deal that's going to make an already great country even greater."

The crowd jumped to its feet in a massive roar. The balloons overhead showered down like a patriotic snowfall. Amid the noise and the blaze of color that framed this snapshot of triumph, I caught Hutchins's eye one more time. It was a fleeting moment, so maybe I'm wrong. But it wasn't the look of delirium you might expect, nor was it a look of despair. It struck me as a look of need, almost a plea, though what he might have really needed from me, I had absolutely no idea.

Hutchins sat at the head of an antique dining table drinking straight from a can of Diet Coke in what must have been the largest hotel suite I had ever seen. Two aides stood on either side, pointing out something on a sheaf of documents spread out before them. I had arrived in the company of one of the Secret Service agents, a man so large that the fabric on the collar of his white button-down shirt didn't appear so much tight as absolutely furious, ready to burst from the immense neck muscles that constantly pressed against it.

Hutchins pulled off his half glasses when he saw me come in and advised me where to sit. He pushed the papers together, straightened them on the table, and handed them to one of his aides, saying to him in that rock-hard voice, "Tell Benny I said to hand-deliver these to Senator Mitchellson Monday morning. I don't care where he is, Washington or Georgia or whatever. Tell Benny to tell Mitchellson that I said I'm ready to meet him halfway. Then tell him if he's not ready to meet me, whether I win or lose, we'll cut his fucking legs out from under him. Tell him he'll need a fucking wheelchair just to get around the Senate floor."

"Yes, sir," the aide said, then sprinted from the room like the Cowardly Lion racing from Oz. As he left, Dalton appeared out of a nearby room and pulled out a chair as if to take a seat. Before he could, Hutchins told him he preferred to conduct the interview in private. When Dalton protested, Hutchins put his hand up, and the conversation was brought to an end. You don't easily question the president. That was a good lesson to take away from this meeting.

Hutchins sat in silence for a moment after everyone had left, and I had no choice but to follow suit. Finally he said, "What'd you think?"

I couldn't tell if he really cared. He had just stood before thousands of cheering, adoring supporters. They were pumping signs with flattering slogans high in the air. They were screaming his name. They were even laughing at his less funny jokes. I should be so lucky. Network television crews were beaming the appearance live into living rooms across the nation, in a precursor of what would likely happen in Tuesday's election, just three days away. And here he was, asking what I thought about it all.

"I thought your tie didn't match your suit."

I don't know where that came from. I was hoping for one of those belly laughs. Instead, he gave me a bemused look and said in a softer-than-usual voice, "This is one of my favorite ties."

He picked up his half glasses and twirled them in his hand. He put them on for a minute and glanced at a sheet of paper in front of him, then pulled them off and placed them back on the table, clasping his hands together in front of him.

"So here's what I have in mind," he said. "You heard me out there. I have lots of thoughts, and the crowds love them, for what they are. But they're little more than unformed ideas. I have to figure out how to translate what's going on up here"—he conked his closed fist against the side of his head—"to the policy-making structures of the West Wing and the rest of that rathole we call Washington."

He paused for nary a moment and continued.

"That's where you come in. First, you help me translate my thoughts into actual policy initiatives. For example, you help me take this American dream idea and spin some real meat-and-potatoes proposals out of it. You figure out how it plays within the White House, how we get people on board. Second, once we figure out a set of proposals, you help create the message around them to sell them to the public. Everyone of my predecessors here has said that's the biggest problem of the presidency, how to communicate your message to the public. You could sit in the Oval and devise a cure for cancer, but it won't do you a damn bit of good if the public doesn't understand what the cure means and if they don't believe that the president is personally behind it."

He broke for a moment longer than before and looked at me hard. He tapped his glasses on the table once or twice and took a pull from his can of Diet Coke. I wasn't sure if he was done yet, so I didn't say anything. Ends up, he wasn't.

"My idea is to announce your arrival in the briefing room on Thursday, two days after the election. I figure you can probably start in the week or so after that. I don't want to rush it too much and have the *Record* pissed off at me. We'll keep Dalton around until right after the holidays, then I have a slot saved for him over in the U.S. Trade Representative's office. He can talk about Rwanda or Chilean imports or whatever the fuck it is they talk about over there. He'll like that."

He wasn't really asking me about this; he was telling me. He wasn't so much looking for a yes or no as a simple acknowledgment that the Thursday after the election would be a good time to make the announcement. I must admit, his strategy did have a certain appeal to it. A weaker man might have said, "Yes, this all sounds good."

Instead, I said, in that unusually formal tone that I seemed to reserve just for him, "Sir, I have no government experience whatsoever. I don't even have political experience. I really don't believe I'm the guy you need in there right now, for your sake."

"Bullshit. I didn't have any presidential experience when I came to the Oval Office, and look at me. I'm up in virtually every poll. This is now my race to lose, and I won't. For chrissakes, the country loves me. Did you see that crowd today? It's almost absurd."

He continued, "I'd rather have someone from outside government than from within. I'd rather have someone who's skeptical of what I'm saying rather than another pansy-assed yes-man. You'd be the first hurdle to any idea. If it doesn't get past you, it doesn't go anywhere. You also understand the news media, and that's exactly what I need. I have to know from inside the White House how these things are going to play inside the press."

I started to believe him myself, started to think that, yes, I could help the president, that I was precisely what he needed, that I could turn his window of opportunity into a reality of success. He was good. I'll give him that. That's probably why he was the president, seemingly destined to win a full term.

Then this voice popped into my mind for roughly the millionth time in the last week—that crystal-clear voice of an aging man who was warning me that this assassination attempt wasn't what it seemed.

Well, we were trying to figure out what it was, Havlicek and me. We were getting up early. We were staying up late. We were burning the phone lines, climbing on airplanes, helplessly waiting for calls from my anonymous voice, hopeful that the next little piece would make the entire puzzle clear. Some of the pieces were starting to come together. I had names to go on now, names like Paul Stemple and Curtis Black. They had a common bond—an armored car robbery some twenty years ago.

We just had to figure out how the past related to the present.

"Mr. President, before I go on with my decision, I need to ask you something. Why did you pardon Paul Stemple?"

I could hear the tick of the grandfather clock behind me, the rhythmic breathing of Hutchins sitting across from me, the soft, absent tap of his glasses against the wooden tabletop. I looked at him and he looked at me, his forehead scrunched into an expression that may have been concern, but may just as well have been anger.

The moment stretched on, the rift of silence widening into a veritable canyon.

"Jack," he finally said, his voice straightforward, betraying neither anger nor surprise, "I don't really know. My best recollection is that Mr. Stemple was going to be pardoned by President Cole. I believe he was on his list after I was sworn in, so I went ahead and issued the pardon. I believe that's the case, though I'd have to double-check."

He had me with that answer. How was I supposed to check with Cole, or get one of his aides to dig up such minutiae in the throes of the last weekend of an election campaign?

As I sat in silence, Hutchins continued, his voice taking on more of an edge. "But here's what I do know. I'm the best goddamned president who'll ever seek your help. That's all you really need to know right now. As far as why I was shot, I'm hoping like hell to find that out as soon as I can. I really don't want to be shot again. I think you'll join me in agreement that it's not a fun thing."

Well, that all seemed like an effective evasion, leaving

me little in the way of follow-up questions. Also, I really didn't have a good enough handle yet on what I was talking about to pursue the line any further. I was fishing, and going back and forth in my mind on whether I should throw out the name Curtis Black. I decided it was premature.

I gave it one more try, saying, "There's something terribly odd about that assassination attempt."

Okay, so now he seemed exasperated. "We have an army of FBI agents working on this issue right now. The only odd thing is that they haven't nailed down an exact motive yet. They will, Jack. In the meantime, you and this guy Havlicek are obsessing over a point that I'm sure will very quickly become clear. The FBI is doing their best work. They're not trying to screw this thing up. They're not trying to cover anything up. Sometimes these investigations just aren't easy, and sometimes they don't work out in the neatly set schedules that you press people demand."

I said, "Maybe you're right," though not for half a second did I think he was.

Then I breathed a long sigh and said to Hutchins, "Sir, I've thought your offer over hard. I really have. I'm honored by it. I was tempted by it. But I can't accept it. I'm a newspaper reporter. Sometimes I don't even think I have any say in the matter. It's just what I do, and what I'll continue to do, and what I sometimes suspect and fear I'll always do."

He stared at me again, silent. My mind flashed to the adoring, applauding crowd in the ballroom from a few minutes before, to all the noise and the festivity, and now to this room, to the sullen silence, to the juxtaposition that was often the president's life. He was the leader of the free world who had once told me he felt anything but free. Forget all his power. Here he was stewing that he couldn't persuade some reporter from South Boston to come work on his staff.

"You're making an enormous mistake, young man," he said, sternly, looking me in the eye. He pushed his chair out and lifted himself up to show me to the door. "We're all done here," he said. "I have some business to do."

I got up and slowly walked over to the door, and when I got within a few feet of him, I stuck my hand out to shake his. He ignored me and said, "This is a decision you'll regret for a long time to come."

seventeen

IT USED TO BE you'd land at an airport in some far-flung city, someone would be there to meet you, thrilled that you had arrived. In fact, that was the reason you had flown in the first place—to actually see the people at the other end. Then age sets in, and with age comes responsibility, and with responsibility come the endless business flights to faraway places where no one particularly cares whether you've arrived in town or not. The only welcoming face is usually that of a reception clerk at the hotel, who asks for your credit card and sullenly punches your name into a computer before assigning you to one of the several hundred identical rooms upstairs. For me, it has gotten to the point that even when I arrive back in Washington from a long trip, there usually isn't even anyone who knows I'm coming home. It may not be a cruel world, but it can be a cold one.

I bring this up because as I stepped off the American Airlines flight from O'Hare to National at 8:30 P.M. Saturday and headed outside for a cab, a familiar female voice said from behind me, "Come here often?"

I turned slowly, not wanting to make a general jackass out of myself in case, as I suspected, the woman was actually talking to someone else. There, walking two paces in back of me, was Samantha Stevens, special agent with the FBI.

"Only when I travel," I said. She flashed me a plastic smile and I asked, "You pulling into town or heading out?"

"Neither. I came to give you a lift." I must have looked a bit startled because she said soothingly, "I'm going to buy you dinner, whether you want it or not."

In fact, I did, even if she may have been the last person I expected to see, making the last offer I expected to receive. It seemed like a good idea. My mind was about to explode, there was so much going on in it. I needed to give it a rest before I briefed Havlicek and Martin the following morning. On the flight back to D.C., I had made a series of calls to lawyer contacts and some police detectives I knew from my days on the Boston crime beat. I didn't learn nearly enough, but what I did learn was interesting. Black, in the words of one veteran investigator, was a Tom Sawyer type, a gang leader who could convince the others to whitewash the fence while he sat back and watched. He had a college education and was widely known on the streets for his brains and his gregariousness—his ability to get along with crooks and to talk his way out of trouble with cops. He was believed to be without a gun on the occasion of the heist, which would perhaps explain why the feds granted him immunity, certain that he couldn't have been the triggerman. His lack of practice might also explain why he was such an awful shot at the golf course that day, assuming that it was him. And yes, he had brown eyes, just like the dead shooter at Congressional Country Club.

What I hadn't learned was where Black had gone and who he had become, and it didn't seem like I was about to. No one even acknowledged that he had disappeared.

That left me with one remaining option: find Paul Stemple. He was the link in this whole equation that I didn't yet understand—not that I understood any of it all that well. The problem was, it wasn't even remotely clear where I was going to find him, or even how I was going to find him. All of this is a longer than necessary way of saying, a friendly face, a piece of fresh fish, and an ice-cold beer seemed like just the quick fix I needed.

"How in God's name did you know I was coming in tonight?" I asked.

"We have our ways," she said, smiling. I made a mental note to check on those ways in the very near future.

"Well, name the place," I said.

"Kinkead's," she said. "Do you have your car here? I cabbed over."

"I do."

We made incredibly vacuous chitchat on the way to the restaurant—the exact kind of conversation I like most. Once inside, she settled gracefully into the booth, sliding her lean body in and then crossing her long legs under the table. She wore her black hair tied back in a low ponytail, scrunched at the end by a small nondescript band. I had never seen her with that look before, and I'm probably not the first to say that she looked ravishing. Put those feelings away right now, I told myself.

We ordered some seafood ravioli and a plate of Ipswich fried clams to start, and I suggested—actually demanded—that she try the pepita-crusted salmon, the signature dish of owner Bob Kinkead. She did.

More chitchat until we both fell quiet as she spooned some clams and a ravioli off the appetizer plates and onto hers. She took a bite, exclaimed her approval in a sound I hoped to hear someday in a different venue, and gave me a searching look.

Out of nowhere, she said, "The only point I want to make before we get too far into dinner is that we need to have a working relationship. I don't know how else to say it other than being direct, so here goes: what I want now is to work with you. That's all I want right now."

Oh, my. There were about a million ways to read that little declaration, and being a guy, I probably wasn't in an effective position to properly interpret even one of them. My first take was that this was good news. She flatly stated that she wanted *a working relationship,* and she had a better understanding of the ground rules under which I work, meaning she needed to continue to bring something valuable to the exchange. This was good. My second take was that she seemed to be saying she wanted no personal relationship, given the way she specifically emphasized *working relationship.* That said, third, she indicated she only wanted a working relationship *right now,* which could be her way of saying we should get this investigation out of the way before we go off and have sex like two angry wolves in the snowy Montana wilderness. Or something like that.

"I'm all for working together." I was obviously playing this safe, never having been one to foreclose prematurely any options.

"Good," she said. "I hear you have some interesting stuff, and by my count, you owe me from the last time."

"Really? What is it you hear?"

She gave me a smile that I wasn't sure how to read.

"Word in our shop is that you and your colleague are on the verge of springing another major story. There's a lot of speculation over what it might be, though I don't think anyone pretends to know for certain."

She paused and eyed me, searching, I'm sure, for reaction. I didn't betray any, so she continued.

"Of course, the hope is that you guys do a story that might answer the question of who the Secret Service shot that day at the golf course."

I still didn't say anything. This was an odd turning of tables for me. Usually, I'm the one prodding, evaluating, trying to elicit any reaction. After years of watching people squirm across from me, I think I came equipped with at least some idea how to carry myself right then. I tried not to bat an eye.

I said, "We're working hard, Havlicek and me. We're getting some leads, and we're following them. But we're not where we want to be yet. Right now, we don't have a story, just a lot of ideas."

I know I was starting to sound like all those jackass cops I had covered all those years, the ones who would say of a sensational quadruple murder case, "We're assembling the forensic, eyewitness, and circumstantial evidence and continuing to pursue further leads. We will solve this case on our timetable, not yours."

We locked eyes for a long moment, not in any intimate fashion—this was, after all, the renewal of a working relationship, as she herself had said—but in an attempt to size each other up. To that end, I contorted my mouth ever so slightly to project the aura of sincerity.

She said, "Well, you boys better put a move on it, or you're going to let a whole bureau of federal agents down." She smiled, and so did I.

I regarded her for another moment. Samantha Stevens

looked outright elegant, in an unfailingly wholesome kind of way—an athlete who will forever retain her physical grace. She had barely a trace of makeup on the perfect lines of her cheeks. The bags under her eyes, as I've said, offered the only sign of her actual age. Every other characteristic screamed of eternal youth.

She seemed unusually poised on this Saturday night, confident, comfortable, able to enjoy the food and the company and still try to accomplish what I was learning was her goal: to leave with more information than she had when she arrived. Looking at her, I had the inclination to rest my hand on top of hers, even for a moment. Instead, I pulled a piece of crusty homemade bread from the basket, took a bite, and said, in a manner intended to goad, "Why don't you tell me what you have?"

She smiled at that, too. "By my calculation, it's your turn."

"I think you've miscalculated." As I talked, she took a piece of bread from the basket herself and playfully bit into it. "Sam, we're actively pursuing a story. I've told you that. We have what we hope are some good leads, but I don't know yet if they're going to pan out. My sense is, and correct me if I'm wrong, that you're not in as active a stage as I am, so it might be better if you helped me rather than vice versa, or at least went first in this exchange."

Truth is, I have no idea about the fundamental logic of this argument. The salient fact to take away is that it marked the first time since I'd known Samantha Stevens that I addressed her as Sam, and that, to me anyway, meant that a significant bridge had been crossed, even if I was yet to learn where exactly that bridge had taken me.

Score one for Jack, even if no one was actually keeping score.

She seemed to think all this over, perhaps even the Sam part. I don't know. As she stared at points unknown, our waiter arrived with our entrees and set them down before each of us. Sam looked her salmon over carefully.

"I guarantee you'll like it," I said. "If you don't, I'll take you home and microwave up some Swedish meatballs."

Opening her eyes wide in horror at the idea, she said, with mock panic, "I'm sure I'll like it."

After her first bite, she did that exclamation thing again, saying, "Oh, my God. This is unbelievable."

"You like?" I asked.

"I love."

Bob Kinkead stopped by the table in full chef's regalia, telling me he'd been watching me on television, and I didn't look as bad as he would have thought. After he left, I gave Stevens a nod, as in, Let's continue.

She said, "Here's what I'm learning about Drinker. He answers only to the director, while I still answer to about two other layers of management. Drinker doesn't speak to my bosses. I can't speak to the director. Drinker barely speaks to me." She hesitated for a second, then said, "And here's the interesting part. I know he and the president talk on the phone all the time—almost every day. I saw Drinker's call logs."

"Would that be so unusual, an investigating agent talking regularly to the victim of the crime?"

"Well, this is no normal crime, and no normal victim. I'll concede, we've only had three presidential assassination attempts since JFK was killed—Sara Jane Moore shooting at Ford in seventy-five, Squeaky Fromme pointing a loaded gun at Ford in seventy-five, and Hinckley shooting Reagan in eighty-one. So there's not exactly a lot of precedent or an FBI manual on how to handle this. But come on, you don't think it's bizarre, an agent and the president talking regularly about the investigation?"

I said, "You know, I was in the Oval Office last week when Hutchins got a call on a line that said 'FBI.' He was pretty abrupt with the caller, said he'd talk to him later. In retrospect, it could have been Drinker. But why wouldn't they speak regularly?"

"Well, they might. But put this in perspective. The president's a busy guy. He's trying to win an election. He doesn't need constant contact with the investigator on the case. If he did want regular updates, he'd be more likely to get them from the FBI director. We're pretty big on the chain of command over there. And it's not like this has been a textbook investigation. I seem to remember reading a few stories on the front page of the *Boston Record* that indicated we were fucking this thing up nine ways from hell."

There's that profanity thing again that turns me on. We both fell quiet, thinking about what Stevens just said. By now, the entrees were done and our waiter had delivered two orders of chocolate dacquoise with cappuccino sauce, and two glasses of port, which he pronounced to be a twelve-year-old Cockburn. Very nice.

I said to Stevens, "Okay, I concede the point. It is unusual those two would be talking as much as you say they are."

She took a bite of the dacquoise and declared she was on her way to heaven. She looked rail thin, yet packed down food like there would be bread lines come morning. She'd make a wonderfully expressive bedmate, I thought, if her partner could live up to the standard set by Bob Kinkead.

She said, "Not to force the issue, but let's put work aside for a while and see if we can chat like two regular human beings."

Truth be known, I still wasn't 100 percent confident that this wasn't some scheme, that Drinker and my new friend Sam weren't conspiring to set me up, playing off each other to learn the existence and the identity of my anonymous informant. I was either getting a remarkable window into the inner workings of a major FBI investigation, or rather an FBI civil war, or I was being played for a farm animal again.

"That sounds good, but just one more thing," I said. "Does Drinker ever bring up this point about the phone call in the hospital room anymore?"

"No, though I have to admit, I'm still curious."

Interesting answer. I decided to take a modest risk. "The name Black mean anything to you in this investigation?"

She looked at me blankly. Either it meant nothing, or she was one terrific actress. She shook her head thoughtfully and said, "Not a thing. Should it?"

My question was designed to accomplish two goals: first, see if, in fact, I did get any response, and second, to gauge in the future whether she had gone and passed this information to Drinker.

I said, "Probably not. Just scratching at dirt."

"No, really. What do you have?"

"Really, nothing solid," I said.

We both sat in silence for a while, sipping our port, collecting our thoughts. She began making small talk, about her first Thanksgiving since her divorce, her driving desire for a Caribbean vacation, her raves about my four-legged blond friend Baker. It became all very casual, breezy, floating on the surface, like a water lily, making no waves, just how I usually like it. Still, here I was, looking for meaning within, and this conversation exposed none of it. We tossed down another glass of port before I paid the bill with my trusty *Record*-issued Visa card. I briefly thought of Martin checking the bill, asking me if the clams were fried in liquid gold. We made our way down the stairs.

For the rest of time, I'll always remember precisely where I was when the events of the next few minutes began to unfold all around me. Actually, it's not as glamorous as it sounds. I was standing right in front of the coat check. I had just found my stub and handed it to the woman when Samantha, who was behind me, suddenly wrapped her arms around my waist and pressed her mouth against my ear.

My first thought was that the second glass of port had kicked in, inspiring an understandable fit of passion, such that she couldn't keep her hands and lips off me. Then I heard her whisper something, and my second thought was to tell her, "Huh? I can't hear you." Good social graces kept that thought in check as I replayed her words in my mind: "Eric—you're my boyfriend."

An agile mind is an amazing thing. Take, for example, mine. I couldn't figure out why she was suddenly calling me Eric, and when exactly I had become her boyfriend— not that I was complaining just yet. I was confused. Then, amid my mental calisthenics, it struck me, within seconds, that her ex-husband, Eric, was probably in the restaurant, and she wanted to do a little role-playing. Well, so much for her fit of passion, but I'd take whatever I could get.

"Eric," she called out. "How are you?" She kept one arm wrapped tightly around me, such that when the nice coat check woman delivered our coats, I had to maneuver my arms around Samantha to accept them.

My back was still to all the action, but I heard a somewhat nasally voice say, "Hey there, Sam. God, this is so great to see you."

I turned around to see a pretty-looking man with blow-dried hair and a dapper red pocket square in a navy blue suit come walking over, his white teeth blazing all over the room. He was tan in November, which explains more than I can describe. He looked to be the type of guy who always got along better with women than men.

"Eric, this is Jack. Jack Flynn." As she said this, she rubbed the back of her hand affectionately against the side of my arm. I thought she was overdoing the lovey-dovey act a bit but didn't think it was my place to say anything. I held out my hand cheerily to shake Eric's, and he gave me an oddly limp-wristed shake. I held in check my desire to call him a pussy.

"Very nice to meet you," I said.

"Same," he said, somewhat dismissively, his eyes drifting back to those of his former wife. I'm not precisely sure why, but I had the urge to punch him in the mouth. Worry not: good manners prevailed once again.

Meanwhile, Samantha was now running her hand up and down my back as we all stood there. Eric turned away for a moment and said, "Hey, Julia, Julia sweetie. Look who's here. Come on over and say hello to Sam."

Up walked an extraordinarily attractive blonde in a skirt so short I wasn't sure if I had accidentally been transported into some sort of adult entertainment lounge.

Eric again: "Sam, do you remember Julia? Julia, this is Sam. You guys met at Nordstrom's that day."

As I stood there, Mr. Manners didn't bother introducing me, and I wasn't sure if it was by intention or stupidity. Finally I stuck my hand out and said, "Julia, I'm Jack Flynn. Nice to meet you." Then I took my hand and softly ran it down Samantha's cheek, the very feel of her skin making my head go light.

Samantha took my hand in hers and kissed it softly. Here I was, thinking I was doing good. I was certainly feeling good. Samantha pulled my hand down to her side, squeezing it with what I first thought was sincere affection. Then I felt her sharp nails dig into my skin, and I almost yelped and jumped in pain. Luckily, I have the discipline of a Marine, and I maintained my smile.

"Coming or going?" I said to Eric.

He just kind of looked at me as if he had forgotten I was there. Maybe the complexity of the question caught him off guard. Julia said, "Just coming. We're going to get a bite to eat at the bar." She seemed nice enough, if not a little daffy, which is maybe what I mean by nice enough.

Samantha absently leaned into me, her body feeling warm and wonderful against mine, even if I was now gin-clear on what a charade this was. She said to Eric, "We don't want to hold you up. We just had a great dinner upstairs and are hurrying out. I'll see you around." She laughed and said, "Seems like we're doing more and more of that."

Proper, mature farewells were made, though I'm not

sure if Eric ever addressed one to me. Julia did, though, and with a smile, creating a kind of bond as the two appendages in this little scene. Outside, on the sidewalk, I said to Samantha, "You almost scratched the skin off my hand."

She laughed in a distracted way and said, "You seemed to be taking advantage in my moment of need." She wasn't quite as flustered as I thought she might have been. Actually, she seemed to be relieved that things had gone this well, especially after that Nordstrom's debacle she had described.

I said, "Sorry about that." I left the intention of my apology vague, whether it was for her running into her former husband, or for my somewhat coarse attempt at physical engagement.

"Apology declined." She said this as she stood facing me, unusually close. The night was cold, the street crowded with cars, the valets bustling back and forth—all of it creating a blur of peripheral motion, even as my eyes focused hard on Samantha, standing in front of me, her face cold and pink and shiny. I could never precisely explain the hints I got, whether they were from her words, her tone, her posture, or her proximity, but inexplicably I placed my hand on her forehead, brushed her hair softly, then let my fingers run down her cheek. She glided closer to me without ever seeming to move, and before I could even think about what was happening, she placed her warm lips fully against mine and kept them there for what could have been an eternity. She pulled back slightly, and I opened my eyes to see hers still closed, her face inches away. So I put my lips on hers again, a kiss that was hard and soft, passionate and affectionate, all at the same time.

Then she pushed me away gently in an almost helpless manner and said, "There's a cab right here. It's better if I just leave." She turned and walked slowly to the curb. As she settled into the taxi, she looked back and gave me an odd, even goofy wave and a smile. I stood on the sidewalk until all I could see were the taillights of her car driving down Pennsylvania Avenue, and I thought, my God, this finally feels like something called home.

As I pulled out my keys on my darkened front stoop, there was a noise from inside the house that I wasn't used to: the sound of someone talking. I froze and strained to hear, but all I could decipher was a low, barely audible mumble. I leaned over the railing to look in the window, but the shutters were drawn closed, as I had left them this morning. I could see a light was on, but that would make sense, given that Kristen had been supposed to drop Baker off earlier in the night. I strained harder to hear, thinking it might be Kristen inside, but it sounded more like a male voice.

Another voice filled my mind. *There are people who would kill rather than see you get to the bottom of this story. You are in danger. Imminent danger.*

A good warning. In the past ten days I had been struck by gunfire, shot at unsuccessfully, punched, and stalked. It was coming up toward eleven-thirty. The only sound was the gentle rustle of crinkled leaves in the chill wind of a late autumn night. There were no passersby, no moon, no lights on in any of the neighbors' houses. Inside mine, the sound droned on.

It could be a stereo, but it certainly didn't sound like it.

Kristen may have left the television on for the dog, though she had never done that before. I admit, I had no idea what it was. I just knew it was something unusual, and right now, the unusual was not going to be good.

You are in danger. Imminent danger.

I thought about slipping back toward my car and calling the police from my cellular telephone. This being Washington, though, it might be a while before they arrived. And it struck me in a wave of panic that if Kristen had dropped Baker off as she said she would, then he was inside with God only knows who. And if the police arrived, it seems one of the first things they always do is shoot the dog. So standing there in frozen silence on the stoop of my own house, I realized I had to handle this myself.

The mind, as I've said, is a funny thing. Miraculously, I remembered that I had left a pair of old pruning shears beside the stoop, in my little patch of a garden in front of my house. I slowly, silently walked down the two stairs, hunched down in the dark, and found them protruding from a pile of ancient, soggy leaves. I at least had a weapon now—maybe not something the NRA would be proud of, but a weapon nonetheless.

With the shears in hand, I stepped cautiously back up on the stoop. I pushed the key into my lock, moving with what I pictured to be the precision of a German surgeon. I strained to hear the voice, making sure it didn't waver or get closer, and I could detect no movement or change. It was a goddamned monotone. What the hell it was, I had no idea. The key pushed all the way in. All I had to do was snap the lock open and burst into the door.

With the key in the lock and the breeze blowing on my

neck, I briefly weighed my options one more time. I knew, inherently, that charging into my own house with a garden tool as my only shield was probably not the smartest thing I would ever do. Hopefully it wouldn't be the last. My mind raced through what I might find inside: some shadowy mastermind of a presidential assassination attempt. Perhaps Assistant Director Drinker. Maybe, in the best case scenario, my anonymous source. Probably some nameless thug ready to carry out someone else's dirty work. But I knew, standing here, that I really had no choice. I wasn't going to leave a helpless dog inside to fend for himself. I had brought myself into this whole situation. The dog was just an innocent bystander.

So without more thought, and perhaps without enough thought, I snapped the lock, threw the door open, and burst inside, holding the shears ahead of me in a way that would allow me to stab anyone in the neck who posed any danger. For a fleeting moment of dangerous glory, I felt like Don Johnson.

"Freeze," I yelled.

The warm air of the house hit me in the face. So did the unmistakable smell of Fritos. Sitting on my couch with his feet on the coffee table and my telephone up to his ear, Steve Havlicek calmly said, "Hold on one second, honey." To me: "Boy, am I glad I'm not some overgrown bush."

At the same time, Baker bolted up from a sound sleep, squinted toward the rear of the house, and ran into the kitchen, barking at the back door. Wrong way, pal. I made a mental note to get his ears flushed out.

I let the shears fall to my side, closed the door behind me, and said breathlessly, "What the flying fuck are you doing in here?"

Havlicek said into the phone, "Honey, I'm sorry. I've got to run. Jack just got in. Seems a bit out of sorts. Yeah. Yeah. I'm at his place. Yeah, we just have to have a chat. Tell Mary I said I'll make it back for her playoff game. Good. Yeah. I love you too."

He hung up the phone, pulled a few Fritos out of the bag beside him, took a sip from a can of Pabst Blue Ribbon beer, and said, "Howaya, slugger?"

"How am I? Jesus Christ, I'm almost dead from a fucking heart attack. How the hell did you get in here?"

"Just a little trick I learned from my days growing up in Dorchester. You don't have a deadbolt on your back door. You might as well just leave the thing open with a sign that says 'Come on in, but bring your own beer.'"

By now, Baker had trotted back out into the living room with a confused look on his face. I knelt down and rubbed behind his ears, relieved that he was all right.

"You scared the hell out of me," I said to Havlicek.

"Sorry about that. Hey, before you sit, grab yourself a beer. I've got some Pabst in the fridge. We've got to talk." As I walked into the kitchen, he called after me, "Grab me another too."

I didn't think anyone drank Pabst anymore, though I noticed I was now the owner of a case of it. Of course, I didn't think anyone outside of grade school ate Fritos either, so I guess I had a lot to learn.

As I slumped down into a chair with a can of beer, Havlicek held out the bag of Fritos in front of my face.

"No, thanks," I said.

"No, really, try some. I bought the pounder."

"No, really, I don't want any."

"You eat dinner?" he asked.

"Where do you think I'm coming from?"

"Good point," he said. He seemed to consider this for a moment, opened his fresh beer, though I don't know if you can ever really call a Pabst fresh, and said, "We've got to talk."

My heart was still pumping, which might explain my frustration. I said, "I thought that's why you were here."

"Right. I'm dying to know what you learned."

Given all the bullets flying around over the last week or so, I didn't particularly like his description. But I put that aside and walked him through every crucial detail of my trip. I told him of the Pigpen, of my discussions with Sammy Markowitz, of the cryptic remarks by Diego Rodriguez, of my deduction about the federal witness protection program, and the confirmation that Markowitz provided.

"So we've got an armored car robber by the name of Curtis Black in the federal witness protection program," I said. "We're told we need to find out his relationship with the president that was just shot. Black's a fellow crook of a guy by the name of Paul Stemple. Stemple's pardoned by the president in the middle of a campaign season."

That summary was followed by a moment of thoughtful silence. Well, almost silence, and probably not all that thoughtful. Havlicek kept crunching on Fritos and swigging his beer. Baker was on the floor between us, snoring. I mulled over our immediate future.

"I know a thing or two about the witness protection program, having covered some issues within it a couple of years ago," Havlicek said. "It's a hell of a well-run government operation. It began about twenty-seven years ago when the feds were trying to bust La Cosa Nostra, and they couldn't break the code of silence. It ends up, it wasn't that these mob underlings were so loyal. It's just that they were scared for their lives. Since then, the marshals have protected about 7,500 witnesses, most of whom, like Curtis Black, are themselves criminals. It's not a squeaky-clean process. It's not even a pretty one. But everyone familiar with it tells me it works."

Havlicek was on a roll and kept going. "The way it goes is, if you have something worthwhile, you cut a deal with the FBI to enter the program. Before a trial, you're given intense protection, typically in some safe house or a hotel suite. You're brought to the grand jury or to court with an army of agents around you. Once you do your thing, or once the other side pleads guilty because they know you're waiting in the wings to testify, that's it, you're given your freedom and a different identity, and you go off and become someone entirely new."

Havlicek looked at me. "Literally, Jack Flynn would cease to exist. Your house would be sold along with just about everything in it. Your dog would be given a new home. You'd pack up a few personal things, some clothes and the like, and the marshals would cart you off in some armored van to a national complex over in suburban Virginia. You get to pick the region of the country where you want to move. They'll help you buy a new house or pay for a new apartment. They might help you with some job retraining and the like so you can get work. They'll get you started on getting new identification, like a Social Security card and a driver's license. You come up with your own personal history, some story of who you are and where you're from. And that's it, suddenly you're out on your own, a whole new person. I'm told that only about three people in the entire marshal's service ever get to learn your new identity—that's how closely held the secret is."

"So the odds of us learning who Black became and where he went are not exceedingly good," I said.

More crunching. He said, "Except for the obvious. Suppose Black is actually dead now. Suppose he's the one sitting in that morgue, the unsuccessful assassin. Suppose it looks like the feds gave a free pass to some armored car robber more than twenty years ago, supplied him with money and a whole new life, and he turns into some sort of presidential assassin."

"The damned question is, why does some robber flunky from Chelsea, Massachusetts, end up shooting at the president, especially after he's taken a ride on the federal gravy train. How does point A lead to point B? And what's the role of Paul Stemple?"

Havlicek replied, "Maybe it was a hired hit. Maybe the guy's in the program. He's settled into his new life. He's working in some menial job, not making the money he was used to making when he was hitting banks and Brink's trucks back in the early eighties. And along comes this offer. Or maybe he seeks it out. You know, calls his old contacts. Maybe it's so good it makes him rich for life."

From the limited knowledge I had of Black, it didn't sound like him. Here was a guy who was always the ringleader, always gliding above the fray, letting others do the dirty work, telling them how to do it but never doing it himself. He was smart, savvy, even worldly. No, he wouldn't be the type to pick up an automatic rifle and take that kind of risk at Congressional just for the cash. He was smart enough to find another way.

"He's too sharp," I said. "He's a chief, not an Indian. He's not going to get his hands dirty like that for the cash."

Havlicek washed down most of a mouthful of corn chips with a pull of beer and said, "Well, maybe he really wanted this president to be dead for some reason."

"That's what bothers me," I said. "And that's what gets to the point of my anonymous friend, who seems to think that if we find out about the relationship between Black and the president, we'll know why this shooting occurred. That's the crux right there, isn't it? And it seems like stating the obvious to say it must have something to do with Stemple, or Stemple's pardon must be some way involved, no?"

Havlicek nodded.

I said, "I know this is all conjecture, but if you play this out a little further, can you assume that the FBI is covering up the identity of the shooter out of raw embarrassment that one of their witnesses went off and made a mockery of them by trying to kill the president? I mean, if something like that gets public, they're going to have the news media and congressional oversight investigators up one side of the program and down the other, and their secrecy is pretty much blown forever. Maybe the program itself is even lost in the media maelstrom.

"So our immediate mission now," I concluded, "is to find Paul Stemple, and find him fast. There's an election at stake in this, and that gives us two days. We find him, we get some answers."

"And on that point," Havlicek said, in a newly dramatic tone, "we're in some luck."

I shot him a curious look. He pulled out his ancient

wallet, shuffled through a collection of cards and old papers, and pulled out a small sheet. He flicked his finger against it and added, "When you first told me about Stemple and the pardon last week, I did a little research on him. I don't like coincidences. I suspected his name might come back into this story."

"So what do you have?" I asked, impressed and embarrassed that I hadn't thought the same way.

"Well, I had to go to hell and back to get this, but I think I have a line on where Stemple is living now, and I think it's right here in D.C. I got ahold of his Social Security number through a contact I have. I used that to nail some of his bank records. I found out that he made some recent withdrawals in Washington. I got some gnome in the Pentagon to tell me he was a Korean War vet, and that he stopped at a local VA hospital last week. I canvassed some short-term real estate brokers on Capitol Hill, where one of the withdrawals was made, and one guy told me he rented an apartment to him. Some skill, some luck." He made a motion to stand up, first placing the nearly empty bag of Fritos from his lap onto the coffee table. "So next stop: his house."

As he stretched his back, Havlicek added, "Jesus Christ. We have a member of the federal witness protection program, Curtis Black, who is in some way involved in an assassination attempt. We have someone taking shots at you. We have a senior FBI official providing us information devastating to his agency. And we have some anonymous source who seems to have all the world's information in the palm of his hand. One quick question: who plays me in the movie?"

I replied, "I don't know. Ernest Borgnine?"

"Screw you. He's about fifty pounds heavier than me. And isn't he dead?"

He ambled off to the kitchen with a few empty cans, calling out, "Give Martin a quick call and let him know you're all right. The guy was a train wreck today."

The hour was late, but Martin picked up on the first ring, as if once again he had been waiting by the phone. I gave him the update on my trip and progress, let him know we were heading out, and told him we'd gather in the morning.

"Boston's all over me to get something good in print," he said, referring to the editors. "Concentrate on a quick— but good—turnover. Meantime, I'll hold them off as long as I can, until we know we're ready to pop."

On his point about Boston breathing down our necks, there is a tendency in this business for the editors back at the main office to think that all us overpaid layabouts down in the Washington bureau are doing little more than waddling over to the Palm for lunch and Morton's for dinner, and in between tapping into the capital's vast public relations machine to be spoon-fed press releases on the latest triumphs of our elected officials. These same God-fearing editors believe that any time we choose, we can simply call up the White House and get the president on the line, or trundle over to the J. Edgar Hoover Building and have FBI commanders invite us into their offices and open up their active case files for us to peruse, all in the name of the public's right to know. Well, Washington reporting is hard work, and what we needed now was persistence and patience—two qualities that Martin understood, God bless him.

When I hung up, I looked at the clock and saw that it

was edging past midnight. My day had begun long before dawn. I wasn't so much tired as physically and mentally demolished. My ribs hurt, and so did my head. Yet it was time to forge on. I was not going to be the guy to hold up this story. Quite the contrary, if Havlicek had a lead, I wanted to follow it.

As we gathered some notebooks and coats, Havlicek asked, "You ever think about what you'd do if you suddenly came into a couple of million dollars? Would you stay in the business? Would you work late at night like this, go through all the deadline stress that we have, all the thankless bullshit? Or would you just kick back and live a life of leisure?"

"What, you just find out you're an heir to the throne of Poland, and they want you to come home and live in the castle?" I asked.

He gave me a look out of the corner of his eye, otherwise ignoring my question. He said, "I get two million bucks, I wouldn't change anything. This whole thing is too much fun." They were the most introspective words I had ever heard him say. Then he added, "Let's go."

"I'll drive," I said.

On the sidewalk, he said, "De Niro."

"What?" I asked.

"De Niro. I bet they get De Niro to play me."

I said, "What, you on heroin? Try Leslie Nielsen."

He smiled and shook his head, this man unlike any other I had ever known.

eighteen

MY CAR WAS PARKED at the curb out front. When I started it up, the engine turned bravely in the cold, dry air of an early-winter's night. Havlicek closed his coat around him in an exaggerated plea for heat.

"Hey, I talked to your FBI friend Stevens today," he said.

"Oh, yeah? You trying to steal my sources?" I asked, jokingly.

He patted the pockets of his coat, looked at me more urgently, and said, "I forgot a tape recorder. You have one?"

"Damn, it's inside." I had started to pull the keys out of the ignition so I could get into my house when politeness once again got the better of me. Knowing I had a spare door key ingeniously stashed under a loose brick in my front garden, I let the engine run so the heat would crank up. "Hold on," I said. "I'll be right back."

I'll never forget his words: "Hurry the hell up. I'm fricking freezing."

Inside, I had hit the third step on my way up to my study, where the microcassette recorder sat on the shelf of an antique bookcase, when I heard the sound. At first, it was like a truck had backfired on the street outside. That was followed by what could have been a plane hitting my house, or an enormous clap of thunder, so strong that the resulting vibrations flung me to the ground, slamming my head against the railing, leaving me in a momentary daze tumbling down the stairs.

In that daze, I recall windows smashing in, the spray of glass, the blast of cold air. For reasons I can't explain, I recall seeing my front door, which I must have left ajar, heave open, and I half expected to see some masked man in a Ninja suit and a machine gun race inside my house. I recall seeing a wave of destruction, as if the whole thing were happening in slow motion—lamps falling off tables, pictures plummeting from walls and cracking on the floor, a chandelier that my wife's family gave us crashing down from above.

Within what must have been seconds, as the noise gave way to a grotesque silence, I understood that something had exploded, probably right out front. I picked myself up without realizing that blood was flowing from a gash in my head and raced out the front door. On the sidewalk and street, in the cold night, the various parts of my car were strewn asunder. A small fire burned in the engine, exposed by the open hood.

I scanned the area furiously, looking for Havlicek. I spotted the door of my car on the sidewalk. The hood was sitting in the middle of the street. There was singed, broken glass everywhere I looked, sparkling softly in the streetlights. Finally, my eyes were drawn to the still form of Havlicek, or at least his tattered body, slumped against my house, his legs splayed open, his head concealed by one of his arms.

I did what anyone would do: I raced over to him, rolled him over so he was facing me, and saw that his skull was cracked open. Blood and God only knows what else poured out of the hole. Half his left ear had been ripped off. He was no longer wearing any shoes, and soot or burn marks covered most of his clothing.

His eyes were closed. My first impulse was to shake him, to yell in his face, to tell him he'd be all right. I knew, though, that if he was alive, shaking him would only cause more blood to flow out of his head. I felt his throat, knowing nothing about where a pulse might be, but in hopes I would suddenly learn. I moved my hand around a couple of different ways, trying to maintain some calm. To my absolute amazement, I found a slow pulse.

"Steve, you're going to be all right," I said, softly. I yanked my coat off and laid it over his form, remembering some first aid guide I must have read somewhere that said you always keep a trauma victim warm. "Stay with me, Steve," I said, speaking gently into his whole ear. "Stay with me. Just stay with me. Hang on. Help is on the way. Everything's going to be all right."

I glanced around the neighborhood and saw several people emerge onto their front stoops, a collective look of panic on their faces. I shattered the odd silence by yelling, "Is there a doctor around?" I got no response. You would think in the heart of Georgetown there would be at least one doctor on my block, but this being Washington, you made your money in television and in the lobbies of Congress, pushing various legislation, not helping those who needed to be nursed back to health. Someone finally opened a door and hollered back, "I've called for help." Nice of you to get involved, I thought.

I turned back to Havlicek. His neck was resting in one of my hands. His garnet-colored blood was dripping onto my wrist and coagulating on the cold ground.

"Everything's all right," I said over and over again, talking, probably, as much to myself as to him. "We're not going to let those bastards beat us," I said. "They're not going to beat us. You're going to be all right."

All of time seemed to screech to a halt out here on the sidewalk of Twenty-eighth Street, amid the morbid ruins that were once my house and car. The silence was still deafening. At this hour, late on a Saturday night, or rather early on a Sunday morning, there wasn't even any traffic. I felt myself start to panic, felt myself want to scream at someone, to assess blame, to seek revenge. Eventually, in the distance, I heard the vague sound of a siren, and over my shoulder, a voice said to me, "Here, I have a blanket and some towels."

A neighbor who I hazily recognized spread the blanket across Havlicek's form. I took the towel and pressed it gently to Havlicek's head, trying to stem the flow of blood. "He's alive," I said. "He's alive, and he's going to be all right."

And just like that, Havlicek opened one eye and looked at me. My heart was pumping so hard it almost exploded through my chest. I hadn't actually believed anything I had said about him being all right.

I looked at him in unabashed amazement and said excitedly, "You're fine, Steve. You're going to be fine. Hear that ambulance. It's about a minute away. Everything's going to be all right. Hang in there with me."

Havlicek tried to mumble something in return, but it was incoherent, the talk of someone weak and in shock. I said, "Don't speak. Save yourself. Stay with me. Stay with me. Help is on the way."

Havlicek being Havlicek, he didn't bother to listen. He continued to mumble. His one eye was open, looking at me. His second eye popped open as well. I told him again to stay quiet. When he still didn't listen, I said, "Steve, do yourself a favor and shut up."

Then, summoning what appeared to be an inordinate amount of energy, Havlicek blurted out, "My pocket."

"Your pocket?" I asked him, still speaking softly, not raising my voice, not acting panicked, although all around us were the parts of what a few minutes ago was my Honda Accord, and before me, my friend was on the doorstep of death, about to ring the bell.

He nodded his head. I fished through his pants pocket, and he looked at me with some exasperation, saying, "Coat."

In the background, the siren kept getting closer, weaving through Georgetown. In the foreground, people weren't so much staring at us as gawking, as if they never had a car bomb explode on their block before in the early hours of a Sunday morning. I reached into the inside pocket of his navy blazer and found a sheet of white paper. I put it in my pocket without looking at it. He seemed content, and closed his eyes.

"Don't go anywhere, Steve," I said. "Hang tough for me. Just hang tough, and you're going to be fine."

I didn't even realize that my hand was on his and that he had been gripping one of my fingers. I didn't realize it until I felt his grip loosen, his hand become completely slack. He gave one hard exhale, and his facial expression changed completely. When I put a finger under his nose, his breathing seemed to have stopped.

I said, louder, "No, Steve. No. You're staying with me here. I need you on this. Your wife, she needs you. Don't go anywhere." The sirens seemed to multiply and got increasingly louder. It sounded like they were only a block or so away. I had my other hand cupped on the back of his head, and despite myself, shook him a bit.

"Come on, Steve. We've come too far. We don't have that much further to go. Stay with me."

With that, I started to breathe into his mouth, to push air into his system. But the sad fact of the situation was that I didn't have a clue what I was doing. It all seemed so futile. When the ambulance pulled up and the EMTs leaped out, I told them I thought he had just stopped breathing a few minutes ago. One of the men put an oxygen cup over his mouth. Another thumped at his chest. Two more raced over with a stretcher. I backed away, fading into the background, almost tripping over what must have been the passenger-side door to my car.

A woman in an official-looking jumpsuit approached me and asked if I was all right. I replied that I was fine, and she said, "You know you have a cut on your head?" She wiped a cloth over it and told me to come with her. I shook my head, never really diverting my eyes from Havlicek and all the men around him. She disappeared and came back in a moment, told me to stay still, and carefully placed a bandage on my temple. "You'll be all right for now," she said. Physically, yeah. The rest, I wasn't so sure.

At that precise point, it hit me—the dog. I turned back and raced toward the house and into the front door, which was open. The inside looked, well, like a bomb had hit it. On the floor in the middle of the living room,

Baker was sprawled out on the rug, the shattered chandelier pinning him to the floor. When I knelt down in the broken shards of glass, he didn't so much cry as whimper, his eyes looking at me in a pleading pursuit of relief.

They say you never approach a wounded dog, that it might even attack its master to protect itself. Screw that. I kissed his muzzle and rubbed his ear and told him he was going to be fine. I very gently pulled part of the chandelier off his back end. I gingerly pulled some shards of glass off his fur. He seemed unable to move, stuck on his side. Whenever my hand or leg went near his mouth, he licked me furiously, almost apologetically. A wounded wolf in the wild he was not.

I made a move to run outside and get help, but when I did, Baker tried to get up, found himself overcome by pain and started to give a plaintive wail. Rather than leave, I covered him with a throw from my couch, scooped him up in my arms, and took him outside into the street. I hoped against hope that the first cop I saw would be a dog lover. A nondog person, they'd just as soon let Baker die in a pool of his own blood. A dog person would carry him on their back to the vet if they had to.

"This dog," I said to a policewoman who seemed to be working some form of crowd control, though the Georgetown crowd would prove more than tame. "He's mine, and he's injured, and he desperately needs some veterinary help. Do you have someone who could rush him to the Friendship Animal Hospital?"

She said, "Well, I'm supposed to call animal control to transport a dog. Technically, we're not allowed to."

She looked concerned, and by her words and tone, I knew I had her. Baker licked my face. I said, "Look, ma'am, this dog desperately needs help. I'd drive him myself, but the insides of my car are scattered all over the street. Please. I'm begging. Please take him."

"Follow me," she said. She led me to a station wagon, opened the back, and I gently slid Baker inside. He kept looking at me, frightened and in pain. I borrowed the woman's cellular telephone, punched out the number for Kristen's house, and told her, in about twenty seconds, of my situation. About two minutes later, she was standing in front of me, out of breath. She slid into the back of the car beside Baker and, lights blazing, they were off.

As I turned back toward Havlicek, a pair of EMTs were pushing his stretcher into the back of an ambulance, about to close the doors. I raced over and said, "I'm with him," and began climbing into the back cabin. One of them gave me a look like he was about to stop me, then didn't bother, which I didn't take as a particularly hopeful sign. The doors shut behind me. Inside, two EMTs worked furiously on Havlicek's head and occasionally pounded his chest.

Within about four minutes, the ambulance slowed to a halt, the doors flung open, and I leaped out of the way. Havlicek was transferred onto a new stretcher and wheeled into the emergency room of Georgetown Hospital. As I tried to follow, a nurse blocked my path and said, "You'll wait out here." By now, I was too dazed to argue. I slumped down in a chair in a hallway, in a situation that was too hauntingly familiar, and tried to piece together the violent puzzle that had been the last hour, and probably Havlicek's final hour.

Before I could put a single fragment of the day in its place, a doctor appeared in front of me. This time it was a man, not a woman. This time he stayed in the hallway, rather than lead me into a conference room. This time, I knew the message before the words came out.

"Your friend, Mr. Havlicek," the doctor said in a tone that seemed aloof, even clinical. "I'm afraid I must inform you that he's dead."

I'd like to report back that I was handling this spate of violence with Bond-like cool, that Havlicek's death only made me angry, and when I get angry, I get even. But save that for the movies. Sitting on that lime-green chair in the hallway of the Georgetown Hospital emergency room, it felt like my entire world had just packed up and abandoned me.

I was, admittedly, frightened. Someone had just tried to blow me up along with Havlicek, or more likely it was just me they were after, and Havlicek was the unwitting victim. Let's put aside questions over who and why for a moment to look at the results.

Havlicek's death had left me without my crucial partner on the biggest story of my life. His death would also mean that I was about to become part of the story yet again, rather than a reporter covering it, just like the week before when I was hit in the assassination attempt.

More importantly, it also left Margaret Havlicek without the husband she adored, something I can relate to. And it left their two children without a father to see them through college. This was a sadness that transcended every other, which is why I finally lifted myself up off that chair, walked slowly, heavily, to a pay telephone around the corner, and dialed the Havlicek household in Braintree, Massachusetts.

It should probably be up to some *Record* official to inform the widow of her husband's death. Problem was, this being two on a Sunday morning, even a newspaper can take a while to mobilize. That very moment, I strongly suspected that a CNN camera crew was standing in front of my house, some blow-dried reporter telling an anchor in Atlanta named Ashley, "All around me are the glass remnants that just a few hours ago were *Boston Record* reporter Jack Flynn's automobile."

Fuck the reporter, and fuck CNN. Now I know how it feels.

"Hello."

It was the unfailingly pleasant, though sleepy, voice of a middle-aged woman, namely Margaret Havlicek, picking up the telephone. She sounded calm, not panicked, meaning she didn't know yet.

"Margaret," I said. "Jack Flynn here." I spoke in the calmest, most soothing tone I could muster. "Margaret, I have some bad news. It hurts me terribly to have to tell you this. Your husband died about twenty minutes ago. We were about to drive to an interview tonight in my car, and he was alone in the front seat while I ran back into the house to get a tape recorder I had forgotten, and it exploded. It appears that someone planted a bomb."

There was silence on the other end as she processed what I had just told her. Then I heard her soft voice say to no one in particular, "No, I just talked to him a couple of hours ago. I just heard his voice. This can't be right. He just told me he loved me." She had become almost too choked up to talk. "Oh, my God," she said, then came the sounds of sobbing, followed by "Oh, my God. Oh, my God," again and again and again.

"How?" she asked, her voice soaked in a cascade of tears. "Who? Why? Why would someone do this?" Her sobbing descended into crying before I could hear her try to collect herself. I felt like a voyeur on my end, the unintended survivor breaking the bad news to the next of kin.

"I was with him at the end," I said. "He was alive after the explosion, then I felt him die in my arms. The EMTs seemed to revive him, but then the doctor declared him dead in the emergency room of Georgetown Hospital."

I paused and listened to her sobs, pictured her sitting on the edge of her bed, surrounded by family mementos, knicknacks, every photograph, every vase, representing some day in their long marriage. Suddenly that house would seem so empty, the future overwhelmed by the past.

"Margaret," I said, "I work with words every day, but I could never find the right ones to tell you just how sorry I am right now." I paused and said, "And I mean this, Steve said just two hours ago how much he loved his life with you, how he wouldn't trade it for all the money in the world. He talked about you and the kids all the time."

"Thank you, Jack," she said through her tears. "Steve really enjoyed working with you."

There was a moment of silence until she asked, "Who, Jack? Who did this to Steve?"

"I don't know yet, but you can be sure we're going to find that out."

I could still hear her sobbing. She said, "I'm going to go now. I don't know what I'm going to do, but I think I should go. Thank you, Jack." And with that, she hung up the telephone to face a life alone that she never wanted or expected.

After that, the call to Peter Martin was relatively easy. He was upset to the point of being choked up, and not just over having the story delayed yet again. And as with so many other times in life, he was able to cut to the chase in a way that even the Washington police didn't seem capable, saying to me, "This means you're in grave danger. I want you out of your house," he said. He didn't know yet that I really had no choice, not to mention doors and windows. "Check in at a hotel somewhere, then call me. I'm going to hire some security guys to watch you, whether you want the protection or not. Be in touch within a couple of hours, or you're fired."

I ambled outside into the cold, coatless, with a bandage over my right eye, dried blood on one of my arms, my hair mussed to the point of wildness. I was not a pretty picture. I flagged a taxi, and as I settled into the backseat, the driver, a man with a turban, turned around and gave me a nervous once-over. I couldn't even smile back. "Friendship Animal Hospital," I said. He thought I was crazy, I'm sure. But he took me there nonetheless, to be with the animals.

When Kristen saw me, she rubbed her palms across her face and followed me with her enormous eyes, just kind of looking at me in mute amazement. When I sat beside her, she said, "The doctor wants to put Baker to sleep. I told her she couldn't do anything until you got here."

I was running low on emotional strength, not to mention physical strength. This news made me feel like I had been kicked in the chest by a mule.

Some sort of veterinary assistant, a kid with a pair of studs in his right ear, led me down the hallway into a visiting room. He opened the door, and I saw Baker sprawled out on top of a stainless steel examination table, tied down. Baker saw me as well. Without lifting his head, his tail whacked the table several times. I leaned over and kissed his muzzle, then gently stroked his soft ears. The kid said, "The doctor will be right with you."

When the door shut behind him, I pulled up a stool and sat. My head was close to Baker's, and I whispered to him, "You are the best boy in the world. You really are." His tail thumped the table again, his head stayed flat. He followed me with his brown eyes. I kissed him again, and he ran his coarse tongue slowly over my soiled face, relieved, I suspect, that he had done nothing wrong to cause all this, that his pain was not some punishment. Dogs think like that, best as I know.

"You are my very best friend," I whispered into his ear. It was the truth, almost from the minute I met him. I got Baker a little under three years ago. At the time, Katherine and I had just moved into our new house in Georgetown and decked it out for the holidays. We dragged in a Christmas tree that soared ten feet. I arrived home from work on Christmas Eve to our plans for a quiet dinner alone. She was sitting in the living room, sipping a glass of red wine, wearing a red satin dress, festive, just for me.

"I'm going to give you your gift tonight," she said. "I'm going to give it to you now."

She pulled a large hatbox out from under the coffee table. I sat on the couch beside her and undid the ribbon. There was no wrapping paper. When I lifted the top, all I saw was a ball of fuzzy blond fur. I looked back at Katherine, confused. She beamed and put her face close to mine. "Pick him up," she said.

"Oh my God," I remember exclaiming. I looked at this frightened puppy, scooped him up in one hand, and held him tight to my face. His fur mopped up a tear that Katherine never saw.

"This is like going to the driving range," she said, imitating my long-held argument for getting a dog. "Same basic swing, plenty of room for error." Baker would be our predecessor to children, our chance to step tentatively into a life of responsibility. Three years later, he is the only living, breathing remnant of our marriage, aside from me, of course. If this veterinarian thought she was about to put him to sleep, she had no idea how wrong she was.

"Mr. Flynn, hi, I'm Dr. Gabby Parins. Sorry to meet you under these conditions."

Coming through the door, she looked up from her clipboard at me for the first time, a pretty young woman with glasses and blond hair pulled back in a tight ponytail. "Oh, my. It appears you've been through some trauma as well."

I explained the situation, the explosion, the falling chandelier, the broken glass. She told me of the extensive injury to Baker's hips, the fractures in both his hind legs. He might never walk again, she said, and he would certainly never be able to run the same way. She could perform surgery, but it might fail, and he could easily die on the operating table, at considerable expense. Her recommendation, given the costs, the pain, the lifetime of a debilitating condition, was to put him to sleep.

"That doesn't seem very humane," I said. "Not to him, not to me."

"On the contrary, Mr. Flynn, given the extent of the injuries here, the multiple abrasions to his skin, the overwhelming possibility of infection, the likely loss of the use of his legs, I think it's the most humane thing you could do right now."

I looked down at the dog, at his profile, pleading with me to make things better, to take him home. I thought of that first night I had him, this vanilla fluffball walking on city sidewalks for the first time, people padding their way in the snowy dusk squealing as they saw him. I thought of the way he moped around the house when I came home from the hospital that awful October day without Katherine, how he sniffed at her side of the bed, waited constantly by the door. I was not about to give him up now, to say goodbye to him and all he represented.

"Doctor," I said, my voice so thick that it surprised me. "Please, perform the surgery. Perform it well. Let's take it one step at a time and decide where we should go from there."

She stood near me in a white coat, with a clipboard in her hand, looking from the dog to its owner. She nodded and said, sweetly, "Okay. I'll do that. I'll do that this morning. We'll both keep an open mind."

While I still stood there, she shot him with a sedative. I rubbed his head until he fell sound asleep. I went out and told Kristen that Baker was going to have surgery. She shed some tears of relief and said, "I knew that's what you'd do." She asked if she could wait with the dog.

I dug into my pocket to see if I had enough money for a cab. When I did, my hand came across a crumpled piece of paper. I pulled it out, and the memory of Havlicek telling me to reach into his coat suddenly pulsed through my mind. Nerves caused me to fumble a bit as I unfolded it, then read the handwritten line: "Paul Stemple, 898 C St., SE, Washington, DC. Apt. 2."

nineteen

IT WOULD BE IMPOSSIBLE to realize how fully my world had just changed. Forget the obvious stuff—that my most esteemed colleague was no longer here to help me, that I would miss him to my core, that I and my newspaper were about to be showered with too much attention at a time when we wanted it least. I had to come to terms with the fact that danger now lurked beyond every corner and in every shadow. I probably should have realized that last week, when someone took a shot at me at the Newseum, but since I hadn't been hurt, I had refused to accept any sort of changed reality. If I had, maybe Havlicek would still be alive.

Marbled into all that danger were answers to the most significant questions that I may ever ask. It seemed evident right then that I had to confront the danger to obtain the information that Havlicek would so badly want me to get. I essentially had two days to the election, two days to answer these questions before Hutchins won his own four-year term.

These were the thoughts racing through my brain as I stood frozen in that antiseptic waiting room, more tired than I've ever been in my life but even more determined to make amends. I asked the veterinary assistant if there were any other exits I might use, like some sort of side or cellar door. He looked at me strangely, but then led me down a rickety set of basement stairs toward a steel door that opened into a small backyard.

Outside, I hopped over the fence into another yard, then another fence to another yard. I don't know where I found the strength and stamina to do it, and I didn't dare start asking myself any needless questions. Eventually, done with my little Bruce Jenner act, I emerged onto a side street in the Burleith section of Washington. I ran behind some hedges and arrived on Wisconsin Avenue. It was after 3:00 A.M., and through the luck of the skilled, I flagged a passing cab and was safely—I think—on my way.

"Capitol Hill, please," I said. I saw the taxi driver eyeing me suspiciously in his rearview mirror, taking in the bandage on my head, the dried blood, the mussed and matted hair. He fumbled around beneath his seat, I assumed to make sure he was carrying his gun.

As he eyed me warily in the mirror and I looked back at him, I said, "I just fell off a turnip truck." He nodded and reached back under his seat, just to be double sure.

On the hill, I asked him to take a drive past 898 C Street, Southeast. It was a two-story brownstone town house in an advanced state of disrepair, on a block of buildings that the current economic boom had apparently overlooked. The bushes in the patch of dirt that passed for the front yard were overgrown. Old candy wrappers, cigarette butts, and beer cans were strewn about. A banister hung precariously off the front stairs, ready, it seemed, to blow down in the first strong gust of wind. All the windows were dark.

"I'll get out at the corner," I told the driver. He appeared relieved, and I can't say I blamed him.

Outside, the air was colder than I had expected, and I remembered that I had left my coat in Georgetown, having covered Havlicek with it. I walked briskly back down the street toward the house, unsure of exactly what I was about to do, but positive that I had to do it. The way I saw it, by morning I would be ordered off the story by the paper's editors for safety reasons, and if I wasn't, then whoever was attempting to abbreviate my life would have learned my whereabouts and would be trying anew.

In front of the house, I took a deep breath and climbed the four stairs to the front door. I knocked softly on the glass window on the decrepit door, which was covered by a shabby curtain, and waited. I didn't hear a sound from within.

I stepped back and looked at the upstairs windows to see if any lights clicked on, but none did. I rang the doorbell, heard a loud buzz inside, and pressed my ear against the window. Still nothing. I looked at the upstairs windows. Nothing again.

I wasn't sure quite what to do. I wished Havlicek was here to jimmy the lock with a knife or a credit card or whatever it was he'd use. The only thing I knew how to break into was a sweat, and I was starting to do that just then, despite the chill air.

For the hell of it, I fingered the doorknob, and to my unbridled amazement, it turned, the door readily creaking open into an entryway that led to a larger room. I stepped inside, keeping the door open behind me. I could either announce my presence and hope for the best, or sneak inside and look for the worst.

"Anyone home?" I yelled. All right, so it's not original, but it gets the job done.

No response, no stirring, no nothing. So I groped around for a light switch, eventually found one, and flicked it on. A bare bulb illuminated overhead, revealing peeling wallpaper covering ravaged walls that rose from a filthy linoleum floor. The only other item in the tiny space was a toilet plunger. Don't ask me why, but I grabbed it.

"Anyone here?" I called out again. Nothing.

I stepped into the main room, felt through the shadows for a few long moments for another switch, and flicked one on. An old, dirty chandelier lit up, and I stood bolt upright in shock and fear. Spread out before me was the living room, ransacked from one end to the other. Right next to me, a desk drawer had been pulled out and thrown to the floor, its contents—some matches, loose change, and assorted papers—tossed about on a thread-bare rug. The cushions of the old, ragged couch had been pulled off and cut open. A small television was smashed on a floor next to its stand. Yellowing shades covered the windows.

My eyes sprinted around the room in search of a person or a body. "God fucking dammit," I said under my breath. I still hadn't moved from where I was standing. Sweat rolled down my face.

"Paul, come on out!" I hollered. My own voice, bouncing off the bare walls, frightened me even more. My mind kept flashing back to the image of Havlicek's mangled ear.

Gingerly I walked through the wreckage of the living room, peering along the floor for any scrap of paper or envelope that might carry someone's name, that someone preferably being Paul Stemple. I saw nothing of any use. Carrying the plunger with both hands, ready to swing, I walked into the back of the house, into the kitchen and turned on an overhead fluorescent lamp with a dangling string. Same drill, same bolt of fear. Cabinet doors were flung open, drawers thrown on the floor, a few dishes broken on the scratched Formica countertops. About a dozen roaches sprinted across the floor to escape the light. All the closet doors were open, which was good, because it meant I didn't have to go through the dramatics of going through them.

I walked back out into the living room, thinking it was high time to get the flying fuck out. But I couldn't help let my eyes wander up the wooden staircase in the far corner of the room to the dark expanse above. I walked slowly toward the steps and stood silently at the foot.

I pushed a switch on the wall, and an overhead light shone on the second floor landing.

"I'm armed," I yelled, the toilet plunger still in my hands.

I started up the stairs, each one creaking louder than the one before. I had no idea what to expect. I didn't even know what I wanted to find. Nothing, perhaps? I just knew I had to go up, to press ahead, to scour every possible corner for any clue as to what had gone so tragically wrong.

On the top stair, the silence was broken by a blur of activity. Something flashed across the scratched wooden floors. I raised the plunger out before me, ready to take a swing at whatever demonic figure was coming my way. My heart nearly came through my chest. I looked down in time to see an immense rat race by my feet into a darkened room and God only knows where from there. I gripped the railing in a combination of relief and for balance. I shook my head and tried to smile at my situation, but couldn't.

That's when I looked closer at the floor in front of me

and saw bloody animal tracks where the rat had just run. He was either bleeding himself or had just stepped in blood. I looked warily, ominously, at the open door from where he had come.

And that's where I headed. I had neither a viable weapon nor a logical choice. I stepped around the railing and down the short hallway, calling out, "I have a fucking gun, and I'll blow your fucking brains out. Come out now."

Nothing.

From my vantage in the hallway, I could see it was the bathroom. I reached hesitantly inside the door, found a light switch, and flipped it on. A pair of rats came scampering through my legs, causing me to nearly vomit. My eyes raced from the toilet to the sink to a pair of soiled towels unceremoniously flung onto the floor. That's when I looked into the bathtub and saw the lifeless form of a human being, facedown in a fetal position, as if in self-defense. In my entire life, I'd never seen a single dead person before, funerals aside. Now I'd seen two in a night.

As I inched toward the tub, another rat leaped out, propelling itself through the air and then scurrying past me. At this point, I didn't really care. As I got closer, I saw that the body was of a white-haired man, wearing a gray sweatshirt, a pair of old khaki pants, and worn white sneakers. I'm no medical examiner, but from the two holes above his left ear, it appeared he had been shot a couple of times in the head. Blood had flowed down the side of his face and formed a puddle in the tub.

I couldn't believe I was doing this, but I put my hand gently on his exposed neck. His skin was warmer than I expected, and still soft. I took a guess that he had been killed in the last few hours.

His wallet lay haphazardly, opened in the tub beside
him, some of the contents spilled around his legs and midsection as if someone had rifled through it before throwing
it back at him. I snatched up a few pieces of paper and
cards—the stub of a bus ticket from Lewisburg, Pennsylvania, to Washington, dated two weeks before, a number for a local social services agency, an address in Silver
Spring with the underlined word, "Rent." No names, no
identification.

I grabbed another handful of papers and sifted
through them, tossing them back into the tub when I
determined their uselessness. The last slip sent a chill up
my spine. It was a torn sheet of lined paper, and on it
were my own work and home telephone numbers, without any name, and, curiously, the main switchboard
number to the *Record* in Boston. Without regards to the
possible criminal repercussions of stealing evidence in a
murder investigation, I shoved the paper into my pocket
and made my way for the door.

In the hallway, I walked as quietly as I could, creeping
down the stairs and toward the front door. I stopped suddenly in the middle of the living room, a vague thought
suddenly crystallizing in my brain. I whirled around,
walked back into the kitchen, and saw what I had thought
I remembered: a telephone answering machine on the
counter.

I pressed a button that said "Greeting," and recognized
immediately a voice that haunted me to my soul. "You've
reached 282-4572. Please leave a message."

It was the voice of my anonymous source, Paul Stemple.
Now he, too, was dead.

Once outside, I bolted up the street toward Massachusetts Avenue. I stopped at a pay telephone, called 911, and in the most casual voice I could summon, informed the dispatcher of a possible homicide at 898 C Street in Southeast. I hung up, found a nearby ATM machine, and withdrew $500, the maximum it would allow. As I flagged a cab, two police cruisers raced past, their lights flashing but their sirens silent. I felt as if I had just gotten away with something, but with what, I didn't yet know.

Regardless of what I looked like, the front desk clerk at the very proper Jefferson Hotel would have treated me with a sense of suspicion, given the hour, which was 4:00 A.M., and the fact that I wasn't carrying any luggage. When he took into account my appearance, which was even more disheveled than before, he called for security, and a nice guard stood politely nearby as I tried to arrange for a room.

"Name, please?" the clerk asked.

"Bird. Lawrence Bird." Bird succeeds Havlicek. It's a Boston thing.

"What sort of credit card will you be using, Mr. Bird?"

"I'm not. I'd like to pay with cash." I pulled the thick wad of new bills from my pocket and put them on the counter.

"Certainly. You have some form of identification?"

"I don't. I was just in a car accident, and I lost my wallet."

"Of course."

He typed on his computer keyboard and gazed thoughtfully at the screen while rubbing his chin.

"Unfortunately Mr., um, Bird, we don't have any availability right now." He said this while looking at his computer. His eyes shifted toward me, and he added brightly, "I'm very sorry."

"Look," I said. "I'm hurt. I'm exhausted. I'm desperate. I have the money right here to pay for a room. I'll check out by eleven in the morning. I will take absolutely any room you have."

I pulled two twenty-dollar bills from the pile, pushed them toward him, and added, "I'll take anything."

He typed for another moment, rubbed his chin a little more, and said, "Oh, good. It seems there's a king bedroom available on the fourth floor that I didn't see." As he spoke, he reached out, gently fingered the $40, and placed it in his shirt pocket.

He printed out a registration form, asked me to sign it, required an upfront payment of $300 and asked, "Will you be needing help with any luggage?"

"All set," I said, smiling without cheer.

Once in the room, I called Martin and told him where I was and my assumed name. Within ten minutes, I was fast asleep.

twenty

I AWOKE FOUR HOURS later thinking thoughts that were way too complex. Foremost among them were the images of Samantha Stevens meeting me at the airport, Samantha Stevens alone knowing that my car was at Kinkead's, Samantha Stevens jumping in a taxicab before I could even offer her a ride home. She was the only person in any way connected to the assassination attempt or the resulting investigation who had monitored my whereabouts in the hours before the explosion. Not good.

I thought of my anonymous source, the grotesque way in which he was forced to die, all because of his mission of truth. I felt as if I had known him, even if we had never actually met. And now he was gone, and with him so much of the information I so desperately needed, now more than ever.

Of course I thought of Havlicek, fighting for the story right to the end, happy with his lot in life, confident that things would always get better, that the truth just lay a day or two away. I questioned whether I could push onward in this story without him or whether it was time to abandon my efforts, then dismissed that latter thought as unworthy of another second's consideration.

Then I thought of Kent Drinker, so desperate for the last week-plus to learn the identity and location of the person who had called me in the hospital that first day.

And a few hours ago, I found that person murdered, just after someone had failed to murder me.

It's a different Tony Clawson. And it's his background that's so interesting and so potentially devastating, especially to my agency.

I played Drinker's strange words out in my mind as I showered and readied for the day. I was exhausted. My head hurt from the cut, my ribs throbbed from last week's shooting. My life had become a life-or-death obstacle course, and right now, I was racing down the homestretch, toward the hopeful confluence of Election Day and some truthful answers about this assassination attempt.

Pink and powdered, I sat down in the fluffy terrycloth robe—I had no fresh clothes—and called downstairs for a laptop computer with Internet access. A few minutes later, a solicitous bellman delivered it to my door.

I settled in at the computer to conduct a cyberspace manhunt. First I checked Social Security Administration records, on-line, for all Tony Clawsons in the country in the last twenty years. For each one I found, I checked for current telephone numbers. If they didn't have a phone number, I checked for death records. If they didn't have a phone number or a death record, I checked for a credit report to see if there was recent activity. It was a frustrating, tedious endeavor, the type of pick-and-shovel work that outsiders assume we layabout reporters have someone else on staff to do.

On about the fifteenth Tony Clawson, this one out in the suburbs of Chicago, I could find nothing—no death record, no phone number, no credit activity. I checked for marriage records. Nothing. I checked, most interestingly, for a birth record, and again, nothing.

I went deeper into his Social Security history and saw that he hadn't been assigned a Social Security number until 1979, when he was listed as forty years old. That was unusual, though not definitive. With every stroke of the key, I learned more, and as I learned more, my pulse quickened to the point of excitement. Clawson, my computer told me, began paying into the system in 1979, and continued for nine years. Sometime in late 1988, he had abruptly stopped paying in.

More keystrokes, more information. Social Security never paid out a death benefit to any Clawson survivors. Clawson didn't appear to have been drawing unemployment payments. There was no mortgage information, no credit activity, nothing. In 1988 Tony Clawson of Rosemont, Illinois, ceased to exist.

This was, of course, interesting because in 1979 Curtis Black had ceased to exist, the year Tony Clawson took shape. Best as I could tell, I felt fairly certain that Curtis Black became Tony Clawson in the witness protection program in 1979, and these records seemed to bear that out. Interesting, though, that Clawson himself then disappeared from sight in 1988. Drinker had implied in my dog park that it was this Clawson who had resurfaced out at Congressional with a gun and a mission. The cryptic words of Diego Rodriguez popped into my mind. *Sometimes people change, and it's tough to keep up with them.* So this is what he meant. But one question still lingered, one very important question: Why?

I was still stuck in the realm of supposition, trying to peer over the wall into the world of actual facts, but with little luck. My gut feeling told me that the truth behind the assassination attempt would say something about this president, something we didn't already know, something he didn't want us to know. I now had just one day to get that into the newspaper, and I was starting to realize what an impossible feat that would be. Maybe Havlicek and I could do it together. But not me alone. Not alone.

The ringing phone crashed through my thoughts.

"I've got two engineers in the lobby," Martin told me, skipping anything in the way of an introduction. "They're going to set up separate phone and fax lines in your room that match your office phone, so you'll get all incoming calls. The phones will also be untraceable, so you can make calls.

"I've also got a pair of security guards standing by the elevator and the stairway on your floor, so no one will have access to your room. I've put down an untraceable credit card to hold your room for as long as you need it."

Hats off to Martin. He was bringing order to chaos, and he didn't even question the rack rate.

"Now tell me what you know. What the hell is going on here?"

"Are you on a secure line?" I asked.

"Affirmative," he said, starting to talk like he really was in a movie. "I've had the office phones swept for bugs every day for the last week."

So I walked him through the bombing scene and aftermath. I told him about making a tentative match between Clawson and Black on the computer. I finished with the part about finding Stemple dead in his bathtub and hearing his voice—the voice of my secret informant—greet callers on his answering tape.

"Jesus Christ," he said. "Havlicek's dead. You're in grave

danger, and we don't even have a publishable story explaining why."

Someone knocked at my door. "Hold on a second," I told Martin.

I yelled out, "Who's there?"

"Phone engineers."

I opened it with the safety chain still fastened like they do in the movies and said, "You have ID?" The first man showed me a badge, and I let him in.

As they set up a telephone and fax, I asked Martin, "Did we get news of the explosion into the final edition?"

"No," he said. "It happened too late. We led with election stuff—the candidates making contrasting proposals on gun control. We had a poll on the front showing Hutchins up six points, just beyond the margin of error."

He paused, then added, "The FBI has called this morning, looking for you. They want to question you about last night. They said you left the scene of the bombing, and they were unable to find you."

Damned right I left the scene. My mind flashed again to Stevens at Kinkead's, to Drinker's inquisition about my source, and then to Stemple in the bathtub. "No way," I said.

"I already told them that," Martin replied. "I told them it was our responsibility now to assure your safety. They said something about filing criminal charges against you and me for suppressing evidence. I told them to go right ahead."

Give Martin credit. He was as far afield as a Washington bureau chief could be from the typical rigors of Supreme Court decisions, Senate committee votes, and election manueverings. But here he was, handling it like a white-collar Clint Eastwood.

"I need some new clothes," I said.

"I'll be there within an hour," Martin said. "I just have to make sure I'm not followed. Stay put until then."

He hung up, the engineers left, and my office line immediately started ringing with requests for interviews, which I didn't grant.

My first call was to Stevens, and was something of a test. When she picked up the phone, I blurted out, "You'll live with Havlicek's blood on your soul for the rest of your life." I hung up before she could reply. It felt good, even if it didn't accomplish anything.

My next call was to Drinker. I took a softer, more pragmatic tack, recalling that he had been seeking to be my new ally. I also didn't want to give up the fact that I knew Stemple was dead. I assumed that he did.

"I'm sorry about your colleague," he said. "That's just awful. We have some agents here who are looking to collect some information from you."

"I'll get around to that," I said. "First, though, let me run something past you. It's my understanding that Tony Clawson used to go under the name of Curtis Black. Curtis Black used to be an armored car robber in Massachusetts, before he entered the federal witness protection program in the late 1970s. Is this something you can guide me on?"

There was a lengthy silence between us, except for the occasional sound of him snapping his tongue in that bothersome way that some people do.

In a very careful, measured tone, he said, "If this is what your information is telling you, I am unable to dispute what you've found."

I rolled my eyes to myself at his lapse into officialese.

"Look, I need more than that right now. I need confidence that I'm doing the right thing. What you're saying, or the way you're saying it, doesn't help me get this into print."

Another long silence, though no tongue snapping.

Then, carefully, Drinker said, "If this is what you've found, then you understand the embarrassment of this agency. You understand why the director wanted to offer up a different photo of Tony Clawson as the suspect, to be honest yet vague at the same time. You understand that it wouldn't reflect well on the FBI to have a former federal witness who lived for a while with a government subsidy and government protection then become an attempted assassin, rather than spend a lengthy stretch of time in jail."

Were the pieces falling into place at last? I asked, "And the motive for the shooting?"

Yet another long silence. "That, I truly don't know," he said. "And the only guy who can actually answer that is still in a Maryland morgue."

I said, "I need to use you as a source, identified only as an official familiar with the investigation. I need that official to say that Clawson and Black are the same guy."

I know that his word would probably not be enough on which to pin a story of this gravity, but it's always good to line up your options.

"Can't," he said, with less hesitation than before. "That'd cost me my job. But give me a while to think of another way."

"Well, that other way better come damned quick. My colleague is dead, and I'm turning into a loose fucking cannon. No telling what I may put into the paper."

"Where are you?" Drinker asked.

"No way," I said.

"You have a fax number?"

I gave it to him, and we hung up. For every question, there needs to be an answer, but for every answer, there always seems to be a new question. And sooner or later, sometimes you just run out of facts, and if not facts, then time.

Five minutes later, my facsmile machine kicked to life. A one-page document rolled out, stamped "Top Secret" about two-thirds of the way up the page, just beneath a letterhead for the Federal Bureau of Investigation, Department of Justice. My eyes raced down the page to see the name Curtis Black, along with his last known address in 1979, in Chelsea, Massachusetts. Beneath Curtis Black was the name Tony Clawson, with an address in Springvale, Illinois, and the year 1979. At the bottom of the page were the words "Identity transition, c/o US Marshals Service."

Obviously Drinker had thought this through pretty damned quickly. I read the document over again. It was glorious in its simplicity. As a rule, you usually have to wade through cartons and sheaves of official papers to come across a jewel like this, and often you risk missing it. This time it was laid out on a platter, direct and easy to understand.

Before I could even step inside, the telephone rang. It was Drinker.

"That going to help you?" he asked.

"It will help, but it doesn't give me everything I need," I answered, not wanting to betray too much appreciation. Never leave facts on the table when reporting a story.

A familiar tone of frustration, even disdain, filled

Drinker's voice. "This lays it right out for you. What the hell else is there?"

I said, "Well, first of all, the last official statement from the FBI was an agreement that Tony Clawson was not, in fact, the shooter. I have no one from your agency saying he was, on the record or on background. Second, I have no motive. Third, I have a loose end left to tie up, a guy named Paul Stemple." I threw that last name out at him to gauge a reaction, to try to figure out just how strong an ally he might be.

There was a long silence again before he spoke. "One, you ask the agency, they will have to tell you that Clawson is still a suspect. Two, you don't need a fucking"—his voice sounded especially tight here—"motive in court. You shouldn't need a fucking motive in the newspaper. Who the hell knows what Black was doing? He was probably doing this for the money. Third, I don't know who or what Paul Stemple is, but he doesn't have anything to do with our case."

I looked over the document again as we talked. It was a beauty. Even the printing was all so neat and clean, the paper crisp. "I'll call you later," I said.

"You either run with this, or I'll go to another paper with it," he seethed. "And this is the last damned bit of help you'll ever get out of me."

The Stemple mention, I'll admit, seemed to shake him up. It may not have been the wisest strategy maneuver on my part—a fear that was fulfilled about forty minutes later. As I carefully tried to readjust the bandage on the cut on my head, my phone rang again. It was Martin, skipping any niceties, telling me in no uncertain words to turn the television to CNN. So I did.

On the screen, a weekend anchor with pouty lips and eyes the size of footballs was just saying, "So we'll go live now to Washington and hear this surprising new development on that car bomb explosion this morning straight from the FBI." The picture flipped to a press conference at the J. Edgar Hoover Building. Drinker was at the podium, looking frazzled. There were a couple of agents behind him wearing badges from the Bureau of Alcohol, Tobacco and Firearms.

"I'll read a short statement, then take just a few questions," Drinker said, gruffly. "At approximately one A.M. today, a car carrying Steven Havlicek, a reporter with the *Boston Record,* exploded on the 1300 block of Twenty-eighth Street in the Georgetown neighborhood of Washington, D.C. Mr. Havlicek was killed in the explosion. The owner of the car, Jack Flynn, also a reporter with the *Boston Record,* was nearby at the time and sustained minor injuries in the explosion that were treated at the scene.

"At this time, the FBI, in conjunction with the Bureau of Alcohol, Tobacco and Firearms and the Washington, D.C. police, have determined that an explosive device was hooked up to the engine of Mr. Flynn's automobile, a Honda Accord, and was timed to ignite several minutes after the automobile's engine started running."

Drinker paused for a while at the podium. Even on television, you could hear the constant flap of camera shutters and see the never-ending flashing of bulbs.

Drinker continued, his face looking grim, "In answer to your anticipated questions on whether we have any suspects, at this time, we don't. But I would like to say that in light of this being Mr. Flynn's automobile that was specifically targeted in this explosion, we are reviewing our own investigation into the shooting on October 26 at Congressional Country Club. So far we have been investigating that shooting as an assassination attempt on the president of the United States. We are now going to review our investigation to determine if Mr. Flynn may have been the intended target in that shooting, as in this explosion, and President Hutchins an unintended victim."

I could hear the audible, collective gasp of my reporter brethren in the room, and trust me when I tell you, reporters don't gasp easily. For that matter, from my hotel room, I could just about hear Peter Martin's jaw drop in our office several blocks away. I could hear Appleton's blood begin to boil in anger and fear that the paper was about to be humiliated on a national stage.

A reporter asked, "Have you learned anything about Jack Flynn's private life that would make you suspicious of such an attack?"

Drinker: "Not definitively, but we are pursuing leads and several lines of inquiry." Not with me, he wasn't. The jackass hadn't even given me the courtesy of a heads-up when we were on the telephone. One minute he was all over my case, the next minute he was leaking me sensitive documents. I didn't know what to think.

A *New York Times* reporter asked what I regarded as the most obvious question of all: "Since Mr. Flynn"— that's how they talk at the *Times*—"was one of the most active reporters in Washington investigating the unsolved shooting of President Hutchins, might that not make him a natural target in this explosion for anyone who fears he is getting too close to the truth?"

Drinker replied, "That is, of course, one explanation, and we are continuing to look at that possibility. However,

I would caution that the attempted assassin is dead. And though we initially investigated the Congressional shooting as a possible conspiracy, we do not have definitive evidence that is the case. So the question remains, under that scenario, who alive would try to kill Mr. Flynn?"

Sitting there on the edge of my bed in the Jefferson Hotel, I felt as if I was watching my life flash before my eyes, or more accurately, collapse beneath my feet. If Drinker had suddenly decided to render me obsolete because I wasn't buying whole hog into his Black/Clawson scenario, this was a clever, almost brilliant maneuver to do just that. By making me part of the game, he was effectively excluding me from it, at least as far as my ability to investigate and report news was concerned.

I looked at my telephone, anticipating that it was about to ring, but it stayed silent. In exasperation, I punched out Martin's number at the bureau but got no answer. Likewise, I got his voice mail at home.

About two minutes later, there was a knock on my door. At least I knew it wasn't Drinker. He was killing me in different ways. I yelled out, "Who is it?"

"It's Peter."

I pulled the door open, and in the hallway before me stood Peter Martin and Bob Appleton, the editor in chief of the *Boston Record*. What, Appleton fly down from Boston on the Concorde? From the fact that they were here, rather than on the telephone, from the look on their faces, from the nasal sound of Martin's voice, I knew this conversation would not be one that I appreciated.

"Boys," I said, as frazzled as I've ever been in my life, every one of my senses screaming for a break, "good to see you."

They came in and settled in my sitting area. We made the appropriate small talk, discussing Havlicek and his wife and the explosion itself and the tidal wave of coverage that was following it.

It was Martin who steered us to the point of their visit. "Jack," he began, "Bob and I have been discussing the events. Bob's worried, and I have to say I agree with him, that with the FBI's theory that you may be a repeated target of some killer, you should not be putting yourself at personal risk any longer by staying on this story."

I had figured this was on the cards. All you have to do is look at the undistinguished career of Bob Appleton, the very definition of a mediocre newspaperman who got to the top by playing it safe, to know this was coming.

"Well," I said, slowly, letting it sink in, "suppose I wasn't the target of a killer at Congressional. Suppose we just side with logic and assume that was a presidential assassin at work. Then let's follow that line of logic and assume that since we were the lead newspaper in the nation covering that assassination attempt, that someone tried to kill us because they didn't like what we were reporting."

I let that sit out there for a minute so even someone like Bob Appleton could understand it. He started to say something, but I cut him off. "This is the most logical scenario. Anyone with a brain knows that. You heard the *New York Times* reporter ask that question today. If this is the case, by pulling me off the story, you are in effect surrendering to whoever killed Havlicek out there today."

Another pause, and then, in a daring tone, "That really what you want to do?"

There was silence in the room. It should have felt

clubby, three guys, successful newsmen, memorializing a colleague who had died and plotting their next move on the biggest story since Watergate. Instead, the feeling, within me, anyway, was one of desolation, a sense of utter loneliness that was on the brink of turning bitter.

Martin said, "Look, Jack, I can only imagine how you feel. Steve is dead. We're all devastated. You've busted your ass on this story, and you've come a long way. Christ, I thought we were going to crack the thing. I really did. But now you've become a part of the story—a big part of the story. The FBI's having press conferences about you, Jack. You're going to be on the front page of every major paper tomorrow. That doesn't work anymore. You know that. You know we can't continue like that."

"Peter, none of our actions, none of my actions, have intentionally made us a part of this story. All we've done is covered it. And even in covering it, we've done everything by the book. It's whoever bombed my car early this morning that made us part of the story. And it's this FBI agent Drinker—and look at his record on this case—who made us part of the story. You want to give in to them now? They don't want me on this story. Don't you get it? Havlicek's dead. My anonymous source is dead. We're knocking on the door of some really serious answers, and you want to give in to them? For chrissakes, I've got valuable documents. We've got this thing all but cracked."

Appleton, who had been watching Martin and me go back and forth as if he were attending a tennis match, spoke for the first time. He bridged his fingers to affect the posture of thought and said, "Jack, we're not giving in, not by any stretch." He spoke slowly, surely, as if every one of his words were some valuable jewel to be savored.

This editorship had obviously gotten to his head. "I'm going to send people down to relieve you. For the time being, I know it's best, for your own safety and for the reputation and future of this newspaper, if you bow out for a while and stay in hiding."

I simply sat there, my elbows on my knees, looking down at the blue carpet in the dark room. I felt like a boxer getting my brains beaten out, unable even to think, longing for relief, but knowing the only relief I would get is from conceding defeat, ending the match, going back to my corner the loser.

"You're making the biggest mistake of your careers," I said, softly, almost as if I weren't even addressing them.

That remark seemed to get under Appleton's thin, chalky skin. Ironically, on a day when they should have been consoling me, offering me any form of help, his tone now changed to that of overt attack.

"We all make mistakes, young man," Appleton said, sternly. "Though this decision doesn't happen to be one of them. Just for the record, I want you to know that I know you were engaging in lengthy discussions with Hutchins about becoming his press secretary at the same time as you were covering this story. Based on that alone, the decision to pull you off the story was made. What happened today just makes it an easy one."

He paused, still speaking slowly, looking me straight in the eye as I picked my head up to match his stare. He continued, "That I consider to be a firing offense. As I said, we all make mistakes, so I'm not going to fire you now."

Appleton looked to Martin and started to stand up. My elbows still on my knees, my voice deflated, I said, "Hutchins pursued me, and he wouldn't take no for an answer, even when I said no. I just used his offer to get a couple of interviews for this newspaper."

Appleton shook his head dismissively. He was on his feet now, leaning toward the door. Martin, still sitting, said, "Jack, you're still a reporter in good standing in my bureau, as far as I'm concerned. My only worry is for your safety. I ask that you not talk to other members of the news media. I ask that you not leave this room until the election is over. There will be no wake for Havlicek. The funeral service is in Boston tomorrow. I'm afraid I have to forbid you from attending. We cannot put your safety at any further risk. We'll continue to foot the bill for all of your protection as long as you don't endanger yourself by leaving. Sandlera and Bartson"—two remarkably ordinary reporters in Boston—"will fly in tomorrow. I'll send them over so they can debrief you. I expect you to tell them everything you know."

Appleton was at the door now. He said to me, "We have your best interests at heart. I'm not sure you could say the same thing to us." Then he walked out.

Martin rose slowly from the wing chair, pursed his lips, and said, "Things will turn out fine, Jack. I'll call you later tonight."

And with that, they were gone. It made me think of the line from Pete Hamill, the journalism icon. Newspapers, he once said, will always break your heart. And now I find out, they can also rack your soul.

THEY LED CURTIS BLACK into the small, dingy conference room, a federal agent and a police detective, pushing him along from behind like he was a common criminal, a pimp, a drug dealer of some sort, someone not worth even a flickering moment of respect.

Inside the room, another police detective sat at a scratched wooden table, smoking a cigarette and paging through a manila file filled with official documents. His smoke gathered in the air of the ventless room beneath the single lightbulb that hung from the ceiling above the table. The stained walls were bare but for one filmy mirror. The room seemed to cast a pall over anyone unfortunate enough to be in it.

At first, Lieutenant Kevin Morrissey didn't even bother looking up, didn't deem his prisoner worth even that much dignity or interest. When he did, as the three men stood by the door, he said in a surprisingly soft voice, "Take his cuffs off."

The detective behind Black pulled out a key, stuck it into the handcuffs, and freed Black's wrists. Black shook them for a moment, trying to regain his circulation.

"Sit down, please," Morrissey said, nodding to the

chair across from him, speaking in that same soft voice. He blew a mouthful of smoke out, and it floated into Black's face. It didn't seem intentional. In a room this small, there was no place else for the smoke to go.

Morrissey nodded at the two standing men, prompting them to retreat quietly out into the hallway. Black heard the door click shut behind them.

Morrissey looked typically Irish, typically Boston—bright blue eyes and a ruddy face, carefully combed graying hair, the build of a former athlete who had tried to care for himself but finally decided to surrender to the effects of time. He sat in his shirtsleeves with a shoulder holster holding his service revolver. He eyed Black from across the table, his gaze drifting from Black's face down to his chest, to his hands, then back up to his face.

"Paul Boyle had two daughters," Morrissey said, his voice still low, easy, almost soothing. "One's sixteen, a junior out at Malden High. She wants to go to college. Smart kid, too, they tell me. Honor society and all that. Pretty girl. The other's thirteen. She's in seventh grade, a good athlete, kind of a daddy's girl type. Liked it a lot, I understand, when he went to her basketball games."

Black gulped hard, knowing where Morrissey was leading him.

"Here they are," Morrissey said, sliding a pair of pictures across the table—one of just two girls standing in the driveway of a modest suburban home, both girls gangly, all arms and legs in the way some teenagers are. They were smiling in an embarrassed kind of way, looking like they were biding time, waiting to do something else. The other picture was a more formal family portrait—a husband, presumably Paul Boyle, and his wife standing up, their two daughters sitting in chairs in front of them. "Take a look."

For a few seconds, Black was riveted by the photographs. Then he felt his head spin, his stomach grow queasy. The smoke continued to float up from the cigarette across his face. He looked away from the pictures at the empty wooden expanse of the table.

"I'm Kevin Morrissey. Lieutenant Kevin Morrissey. I assume you've been read your rights?"

Black continued to look down.

"Well, it's probably worth repeating the highlights. You have the right to remain silent. You also have the right to a lawyer. If you should want a lawyer, we will cease talking to you immediately and give you the opportunity to call your lawyer. You are free to do that any time you please."

Morrissey paused, and his voice became more confiding. "My advice to you right now, Curtis, is that a lawyer would not help and may well hurt. We can work together a lot more easily without someone getting in the way right now." Change of tone again, back to the original one. "But again, that's your call. You do have the right. I just want you to know that."

Black nodded and said nothing. He didn't have a lawyer, didn't even know a lawyer. A lawyer was never part of his program, never necessary, not until the FBI and Boston Police had showed up at his Chelsea apartment that afternoon.

Morrissey eyed him expectantly, nodded himself, and said, "So what went wrong? You don't usually kill people, Curtis. That's not your style. And look at this guy. Good husband. Good father. You know he was an usher up at

St. Paul's Church. He's dead. And look at his family. They've got to live a life without him. I wonder if those girls will even be able to go to college now."

He said this not in a taunting tone, but flat, matter-of-fact, curious.

Black sat in silence. Morrissey took a last puff of his cigarette, stubbed it out on the table, tossed it on the floor, then lit up another one.

The smoke continued to wash over Black's face. The faces on the photographs smiled up at him. The room seemed so painfully small and shrinking by the moment, the stains on the wall clawing at him.

Morrissey said, "You ever hear of the charge of felony murder?" He paused, got no reaction from Black, and continued. "We have it here in Massachusetts. It's when a victim dies in the commission of a felony, just like last week on Hanover Street. Everyone involved in that felony, whether they pulled the trigger or were some flunky driving the car, they're all going away for life. That's the sentence: life."

Morrissey was silent. Black gazed down at the table. This, he was coming to realize, was the dreaded climax not only of a tortuous week, the longest, most painful week of his life, but the climax of what had until then been a successful career of crime. Successful criminal careers, he was realizing, don't end with a banquet and a gold watch. One way or another, they usually end in court, then prison. For the last seven days, Black had awaited his destiny. He could have fled like a couple of the others, just taken his cash and boarded a plane and gone somewhere he had never been before, never to return. But he couldn't bring himself to do it. Some odd part of him, a part he had never felt before, kept him back, told him he had to face the consequences of that deadly dusk on Hanover Street. He had already lost his wife and their son in a hit-and-run crash the year before. After that, he felt he had nothing left to lose.

"We have an informant," Morrissey said, his voice still so calm, so easy. "This informant tells us that you were recruiting for a job a couple of months ago. You were getting ready for a heist. This heist."

Morrissey paused, stubbed out another cigarette, and threw it on the floor. Black continued to look down at the table, away from the photographs.

"We have a witness, an employee of the city of Boston's Transportation Department, Parking Enforcement Division. He saw someone double-parked in that blue cargo van outside of the bank. He tried to get that person to move, then wrote out a ticket. He picked your photograph out of a lineup, an old FBI surveillance photo we have, and identified you."

Black flinched, his almost imperceptible movement the only betrayal of a wave of sheer terror working its way up his spine. If there was even a scintilla of doubt about his fate, it was decided with those foreboding words. *We have a witness.* Black lifted his head up. His eyes rested on Morrissey. The two men locked stares in total silence.

"There is a way out," Morrissey said finally, the two men still eyeing each other, Black in desperation, the detective providing at least the veneer of help. "There's a way out." He shuffled some papers around purposefully. "Let me tell you how."

Black continued to stare at Morrissey, who lit up yet another cigarette, took a fast drag, and put it down right on the table.

"I don't believe you fired the weapon," Morrissey said. He paused, letting that thought hang out there with the cigarette smoke and the awkward adolescent smiles of Paul Boyle's two daughters. "Judging from where we believe you were during the commission, and the ballistic tests, we don't think you could have fired the weapon."

Silence, Black just staring back.

"Not your style." Morrissey raised his graying eyebrows. "And who knows, I may be able to find another witness who says you never got out of that van, which would make it impossible for you to have fired the gun, because Mr. Boyle was shot by someone standing over at the doorway to the bank."

Black continued to stare at him, his blank face masking a hurricane of thoughts and questions churning in his head. What kind of deal? Could he avoid doing time? What would that mean to the rest of his life? What would it mean to the others involved?

Morrissey continued, "So we cut a deal, me and you. I'd still have to convince the FBI to go along with this too, and they're not as easy and they're not as eager, but the worst of the charges in this case is in state court, this felony murder count. Life in prison, just for being there. It takes a long time to live a whole life in prison, you know."

Black could only imagine, which is what he was doing sitting in the chair trying not to breathe in the smoke, trying not to let his eye linger on the photographs of Paul Boyle's two daughters, trying not to let his guard down and be trapped by this man across from him.

"We cut a deal," Morrissey said. "You give me the names. You tell me who fired the shot that killed Paul Boyle. You tell me who else was involved. I'm especially interested in a convict by the name of Rocco Manupelli, who has strong connections to the Boston branch of La Cosa Nostra. You help us, we protect you, we put you in the federal program, we send you out of state with a new identity and a new way to make a life, an honest way to make a life. You make out. We make out. The only losers in this thing are the fucking murderers who killed this man." With that, Morrissey reached across the table and waved the Boyle family portrait in front of Black's face. "These girls don't have a father."

Black stared at him, still silent. He wondered to himself if he could do it. Could he be a rat? He didn't know these guys well. He didn't owe Manupelli anything. They had bungled the job. He had it teed up perfectly for them. Just follow orders and adhere to the plan, and they'd be all set now. And what was the alternative? If he didn't rat, what would happen?

As if reading his mind, Morrissey said, "And think about it. You're the only one we have right now. If you don't cough up the others, we come down on you in state and federal courts with a fury the likes of which you've never seen before. You'll never see a free day for the rest of your life. You won't even make bail."

Morrissey stubbed out another cigarette and flicked it on the floor. Black just wanted out of this room, out of his life, for that matter. He needed time to think. He should talk to a lawyer, if he could find one. He knew that much. That thought emboldened him to speak.

"We may have a deal. I need to speak to my lawyer first," he said.

Morrissey jumped up out of his seat, the chair almost falling backward because of his sudden force. He yanked out the chair closest to Black and sat back down, their faces now a few inches apart.

"This deal holds right now," Morrissey said, almost seething. "You get a lawyer involved, that creates a whole new level of bullshit I have to go through. I still have to talk those jamokes from the federal government into this. If you hesitate, I hesitate. Let me state it another way. You call a lawyer right now, I want to be the one who swings that prison door shut on the rest of your life."

Black put his hands up to his head, through his hair, across his forehead and eyes. When he opened his eyes, he was accidentally staring at those pictures, the smiling girls, the dead father, the times past they would never have again.

Looking at the photos, Black said, "I'll give you the guys." His voice was so low it was barely audible. Morrissey still sat right next to him, still just a few inches away.

"How many?"

There were five involved, plus him. Black hesitated. "All four," he said.

"Who was the shooter?"

"I don't know." As he said this, he thought of Stemple pitching his handgun into the harbor.

"Bullshit. How the fuck do you not know?"

Black gulped. "They wore masks and identical clothes. They were a good distance away from me. It was getting dark. I couldn't tell which one it was."

"Fuck it. No shooter, no deal." Morrissey got up as he said this and walked the few steps to the other side of the room, then turned toward Black, leaning on the table with his two hands.

Black's mind went into overdrive. Does he make it up? Does he tell him Stemple because it was Stemple who ditched his gun? But maybe Stemple fired a shot that missed. Does he tell him Rocco Manupelli because he doesn't like Rocco, thinks Rocco was destined to fuck this thing up, knows that Morrissey wants to hear that it was Rocco who was the killer?

Black said, "Then no deal. I don't know which one fired the deadly shot."

Morrissey lit up another cigarette and walked a slow lap of the table, cutting close behind Black.

"You're missing a guy too, right? Five guys at the scene, including you, and a driver at the fish pier, right? We have witnesses."

Black said, "Three guys were on the guard when he came out of the bank. One guy was on Boyle. I was in the van."

"Yeah, and what about the driver at the pier where you dumped the first getaway car?"

Black hesitated, collected himself, and said, "There was no other driver. We planted a car there, and when we got there, I drove."

Morrissey shook his head. When he spoke, his voice sounded tired now. "Bullshit again. I know how you work. You wouldn't risk leaving a car there unattended and having it be towed or watched or whatever. You like having a man on every job, a live person. You don't leave things to chance."

Black thought of his getaway driver on the pier. Older guy, no record, not even any criminal experience. He had needed the money, but didn't need it so bad he wanted to be part of the holdup. He took the driver's job for a smaller cut and said it was the only job he'd ever do. Black recalled the way the driver watched as the men arrived on the pier, angry and scared. He had watched as Black vomited, then fearfully asked what had gone wrong.

Black would spare him. He'd spare him. To Morrissey, he simply shook his head.

In response, the detective tossed his half-smoked cigarette, still lit, against the wall and strode silently out of the room, flipping the door shut behind him.

Maybe five minutes later, the door opened and another man in a navy blue suit entered the room.

"Curtis," Morrissey said, "This is special agent Kent Drinker of the FBI. He's a liaison between the bureau and the witness protection program. He, along with the U.S. attorney here in Boston, has to sign off on anyone entering the program."

twenty-one

Present Day
Monday, November 6

THERE IS NOTHING LIKE a funeral to spur a dreaded bout of introspection. First off, I defy anyone who has ever sat at such services to say they haven't looked around the room and wondered how many people they might attract to theirs, what the mourners might say, how sad those closest to you would be. I mean, I admit, I joined the National Press Club just so it would take up another line of my obituary and because maybe the club's board of governors might feel compelled to show up at the church, even though they had never met me and I don't even vote at the club elections.

I bring this up because as I gazed across the vast expanse of the Sacred Heart Church, at the hundreds upon hundreds of people crammed into the pews to mourn Steve Havlicek's passing—the Little League coaches, the fellow PTA members, the governor of Massachusetts, the entire congressional delegation, the high school and college classmates, the kids who grew up on the same block, the Neighborhood Watch members from down the street, I couldn't help but fear that my own death wouldn't lure any more than a few of Boston and Washington's better-known bartenders and the couple of interns who I used to take out to lunch as another excuse to use my company credit card.

Second, these occasions serve as an abrupt reminder of our own mortality, especially this one, especially for me. I don't think I need to remind anyone, I was supposed to be in that car when the bomb went off. I was supposed to be dead. The only thing that saved me is my mediocre memory—forgetting the tape recorder—and a sense of courtesy that harks back to a more chivalrous time. Had I pulled the keys out of the ignition and left Steve Havlicek in the cold to open my front door, I'd be somewhere between heaven and hell right now, the good Lord and Satan engaged in a game of dice to determine my eternal destiny.

Martin had warned me not to travel to Boston for Havlicek's memorial service. Well, screw Martin and his warnings. I felt like I didn't have a whole lot left to lose. So come Monday morning, I snuck out of the Jefferson through the kitchen, hailed a cab to Baltimore-Washington International, the farthest away of D.C.'s three airports, and grabbed a flight to Logan.

Anyway, like I said, the funeral, held in Havlicek's native Boston neighborhood of Roslindale, was packed. Margaret Havlicek, in a dignified black dress, sat in the first row, flanked on either side by her two children, both of whom, notably good-looking, seemed to have more of her genes than his, at least from an aesthetic point of view. The publisher of the *Record* was there, as were all the top editors and representatives from the other major newspapers. Everyone knew Havlicek, and to know him was to like him. I knew that better than anyone.

Despite the sickening session with Appleton and

Martin the day before, I was treated with an utmost sense
of respect and dignity, even if I had been ordered to stay
away. Margaret Havlicek had even called me in Washington and asked me to deliver a short eulogy. Once I was
there, General Ellis, the publisher, pulled me aside and
lauded what he described as my "constant acts of hero-
ism" on the story. Appleton himself stopped at my pew as
he walked slowly down the long aisle and put his hand on
my arm. I quelled my first impulse, which involved a kid-
ney punch.

For me, if I looked beyond the languid angst of it all,
the forever sadness that would mark this day, it was good
just to be out of that goddamned hotel room. I mean, I
love a nice hotel as much as anyone, and more than most.
But I had been held captive at the Jefferson Hotel all day
Sunday, not even allowed to leave to visit my recuperating
dog, who, by the way, seemed to be doing better, according to Kristen and Dr. Parins.

In church, Havlicek's oldest son, Paul, walked slowly
up to the altar to deliver the first eulogy of the morning.
He told of how his father never missed a single one of his
baseball games as a kid, how he would fly home through
the night to drive him to hockey practice in the cold
predawn hours of a Boston winter morning, how he took
an adult course in advanced calculus at Roxbury
Community College just to help him with his homework
in advanced-placement math. He recalled how his sister's
junior high gymnastics coach quit in the middle of one
season. I remembered that. The coach was actually
indicted for having sex with a minor, but Paul wisely left
that part out, given the surroundings and the occasion.
So with the season on the brink of shambles, Steve

Havlicek stepped in as the new volunteer coach, even though he knew about as much about gymnastics as Elvis knew about weight control. For the next month, he left work early every day. He told the team if they won the division title, he would learn how to do a backflip. They did, and he did, though he had a lot more trouble than the group of young women.

As Paul left the altar, there wasn't a dry eye in the house, nor a face that saw a wide smile. His departure was my cue to speak, and I walked to the front of the church, the guy who could and probably should be dead instead. Perhaps, I thought as I walked in the eerie silence of the massive church, it had been time for me to join Katherine in some form of afterworld. Perhaps I had defied destiny by mistake.

That aside, I told the gathered mourners of my first days at the *Record,* of this funny man named Havlicek who immediately insisted that I take him to lunch so he could show me the ropes, but was so busy eating that he only had time to tell me what a great guy he thought I was, and oh, yes, I could feel free to use the company credit card to pay the tab. After that, though, he was always the first one with a compliment, a suggestion, a bit of valuable advice.

In the last week, I saw more of him than I ever thought possible. That line seemed to raise a few chuckles. I talked about his brutal work habits, his ability to stay up around the clock, his commitment to the story, his steady stream of scoops, his unfailing good news judgment, his generosity as a colleague.

I mentioned the moments before the explosion, how he looked at me in my living room and asked if I would change my life if I inherited a couple of million dollars. Some people in the church laughed, understanding that it was a typical Havlicek question. I described his answer, how he said he wouldn't change a thing. This whole endeavor, he said, is too much fun, too worthwhile, to alter even a single part.

"Margaret, he loved you more than most people realize is possible, and we need only look around this church today to see the breadth and depth of the love so many people felt for him. Steve," I said, as the sounds of sobbing rippled through the cavernous room, "it's been not just a pleasure, but an honor. You were the best I've ever met."

As I walked past the thirty or so rows of pews to my seat near the back, I passed Samantha Stevens, standing on the end, watching me intently, tears streaming down her cheeks.

After the service, I stood in the back of the church, in a crowd of *Record* reporters, and watched sadly as Stevens walked by, alone. She circled back around and approached timidly, silently, searching my eyes with hers. Speaking so softly that she barely moved her lips, she said, "Drinker doesn't like to lose."

I thought that an odd thing to say. Lose what?

I replied, "Who killed Havlicek? Who planted that bomb?"

She shook her head slowly and sadly. "I don't know."

"How did you know I was arriving at National Saturday night, and why did you meet me?"

"I just wanted to see you. I called Havlicek up, and he told me when you were coming in."

That answer nearly caught me short, but I refused to

let it. Through gritted teeth, I asked, "Why did Curtis Black or Tony Clawson try to kill the president?"

She continued to stare at me, not coldly, but with heart. "I don't know."

I was growing angry, seething, but still quiet. "What is it you know?"

"I only know that I was never involved in anything to do with that explosion, or with Drinker. And I only know that I don't want to see you hurt in any way at all."

And with that, she turned and walked slowly away.

My third point about funerals, that perhaps I should have made earlier, is that they make me think of everyone else who has died in my life. In the cemetery, as the priest droned on too far away for me to hear, I thought of my father in the pressroom of the *Record*, putting in an honest day's work for an honest day's pay. I thought of my mother, dying of a broken heart after my father's death.

And of course, I thought of Katherine, who was supposed to be here with me during difficult times like these, my constant companion for my entire life. We should be preparing for another holiday season, making plans for family visits, keeping a camera nearby for our baby's first steps. Instead, I had no one to share with, nothing to look forward to, not even a steady job.

What I did have, though, were bodyguards, two of them whom I paid $300 apiece, plus airfare, to join me on this Boston excursion. In their somber suits, at least they were dressed like the mourners, and their presence allowed me some comfort, though I still found myself peering around suspiciously at the gathered crowd.

Which is exactly what I was doing when Gus Fitz-patrick emerged from a cluster of people and walked slowly my way with his trademark limp. I held my hand out, and he shook it silently, then reached his other arm around and rubbed the back of my shoulder.

"It's really nice to see you, Gus," I said, and this was one of those occasions when I really meant it.

"It's really nice to see you," he said. "Thank the good Lord you're alive."

He looked me up and down and then said something that rocked me to my core.

"Nothing is still as it seems," he said, staring me in the eye. "Do not yet believe anything that they tell you."

My jaw dropped in an almost stereotypical way. The identical words of my anonymous informant, Paul Stemple, rang through my mind.

"Gus," I replied, trying to maintain composure. "Do you know what you're saying?"

He nodded and remained quiet.

"What's going on here?" I asked, my tone urgent but my voice low, so as not to attract attention.

Gus stood silently.

In the void, I said, "Havlicek is dead." Well, admit-tedly, I was speaking the obvious, given that his casket was sitting about twenty yards away in front of the hole where it would momentarily be placed. But in newspa-pers, that's often what we do, state the obvious. Why else a front-page headline that reads "Reagan Beats Mondale"?

"I feel horrible about that," Gus said. "You know I do."

I bore in on Gus. Gus bore in on me. He finally shifted his gaze to look over my shoulder, and I glanced back to see the priest throwing holy water on the casket and sprinkling it into the hole in the ground. The burial was unfolding about thirty yards away, a good-sized chip shot, outside of easy hearing range.

I felt, to say the least, confused. My mind raced through every crucial moment of this case, but I couldn't find Gus's footprints anywhere and had no idea why he was here now. I didn't even know enough to ask anything, so I repeated myself, saying, "Steve Havlicek is dead." As I said it, I was surprised to hear my voice crack.

More silence, until Gus said, "Come with me, Jack."

I thought about Martin and Appleton huddled amid the mourners, about their orders for me to return immediately to Washington, about my dubious status at the newspaper. I looked at my bodyguards and gave them a little hand signal to follow me. Then I thought about Havlicek, about the way his grip loosened on my hand Sunday morning in the unforgiving aftermath of the explosion, about his wife's voice on the other end of the line when I told her that her husband was dead.

So I nodded at Gus, and he, for no apparent reason, nodded back at me, and we disappeared over the other side of the hill, meandering among the ancient oak trees and tombstones.

The two of us stood on the end of the Boston Fish Pier in a remote loading area beside the ancient brick auction house as the pale November sun seemed ready to surrender to the chill of another New England winter. On one side of us, the magnificent city skyline rose toward the heavens, the steel-and-glass buildings splashed with light. On the other side, the harbor sparkled and rippled in the autumn breeze. Planes from Logan Airport thundered overhead as they ascended to destinations unknown.

Gus looked at me and spoke for the first time since the graveyard. "Are you familiar with Paul Stemple?" he asked.

"I saw him yesterday morning," I said. "He's dead. Murdered." Here he was, a man who held secrets that could probably shake our democracy to its core, and his passing was marked only by a newsbrief in the *Washington Post* under the headline "Capitol Hill Transient Slain."

Gus grimaced and shook his head slowly. "I had a feeling," he said.

Much as I love Gus, standing there watching him, I couldn't contain my anger, even with the prospect of an imminent explanation. "As I've said, Havlicek is dead. I couldn't have been warned about this? You couldn't have helped us out—some real goddamned help—instead of this pseudo-intellectual gamesmanship?"

We had driven from Roslindale to the waterfront in collective silence, the only sound in Gus's car being the all-news AM radio station broadcasting blurbs from a speech President Hutchins had delivered that morning in Cleveland, Ohio, on the eve of the election. The reporter said that after a final blitz from Detroit to New York City, Hutchins would be back at the White House tonight. Democratic nominee Stanny Nichols, the reporter said, was spending election eve scouring the crucial electoral state of California for last-minute support.

When we had arrived at this barren concrete loading zone, Gus simply got out of the car and stood in the brisk outdoors air. I, of course, followed him.

To my pending question, he stayed silent, either thinking about what I had asked or ignoring me. I only became angrier. What, he hadn't prepared for this moment? After all this, he didn't know what he was going to say?

I glared at Gus in a way I never thought I could or would and said, "What the hell is going on here? What the hell is going on?"

Gus leaned back against the hood of his car, a navy Oldsmobile bought with cash, no doubt—money saved from decades of hard work alternating between the evening and overnight shifts in the pressroom. He looked extraordinarily uncomfortable in his shirt, tie, and jacket, and it struck me that I hadn't seen Gus dressed this way since Katherine's funeral. Then it occurred to me to put that thought out of my mind right now. I had to concentrate on the issues at hand.

Lingering silence. Endless silence.

I said, "Gus, you brought me here to tell me something. What is it?"

"This isn't easy," he said. He fell quiet again, and I regarded him more closely—the long forehead on such a short man, the fatherly eyes, which at the moment held the anguished embarrassment of a child, the leathery skin baked from too much sun over too many summers, the way he stood with one leg always bent at the knee because the other leg was two inches shorter.

He broke my train of meaningless thought and said, "I know Curtis Black."

This time I stayed quiet, waiting, expecting.

He said, "I know Curtis Black. The guys in that armored car robbery, they fled Hanover Street in one getaway car with the money, drove along the waterfront, and came to this very spot. I met them here in a second car, and we all drove from here down to a storefront in Providence, where we split up the cash. My take was somewhat smaller than the rest because I wasn't at the scene."

I looked at him in shock. Gus, my Gus, a common criminal, part of a gang of killer armored car robbers. A man died that day, a young husband, a father, if I remembered right from the newspaper clips, shot in the neck during a heist on Hanover Street. And Gus was a part of it—not the direct cause, if he could be believed, but an accessory nonetheless.

Gus stood there watching me. My mind became a blur. So many questions to ask, so little ability to ask them. I was, in the parlance of the pop psychology that so many of my journalistic colleagues indulge in, conflicted. On the one hand, I didn't want to believe what he was saying. I didn't want him to be involved in anything like this. On the other hand, if he was, he would be forthcoming with the explanations I needed to this seemingly inexplicable, impenetrable mess.

"I don't get it. If you were involved, why weren't you arrested like the others? Why didn't you go to prison? How did you end up at the *Record?*"

Gus was still leaning against the car, almost sitting on the hood, his arms crossed. I was standing facing him.

"Black didn't give me up," Gus said. "When he turned government's witness, he denied there was a second getaway driver. Two of the other guys, probably hoping to get leniency, kept insisting to the feds there was another driver, but they didn't even know my name. It came down to Paul Stemple. He fired a shot that day, but meant to aim high—a warning shot. The guy next to him, name of Manupelli, fired a shot too. Stemple was always racked by guilt over the possibility that he killed the guard, that the whole thing was his fault. So he refused to give me up because he knew I didn't have anything to do with the death. The U.S. attorney himself asked Paul if there was a second getaway driver, and Paul told him no."

I shot a glance toward my bodyguards standing by their rental car about forty yards down the pier, though perhaps *shot* is the wrong word to use at this point. I don't know. I didn't feel like I knew much of anything anymore, even as I was learning new things by the second. I returned my gaze to Gus.

Gus said, "So I went to your old man. We knew each other growing up. I told him I was desperate, that I was in a lot of trouble, that I needed his help. I mean, I didn't get involved in this robbery just for kicks. I'd like to tell you I needed the money to pay for something for the kids or medical bills or something. Something. But I needed it because I got in some gambling trouble, and if I didn't come up with some cash, I was going to be in some serious health trouble, maybe even dead."

Standing here on the Boston Fish Pier at high noon on election eve, I mused that you know people, but you don't really know them. You know them now, so you think you've known them always, as if everyone follows the same cookie-cutter path in life from young adulthood on to marriage, parenthood, or whatever. In fact, what you see or even imagine is little more than an outline, a silhouette, and perhaps a deceiving one at that. What you don't see is the text and the texture, the private drama that makes up a human life.

I was both stunned and spellbound. I didn't say anything—one, because I couldn't, and two, because I didn't want Gus to stop. Never interrupt the steady flow of crucial information to hear yourself speak.

Gus took the silent bait. "Black didn't give me up, and I owed him for that. But Black didn't give me up for a simple reason. Had he given me up, I would have made a pretty damned good government witness. I couldn't have been involved in the shooting. I didn't mastermind the thing. I was just a grunt driving a car, trying to make some dough to keep my legs from getting busted. Had I been a federal witness, Black would have gone to jail."

He paused only long enough to look me hard in the eye and catch his own breath. This whole thing seemed to be like penance for Gus. I suspect he regarded me as some sort of keeper of the truth, being in the newspaper business and all, and here he was letting the truth be known for the first time, so many years after the fact.

"So I owe something to your father. He was a shift supervisor at the *Record*, and he got me a job when I needed it most. And I owe something to Mr. Stemple, and here I am taking care of two debts by trying to help you." A pause, accompanied by a watchful gaze over my face, then, "Does this make sense?"

"It does, yeah, if I knew what it is you were trying to help me with. I don't mean to beat a dead horse, but one of the two reporters on this story was killed. And the other one, me, despite all your attempts to help, has more questions than answers. I know Curtis Black is involved. I know he tried to assassinate the president of the United States. But I don't know why, and I don't have proof. In other words, so many days and so much tragedy, and I can't even get a news story out of this. So nothing personal,

Gus, but you haven't done a whole lot by me yet, not, at least, as much as you probably intended."

Gus looked at me in a curious way, speaking, it seemed, without talking.

"You have it partly right," he said.

I whirled toward him and asked, pointedly, "What do you mean by that?"

He fell mute. I softened my tone. "Gus, you want to help. I trust you on that. So help me. No more hoops. No more hurdles. No more being cryptic. Help me."

There was more than a hint of desperation in my voice, but at this point, so what? Gus stood up a little straighter, though his leg was still bent in that familiar way it always is.

He said, "You know Curtis Black went into the witness protection program, right? We've established that."

I nodded.

"So he gets a new identity. I don't know what happened to him in the program. I heard he vanished—abandoned his new, government-issued identity and got a third identity on his own."

This coincided with the government records that I had seen the previous morning, which showed that Clawson vanished in 1988.

Gus continued. "So he's running around, and no one knows who he is: not the government who gave him a free ride on a felony murder offense, not the guys he betrayed and put away for the rest of their lives.

"No one knows who he is," Gus continued. "No one knows where he is."

I asked finally, "So then why does Curtis Black take a shot at the president?"

Gus looked at me long and hard, leaving the sensation

that he was looking through me, into my mind, willing information to me.

"He doesn't," Gus said, still staring at me. Abruptly he turned around, opened his car door, reached beneath his seat, and pulled out a copy of that morning's *Boston Record*. He shut the door and held out the front page in front of me.

I looked at a pair of side-by-side colorful photographs taking up much of the top half of the page. The first one was of Senator Stanny Nichols working a ropeline at an event in Los Angeles, leaning over the yellow tape, both his hands stretched out for the thronging crowd of Democratic supporters to shake. The second one, right beside it, was of President Clayton Hutchins standing behind a podium on the tarmac of the Milwaukee airport, a lineup of fully uniformed policemen standing behind him in an anticrime event, and behind them the distant outline of Air Force One.

Gus pointed slowly at Hutchins, his finger lingering on his face for a few seconds. He looked me in the eye and slowly, somberly, said, "That's Curtis Black."

And just like that, so many pieces fall into so many empty places, a picture suddenly emerging from all the disparate parts, though it didn't yet become entirely clear. I stared at the photograph, then at Gus.

"He's had some cosmetic work done," he said. "He's worked on his speech patterns, his Boston accent. But it's him. We knew it was him, but we couldn't be sure, so from prison, Paul sent a message to him when he was vice president, through a brother-in-law who was a big fundraiser. The message said simply, 'Paul Stemple knows and needs to be pardoned.' And lo and behold, he was."

My head was swimming, my hands visibly shaking, my voice weak from mental exhaustion.

I asked, "So if Black is the president, not the would-be assassin, and all the other men in the gang are dead or in jail, then who shot at Black, and why?"

Before he could open his mouth to answer, I felt another piece of this nearly completed puzzle jamming into place. No one shot at Hutchins. Someone shot at me. I was the first man struck. Drinker was right when he floated that theory, though for all the wrong reasons. I was the intended victim of someone who was trying to maintain Hutchins's secret.

Gus said, "We can't prove it, but my belief is that it was you they were gunning for, not Hutchins. From what I've heard inside the *Record,* you were nosing around on this pardon early on, and they must have been trying to get you out of the way. Someone was. I just don't know who."

There was a long silence between us. The chill breeze continued to rustle through my suitcoat, though I didn't actually feel cold. Planes continued to rumble overhead, though I didn't hear a sound.

"Why didn't you just tell me all this to begin with?" I asked, a dose of aggravation seeping into my voice. "We could have avoided a lot of tragedy."

Gus shook his head slowly and looked down at the ground, then back up at me. "I think I have a pretty good idea about how you work. God knows, I've been watching you since you were greener than a meadow. I've known you a long time, Jack. If I just gave you what I had, anonymously, you would have dismissed me as some sort of crackpot and never checked the information. If I had come to you on the record, I would have destroyed my entire life. My wife doesn't know about this armored car heist. My daughters, they don't know about this armored car heist. You're the best reporter I know. I wanted you to figure this out on your own, without my direct involvement, and come to the answers yourself. It almost worked."

I said, "So you won't go on the record? I need you on the record on this."

Gus shook his head slowly. He said, "I just can't. I busted my hump to recover from where I was. I've made a life for myself. I'm happy. My wife is happy. I can't destroy all that now."

"Who killed Havlicek and Stemple?" I asked.

"That part, you're going to have to learn on your own. It's either Hutchins or the FBI. I just can't tell you who."

Standing there, I suddenly felt the driving urge to get somewhere fast, though I wasn't quite sure where I needed to be. I was sitting on information that no one else in the world had, but I wasn't quite sure how to let anyone else know.

I nodded slowly to Gus. I couldn't well be angry, but I was somewhere shy of appreciative. "I've got to get out of here," I said.

"You have what you need?"

I don't think he meant luggage. "I have, I think, whatever I'm going to get."

I looked back at my bodyguards and gave them a wave to approach. Their car started, and they raced up to where we were standing. Gus took a step toward me, reached his arm out to hug me, and I fell into his embrace. As we stepped back from each other, he looked me in the eye and said, "You're a man of words. Me, I'll never be able to tell you how sorry I am. For everything."

He smiled and hit me softly on the shoulder with his open fingers. Then he added, "You're on your own now, and for you, with your talents, that's not a bad place to be."

twenty-two

SO ON YOUR OWN really means being on your own. It means having a newspaper that doesn't want you on the story. It means having a key informant who has nothing else to give. It means having an FBI that may be trying to kill you rather than help you. It means returning home to Washington to nobody and nothing but the presence of imminent danger.

After all that had gone on that day, with all that was left to come, my hotel room seemed depressing, if I had the time or inclination to be depressed, which, right now, I didn't. As I fired up my laptop, I leaned back in my chair and pondered what I had. The president of the United States was a former armored car robber named Curtis Black who had entered the federal witness protection program at the invitation of the government under the name of Tony Clawson, switched names again to Clayton Hutchins, became a prominent businessman in Iowa, was elevated to the governorship by the eleventh-hour whims of a fickle electorate, was nominated vice president without a public vote, became president when his predecessor dropped dead, and was now one day away from being elected to a full term.

How did I know this? Well, two of his cohorts on the armored heist told me—one who was now dead, another who wouldn't allow me to use his name.

While we're at it, let's not forget that the Federal Bureau

of Investigation was trying to kill me and had succeeded in killing my colleague, Steve Havlicek. And how did I know this? Well, the suspicions of those same criminals and my own gut instinct.

All this would go over big with Appleton—trying to end the Hutchins presidency on the word of two admitted criminals, but without the benefit of sharing their identities with our readership. I couldn't help but smile to myself. My sourcing, if that's what you want to call it, was so weak as to be laughable. I knew the facts. I just couldn't put them in the newspaper. I imagined the pitying look on Appleton's face when he fired me, or maybe he'd just do it by telephone, and all I'd get would be the pseudo-sympathetic tone of his voice.

I flicked the television on and turned to CNN's *Headline News* to see where Hutchins was campaigning. A couple of minutes later, the network played footage of him speaking to a huge rally at Rockefeller Center in midtown Manhattan, urging his supporters not only to vote themselves but each to bring a family member and a friend or neighbor to the polls—all, he said, "To guide our own destiny, to renew that most sacred of institutions, the American dream."

The camera showed men and women and children laughing and applauding and shouting high into the air. Balloons, red, white, and blue, fell from the sky, framed by the mammoth skyscrapers of New York. I stared hard at Hutchins, at his features, his smile, his face, his eyes, his graying hair. Frustrated, I flicked the picture off.

So do I call Martin? I decided it wasn't the right time yet. I decided I wanted to be armed with more information before he raced over and threw me off my game. On a legal pad, I scribbled down the names of people I needed to call: Sammy Markowitz, Kent Drinker, Clayton Hutchins. Neither Markowitz nor Hutchins would be particularly easy to raise, though I imagined by now, Drinker might well be all too easy. Chances were, he would find me before I even began looking for him.

Which, of course, begged the question: which was, the killer FBI agent—Drinker or Stevens, Stevens or Drinker? Or both? Stevens was an obvious suspect, given her mysterious presence at the airport. But then I recalled Havlicek telling me in the car before he died that he had talked to her that day. He just didn't explain what he had said. Perhaps he really had given her my arrival time.

Well, I wasn't going to answer that question now, so I flipped through my datebook for Markowitz's number. When I called, some dullardly gentleman picked up the telephone, announced the name of his fine establishment, the Pigpen, then yelled to someone nearby, "Hey, leave the fucking jerky alone. I'll get it for you when I'm done." Pause, then, "Yeah, what."

"Is Sammy there?" I asked.

"No."

Great. This song and dance all over again. I said, "Well, when he gets in from church, could you tell him that Jack Flynn called. Tell him it's urgent that I speak to him."

"Hol'on a second," the man said. I heard him ask someone else, "Hey, Rudy, the boss go to church or somethin'? Isn't he in his booth?"

There was no pulling one over on this guy. A long pause followed, then the phone rang, then Markowitz's voice said, "You have nine lives? Hate to tell you, but I think you're down to about two."

I wasn't much in the mood to make funny with him, given the day. "Sammy, I need you to tell me something, and I need you to be straight. Is there anyone up there in your world who'd be worried about me digging around on Curtis Black? Let me take it a step further. Is there anyone up there who'd kill over this? His cohorts in that failed robbery? Debtors? Anyone you can think of? And is there anyone who would want to kill Black himself if they found out who he is or where he is?"

There was silence. I heard the flick of his lighter, the sound of him inhaling a cigarette, then blowing smoke out toward the decrepit environs of his bar. "No," he said. "Black kind of became a nobody when he left, and that was a long time ago—over twenty years. We don't hold grudges that long in my business. Only in the movies. Too much money to be made." He paused as if he was calculating something, like that day's bookmaking receipts maybe, then added, "And I'm tallying the people up here. Everyone involved in that particular heist is either still in jail or dead. There's no one free who gives a rat's ass about Curtis Black."

I asked, "You're absolutely sure?"

He paused again, then said, "Yeah, unless there's something going on I don't know about, but that's at best unlikely. Yeah, I'm sure."

I said, "Let me ask you something else. You by chance mention to anyone that I was talking to you about Curtis Black? If you did, no hard feelings. But I'm at a point in my story that it would be really helpful to know."

There was another long pause. I could hear him puffing on his cigarette. I could hear the mindless chatter of his small-minded clientele in the background, some woman on a jukebox singing a country song about a car stealing her man or maybe her man stealing her car. "No," he said. But it was the way he said it, anything but firm. He sounded uncharacteristically weak, begging more questions.

So I asked him one. "Who? Who'd you tell? I need this."

I heard him take a deep breath, then let out a mouth full of smoke. "A fed, some fucker by the name of Drinker—I told him he should own a bar with that name. He came by, wanted to know what I knew. He kept pressuring me, wouldn't get out of my face. He was raising your name. After a while, I just had to get him out of here. I told him you were looking into Black." Another long pause, then, "I don't normally say this, Jack, but if I hurt you, sorry."

Dimed by a lifelong crook. "Great. An apology. That means a lot."

Sammy said, "Look, I'm getting old. I'm in the market for friends, not enemies, and he was offering me friendship, said he'd keep an eye out for me, rather than on me."

I said, "Do me a favor, Sammy. When you screw me over again, just let me know about it, would you?"

Next, I called the White House switchboard and asked to have Royal Dalton paged in New York. This would be my most significant problem. My past dozen days aside, a reporter doesn't just get in to talk to the president of the United States at will, especially on election eve. In fact, most reporters never get the chance to see the president one-on-one in their entire lives. The only time they are able to question him is on national television, at one of his rare press conferences—a venue that wouldn't work particularly well in this situation. Just imagine, me standing up in the East Room of the White House and saying, "Sir, we are pursuing a story saying you were once Curtis Black, an armored car robber in Massachusetts. Do you care to confirm that fact here, and if so, is it true that the FBI has killed reporter Steve Havlicek in its effort to protect you?" Either the stock market would drop one thousand points in the day, or I'd be led off the grounds in a straitjacket by men who would load me into the back of a blue van and say repeatedly, "You're right, the whole world is out to get you. But trust us. We're your protectors."

Ten minutes later, my telephone rang back. An officious-sounding twenty-something said, "This is Hamilton Carr. Could I help you?"

First off, I hate when someone returns someone else's phone messages. Second, I hate it more when they just assume I know who they are. This, by the way, is standard procedure in Washington, the world's self-importance capital.

I said, dismissively, "I don't think so. I'm trying to reach Royal Dalton."

"Well, can I help you with something?"

"Sure. You could take a message and pass it on to Royal Dalton. Ask him to call me at the number you just dialed."

Exasperated, young Hamilton said, "I am the duty person in the White House press office today. How can *I* help you?"

Equally exasperated, I said, "You can do your duty by calling Mr. Dalton, telling him that Jack Flynn said he has a significant story running in tomorrow's paper on the presidential assassination attempt that requires an adult's attention, and asking him to please call me at the number you just dialed. Tell him I'll be here for ten more minutes."

Sure enough, about three minutes later, Dalton was on the other line, himself exasperated. "It's the day before the election," he said in that thin voice of his. "What could you possibly be doing?"

"Trying to hold this democracy together, a task that you people aren't making any easier," I said. "Here's my problem. I need to talk to Hutchins. I need to talk to him about a subject that only he knows about and that only he will want to know about. I need to talk to him tonight—"

"Absolutely no way. We just gave you time with him on Saturday, and best I can tell, you haven't done anything with it."

I said, angry, "Well, we've had a few things happen since then, like a car bomb and the death of my colleague." I paused. He stayed silent, so I asked, "Where are you?"

"We're at Kennedy. We're about to board Air Force One back to Andrews."

I said, "Would you relay a message to Hutchins? Tell him I'm doing a story about Curtis Black, with some new, crucial details that could prove, well, explosive." Much as I enjoy my own puns, especially those with a double entendre, I didn't particularly like that unintended one.

He replied in that superior tone of his, "What in the world are you talking about? I'm not going to relay a message like that, even if I could. Tell me what you're working on, and maybe I can get someone else at the White House to help you out."

I said, "I'm going with a story tomorrow. It's potentially devastating to Hutchins, especially if his own staff prevents him from responding. If you don't tell him I'm trying to reach him, you're going to be screwed. Take my word for it, Royal."

"You know I can't go to him on the night before the presidential election with no information."

"On this one, you have to, or you'll regret it for a long time to come. Have him call me. I'll be here."

He didn't reply, leaving another moment of gaping silence. I added, "Remember, Curtis Black, crucial details, explosive. Tell him that."

Now I'd be lying if I said I wasn't getting any satisfaction from this, working the telephone, putting pieces together, inching closer to the answers that Havlicek and I had pursued to his death. I was back in my element, even if no one wanted me there. But it doesn't matter if they did or didn't. In newspapers, at the end of each day, the only thing that matters is what you can get into print.

The telephone rang. I picked it up, and it was Lincoln Powers, the chief of staff.

"Young man," he said in a spare Texas twang, "I brought your request to the president, and the president said, verbatim, that he doesn't know what you're talking about and has nothing to say."

I replied, "Well, could you tell the president, verbatim, that tomorrow's *Record* will carry a story detailing the transformation of Curtis Black, and it will no doubt have a profound impact on the election. I'll be at my phone for a short time only."

Well, that last part was a lie. Actually, I'd be glued to my phone waiting, but why give them the confidence rooted in your own anxiety?

About ten minutes later, the telephone rang again, and miraculously, or not so miraculously, it was that familiar voice of President Clayton Hutchins. Every half-cocked bluff was working like a charm. Without introductions, or even enthusiasm, he said, "Curtis Black. What the hell does that mean?"

"I think you know, sir," I said, trying to sound sympathetic to someone who was about to be found in a life-defining lie. "I uncovered some crucial new information on Curtis Black and his current identity."

"I don't know what the hell you're talking about, young man," he said. He sounded sincere, but politicians usually do.

I replied, "Sir, I've talked to other members of the gang on that Wells Fargo job. They know who you are. They are willing to go public with their information." Well, not exactly, but why get bogged down in the mundane details of sourcing a story?

"Young man, I don't have the slightest fucking idea what you're fucking talking about, but be aware you're talking to the president of the United fucking States of America."

Employing an old reporting trick, I let that hang out there, my implicit accusation, his pathetic response. This wasn't so much a pause as a protracted silence. I pictured him sitting in his office on Air Force One, the plane preparing for takeoff, a small army of aides and servants outside his study door. He was the most public and most private man in the world.

Now I understood what Stemple was saying on that very first day he spoke to me, all that stuff about nothing being as it seems, the strange complex motives involved.

At least, I think I understood. More important, I think I was about to know in such a way that I could write about it.

Then, in a tone I had never heard before, his voice so thick it barely sounded like him, he said, "I'm in New York, on the runway, about to get airborne. Why don't you come over to the White House when I get back, and we'll talk."

"That would be helpful, sir," I said. "What time?"

"Seven." We hung up, leaving just one immediate question, at least for me: would someone try to kill me before I could get in?

At this point, I had no choice but to call Peter Martin, who snapped up the telephone on the first ring as if he had been waiting for my call all day. Just as Havlicek preserved the story in the moments before he died and passed it on to me in the form of Stemple's address, I needed to make plans in case I came in harm's way.

"Well, we were right about one thing," I said. "Curtis Black was definitely involved in the shooting. Only he was the victim, not the attempted assassin."

Martin said, "What? What are you talking about?"

I said, "Here's the short version. Curtis Black is the president of the United States. One of the guys from his old criminal gang told me so today." I paused and added, "Take this one to the bank."

"I don't understand." You don't hear Martin say that all that often.

I said, "Curtis Black became a federal witness. He came out with a new identity, that of Tony Clawson. A few years later, he ditched the name Clawson and assumed the name Clayton Hutchins, who, I have a raw hunch, was an actual person who had died very young. He's a smart guy. He went off and made a fortune in computer software. He came into politics almost unwittingly. He became governor of Iowa at the last minute, and then he rose up almost in spite of himself. And when it was time to run for president, think about it. He had a fabricated background. It was real, but it wasn't. It was chosen as a best-case scenario, so there could be nothing wrong with it, except it was a lie. Remember when David Souter won confirmation to the Supreme Court? One of his best qualities was that no one knew anything about him because he was such a recluse and never wrote anything down. This is like that. In a media age when all we do is look for scandal, he didn't have any because his whole life was made up. And fortunately for him, we all found scandal in his opponent, so we were distracted."

I could hear Martin breathing heavily into the phone, playing out every angle of this story, every possible thing that could go wrong versus what might be right.

"You have it firm enough to go with?"

"No. But Hutchins has agreed to see me. I'm heading over there in about an hour."

"Is it safe for you to go?" Good question; Martin getting his bearings.

"Don't know, but it's even less safe not to go."

"All right. I'll be in the office when you get back. Be careful, and be good."

When I paged Drinker next, he returned the call before I could even lean back in my chair.

I said, "I need to speak with you soon. I'm ready to go with a story and want to go over some angles. You know as well as I do that I wasn't the intended target at Congressional. I'll give you one final chance to help."

He replied, sounding sincere, "Go ahead."

"No. In person. Meet me in the lobby of the Four Seasons Hotel in twenty minutes. And just so you know, I've already written everything I know down and passed it on to my superiors. Don't fuck with me. It won't do anyone any good."

Maybe it was rude to leave him hanging in a hotel lobby on the night before this historic election. But maybe it was ruder still to kill Havlicek in cold blood, and try to kill me. Screw him.

I paused and ran my fingers over a picture I had in my luggage of Katherine, eight months pregnant, sitting at our patio table, her chin resting on the palm of her right hand, smiling at me. "This is it," I whispered. Then I snuck out the back, through the kitchen.

It was after dusk, chilly. I scanned the parked cars, checking to see if any of them pulled out and followed me as I walked, but none did. I had the feeling that death waited around every corner. I headed down Sixteenth Street with a baseball cap pulled low over my head and flanked by the two gentlemen I had assigned to protect me. I ducked into the Hay-Adams Hotel, just across Lafayette Park from the White House. I sat at the bar, ordered a Coca-Cola, and wrote out the lead to my story dozens of times on the keyboard of my mind, glancing constantly at the door all the while.

About forty minutes later, out the tall windows, I could see Marine One descending from the sky and disappearing from view to land on the South Lawn. One more time, I pulled my cap low, and hurried straight across the park at a pace that was closer to a trot than a walk. At any minute, I felt, my life could end. I also felt as if my destiny was out of my hands.

I arrived at the northwest gate, where I flashed my badge to a Secret Service agent. I felt safe on the White House grounds, maybe wrongly. The agent buzzed me in with a bored nod. An interview like never before.

Truth be known, I didn't have anything close to what I needed to get this story into print. Like I said, I had the word of two admitted felons, one of whom was dead. I don't think even the *National Enquirer* would go to bed with this one.

So what I needed here, like a good cop trying to create an airtight case, was a confession. And just as a good detective uses the power of the law to scare the bejesus out of suspects, I needed to use the power of the written word to intimidate a president on the verge of his own election. I needed him to think that his fate had already been decided, at least in terms of the coverage in the *Boston Record*. I needed him to think about the inevitable onslaught to come, the media maelstrom that would follow my story, the classic feeding frenzy from which there would be no escape. I needed him to believe that the best and perhaps only way out was an honest admission of fault.

When I was led into the Oval Office, Hutchins was sitting at his desk in shirtsleeves and a crisp red tie loosened at his neck, the top button undone. He was alone. Dozens and dozens of lawyers and dozens more political advisers and newly minted friends in every corner of official Washington, and he chose on this evening to handle this topic alone, just as I suspected he would. That, in itself, was interesting.

He held a heavy lowball glass in his hand, and the glass was filled with about three fingers' worth of what looked to be whisky and ice. As I sat in a chair in front of his desk, he nervously slid the glass around, causing the cubes to smash softly against each other. He brought the glass up to his face and absently took a sip.

"You believe in redemption?" he asked me, his voice deep, animated, breaking the heavy silence like a clap of thunder.

I considered that question for a moment and replied, "I do, sir. There's something very human about it, something almost moral, and something uniquely American. We have the right to screw up. More important, we have the right to another chance, at least in most cases."

He pondered that for a minute, shook the ice around in his glass again, and took another sip.

"It's election eve," he said, looking me in the eye. "My pollsters informed me this afternoon that I'm going to win. You care for a celebratory Scotch?"

Why not? Create a mood of confidence, two men exchanging secrets. "If it's convenient, sir."

He pressed a button on the side of his desk, and a dark-skinned steward, Indian-looking, came silently through a side door. "Raj, get my friend a Johnnie Walker, please," Hutchins said. To me, "Rocks or no rocks?"

"No ice."

"Neat," he said to the steward, who turned and walked quietly out the door he came in. Hutchins called out after him, "Make it a double, Raj. We're celebrating."

After I got my drink, Hutchins bore into me with his eyes. "I watched you guys go after my opponent early in the campaign. Christ, what did he do? Fudge some information on his mortgage application or something ten years ago, and you guys try taking him down, try ruining his political career. You were throwing around half-truths and nontruths and buying into anything you were fed. I thought it was sickening then, but it helped me, so I kept my mouth shut. The guy, he wins his party's nomination. He's sacrificing his time, his livelihood, his fucking reputation. He's on the doorstep of the White House, for God's sakes. He's campaigning all over the country twenty hours a day for something he believes in, even if that something is only himself. Christ, he should be applauded. He's part of the elite. And you guys won't cut him a break." He paused and laughed a breathy, bittersweet laugh to himself.

He looked down at his drink, took another sip, and continued. "And now here I am. I'm on the verge of winning the election. I'm going to get my own four-year term. Things are going all right. We're getting a good team in place, even if you're not on it. The economy's doing well. Wall Street breaks a new record every other day. And you guys, you're bored. You're fucking bored. You need something else, something to get your teeth into. So you turn on me because that's just what you do. You can't help yourselves."

He stared at me. Maybe glare is a more appropriate word. I stared back. That's easy to do when you're in the right. He eventually averted his eyes, giving me some small victory. He said, decisively, "All right, tell me what you think you know."

I took my own sip of Scotch. I don't particularly like whisky on the best of days, but the taste seemed especially harsh tonight, almost medicinal.

After grimacing, I showed him all my cards. It was coming up on 8:00 P.M. and I didn't have the time or the creativity to do anything cute. "Sir," I said, "you are living under an alias. You were born Curtis Black. You were a convict in Massachusetts. You turned government's witness. You were relocated under the federal witness protection program under the name of Tony Clawson. After being in the program for eight or nine years, you switched names a second time, to Clayton Hutchins. Through a combination of luck, timing, and skill, you have risen to the top of the world."

This time, he laughed a devilish laugh, then leaned back in his high-backed leather chair. "I'm the fucking president of the United States, young man. President Clayton Hutchins. What you have is some cockamamy story that's probably been put out by my political opponents in a final, desperate attempt to defeat me. You're embarrassing yourself by even bringing it up."

If that was true, what was he doing sitting here with me alone in the Oval Office on election eve drinking a Scotch whisky?

"Sir," I said, always talking to him in that formal way, "I have two men involved in the armored car heist on the record—"

"Bullshit," he said harshly, leaning forward this time. "Armored car heist? There's no fucking armored car heist. You've been set up, by my opponent or someone who is desperate to make sure I don't win. Check my fucking biography. I was never involved in any fucking armored car heist."

He was pursuing the precise strategy that I feared the most—a hard-and-fast denial, followed, no doubt, by complete inaccessibility, at least long enough to be elected president the next day. Basically, what he was doing was issuing a challenge, daring me to go with the information I had, which he realized was pretty damned flimsy. His arguments would be almost identical to the ones I would hear from the paper's editors, from Martin to Appleton, as they tried to protect the institution from libel and shame.

There are a lot of reporters, mind you, who are all too willing to stretch their information in stories, to make supposition appear as fact with a few careful twists of phrases and subtle caveats. I'm as willing as anyone to stretch my information, but I do it before I write the story, like now, as a device to achieve the truth.

"Sir," I said, "we have a source, someone familiar with your transition into the witness protection program, who is helping us out. Later tonight, this source, who has intimate knowledge, will agree to go on the record to discuss your case. He is familiar with all the details—the initial criminal charges, the name change, the cosmetic surgery."

I eyed him carefully to see if I was having any effect. I couldn't tell. Hutchins shook his glass some more and gazed back at me with a look that was tough to read.

Maybe I was just having a tough time with perspective. I was physically exhausted and mentally drained, and perhaps because of that, Katherine's image kept rolling through my mind. I thought of that ride to the hospital the year before. I thought of how she put her face against my shoulder and held my arm and kissed my hand and told me that she felt as if she were born to have children with me. She told me that even after we had our baby, I would always, always, be the most important person in her life, the one she cherished the most, and that I had damn well better feel the same way about her. And I did. I did.

Which is why ever since, the emptiness had been so overwhelming, the loneliness unbearable, even when I wasn't alone.

Then, sitting there in the Oval Office, I had another thought, as if Katherine had all but whispered it to me in this time of need.

"Sir, it's god-awful to have your wife and child die the way yours did," I said. "Unbearable." I paused for a long moment, then added, "I understand that all too well. I understand what it can do to your heart, to your mind, to your very sense of being. It can change everything, even if you don't realize that it's changing anything at all."

That was followed by a long stretch of silence. He wasn't looking at me, but rather down at his glass, if, in fact, he was looking at anything at all.

I said, "You don't need me to tell you how much of a monumental success you've become," I said. "And against all odds. I have a hunch you didn't turn to crime until after your wife and son died, when you didn't know what else to do. I have a feeling that their memory gave you an awful lot of support when you left crime behind and started your new life. I have a feeling that you miss them now in a way that only the two of us could ever really understand, that you'd like to be true to them, that you want to stop living this lie."

He still stared down at his desk. I couldn't be positive, but I thought I saw a drop of water—a tear—roll off his face and splash into his glass.

I paused for effect more than anything else, took

another deep breath, and said, "Sir, tomorrow morning, I'm fairly certain I will have a story on the front page of the *Boston Record* explaining that your past is fictitious, that you are a rehabilitated felon." I then added in an admittedly lame attempt at humor, "At least I think you're rehabilitated."

He didn't laugh.

Behind me, on the other side of the office, the burning logs in the fireplace snapped several times, sounding like gunshots, making me jump, but imperceptibly so, I hope. Darkness engulfed the room, the reflection of the desk lamps shining on the inside of the French doors and the tall windows. In front of me, Hutchins held the glass in his hand on the surface of the desk and shook it back and forth again, then lifted it to his mouth for another sip. He still hadn't met my eyes. The quiet seemed interminable.

"I am Clayton Hutchins," he said finally, looking up, his voice softer, his tone less resolute. "The government says I'm Clayton Hutchins. All my records say I'm Clayton Hutchins. I have a birth certificate. I was home-schooled by parents who have since died. I worked on a farm, went to college later in life."

I stayed silent. I saw that his cheeks were damp. I shook my head slowly in a sign of disappointed disbelief.

More silence. He took a deep breath, focused on some point beyond me, and said, "It's one thing I always liked about you, Jack, one thing that always drew me to you. You know what it's like to have everything taken away from you by some arbitrary hand. You know what it's like to lose everything you've ever wanted, all of your hopes and all of your dreams and all of your expectations for the future, all in one incomprehensible act of a God who you could never, ever even pretend to understand. You know what it's like to live the rest of your days knowing you can never get it back, no matter who you are, even if you're the president of the United States. You know all that."

I was riveted, fearful that even the slightest movement or noise would stop his inevitable confession.

He continued in a louder, firmer voice. "I paid a steep price. I struck a deal. I traded in my entire life, or what was left of it. You know what that's like, to give up your life? And now that I've turned myself around, now that I've made it on my own, you're going to hang all that around my neck and choke me to death, all over again?" He pronounced those last three words by punching out every syllable.

"I deserve better," he said. "You know that."

He paused, stared down at his glass, at the ice melting into the whisky, and added, far more softly, "This wasn't part of any deal."

I probably should have felt pity. But all I really felt was relief. Sitting in the Oval Office on deadline on the night before the election with the president of the United States, I had him cold. I had my story. I even had my quotes, which I repeated in my mind several times to help commit them to memory.

"Sir, you may be right. It wasn't part of the deal you had with the government. But you had a deal with the American people, and that deal was to tell the truth, to let them know who you are, to be judged on the whole rather than just the past few years."

His voice grew louder. "I did tell them who I am, dammit. I am Clayton Hutchins. I made my money on my own, with no help from anyone. For chrissakes, I gave up a lucrative life to be Clayton Hutchins. I succeeded. And now you're about to burn me with my own success? Where's the fairness in that? Where's the fucking fairness in that?"

He pounded his fist on the desk as he asked these last questions. I remained silent, taking in this remarkable situation. Hutchins started up again, seething. "You think I've been a bad president? You think all those people who are planning to vote for me tomorrow believe I'd make a bad president for the next four years? You think my policies aren't carefully thought out? You think I've been corrupt? No, goddammit. No."

He took a long, final sip and slid the glass aimlessly across his desk as he reclined in his chair. "Raj!" he yelled. The steward appeared silently in the doorway. "Another Johnnie, please."

"Sir," I said. "The voters have a right to know who they voted for. They have a right to know your background, your experiences, the truths in your life, and the lies. All of that shapes who you are, and dictates how you'll act in the future as the country's leader, in times of good fortune and in times of crisis. The voters have the right to the truth."

He shook his head dismissively. "But I struck the deal with the government. I honored my part, they honored theirs."

"Sir, with all due respect, the people are the government. Yes, it's a cliché, but it also happens to be the truth. And the people have a right to know."

And I believed this. Light, sunshine, is an amazing thing. It keeps a democracy vibrant by keeping the people informed. Informed people are usually wise people, or at least practical. Was there self-interest in this story? Of course. I'm in this business to break news, to tell people that which they don't already know, to place important facts in the rich dialogue of our nation. This wasn't about his sex life or some ancient two-bit misdemeanor. This struck at the very foundation of who our president is, and in this case, was.

He stood up and stared down at me from across the desk, then walked toward the French doors, slowly. He stopped and looked out into the Rose Garden, black but for a few spotlights shining on some chrysanthemums standing sentry against the autumn breezes. Then he walked slowly over to the fireplace and stood there for a moment, gazing at the unfinished portrait of George Washington hanging over the mantel. I sat in silence, following his movements, thinking of the office. I remembered hearing how Ronald Reagan, on his last morning as president, walked slowly from the residence to the West Wing and found it completely darkened and empty. Everyone had cleaned out their offices the night before. He wandered aimlessly around the Oval Office, absently letting his hand drift across the furniture, the walls, all that history, some of it made by him. Then he saluted and walked out the door, alone.

From across the room, Hutchins said to me, "How about a deal? How about I resign, Wednesday morning, win or lose. I'll send my resignation up to the Congress. I'll schedule a speech and tell the public I have some illness or something like that. We'll figure that part out. I'll give you an exclusive interview about it tomorrow night, after the results are in, for Wednesday's paper. You alone, on the details of my resignation. And you agree not to write anything about my past."

He paused and looked at me dejectedly, expectantly, seeking a reaction that he wouldn't get. In fact, it wasn't a bad deal under most circumstances, and would alleviate a lot of bullshit I was about to face, I'm sure, from Appleton and Martin. But there was one essential problem with it. It was another lie.

"I can't, sir" I said. "The public is entitled to the truth."

A flash of anger spread across his face. "The truth is," he said, in something just short of a yell, "the truth is that I've been a damned good president. That's the fucking truth. You want the truth, print that."

"I will, sir. Any story will note your policies, your successes. It will note your popularity. It will also inform voters of your past. They can decide what they want to do with that information."

He collapsed into one of those pale yellow chairs where he was often pictured on television during photo opportunities with some visiting foreign leader. He rested his elbows on his knees and stared at the carpet in front of him, looking increasingly despondent. "I tried to save you," he said.

I assumed I must have heard him wrong, so I asked, politely, "Excuse me, sir?"

"I tried to save you, and I tried to save your cohort, Havlicek. And this is the payback I get."

I stared at him as he continued. "When you started asking around about Paul Stemple last month, Drinker just wanted to kill you. Just kill you, no questions asked. Put an end to our fears. I wouldn't allow it. I had another plan. I said I could hire you, give you the job as press secretary. You seemed talented enough to do the job. You'd be on our side, and the questions about me and Stemple would never be asked again. They'd go away forever. I had no idea he was going to try to kill you at Congressional that day."

I gulped hard at this matter-of-fact revelation. "So that wasn't an assassination attempt on you? That was really an attempt on my life?"

"It was, but believe me when I tell you I didn't sanction it. My intent was to hire you. That was the point of golf that day, not to kill you."

By now I had moved over to sit on one of the settees perpendicular to his chair. A single lamp lit this side of the room, leaving both our faces in virtual darkness as we talked, as if we were both sitting just offstage, just out of the limelight.

I asked, "Why Drinker? What's his motivation?"

Hutchins flashed me a wry look. "Isn't self-motivation always the best motivation?" he asked. I stared at him but didn't answer. He said, "He expected to be named the director of the FBI soon, by me, once I became elected, and his expectations were probably going to be fulfilled. He knows my goddamned secret. He was involved in the case way back when, and when I was about to become vice president, I had no choice but to call him up and make it in his own interest to keep my past the past."

You never know what people might say in times of triumph and tragedy, how much information they may divulge, the depths of their emotions, and this soul-bearing exercise in the Oval Office was certainly proof of that. In some odd way, Hutchins began to look relieved talking about his past and the efforts to conceal it, so I continued to press him, and perhaps my luck as well. "So it was Drinker who killed Havlicek?"

Hutchins nodded.

"Why?"

"You wouldn't take the press secretary's job. My plan failed. He also believed that Stemple began providing you with information after the Congressional shooting, and he couldn't find Stemple to kill him at first, try as he did, so he figured it was easier to kill you. And you guys wouldn't buy into our line that the dead assassin was a federally protected witness named Tony Clawson, which would have been embarrassing for the FBI, but would have assured that no one would ever associate me with Clawson for the rest of my life. I tried fending Drinker off by pushing and pushing you to take the job. You set yourself up by refusing to come aboard."

If I thought about that too hard, the calculation would sicken me. With that logic, I had caused Havlicek's death a number of different ways. But right there and then, I refused to dwell.

It was after eight-thirty and heading toward nine, the deadline for our first edition. I assumed I had blown that already. I steadied myself on the couch and said, "Sir, I appreciate your help, but I have to leave. Is there anything else you want to make clear to me about your past, about the election, about your plans for the future? More to the point, if we run a story tomorrow, and we will run a story tomorrow, do you plan to resign in the light of these allegations, or will you remain in office for as long as you are able?"

He sat with his elbows on his knees and his head pointed straight down at the floor, as if in prayer. He looked up at me from the uncomfortable crouch and said, "I don't know. I just don't know right now."

I nodded. Why should he? I got up and started slowly, quietly for the door. When I got there, he said softly, "So no deal?"

"I have an obligation, sir."

"You know, you fulfill that obligation, it's the end of me. Have I really been that bad a person? Do I really deserve this?"

As I turned to walk out the door, he was still sitting in that chair by the fireplace, hunched over, looking nothing like the man I saw on the golf course on that brilliant October morning eleven days before. He said to me in a voice as plain as white paper, neither loud nor soft, angry nor sad, "You should believe in redemption. And if you do, you should honor that belief." I stopped walking while he talked, not wanting to be rude. He wasn't even looking my way anymore. When I began walking again, I heard him say, as if to himself, though perhaps to me, "You more than anyone else should understand my grief."

twenty-three

I GULPED IN THE fresh night air as I stepped outside the West Wing and onto the North Lawn of the White House. Nearby, anchors for some of the cable stations, Moose Myers among them, did stand-ups for their pre-election specials, all of them holding their microphones to their mouths, the glowing building as their backdrop, so completely, exquisitely oblivious to the news that was about to crash over the country.

I strode toward the northwest gate, looking out into the patch of black on the other side that was Lafayette Park. I stopped for a second on the White House drive. As soon as I stepped outside of that gate, I was fair game. Drinker could be sitting in that park right now, lurking, waiting, watching me, fingering a gun or a knife shoved into his overcoat pocket, his collar turned up against the breeze. He could be posing as a tourist with a windbreaker and a camera. He could be hiding in a doorway with a ski hat pulled down low over his forehead. He could slash my throat as I walked on an otherwise barren street, grab my wallet, and leave me bleeding to death beneath a street-lamp on a littered city sidewalk. Isn't it ironic, the papers would point out, that a well-known reporter who had survived a shooting and a bombing was finally felled by what was probably a crazed drug addict in search of a few bucks, and isn't Washington, the nation's capital, a disgrace?

Time was my enemy here. Staring into the abyss of that park, I quickly turned around in the drive and began to trot toward the walkway that led to the adjacent Old Executive Office Building. Technically, it was off limits with my press pass, and at any juncture, the Secret Service uniformed officers could stop me, even detain me. But detention, I quickly calculated, was preferable to a violent death. At least I could probably make a phone call, most likely to Martin, and dictate what I had.

The guard shack between the White House and the ancient and ornate OEOB, which once housed the Department of War, was usually empty. I scurried down the stairs, across an alleyway, and into the loading entrance. I wended my way through a maze of wide, empty hallways, my wing tips clicking on the hard tile floors and echoing off the walls. Every doorway seemed dangerous. Every turn seemed pivotal. It felt like I had walked a mile before I finally saw a red, illuminated Exit sign. I rounded a corner, saw three officers chatting at a station, summoned every ounce of calm that I could find, and casually walked toward the turnstyle. One of the agents matter-of-factly buzzed me out, and I was on my way.

Out on Seventeenth Street, the luck of the skilled came through once again, this time in the form of a taxi-cab happening by just as I hit the curb. The elderly, grizzled driver was aggravated when I directed him to my office just a few minutes away, so I said to him, trying to lighten the mood, "Who do you like in tomorrow's election?"

"Is there even a question?" he asked. "Hutchins, all the

way. The stock market's up. The economy's so good that even I own stocks these days. And he's honest. Look at that other creep. He lies. They all lie, I guess, but Hutchins lies less."

Well, brace yourself, old man. Brace yourself.

In front of my office, I slipped him a fin for his time and opinion and made a dash for the front door, all, fortunately, within full view of a very friendly building security guard named Alan. I ran past him, boarded a waiting elevator, and ascended to my office, a place I had feared I would never see again.

The bureau, I was quite sure, was probably as safe a venue as any, and more comfortable than most. A writer likes familiarity. A reporter does as well. This was not a story I wanted to type from the small desk of my hotel room, nice as my hotel room might be.

By nine at night, my office was a shadowy shade of gray, with the hazy green glare of so many computer screens casting the only light across the vast room. I knew this bureau better than I knew anyplace else on Earth, yet it seemed somehow different now, eerie. Speaking out loud, I told myself I needed to calm my nerves, saying, "You have to relax." Even the sound of my own voice made me jumpy, but not nearly as much as the sound I heard next, that of someone else speaking to me in the dark.

"Who are you talking to?"

The new voice made me just about leap through the ceiling. My eyes darted about the room until they came to rest on Peter Martin, sitting in the dark at a computer screen just across from mine, flipping through wire stories.

"Jesus Christ," I said. "You're going to scare me to death."

"Actually, it's you who scared me. You should be at your hotel. I've been waiting here for you to call." He paused, then said, "Tell me what you have."

I sat down at my computer. He drew his chair up closer, and I slowly, carefully walked him through my session in the Oval Office. I read him some Hutchins quotes that I had furiously scribbled on a legal pad just after I had left the West Wing.

After my ten-minute monologue, Martin looked stricken, as if he might get sick right there on the newsroom rug. In the heavy silence, my telephone rang, the sound crashing into our thoughts. I suspected it might be Hutchins, trying to sweeten the deal for cooperation, but when I picked up the receiver, I heard only dead air, followed by the click of someone hanging up on the other end. It made my skin crawl, even if I didn't fully appreciate or understand why.

Martin, on the other hand, seemed not even to notice. Staring not so much at me but through me, he said finally, "You use tape?" he said.

"No."

"You took contemporaneous notes?"

"Well, right afterward, from memory, in the briefing room on my way out the door."

His questions made me question myself, but I had done the best I could. I knew that much.

"Incredible," he said, softly. "This whole thing is incredible." As he spoke, he leaned over and picked up the telephone. Punching out a number, he added, "Appleton's not going to like the circumstances—your involvement when you were supposed to be sitting in your hotel, the lack of a tape recording—but I have no doubt you did exactly what you should have done."

He talked on the telephone for a few minutes with Appleton, hung up, and said to me, "Write something out. Appleton wants to see it before he figures out what to do. He says there are no guarantees."

No guarantees. I wasn't sure whether this proclamation was infuriating or hilarious. Here we had the president of the United States, dead to rights, in an absolute lie that defined his entire life. I had risked my life for this story. Havlicek had lost his. And we had some pencil-pusher of an editor in chief sitting in his million-dollar house in a wealthy suburb of Boston impatiently telling us that there were no guarantees he would run the most important story in the country. Screw him, and while we're at it, screw this entire newspaper business as well. But not before I write this story and get it into print. Call me a fool, but I'd rather like to inform the voting public that the guy they were about to elect as president is a former armored car robber.

So I settled in before my computer and began to write. And I wrote and wrote and wrote, what I immodestly consider one of the best stories I've ever put together under deadline pressure. My fingers danced like magic across the keyboard. My mind clicked on more cylinders than I knew I had. It was a complex story with a very simple core: The president of the United States is not who he said he was. I wrote of the Oval Office interview, of his belief that the FBI was behind the shooting, and how the intended target was me. As promised, I talked of his successes as president and the lofty approval ratings that came along with it. I explained the 1979

Wells Fargo heist, the deal that Curtis Black struck with the U.S. attorney, his disappearance from the program in 1988.

When I was done, I punched out the number to Martin's office, where he had wandered to watch television and pace nervously while I did my work. He came out to my desk, and for fifteen minutes he sat in front of my computer in absolute silence, his fingers not typing in a single change as he paged through the story. That silence was finally broken by my ringing telephone. Again, dead air on the other line, followed by a click. I didn't like that at all. I looked suspiciously across the expanse of the bureau, at the empty chairs and the dormant computers. It all looked like some sort of barren Broadway set after the actors had long ago gone home.

"Fucking brilliant," Martin said as I walked back to my desk. "If we don't run this story, I don't want to be a part of this company anymore. You have my word that I'll quit."

"Let's just all calm down," I said. "It's only the president and the future course of America at stake." Neither of us laughed. "Let me give it another quick read," I added.

Martin stood up, told me to hurry up, and nervously walked back and forth behind me. I sat down at the terminal and scanned the words. By now, concentration was difficult. The two telephone hang-ups nagged at the core of my brain. All around me, the silence wasn't so much deafening as frightening. Outside in the hallway, a buzzer began sounding, and my stomach knotted up, until I realized it was just the facsimile machine. Another phone rang in the far corner of the bureau.

At that exact moment, the oddly melodic sound of shattering glass spilled into the room from the hallway beyond. My skin tingled from the noise and what it likely meant. Martin and I looked at each other in silence, and without a signal or a spoken word, I started walking slowly, quietly, across the room toward the door. I don't know why I got up and he stayed with the story. Probably we were just further defining our lifetime roles.

As I got halfway toward the hallway, my body so tense my arms and legs may as well have been wooden boards, the murky figure of Kent Drinker appeared in the doorway, looking much as he did that night when he emerged from the dark while I threw a ball for my dog, only here I suspected he wanted to do something more conclusive than chat. As nervous as I may have been, the very sight of him in my newsroom, daring to invade a place I always considered a sanctuary in the self-important and even corrupt culture of official Washington, made me livid—not so much defensive as emboldened.

"What are you doing here?" I yelled. It wasn't an inquiry but a warning.

He continued walking toward me, maybe fifty feet away, holding a gun in front of his chest with one hand, the barrel pointed at what I estimated to be my forehead.

"You don't fuck with me, and you don't fuck with the FBI," he said, answering my question, even if he hadn't actually tried.

"I want you the fuck out of this building," I replied,

That demand didn't seem to hold any sway. Drinker continued to walk toward me, around a clutter of desks. I stood frozen in the middle of the room. I'm not sure what Martin was doing behind me, because I didn't dare turn my back to look.

In the heat of the moment, I figured it was best to try to engage Drinker in any way possible. Conversation buys time. Time buys the opportunity to be creative. Creativity might help me get out of this situation with some semblance of my health, or at least life.

So I asked, "What is it you want?" Of course, I knew the answer to that already. Unfortunately for me, his intention was to make sure that I wasn't about to transmit a story to the *Record* that would include details of Hutchins's past life and suspicions that the FBI—specifically he—had killed Havlicek and tried to kill me in an attempt to block the truth from being known. Even less fortunately for me, he also wanted to make sure that I wouldn't live to tell anyone about what I knew. Of course, the reason he hadn't killed me in the prior twenty seconds was because he didn't yet know if I had sent the story yet.

"Fuck you," he said, maybe twenty feet away from me by now.

I was standing by Michael Reston's computer. I knew this because on his desk was a metal-framed photograph of Reston standing in front of the Supreme Court with the chief justice, both of them smiling as if they were soul mates. The picture spoke volumes about our favorable court coverage, but no need to get bogged down by such journalistic issues right now.

Drinker was circling desks in silence, still coming at me. He was hunched down, as if ready to do battle. I thought about picking up the photograph and flinging it at him, in expectation that he wouldn't shoot back because if I were dead, he would never know the damage I may have already done. Then I thought, if I ruined this photo, Reston would kill me anyway, so either way, I lose. My eyes quickly drifted over his desk, to a huge, hardcover legal volume, and then to his telephone. I could throw the book, which weighed more, but the fluttering paper might slow the velocity. I saw that on television once. The telephone was sleeker and harder. Of course, there was the general problem of the cord, which might slow down the throw, or even stop it in midair. I knew for a fact, though, that the cords on these phones stretched about a dozen feet, because I often liked to walk around my desk and talk at the same time.

Here goes. Drinker was but fifteen feet from me now, a free throw in the NBA. I waited another second for him to get within range, and in one quick swoop I picked up the phone and fired it at his head. Mind you, in Little League, back when I was twelve, I once pitched a no-hitter, and in the dog park in Georgetown, I am widely considered to have the best arm in the neighborhood, at least among those who are inclined to think about such things.

And I'll be damned if this throw didn't prove it. Drinker ducked, and the phone smashed into his wrist, causing the gun to fly out of his hand and slide underneath a nearby desk. He shook his wrist violently in pain, scanned the floor quickly for the weapon, then looked at me with a hatred I hope never to see again.

I was very temporarily elated, pleased at my decision to choose the phone over the picture frame or the book, and wondered if this was what the nice ad people at AT&T had in mind when they coined the slogan "The right choice."

"You fucking cocksucker," Drinker said. And he started toward me at a faster pace, almost a run, but something more controlled, more determined. Tellingly enough, he seethed the words, "You should have been dead at Congressional."

Um, Peter, I thought to myself, anytime you want to help out here, please feel free. I shot a glance back and saw him at the computer keyboard, and I realized quickly that he was transmitting the story to the *Record*. Good to know where I stood in the scheme of things.

When I turned, Drinker saw what I was looking at, and that made him panic. He charged me with the force of a linebacker, smartly throwing his forearms into my sore ribs and lifting me up off the ground and onto Reston's desk.

As Drinker started to move past me, I collected myself and dove off the desk for his leg, bringing him down in a heap, the sound of him screaming as he fell on his bad wrist filling the room. I punched him once in the face before he even knew what had hit him. Problem was, that didn't seem to faze him much, or at least it didn't impede his ability to knee me in the ribs and cause a measure of pain that I hadn't thought possible.

As I saw stars, Drinker, free from my grip, raced across the room. From my perch on the floor, I could see Martin back away from the computer and stand aside. I could see the story quite literally scrolling across the screen, as it does when it is transmitting. When it finally arrives at its destination, the computer beeps twice and the screen says, "File sent without errors." If we could see that now, it would read like poetry.

Drinker arrived at the computer with an absolute cognizance of what was happening. He started pressing keys immediately, hitting what was probably the escape button again and again and again. Still, the story continued to scroll.

Frantic and frustrated—never a good combination— he picked the keyboard up to rip it out of the terminal, in a last, desperate attempt to save himself. Standing now twenty feet or so behind him, I assumed he finally had us, that the force would cause such technological havoc that the whole computer would shut down or explode and the story of Hutchins's past would end up in some netherworld of information. And we, of course, would end up dead.

Martin must have thought the same thing, because at that second, the slightly built Washington bureau chief of the *Boston Record* lunged for Drinker and shoved a ballpoint pen deep into the side of his neck. Drinker collapsed, his eyes bugged out. The keyboard tumbled out of his hands and dropped to the floor, and as it did, the monitor beeped twice and the words "File sent without errors" flashed across the screen. Drinker rolled around on the ground, moaning, the pen still protruding out of his neck. Martin leaned on a desk, disheveled, licking a cut on his finger. I stood back in something of a fog, taking it all in. You'll forgive my lack of restraint in thinking for a brief moment, as I looked at Drinker's neck, that the pen is indeed mightier than the sword.

Anyway, Martin casually picked up the telephone

and called for an ambulance. I picked up Drinker's gun and told him, "You try to stand up, you're dead." As I stood guard, Martin made a second call, this one to Appleton.

"Yeah, you're right," I heard Martin say. "This really is a pain to have this story move so late at night."

twenty-four

So HOW IMPORTANT IS truth, anyway? I don't mean small truths, and conversely, small lies, like, "Honey, you look great in that dress." No, I mean larger, consequential truths, along the lines of "Are you having an affair?" and "Are you really behind me on this?" Sometimes lies hurt. Sometimes truths hurt more.

Of course, in the news business, we don't particularly care, and maybe that's part of both the problem and the majesty of the profession. We aim only for the truth, or what we think is the truth, or what may well prove to be the truth. Of course, all this is seen through the prism of time and competition and the driving need to be different and interesting, even while being mostly the same. When Moose Myers is doing a stand-up from the White House lawn twice an hour for CNN, when the *New York Times* and the *Washington Post* have an army of Ivy League graduates swarming for any scrap of news they can push their WASPish white teeth into, truth can suffer, even in the most indefatigable and valiant pursuit. Facts are molded to beliefs, decisions are rushed on deadline, calls aren't made for lack of time.

And in Washington, in politics, lies aren't told out of

convenience, but out of necessity. No candidate or public official in his right mind will stand before a thronging crowd of supporters and yell out, "Read my lips, I will raise your taxes," or tell a pack of nearly snarling reporters, "I absolutely had sexual relations with that woman." Lies are so ingrained into the Washington culture that sometimes people don't even realize they're telling them. Facts are simply contorted to conform with beliefs, melded to the moment. It's the American way.

So is the truth even important anymore? Do we really need it, in life, in the body politic, or is it just better, easier, to go with what feels good, to tell lies, to accept them, with the understanding that even if lies hurt, the truth too often hurts more? Well, I don't mean to climb too high on a moral pedestal, but I'm still a fan of the truth. Always have been, and expect I always will be. Truth is an immovable foundation. Lies shift and collapse. With truth, even at its most painful, you can address it, build on it, and move on. I happen to have a rather high regard for the public. I believe they can take the truth, decide if it's important, and make sound judgments on the people put before them. Which is why journalism, for all its drawbacks, for all the twits like Appleton who hold too much power, is still a good and decent calling.

Which brings me to the issue of Clayton Hutchins, or Tony Clawson, or Curtis Black, however you want to refer to him. Do I believe in redemption? Yes. I meant it in the Oval Office when I told him there was something uniquely, importantly American about it. I also believe the public had a right to know who he really was and how he got there. There's something American about that as well. The free flow of information, of truths, is arguably the most significant attribute of a democracy.

Hutchins won the election. He won with 50.4 percent of the popular vote, and took the Electoral College by a nine-vote margin over Senator Stanny Nichols. On Election Day, the networks devoted full-time on-air coverage to the pursuit of the *Record* story, quoting liberally from our pages until the early evening, when they were finally able to confirm key aspects on their own. The all-news cable stations nearly burst at the seams. The Internet all but exploded from overuse. The bottom line: the people, the voters, knew what they were doing, and enough of them believed in the concept of redemption. Or maybe they were just happy with the rising stock market. Either way. The president as our first form of entertainment is not a novel concept. As has been said before, they don't limit your miles on Air Force One or your use of the White House by your margin of victory. Hutchins was the president for the next four years.

I think. An independent counsel was named by the attorney general to investigate the president's possible role in Havlicek's death, though truth be known, I don't believe he had any. Not Black's style, not then, not now. The Democratic-controlled Congress appointed a select committee to probe possible election fraud and abuse of power. The ever-dignified vice president, Ted Rockingham, met reporters on the White House driveway and pleaded with the country to give Hutchins the benefit of any doubts. Whether he'd get it, whether he'd need it, who really knew.

These were the thoughts I was thinking as I kicked my feet up on my desk after another difficult deadline on Wednesday night, the day after the election. It was the end of a whirlwind day of Washington events, capped by an Oval Office address delivered by Hutchins in which he portrayed his own redemption as being part of the American dream he had long espoused, the American way. Now, he said, it was time to heal, both himself and the country, and he would like to see the job through.

Ironically, while Hutchins, the admitted criminal, spoke, Drinker, the law enforcement agent, was being detained under heavy guard at a military hospital just outside Washington, facing a battery of federal and local charges, among them conspiracy to commit murder. You know what they say in Washington: it's never the crime, always the cover-up. Dozens of FBI agents were working with D.C. police to try to determine who actually fired the shots out at Congressional. They had a body. They just needed an identity to go along with it.

And me? I've been running crazy with the story. We did a takeout on the early years of the real Clayton Hutchins, the only child of deceased parents who died by his own hand, all alone, in his early twenties, only to see his name and childhood resurrected by a man who would become president of the United States. I received an invitation from Hutchins's secretary to join him for dinner on Friday night. That would be interesting. Meantime, every television interviewer from the smallest cable channel to the biggest network has tried to book me for their show. To each, I say, I don't talk, I write.

And television is the least of it. That day, a Hollywood producer called me at work, trying to buy my story for a substantial six-figure sum.

"Is Ernest Borgnine still alive?" I asked him.

"Um, I'm not really sure, why?" he replied.

"When you find out, give me a call," I said, and hung up. I haven't heard back from him, which is just as well.

Well, on this Wednesday night, after deadline passed, after the bureau cleared out, after even Martin left, I wandered over to Steve Havlicek's desk, sat in his swivel chair, and ran my hands over some of his things, which were still laid out on his desk exactly as he had left them. He had a mug with the words "World's Best Dad" on it. He had several legal pads scattered about. He had a Cross pen with his name on it, which I thought was unusual. I had never seen it before. Inside his top drawer, he had a pound bag of peanut M&Ms, opened and mostly gone. I pulled a box out of the supply closet and packed his stuff slowly and carefully into it, leaving out the autopsy report on the mystery man who fired those first shots at Hutchins and me. Good taste prevails once again. I wrote out a quick note saying, "Margaret, we all miss Steve more than we can ever say. This story is happening because of him. Very best, Jack." I dropped the note in the box, sealed it up, and left it for Barbara to ship to Boston.

As I walked out, I had the feeling of accomplishment, so much so that after I got home, I walked down to the cellar and pulled out a couple of folded-up moving boxes. I climbed the stairs to the second floor, hesitated for a moment in the hallway, then pushed open the door to the nursery.

Inside, slowly and surely, I took several stuffed animals out of the crib, removed the tiny cotton blankets and sheets and folded them up, placed them in a box, then lugged it down to the cellar. Back in the nursery, as Baker sprawled out on the Winnie-the-Pooh rug where I had slept a couple of weeks before, I unpacked the toy chest, putting each stuffed bear and dog carefully into one of the boxes. I threw away the dried-out jar of wet wipes. I took the few pairs of infant pajamas out of the drawers and put them into the box. I was picking up a Gund bear on top of the bureau when I heard a knock on the door downstairs.

Baker, of course, was thrilled. He limped down ahead of me. I pulled the door open and there stood Samantha Stevens, a special agent with the FBI. It must have been raining out, because her hair was matted to her head. She held a bottle of wine beside her.

"I got your message this morning," she said, standing on my stoop. "Thanks again for the apology."

I said, "Don't mention it. I got your message this afternoon saying I'm not such a jackass."

She smiled mischievously and said, "You're not."

"Come in."

She stretched out her arm and handed me the bottle of wine. "Peace offering," she said. I hadn't seen her since Havlicek's funeral. I hadn't spoken to her—a couple of passing conversations aside—since we kissed on the sidewalk outside of Kinkead's.

As I took the bottle, she pointed to my hand, which still held the blond teddy bear, and said, "New toy?"

I didn't laugh. "Old toy, actually," I replied.

She quickly understood what I meant and studied my face for a moment while I studied hers. We were both quiet, though I'm not sure if it was out of awkwardness or relief. She followed me into the kitchen, and I put the bear down on the counter to open the bottle of wine. When I turned around to face her, she drew close in that way she does, hardly seeming to move at all.

She put her face against mine and kissed me on the lips, not passionately, but warmly, then she pulled away, her eyes closed for a second, then open, looking into mine. That's when I kissed her, bringing my hand up to caress her wet hair. It was a long kiss, again, not so much passionate, but warm, strangely familiar, so natural.

She said, barely moving her lips, "I missed you." I glanced at the dog lying on the floor behind her, at the stuffed bear sitting on the countertop. I stared into her eyes for a few silent seconds and said, "I missed you too."

And at that moment, a future seemed to emerge from the past, like life from ashes, like wine from old grapes, something with a bit of whimsy and so much more.

"Good," she said. "Don't be a jackass again."

"I'm promising you," I replied. "I won't."

Acknowledgments

Special thanks to Ande Zellman, my first and best reader and the one who encouraged me the earliest and hardest to write something other than the daily news.

To Richard Abate and the elite team at International Creative Management, who gave me equal doses of encouragement and expertise.

To George Lucas of Pocket Books. His talent with words is exceeded only by his way with people. This book wouldn't be this book without his deft hand, his vivid imagination, and his seemingly blind faith in the writer fortunate enough to pen these pages.

To my sister Carole, who helped me with the medical scenarios contained within, to my sister Colleen, who didn't so much encourage as provoke me into this endeavor, and to my mother, who's always been there for everything else.

To the great people of *The Boston Globe;* especially Michael Larkin, who hired me too many years ago and still edits me now; Matt Storin, the editor who has entrusted me with the greatest jobs I will ever know; David Shribman, the wisest and warmest of bureau chiefs in a city—Washington, D.C.—that has gotten all too cold. Thanks as well to Greg Moore and Helen Donovan for their confidence. It's a crazy, wonderful way to make a living, this business of newspapers, and there's no better place to do it than the *Globe.*

Visit
❖ **Pocket Books** ❖
online at

....

www.SimonSays.com

....

Keep up on the latest new
releases from your favorite
authors, as well as author
appearances, news, chats,
special offers and more.